David Lagercrantz

DARK MUSIC

Translated from the Swedish by
Ian Giles

MACLEHOSE PRESS
QUERCUS · LONDON

First published as *Obscuritas* by Norstedts Förlag, Stockholm, in 2021

First published in Great Britain in 2022 by

MacLehose Press
An imprint of Quercus Editions Limited
Carmelite House
50 Victoria Embankment
London EC4Y 0DZ

An Hachette UK company

A CIP catalogue record for this book is available
from the British Library.

ISBN (HB) 978 1 52941 319 9
ISBN (TPB) 978 1 52941 318 2
ISBN (EBOOK) 978 1 52941 320 5

This book is a work of fiction. Names, characters,
organisations, places and events are
either the product of the author's imagination
or used fictitiously. Any resemblance to
actual persons, living or dead, events or
particular places is entirely coincidental.

10 9 8 7 6 5 4 3 2 1

Designed and typeset in Cycles Eleven by CC Book Production
Printed and bound in Great Britain by Clays Ltd, Elcograf S.p.A.

Praise for David Lagercrantz's books in the *Millennium* Series

"Salander and Blomkvist are just as compelling as ever . . . Fans of Stieg Larsson's captivating odd couple of modern detective fiction will not be disappointed"   *New York Times*

"Lagercrantz pulls it off, and with a great deal of style . . . Elegantly paced, slickly executed, and properly thrilling . . . A welcome treat"
                                                                        Observer

"Lagercrantz has constructed an elegant plot around different concepts of intelligence . . . His continuation, while never formulaic, is a cleaner and tighter read than the originals"   *Guardian*

"David Lagercrantz has done well . . . *The Girl in the Spider's Web* conveys the essence and atmosphere of Larsson's *Millennium* novels. He has captured the spirit of their characters"   *The Times*

"Lagercrantz's real achievement here is the subtle development of Lisbeth's character; he allows us access to her complex, alienated world but is careful not to remove her mystery and unknowability. Lisbeth Salander remains, in Lagercrantz's hands, the most enigmatic and fascinating anti-heroine in modern genre fiction"   *Financial Times*

"I found that I kept forgetting for several pages at a time that I wasn't reading genuine Larsson . . . One devours Larsson's books for the plots, the action, the anger, and most of all for Lisbeth Salander . . . Lagercrantz has caught her superbly"   *Daily Telegraph*

"Lagercrantz has more than met the challenge. Larsson's brainchildren are in good hands and may have even come up a bit in the world"
                                                                Wall Street Journal

Also by David Lagercrantz in English translation

DARK MUSIC

2003

ONE

It was meaningless bullshit. The lot of it.

Chief Inspector Fransson was delivering a long, peevish exegesis about what an idiot the assistant commissioner was and Micaela Vargas could no longer listen. It was too hot in the car, and the splendid mansions of Djursholm lay outside.

"Did we go past it?" she said.

"Calm down, young lady – this isn't exactly my usual stomping ground," Fransson said, fanning himself with his hand.

They drove on down towards the water, stopping at a tall gate with a CCTV camera and an entryphone. It opened after a few words from Fransson and they rolled into a large courtyard, past a fountain and up to a sumptuous mansion built from ochre-coloured stone, its large windows and colonnaded frontage overlooking the sea.

Micaela felt more nervous still. She was a local community beat cop, but this summer she'd become part of a murder inquiry because she possessed certain knowledge about the suspected assailant, Giuseppe Costa. She had mostly been tasked with running errands and doing basic checks. Nevertheless, she had been permitted to come along today to visit Professor Rekke, who would be able to assist them with their investigation – or so the assistant commissioner said.

White stone steps led up to the house, and standing on the terrace at the top was a woman in ivory cotton trousers and a blue blouse that fluttered in the wind.

"I suppose that must be the wife," Fransson said.

The woman looked like a film star. Micaela got out of the car feeling sweaty and uncomfortable, and crossed the raked gravel to the house.

TWO

Four days earlier

More often than not, Micaela would arrive at work early. But that morning, she was sitting in the kitchen eating breakfast although it was past nine o'clock. The phone rang. It was Inspector Jonas Beijer.

"We have to go see the assistant commissioner," he said.

He didn't say why. But it was clear it wasn't optional. She went to the mirror in the hall and pulled on her sweatshirt, an extra large one that sat on her loosely. *You look like you want to hide*, her brother Lucas would have said. But she thought it suited her. She brushed her hair and combed down her fringe so that it almost concealed her eyes, then headed off to the Tunnelbana.

Micaela had just turned twenty-six. There weren't many people on the Tunnelbana. She had a whole group of seats to herself and was soon lost in her own thoughts.

It was no surprise that the case interested the top brass. The murder itself might have been an outburst of madness, a drunken act. But there were other elements that explained the attention on the investigation. The deceased – Jamal Kabir – had been a football referee and a refugee from Taliban-controlled Afghanistan, and he had been beaten to death with a rock after a junior football match at Grimsta IP. It went without saying that Assistant Commissioner Falkegren wanted a piece of the action.

She got off at Solna Centrum and continued towards the police station on Sundbybergsvägen, thinking to herself that today was the day she would put her foot down and tell everyone what she thought was wrong with the investigation.

Martin Falkegren was the youngest assistant police commissioner in the country; he was forward-looking, and wanted to keep up with what was new. People said he wore his ideas like medals across his chest, which he guessed was not meant kindly. But he was proud of his openness, and this time, yet again, he had tried a different approach. They might get angry. But, as he had told his wife, it was the best lecture he had ever attended. It was worth a try.

He set out extra chairs and bottles of Ramlösa mineral water as well as two bowls of liquorice his secretary had bought on her mini-cruise to Finland, and listened for the sound of footsteps in the corridor. No-one seemed to be on their way yet. For a moment he pictured the investigating officer, Carl Fransson, standing before him, with his hefty body and critical gaze. Frankly, he thought to himself, he couldn't blame him. No detective wants the bosses involved in his inquiry.

But these were special circumstances. The murderer, a batshit, narcissistic Italian, was manipulating the shirts off their backs. It was an embarrassment – nothing less.

"Sorry, am I the first to arrive?"

It was the young Chilean officer. He couldn't recall her name, but he remembered that Fransson wanted her off the team – he'd said she was bolshy.

"Welcome. I don't think I've had the pleasure," he said, proffering a hand.

She took it in a firm handshake and he looked her over from head to foot. She was short and stocky, with thick curly hair and a long fringe combed down over her forehead. Her eyes were big and restless and shone with a dark intensity. There was something about her that immediately attracted him yet also kept him at a distance, and he was tempted to hold on to her hand a little longer. But her expression warned him against that, and he muttered instead:

"You know Costa, don't you?"

"I know *of* him," she said. "We both come from Husby."

"How would you describe him?"

"He's a bit of a showman. He used to sing to us outside the flats. He can get pretty aggressive when he drinks."

"Yes, that much is obvious. But why is he lying to our faces?"

"I don't know whether he's lying," she said, and he didn't like that.

It was inconceivable that they might have the wrong guy. The evidence was substantial and they were preparing to charge him. All that was missing was a confession. But he didn't have time to tell her that. He heard the others approaching along the corridor and stood up to congratulate them.

"Good job. I'm proud of you chaps," he said, and while he might have tried harder to include the Chilean girl, he did not correct himself.

His attempt to sound collegial was unsuccessful.

"What a senseless incident. And all because the referee didn't award a penalty."

He was just trying to get the conversation started, but Fransson seized the opportunity to lecture him and said it was far more complicated than that. There was a clear motive, he said, which might not be a motive to the likes of you and me, but it was to an alcoholic football dad without any impulse control who lived for his son's successes on the pitch.

"Yes, yes, of course," Falkegren said. "But my God . . . I saw the match tape. Costa was completely insane, while the referee . . . What's his name again?"

"Jamal Kabir."

". . . while Jamal Kabir was the picture of calm. Talk about poise."

"That's what they said."

"And him waving his hands. Elegant, right? As if he were controlling the whole match."

"It is a rather unusual style, it's true," Fransson said, at which point Martin Falkegren turned his gaze away from him and resolved to regain control of the conversation.

He wasn't there for chit-chat.

Micaela fidgeted. The atmosphere was not exactly relaxed, despite Falkegren trying his best to be one of the guys. But that was a hopeless project from the very start, and not just because he always smiled. He wore a shiny suit and loafers with tassels.

"How's our evidence looking otherwise, Carl?" he said. "I spoke briefly with . . ."

Falkegren looked at her. But he couldn't remember her name, or his thoughts were elsewhere, because he left the sentence hanging until Fransson interjected and outlined the evidence. As always when he spoke, it sounded convincing, as if all they needed was a verdict. That might have been why the assistant commissioner wasn't really listening. He muttered:

"Absolutely. None of the evidence is directly weakened by the observations in the P7."

"I think that's right," Fransson said, and Micaela looked up from her notepad.

The P7, she thought. The bloody P7. She had got hold of it some ten days ago and still wasn't entirely clear what it was. It seemed to be a report on the preliminary examination conducted by the forensic psychiatrist. She had read it with a certain degree of expectation, and had been disappointed almost right away. Antisocial personality disorder was the conclusion. Costa was, in other words, some sort of psychopath. She didn't believe it.

"Exactly," said the assistant commissioner with new fervour in his voice. "That's the key."

"Well, maybe," Fransson said, fidgeting.

"It's still important to get a confession out of him."

"Of course."

"And you've come close?"

"Up to a point."

"I happened to play a role in that drama, didn't I?" Falkegren said, and for a moment no-one responded even though they understood full well what he meant, which was why it was no surprise when he added:

"I asked you to try a new interrogation technique."

"Yes, right, it was a good tip," Fransson muttered, taking care to sound grateful but not too impressed.

After the P7, Falkegren had suggested they stop pushing Giuseppe Costa and instead ask him to engage in some verbal introspection, which had sounded a little odd. But Falkegren stood his ground. "His self-image is grandiose, and he thinks he knows everything about football," he had said, and eventually they agreed to give it a go. One day, when Costa was boasting more than usual, Fransson had tried to provoke him.

"Surely, given your extensive experience, you must be able to tell us what's on the mind of a person who does something as senseless as beating a referee to death," he had said, and Costa sat up and spoke with such empathy that it felt as if he were making an indirect confession. It was certainly an interesting moment in the investigation. But Micaela had not understood until now that it had been such a moment of pride for Martin Falkegren.

"It's a well-known trick. There's a famous example," he said.

"Is there really?" Fransson replied.

"A young journalist interviewed Ted Bundy in prison in Florida."

"Sorry?"

"None other than Ted Bundy," he repeated. "The method was very successful on Bundy. He'd studied psychology and when he was given the chance to shine as an expert, he opened up for the first time." Micaela was not alone in looking sceptical at this point.

Ted Bundy.

He might as well have name-dropped Hannibal Lecter.

"Don't get me wrong," Falkegren said. "I'm not making comparisons. It's just that there's new research in the area, and new interrogation techniques, and in the police we . . ."

He hesitated.

"Yes?"

". . . have major knowledge gaps. I would even go so far as to say we've been naive."

"Really?" Fransson said.

"Oh yes. The term psychopath has long been considered antiquated and stigmatising. But that's changed, thank heavens, and just the other day I was at a lecture – a fantastic lecture, I must say . . ."

"I can tell."

"Exactly. It was thrilling. We were all glued to our chairs; my goodness, you should have been there. The lecturer was Hans Rekke."

"Who?"

The men looked at each other. It was clear none of them had heard of him, and that they had no intention of getting up to speed.

"He's Professor of Psychology at Stanford University – an incredibly prestigious position."

"Impressive," Fransson said with audible irony.

"Truly," the tone-deaf Falkegren replied. "He's been cited in all the leading journals."

"Fantastic," added Ström, just as ironically. Axel Ström, the oldest in the group, was approaching retirement age.

"But you mustn't think he's off in the clouds – he's not. He's a specialist in interrogation techniques and has helped the San Francisco Police Department. He's amazingly sharp and knowledgeable."

These words did not hit the mark either; rather, they reinforced the "us and them" feeling in the room. It was him – the boss and

16

career-ladder climber who had gone to a lecture and seen the light – versus Fransson and his blokes, the hardworking, rational police detectives with their feet on the ground, who didn't immediately fall for every new fad.

"Professor Rekke and I understood each other right away – we hit it off," Falkegren said, thus managing to imply that he was hyper-intelligent too. "I told him about Costa."

Fransson raised an eyebrow. "Oh, you did, did you?"

"I told him about his grandiose and narcissistic traits, and the somewhat ticklish situation we're in, without any forensic evidence," Falkegren said.

"OK," said Fransson.

"And that was when he mentioned that trick with Bundy, and said we might want to try it."

"Well, that's good, now we know the background," Fransson said, eager to draw the conversation to a close.

"But then afterwards, when it was such a success – when Costa really opened up – I thought to myself: Good God, if Rekke could help us like that from a distance, just imagine what he'd be able to do if he was more familiar with the case."

"Hmm, yes," Fransson said, looking troubled.

"Exactly," Falkegren continued. "That's why I asked around a bit . . . Well, you know I have my contacts. Nothing but praise. Sheer praise, gentlemen. I therefore took the liberty of sending our files over to Professor Rekke."

"You did *what?*" Fransson exclaimed.

"I sent the investigation to him," Falkegren said, and it was as if they hadn't quite understood.

Fransson leaped to his feet.

"For Christ's sake, that's a breach of confidentiality during the preliminary investigation!"

"Calm yourself, calm yourself," Falkegren said. "It's nothing like that. Rekke will be like a member of our team. After all, he has his own duty of confidentiality as a psychologist. If I'm perfectly honest I think we need him."

"Bullshit!"

"You've done a good job, as I said, no doubt about it. But you don't have a watertight case. You need a confession, and I'm convinced that Rekke can help you with that. He tracks contradictions and gaps in witness statements like no-one else."

"So what is it you think we should do?" Fransson said. "Let the professor take over the investigation?"

"No, no, for God's sake. I'm just saying you should meet him and listen to him. See whether he can give you a new way in, a new idea. He'll see you at two o'clock on Saturday at his home in Djursholm. He promises to have reviewed the files by then."

"There's no bloody way I'm using another Saturday off for some pointless crap," said Ström.

"OK, OK, fair enough. But I'm sure a few of you can go. What about you?" Falkegren said, pointing to Micaela. "In fact, Rekke asked about you in particular."

"He asked about me?"

She looked around in concern, convinced it was a joke.

"Yes, you led some interrogation with Costa that he thought was interesting."

"I can't imagine—" she began.

"Firstly, Vargas can't go alone," Fransson interjected, turning to Falkegren. "She doesn't have enough experience, not by a long shot, and secondly, with all due respect, Martin, you could have informed us in advance. You went behind our backs."

"I admit that. You have my apologies."

"Well, it is what it is. I'll tag along."

"Good."

"But I don't intend to follow one word of the professor's advice if I don't like it. I'm heading this inquiry – no-one else."

"Naturally. But do go with an open mind."

"I always have an open mind. It's part of the job," he said, which made Micaela want to snort or say something crushing.

But as usual she held her tongue and nodded with a serious expression.

"I'll tag along too," Lasse Sandberg said.

"Me too," said Jonas Beijer. And that was that.

The following Saturday, they met outside the police station and headed off to the big house in Djursholm: Vargas, Fransson, Sandberg and Beijer.

THREE

Micaela remembered when she had found out. It was the day of his arrest. It was half past eight in the evening, and she was going to visit her mother on Trondheimsgatan. It was early June, but the air had the chill of an October day, and the area outside the flats was full of people. When she got closer, upset faces turned towards her, and within the space of a few minutes she had the highlights.

Giuseppe Costa, or Beppe as they called him, had killed a football referee. His son Mario's team, Brommapojkarna Academy under-17s, had been playing, and towards the end of the second half Beppe had run onto the pitch, heavily inebriated, and begun stirring things up, lashing out. It had taken five or six people to wrestle him onto the turf. Afterwards, when everyone had thought the situation had calmed down, he had reportedly followed the referee with a crazed look in his eyes.

"That sounds completely insane," she said, and went up to her mother, who was on the walkway outside her flat looking down at everyone below.

Her mother had her long grey hair down and was wearing slippers without socks and a new floral hippy blouse. There was a stiff breeze and she looked worried, as if she were afraid something had happened to one of her sons.

"*De qué están hablando?*" she said.

"They say Beppe's killed a football referee," Micaela replied. Her

20

mother was relieved that Simón hadn't done something idiotic again, or potentially fatal. Later, when they were eating dinner, she brought it up again.

"Only to be expected," she said.

Not that Micaela gave it much thought at the time. It was just the kind of thing people regurgitated, she assumed. But afterwards it had bothered her. It suddenly felt as if Beppe had been born to kill a ref. The whole of Husby erupted with rumours and old stories that paved an inevitable path to murder, and perhaps that was why Micaela relayed other things too. One incident in particular that stood out.

She had been only eleven or twelve at the time, and back then she'd heard about Beppe pretty often. Fights, scenes at the bar in Husby, rowdiness and shouting from his flat.

In those days, Simón, her eldest brother, was into hip hop – sometimes it felt as though hip hop was the only thing not killing him – and like so many others he was afraid of Beppe. The lads who played Eminem on their boomboxes, Beppe would kick them around the square. But Beppe must have realised that Simón was in desperate need of validation because he made some sort of approach, and one day he took him aside and they rehearsed. Later that night Beppe stepped right up to the barbecue area outside the flats and whistled. He was going to do a song, he said.

"Not now. We don't feel like it," people shouted.

"Shut your gobs. I've got something special for you," he said, beckoning Simón over.

Simón waved dismissively, and seemed just as awkward and lost as ever. But then he did a couple of dance moves she'd never seen before. And when he and Beppe rapped "I'm the lost son with a life of crime, I'm the one they're calling in to nine-nine-nine", the song Simón had written, Micaela couldn't think of a time when people had shouted with so much glee outside the flats.

It wasn't so strange, really. She guessed that all murderers had done good things too. Yet it lingered with her, a kind of unsolved mystery. She told the story a couple of times after the murder and eventually heard from Jonas Beijer that Beppe himself wanted to speak to her.

"Would you say there's a conflict of interest in your relationship with Costa?" Beijer asked.

"I don't know," she said.

But Beijer didn't seem to hear her hesitation, instead telling her to "establish contact and see if you can get him to talk". It was a long shot, of course. Nothing had worked so far. Costa had barely managed to stay on topic during questioning, and hadn't even admitted to what everyone could see on the video footage from the match.

As ever, she prepared meticulously, and on the morning of June 10 she went down to see Beppe. He was sitting alone in the interrogation room, smoking a cigarette. His enormous, dishevelled figure seemed to have shrunk, and he smiled uncertainly.

"I hear you're saying good things about me," he said.

"I say a lot of shit things too."

"I liked your old man," he said. "We confided in each other."

"We all confided in him."

"But he was a stand-up guy," Beppe said, and he looked so contrite and unhappy that she had to feel sorry for him.

He seemed to have the whole world against him, and perhaps that was why – in an attempt to conceal her sympathy – she went in hard. Afterwards she was told that she'd drawn out a lot of new information. Jonas Beijer congratulated her, and she surprised herself by saying, "He's hiding something," which made an impression.

She could feel it right away, as if she had passed some kind of test, and the next day she was invited to join the investigation.

"We need someone with a bit of perspective," Beijer said, and while she realised immediately that not everyone would welcome her with open arms, she was overwhelmed.

It was a big step, suddenly going from beat cop to investigator on a murder case everyone was talking about, and she began to dream that she would end up a chief inspector – or perhaps even a chief superintendent. In those first weeks, before the doubts crept in, she was indescribably proud and purposeful.

FOUR

On the Saturday they were due to visit Professor Rekke, there was nothing about the murder in the paper for once – not even an opinion piece on violence in football, or on the persecution of referees, or of children. Nothing.

That was why she read only the international news, just like her father back in the day, and there was very little coming out of Iraq. The war was officially over, even if it wasn't over in practice. Every day, more suicide bombs were being detonated over there. It felt like there was a long way to go before Western-style democracy rose from the ruins.

The sun was scorching in the plaza at Kista torg. She had got up from her kitchen table and was heading for the wardrobe when the telephone rang. It was Vanessa, her best friend, and as it was Saturday morning Micaela guessed it was a report from the party scene. This time it was a long, rambling account of a "mad-clingy Swedish boy" who had tried to have sex with her on the bus home.

"Get out," she said.

"It's the truth," Vanessa said, and when they hung up Micaela let out a small laugh but she wasn't really amused – it was a variation on a story she had heard a hundred times before.

She opened the wardrobe and laid out her dresses and skirts on the bed, resisting the temptation to call Vanessa back and ask for advice. She chose an outfit that was dressier than her usual: a black skirt, red

T-shirt and denim jacket that was perhaps a little on the small side and stretched over her breasts, but which she liked nonetheless, finishing with some white trainers.

On the Tunnelbana she felt surprisingly full of expectation. After all, this was a different kind of assignment, and the professor had mentioned her specifically, or at least that was what they'd said. That was pretty cool. As the train passed through Kista, Hallonbergen and Näckrosen, she rehearsed what to say to her colleagues, and when she got off at Solna Centrum there was something light and effervescent bubbling in her body. But that all died in the car park. It didn't take more than a look – Lasse Sandberg's squinting, scrutinising look that always made its way down to her hips.

"Hello . . . Check out Vargas, all sexed up for the professor," he said.

"I thought—" she began.

"Maybe she never made it home last night," Fransson added.

"It's not always easy to find the time to change between shifts," Sandberg said, which wasn't worth a reply.

She got into the back seat of Fransson's Volvo 745 next to Jonas Beijer, who gave her a sympathetic smile. She lowered her gaze to her nails and wondered whether it had been an idiotic idea to paint them. When she looked up again she was blinded by the sun.

It was a hot day, without a cloud in the sky, and it wasn't much cooler inside the car. Something was wrong with the air conditioning, and the men soon became sweaty and loud. Fransson was describing the hellish pain he'd felt in his hand after shooting practice on the firing range at Hagalundshallen earlier that morning.

"It was like my whole hand was on fire," he said.

As always, he dominated the conversation, and in the absence of anything else to do Micaela observed how Beijer and Sandberg mimicked his tone. If Fransson was whining, they whined too; if he was laughing, they grinned along, and they never chuckled harder than when united against the butt of all their jokes, Assistant Commissioner Falkegren. He was such an unbelievable moron, with those stupid tassels or whatever they were on his shoes . . .

Eventually Micaela had had enough. She longed desperately for any conversation she hadn't heard a hundred times before. But then they glided into Djursholm, past the big, expensive houses, and she lost herself in other thoughts.

Djursholm was at the other end of the Tunnelbana line. The people who lived here were born clutching a winning lottery ticket, while those in Husby were like shrapnel – the debris from faraway explosions. It was Simón who had made that comparison.

"I don't need to read the papers to find out what's happening in the world. I can see it from my neighbours," he had once said, possibly because he had never read the papers, or anything else for that matter. But he did have a point.

When there was war or revolution somewhere in the world, those affected came to Husby, and refugees always brought a little piece of the war with them. As children they had learned to deal with the aftermath.

Red-headed with freckles, the woman on the terrace appeared to be thirty-five or forty. She had a slender, supple figure that seemed peculiarly slight in the sunlight and made them all feel thickset and heavy as they approached her. But worst of all was her beauty. She was so beautiful that they contracted into themselves, and this was not helped by the fact that she received them with such exquisite kindness.

Micaela tugged nervously at her skirt and stayed behind Fransson. He was not usually deferential, but even he seemed lost – especially when they stepped inside the house . . . What were they meant to say?

Falkegren with his suits and tasselled shoes was one thing, but this was something else entirely. Large, beautiful paintings hung on the walls, the ceilings soared, and every single item of furniture exuded style and class. From an adjacent room they could hear a violin being played in delicate, melodious tones. Micaela was speechless. The woman – who had introduced herself as Lovisa Rekke – looked irritated.

"Dear God, I told her to stop," she said apologetically, then shouted, "Julia, that's enough!" The violin fell silent and a girl of seventeen or eighteen emerged from the door on the left, no less ravishing than her mother – absurdly sweet, with curly hair and clear blue eyes.

"Sorry, Mamma, I forgot," she said, and it was more than Micaela could bear.

They were all taken aback, lost for words. No-one said: "Good grief, the music was wonderful," they just stood there, dumbfounded and awkward. Julia Rekke took the initiative, held out her hand and said: "What a pleasure it is to meet you."

Micaela couldn't conceive of a better example of the gulf between the classes: a teenager had transformed them with her poise into a flock of lost sheep. Micaela was filled with a desire to smash a vase or tear down a painting. But there was something else.

She began to think about Rekke's academic articles. She had skimmed them during the week, and had found no suggestion whatsoever that he had cooperated with the police, as Falkegren had said, or that he was even interested in acts of violence. Rather, Rekke discussed errors in thought, hoaxes perpetuated by our brains because of preconceived notions and false ideas. It was probably true – as Fransson had said – that most of it was splitting hairs, intellectual dexterity. Yet something there spoke to her: a clarity, she thought, a sharpness she had been missing.

"Where is he?" Fransson asked in irritation.

"A fair question," Lovisa Rekke said. "I imagine he became pre-occupied with something."

"We don't have all the time in the world."

"I'm sorry – I do understand. I'll go and fetch him. Please take a seat," she said, pointing to a white suite of sofas beside a bronze statue of a girl curtseying, and they sat down to wait.

It may not have been that long, but it felt like an eternity before the lady of the house came downstairs and apologised again, and when they were left alone a second time it was clear that the waiting and the house were having an impact on the others too.

They were twitchy with expectation. Not even Fransson was impervious. He began to fiddle nervously with his wristwatch, an IWC Schaffhausen he had inherited from his brother that he insisted was well beyond his means.

"Maybe the professor has something important to tell us after all," he said, and it was then that they heard rapid footsteps descending the curving staircase, and saw Hans Rekke hurrying towards them.

FIVE

Later, Micaela would wonder what they actually knew that day, and of course it was much less than they realised. But at the time the murder case appeared quite simple, in spite of its brutality. There was nothing sophisticated about it, no sign that the crime was anything other than spontaneous. It appeared to have been an explosion of madness, all the more spectacular because the victim had his own luminosity.

Jamal Kabir was thirty-six years old when he died. He was a handsome, lean man with an upright posture and a misaligned jaw from having been assaulted and tortured in Kabul. Many people talked about the sorrow he radiated, and it was perhaps no surprise that rumours swirled around him. But during the investigation they had heard only good things about him, and he was well known as an experienced referee and coach.

During the Taliban regime, he had fought for the freedom to play football in Kabul. It hadn't been easy, he had told the Swedish Migration Agency. The regime kept announcing new rules about the length of sleeves on jerseys and trousers, and the extent to which players were allowed to celebrate goals. But he had fought for his football. He regarded it as vital, he said. All other entertainment was prohibited. No music was allowed. No-one was permitted to watch films or theatrical performances. Books were burned. Women were shut away or hidden beneath burkas, and there were regular public executions at the city's Ghazi

Stadium, as if murder and mutilation had replaced football as the main form of popular entertainment.

It seemed to have become an existential issue for Kabir to ensure that people were offered something else, and he arranged matches and tournaments for juniors. This made him popular, or so he said. People came to thank him. But he encountered more and more problems with the authorities, and in the end he was arrested, then tortured. There were question marks over his background, and Micaela thought the accounts of his capture were not entirely credible. But the Migration Agency had seen medical evidence that the Taliban really had set about him. There was no doubt that he had been badly assaulted.

According to the autopsy report, he had old fractures to his ribs and his jaw that hadn't been sustained during the murder. There were pale scars visible on his wrists left by some kind of chain, and there were traces of frostbite on his chest. He had fared badly, yet he hadn't lost his fighting spirit. When he arrived in Sweden in November 2002, he immediately resumed his activities from Kabul, but in his own way. While still in the refugee reception centre in Spånga, he sought out the local football pitches and made contact with the boys' teams training there.

"It became my way of surviving," he said.

He fetched balls and set out cones; he offered advice and praise. Before long he was given the chance to referee junior teams' matches, and one thing was obvious: he knew what he was doing. People noticed him, not least because he moved around the pitch in an unusual way, and little by little he was given greater responsibility. In the end he was appointed referee in the national top flight for juniors, and in May, three weeks before his murder, the *Sportspegeln* magazine show came to film him. That was why several onlookers recognised him when he stepped onto the turf at Grimsta IP on June 2. It was certainly why one witness, Ruth Edelfelt, the mother of one of the players, saw him as a war hero, while others spoke a little pompously about the melancholy in his demeanour.

They knew that Kabir had been allocated a flat on Torneågatan, in the Akalla suburb, and was working extra hours at a motorcycle-repair shop, just as he had done in Kabul. The police had received no information to suggest that he was under threat or felt vulnerable. He looked confident as he blew the whistle to start the match just before one o'clock. There were two video recordings of the match. Both teams – Djurgården and Brommapojkarna under-17s – had been filming it, and it was obvious in the footage that Kabir was single-minded and focused. Even if he occasionally glanced at the sky.

There was a storm brewing. It was unusually cold for summer, and the spectators were all wearing coats or tracksuits – all except for one man, in shorts and a pale-blue Napoli jersey with the word Buitoni emblazoned across it. The jersey was important to him. Micaela knew that better than anyone. Back in the day, Beppe used to drone on about Napoli's golden era in the eighties, and the jersey was a replica of the one the team had worn when the club won Serie A with Maradona up front.

The jersey had started off clean – possibly even ironed – and Beppe had been in a splendid mood. He had every reason to be. He was the father of the biggest star on the pitch, Mario Costa, and for a while he wandered around drinking from a green Gatorade bottle that probably contained something other than water, bragging about his lad. But as so often in his life, his mood changed, which may in part have been down to the weather – in the middle of the second half, it began to lash with rain. But more than anything, it was the match itself. Djurgården pulled level, and Beppe began to yell – most of all at Kabir.

"You fucking blind or what? Blow the whistle!" he bawled, though for a long time no-one took any notice. There were other things to concentrate on. The score was 2–2, and the game became increasingly exciting and intense, especially in the dying minutes when Mario got possession of the ball just outside the box, ghosted past two or three players, and was about to shoot when he was felled.

"Penalty! For fuck's sake, penalty!" Beppe shouted, and for once he was probably right.

It looked as clear as day in the footage when they played it back, and Kabir seemed poised to blow his whistle. Yet he never did. No penalty was awarded, and Mario lay injured in the penalty area, shouting, while Beppe rushed onto the pitch and all hell broke loose. Beppe was beside himself, which perhaps was why so many people described Jamal Kabir as dignified – at least, that was what Micaela thought.

Kabir's calm demeanour was in absolute contrast to Beppe's fury; in the last footage of him alive he radiated a sense of being in full control. It was as if his body language was saying: *You can't shake me*. But then something happened. The footage ended abruptly when someone knocked into the camera. After the coaches and parents had managed to haul Beppe off Kabir and calm the situation down, Beppe took a seat in the stand and drank from a new sports bottle that definitely didn't contain water either. It was then that Kabir left the scene, and almost everyone else left at the same time, even Mario, who was in pain and didn't wait for his father. The arena emptied. Only Beppe and the caretaker were left.

But Kabir didn't get far. He stopped on Gulddragargränd just outside the sports centre and checked his mobile in the rain without making a call or sending a text. According to one witness he looked indecisive, worried, or on his guard, at least. Then he vanished into the grove of trees in front of him.

Micaela had never understood why; it was hardly a shortcut, and it was uphill and covered in brushwood. But in he went, never to be seen alive again. It was noteworthy that at around the same time Beppe had got up from his seat and disappeared off in the same direction, muttering dreadful profanities about Kabir.

No-one could say with any certainty what had happened in those crucial minutes – only that it must have been sudden and violent and, no matter how you viewed it, things looked serious for Beppe.

He had proven himself capable of real violence. And he'd had a stone in his hand as he staggered along after Kabir, heading towards Gulddragargränd.

He emerged bloodied from the woods where Kabir lay dead with his skull crushed, and there was CCTV footage from the Tunnelbana which showed him sitting in shock, his T-shirt covered in dark stains.

It would seem he had a motive, an opportunity and the character to have committed the deed.

SIX

Hans Rekke hurried down the curving staircase wearing jeans and a blue linen shirt with the sleeves rolled up, and sat down next to them on the sofa with a slim plastic folder in his hand, his left leg twitching, like a runner who had stopped only reluctantly.

"I'm so sorry," he said.

It didn't feel like he meant it. Unlike his wife and his daughter, he didn't look any of them in the eye. He didn't even shake their hands. He kept his eyes on the floor, his expression troubled, and placed the plastic folder on the coffee table. Micaela was struck by his body, which could have belonged to an athlete – a middle-distance runner. He was lean and tall, with sinewy arms. But his most striking feature was his hands, so small-boned and graceful that she instinctively looked down at her own fingers. She had labourer's hands, she thought, as she gazed out through the window at the sea beyond, uncomfortable. When she looked back the professor was staring at her, and it was not just embarrassing: it felt wrong.

She was a nobody on the team – an intern, basically. He should have been looking at Fransson, but he was looking at her, and although she turned her head away again immediately, she had time to take note of his face. He wasn't beautiful like his wife and his daughter – rather, he was hawk-like, chiselled, with a luminous charisma and pale-blue eyes that seemed to see straight through her.

"Well, we might as well get started then," Fransson said, annoyed again.

"Yes, yes, sorry, of course," Rekke said, looking at the others in the group with the same intensity.

"I gather Assistant Commissioner Martin Falkegren sent you our preliminary investigation," Fransson said.

"Certainly . . . exactly . . . yes."

He sounded distracted.

"And . . . ?" Fransson said.

"And what?"

"What's your perception of Costa?"

"Costa?"

Rekke looked out at the gravel and their car, absorbed, it seemed, in a different line of thought.

"Surely you've read the files? If not, this visit is pointless."

"I've read them."

"Good," Fransson said, fidgeting with his watch. He still seemed nervous. "Because we're looking for a way to get our suspect to confess."

"I've gathered that."

"OK, great. Because you've already helped us, indirectly. Apparently we made use of a method you referred to, one that was used – if we've understood correctly – by a journalist interviewing Ted Bundy."

Rekke once again averted his gaze and looked towards the fountain outside. He seemed self-conscious. "I was being an idiot, it's not that good a story, really."

"Isn't it?"

"Stephen Michaud – the journalist – didn't get much out of Bundy, I'm not quite sure why I mentioned it. I think I must have wanted to say that I believe in flattery. What's the old saying? The praise we receive is inversely proportional to the amount we deserve."

Carl Fransson appeared to contemplate these words, and not entirely

35

understand them. He leaned forward, stretching out his right hand in an odd movement.

"Yes . . . perhaps . . . but in this case it really turned out—"

Rekke interrupted him. "You were on the firing range with your pistol this morning."

"What . . . yes . . . how did you know?" Fransson looked at him in surprise and withdrew his right hand, crossing his arms.

"Just a guess, nothing to worry about. But I apologise. I interrupted you."

"As I said," Fransson continued, even more uncertain now, "we're interested in knowing what more we can do to get him to open up, especially taking into account his personality disorder."

"You're alluding to the conclusions in Per Wärner's P7?"

"In part, yes. But we have also noticed ourselves how he behaves and how he brags."

"Grandiose?"

"Exactly. Grandiose, and impulsive. A psychopath, to put it plainly. Or do you have a different view . . . as an expert?"

"As an expert, I'm of the opinion that very many people want him to be a psychopath," Rekke said.

"How do you mean?"

"How to put it? There's something about that word that is enlivening, is there not? A shot of whisky in your coffee, an aperitif to offset the boredom of everyday life."

"Now you've lost me," Fransson said.

"I apologise. I have a tendency to be cryptic."

Rekke fell silent, his eyes glassy. It was as if he were constantly entering into and emerging from intense concentration.

"I like your watch – it's a stylish, classic piece," he said.

Fransson looked down at his wrist.

"What . . . oh . . . thanks."

"But the crown appears to be damaged. You should get someone to look at it. Otherwise it'll come off."

"There's nothing wrong with the crown," Fransson muttered, angry now, tugging at his shirtsleeve to hide the wristwatch.

"But more to the point: was it really such a good idea to get so worked up over the P7?"

Fransson started.

"What do you mean?" he said.

"*Munvig*, for example," Rekke said. "Is that a common word nowadays?"

"Er . . . no . . . I don't believe so."

Fransson glanced at the others as if to say: *Do you see? He's impossible to talk to.*

"Well, what do you say?" Rekke said, turning towards Micaela. "Is that what you say in your neck of the woods? That was a *munvig* guy I met yesterday."

"No, not exactly," she said.

"Yet it appears three times in the preliminary investigation files. How can that be?"

"I don't know," Fransson said.

"In that case allow me to explain," Rekke said. "*Munvig* is a poor translation of the English word 'glib'."

"Glib?"

"Quite. Swedish dictionaries tend to define it using several words: 'smooth-tongued', 'loquacious', 'superficial'. But when Mia Hjerlingm did her Swedish translation of Robert D. Hare's *Without Conscience: The Disturbing World of the Psychopaths Among Us*, she chose one word instead of several, and that was *munvig*, which took hold, especially since it ended up at the top of Hare's psychopathy checklist. *Munvig* and charming is what the Swedish translation says."

"I don't understand," Fransson said.

"The word took hold and began to appear in more popular works, or what we might describe as more light-hearted books, such as *How to Uncover a Psychopath*."

"Oh, right," Fransson said, clearly discomforted.

"Exactly. And you and Inspector Sandberg have read that book, have you not?"

"What's that got to do with this?"

"You allowed your opinion to be coloured by it," Rekke said calmly.

"Are you claiming we made it up?"

"No, no, not at all. It's merely that your perspective was altered slightly, as happens to us all when we read books that fascinate us. But the troubling thing here is that there was no dissenting voice, no *advocatus diaboli*, no *via negativa*."

"Sorry?"

"You were all – well, almost all – looking for the same thing."

"And that was . . ."

"To corroborate the conclusion in Per Wärner's P7, which is unfortunate, and not just because Per is an idiot."

"Is he an idiot?"

"Yes, by and large. It became a vicious circle and strengthened the tendency in the inquiry that we psychologists usually refer to as 'confirmation bias' or 'group polarisation'."

"What?"

"You use the term 'tunnel vision' in the police, don't you?"

His words went through the team like an electric shock, yet Micaela saw that the men didn't at first grasp what he was saying. Fransson gaped. Then he bellowed in a combination of anger and confusion:

"What the hell are you implying?"

Rekke met his gaze for a second or two, then turned to her.

"It's particularly common in homogeneous groups with a strong leader. Do you have a strong leader? What do you say, Micaela?" he said. She jumped – and not just because he knew her name. Something dark ignited within her – perhaps even a thirst for revenge.

"Now you're going too far," Fransson hissed, and Rekke looked as though he wanted to leave.

His left leg began twitching again, just as it had done when he sat down. But then he blinked slowly and straightened his back as if he was about to go on stage. He fixed his eyes on a point above Fransson's head.

"We can start with the first witness statement," he said.

"Which witness would that be?"

"The caretaker at Grimsta IP, Viktor Bengtsson," he said. "He sees Costa bend down and pick up something from the running track, at the edge of the football pitch; he doesn't know exactly what. But, step by step, you seem to put a stone in Costa's hand. 'Could it have been a stone?' Detective Inspector Axel Ström asks on page 138 of the interrogation report, and gets a 'Yes, maybe' in reply. Afterwards, it's a fact that Costa had a stone in his hand. Isn't that a little strange?"

"We haven't taken it as fact."

"And then we have the profanity. Bengtsson hears Costa cursing the referee. But is Costa really saying 'I'm going to kill that bastard'? Initially, reference is made only to profanities in general. Bengtsson says: 'He looked like he could kill someone.' But somehow, that is transformed into words coming from Costa's mouth. Bengtsson's memory is embellished."

"That's not true. We've posed critical questions all along."

"Ostensibly, perhaps, but not in practice. Regardless, I think Bengtsson's statement is pretty good in comparison. Things are worse when it comes to young Filip Grundström."

"What's the matter with him?"

"He's a sensitive lad, right? He's able to read your wishes, and I sympathise with that. What didn't we all do at that age to secure fifteen seconds in the limelight? Filip saw Costa with a dirty Napoli jersey. But exactly where is not clear – not at first. He becomes more certain, and then, hey presto, Costa staggers out of the forest next to Gulddragargränd, and in the same moment the red muck on his top becomes blood. Isn't it funny? How one assumption reinforces the other, and how that, in turn, affects the way you speak to other witnesses."

"That's an outrageous suggestion," Fransson said, half rising, only for his heavy, ungainly body to sink back down again.

"Perhaps . . ." Rekke said. "But you become increasingly selective about which information you take an interest in, and I can't understand why you suspect Costa to the extent that you do. His account is nuts, I admit. But the funny thing is that the truth is often like that, off the wall. Why couldn't he have walked in the ditch that runs alongside the road? He was wet and angry, he might as well get wetter and angrier. And why couldn't he have have fallen and hurt his elbow and seen a green clothes hanger on the bank of the ditch? A green clothes hanger."

"What about it?"

"Nothing, really. It's just an odd detail that caught my eye. I couldn't understand why he would mention it if he were lying. A hanger, maybe, but a green one? How many green clothes hangers have you seen in your life?"

"I don't know."

"Nor do I, but here's one in any case."

He produced a Polaroid from his plastic folder, and to Micaela's surprise – and excitement – the photo showed a green hanger in a ditch.

"It was a little further away than I'd expected," he said. "I had to root around a bit."

"So you've been out there?" Jonas Beijer said suddenly, as if he had just woken up.

"Yes, but not for the hanger. I was interested in the mud and the water."

"Why?" Fransson managed to spit out.

"The lakes and marshes out there are dystrophic and acidified. There's a lack of lime, which turns the mud a red-brown shade and makes the water in the ditches look like watered-down blood. I wanted to conduct a little experiment."

"What experiment?" Jonas Beijer said.

"Nothing scientific. Just a small comparative study, this time in black and white – grainy black and white," he said, pulling out two more photographs from the plastic folder.

One of them was all too familiar to them. It was Giuseppe Costa, a full body shot of him sitting on the Tunnelbana, looking dishevelled in his stained Napoli jersey. The other photo depicted a tall, slim figure smiling cautiously at the camera.

The man was Rekke himself, and he was also wearing a dirty T-shirt.

"The lengths we go to in order to understand," he said.

"So you threw yourself in the ditch too?" Fransson said.

"I settled for rubbing the top in the water and mud, then putting it on and walking up to the Tunnelbana station at Vällingby. But that was interesting. Remarkable, is it not, how similar the two tops look?" he said, and they really did. Micaela couldn't help feeling a pang of shame.

Had she ever thought the CCTV footage was especially convincing?

"So you mean there was never any blood on Costa's top?"

This was Jonas Beijer again. He seemed to be gathering his thoughts.

"That's exactly what I mean."

"Why did he get rid of it so quickly then?" Fransson snapped.

"I don't know."

"You don't know?"

"No," Rekke continued. "But perhaps we'll have to take him at his word. The jersey was dirty and tattered, splitting at the seams in two places. Perhaps he didn't feel like washing it. Why do you assume that it was important to him?"

"So you don't see any cause for suspicion, none at all?"

"Of course it would have been better if we'd found the jersey. But there are other issues that are more disturbing – don't you agree?" Hans Rekke said, looking at Micaela.

"What . . . no . . . I don't know about that," she said.

"No? She asks different kinds of questions. She has a different focus to her gaze, and perhaps it makes a difference that she . . ."

He looked at her intensely again, and she felt uncomfortable, ill at ease, as if he was going to articulate a truth she didn't want to hear, and perhaps he noticed that too. He fell silent, then changed tack and moved on to Costa's previous assault case as described in the investigation.

"What sets it apart?" he said.

"Violent aggression," Jonas Beijer said, as if he had changed sides and was now one of Rekke's pupils.

"Exactly, but there's something else, isn't there?"

"What?"

"An absolute bloody racket, in short. Each time Costa's attacked someone, he's shouted and bellowed. But what happens when Jamal Kabir is killed?"

"We don't know."

It must have been quiet, Micaela thought to herself.

"No, we don't," Rekke said. "But there are a few things we *do* know. Jamal Kabir doesn't turn around. No blows land from the side or front. Every blow is aimed at the back of his head. It doesn't seem credible that he was warned in advance by shouts and profanities. But above all—"

"What?" barked Fransson.

"The blows come from above. The cranium and the skull seem to have been crushed by extreme force. The fractures have, as it were, continued in the direction of the trauma. But with one blow it's different; it has made the skull expand momentarily – it's detectable from the protuberance in the Y-shaped crack formation. And what does that indicate?"

"That the blow came from below," Micaela said suddenly.

The thought had already occurred to her.

"Exactly, and which of all the blows ought to have come from below if Kabir fell forwards?"

"The first."

"Quite. And how tall is Costa?"

"One hundred and eighty-seven centimetres."

"And Kabir?"

"A hundred and seventy-three."

"Hence, an educated guess is that the murderer is probably shorter than Kabir, not taller. But above all, I cannot associate this type of cold, methodical rage with Costa's personality, because – to answer your first question: Costa is no psychopath. He's too sentimental and anxiety-driven."

"So what is he, then?"

"He's an alcoholic and an extrovert. He's proud and he's bitter. Without doubt he can be violent. But he didn't kill the referee. You are mistaken," Hans Rekke said in a voice that sounded neither triumphant nor superior, merely apologetic.

Nevertheless his words felt like a slap, even more so since they were sitting in his large house, and because at that moment Rekke seemed so sophisticated with his tall, slim figure, as if every part of him was superior.

Micaela was not surprised in the slightest when Fransson stood up.

"I've heard enough," he spluttered.

"Really?"

"You quite clearly know nothing about police work," he spat, at which point Rekke also stood up and looked at the chief inspector with the same melancholy smile.

"No, perhaps not," he said. "But still, I see certain patterns, and I advise you to check that recording of Kabir just after the final whistle."

"For Christ's sake, we've seen it a thousand times."

"I don't doubt that. But isn't it strange how calm Kabir is, while Costa continues to shout and bluster? It's as if he reads him to a tee: just another nutter, he seems to think to himself. But then suddenly, just before the camera takes a blow, what happens? He looks diagonally to the right and sees something else and he is frightened."

"His gaze is just flickering."

"Is it really? I believe—"

"I'm not interested in what you believe. I'm done with your bullshit."

"I'm sorry about that."

"Well, thanks for having us," Fransson said, and he made for the front door.

For a moment the others didn't know what to do. The change of direction was so sudden and confusing that Beijer and Sandberg ended up swaying on the spot, as if they wanted both to follow Fransson and to stay with Rekke. But eventually their impulse to stand by their boss won out, and only Micaela was left standing beside the bronze statue, deep in concentration.

"What is it you believe?"

"What . . . ?" Rekke said, not quite with her.

"You think there was someone else there on the touchline, someone we haven't yet spotted?"

Hans Rekke looked at her, not as he had before, but as if the interest he had shown in her recently had been purely intellectual – as if she had been just another thing he had inspected.

"Perhaps," he said hesitantly, and she wondered whether she ought not to leave too. But then she thought about the referee and his gloomy demeanour on the pitch.

"What about Jamal Kabir, then? What do you make of him?" she said.

Rekke seemed to come back to life. He looked at her with a puzzled expression.

"I don't trust him," he said. "Not just because of the gaps in his story. It's his old injuries, too. I recognise them. It's as if they point to . . ." he began, fervour returning to his voice.

But he didn't have the chance to finish. Agitated voices were audible from the hallway as well as the sound of footsteps, soft, tentative steps that seemed afraid to interrupt. It was Rekke's wife, who had stepped out of the kitchen and was now looking at them quizzically, perhaps in annoyance. At the same moment they heard the front door slam. All three of them went in that direction, past the daughter, Julia, who watched them with a curious, almost greedy expression. Micaela heard Rekke whisper:

"She's our little spy."

"What?" she said.

"You have to guard your secrets," he said.

His tone was playful, as if he had completely forgotten about the slamming door. Micaela couldn't summon the energy to care.

As she emerged into the sunshine her steps felt sluggish. She looked down at the raked gravel. Fransson and Sandberg were waving at her impatiently from the car, and she swore to herself, absorbed in her thoughts. Suddenly she turned around, with a feeling that she was being watched again, being observed with the same sharpness and intensity as before. But it was just her imagination.

Over by the veranda Rekke briefly put an arm around his wife's waist before disappearing into the large house with light, nonchalant steps, as if the meeting had for him been no more than a footnote, a halt en route to something more important. At that point anger and humiliation washed over her.

She got into the car with a determined expression, and was hit by the stifling heat inside.

SEVEN

August 4, 2003

Fransson's huge body froze.

It almost looked as if he had the cramps. He had been in an unusually good mood for the last week, and that was because the visit to Rekke had been brushed aside. The professor's run-through now seemed like an illusion – a magic trick that had confused them in the moment, but which meant nothing once they returned to harsh reality. Throughout the month of July, Fransson and the team had worked on the same hypothesis as before, doubtless helped by the fact that Giuseppe Costa was at last on the way to confessing, without them having to resort to any psychological tricks.

He had simply gone to pieces, sinking into a state of resignation and confusion. "I don't know" was now his response to the question of whether he was guilty, as if he were opening up to the idea that the crime might have occurred during a blackout. On the whole, his guilt seemed just as evident as before, and Chief Prosecutor Mårten Odelstam was preparing to file a charge of murder, or at least manslaughter. Life on the team was, in other words, much the same as usual, and Fransson yearned to be up north in the Oviksfjällen mountains, fly fishing. He longed for it all to be over, for a time when the newspapers would stop writing about it and griping, and the damned assistant commissioner would stop calling him and agitating. But when did life ever work out the way you wanted it to?

On this particular morning, Micaela Vargas stepped into the open-plan office with a determined stride, and it was immediately obvious that there was something different about her. It wasn't just that she was wearing a skirt and heels. It was also . . . her smile. For the first time since they'd been at Rekke's and she'd got her knickers in such a twist that she'd swallowed everything he said, she didn't look so goddamned troubled, and it was a moment before he realised that she was looking at his hands. What the hell was up with his hands? She seemed to be clutching something, a small, shiny pin-like object. The fuck . . . ? It was the crown from his Schaffhausen. At first he didn't understand, or perhaps he thought he could just push it back on and pretend nothing had happened. But then it dawned on him. His two-hundred-thousand-krona watch had broken.

"Jesus fucking Christ," he shouted, standing up with a groan, and then it was not just Vargas glowering at him, but the rest of the team too.

He mumbled something about needing to get to the watch department in NK – he needed to fix this right away. And yet he was unable to move. He stood there, gripped by a sudden unease, and perhaps that was why he was looking at Vargas, who had somehow started all this. She had sat down at her desk, and whereas before she had just been smiling, she now appeared disturbingly decisive. Her shoulders and back were tense as she grasped her mobile. Fransson was struck by the realisation that she was calling the professor.

Bloody Rekke.

For a while, Micaela had hoped he was wrong. It was too much that he had sat there in his big house, with his beautiful wife and his perfect daughter, and known better than they did about everything. But the more she tried to dismiss his words, the more they haunted her, and in the end she could see quite clearly what she had felt only as a knot in her stomach before: they were on the wrong track. Not that anyone listened to her. The bloody morons were far too worked up over the fact that Beppe had fallen into a state of deep crisis and no longer had it in him to issue denials or tell tall tales.

When she lodged her objections, she was met with nothing but embarrassed looks and empty promises, and eventually – a week after their visit to Djursholm – she resolved to contact Professor Rekke. It went against protocol. She didn't want to be made to feel like a small, exotic bird being inspected from above, and even less like that bronze girl curtseying obediently. But still, she gathered her courage. This wasn't about her, it was a murder inquiry, and one evening at home in Kista, after she'd had a couple of beers and spent an hour on the phone to Vanessa, she dialled his number. She was sitting in her kitchen looking out the window towards Kista church. A woman's voice answered. It was Lovisa Rekke. Feeling decidedly nervous, Micaela explained in a roundabout way who she was.

"Oh, hello!" Lovisa said, as if delighted that Micaela was calling.

"I wanted to speak to Professor Rekke," she said, uncertain of how to refer to him.

"I'm afraid he isn't at home. I hope he didn't upset you too much during your chat. He can be a bit rude sometimes. But he means well."

"I think what he said was true."

"That doesn't surprise me at all. Sometimes it's as if he can see through the walls. Julia and I joke that we have to hide our secrets well."

"How can I reach him?"

"He's gone back to Stanford. But I'm sure he'd be delighted to talk to you. He liked you."

It wasn't exactly that Micaela believed her . . . yet it boosted her self-confidence, and as she took down his mobile number and email address, she felt a sudden sense of expectation, as if he might not be so bad after all. But then he didn't pick up when she called, and no matter how many times she emailed, he didn't reply. Still, she couldn't shake off his words, and on her way to work a few days later she called Lovisa Rekke again.

She could tell straight away that something had changed. Not that Lovisa was unpleasant. "Oh dear, what a pity," she said. But there was something new, something chilly in her voice, as if she wanted Micaela to keep away.

Micaela refused to give in, especially since she'd uncovered new information. She had gone out to Grimsta IP and seen all of them again: the coaches and parents – all those who had rushed over to Giuseppe Costa and wrestled him to the turf. She knew them pretty well by that stage. They were well-meaning middle-class dads, proud of their boys. But that evening it was like being down at the police station. The atmosphere was more hostile, and they looked at her with annoyance, even Niklas Jensen.

Jensen wasn't much taller than she was. He had a red beard and small, screwed-up eyes, and he was older than the other dads – perhaps as old as sixty. Usually he liked small talk and would smile kindly at her. But this time he just stood there by the touchline in his Brommapojkarna tracksuit, staring at the lads on the pitch with a dissatisfied expression.

"Thought you'd cleared this up?" he said, without bothering to look her in the eye.

"I'd like to check on a few things," she said. "Before, you listed who was in the vicinity of the fight."

"I was standing pretty far away. I didn't get that good a look."

"I know," she said. "But are you sure you included everyone? Did anyone walk by? There could have been someone you missed."

"I find that hard to believe."

"But if you think—"

"No," he said.

"Absolutely certain? If you ask me, it's clear from the video that Kabir was scared by someone passing by, and you must have been in the perfect position to see who it was."

"That would be the old man."

"The old man?"

"I already mentioned him."

"No," she said.

"I mentioned him to Inspector Sandberg."

Bloody Sandberg, she thought. Had he not bothered to note it in the transcript of the interview?

"I haven't seen that in the files."

"Hmm, well, it wasn't important. He just walked by briefly. Then he buggered off," he said.

"Which way?"

"Towards Gulddragargränd."

"What did he look like?"

"He was an Arab too, bald, fairly short and hunched over, maybe with a limp. He was easily seventy, or more like eighty, actually. Wearing a green jacket. I didn't get a good look at him, I don't suppose any of us did. We were otherwise occupied."

"Damn," she said with such vehemence that Niklas Jensen added:

"Come on, it was just some decrepit little man."

But this decrepit little man they had missed, or even ignored, had somehow frightened Kabir. She had been convinced at once that she was onto something significant, and since then she had turned everything upside down, searching for a better description. But hardly anyone had seen the man. Apart from Jensen's statement she only had two sightings, both from a distance. Still, there really had been an old man with a limp at Grimsta at the time of the murder, and it was a lead she needed to get to the bottom of. She was also obsessed with what Rekke had been on the verge of saying in relation to Kabir's injuries when their conversation in Djursholm was interrupted.

She had the impression that it was important. She wasn't satisfied with the medical examiner's assertion that every single blemish on Kabir's body had been gone over ten times. She spent hours looking at the pictures from the autopsy as if they were maps, secret ciphers that could be decoded, and she needed to get hold of Rekke to discuss what she could see – or thought she could see.

On several occasions she'd had the phone in her hand and dialled his number only to hang up before it started ringing. Only now, when the crown on Fransson's watch had fallen off, did it suddenly feel easy. This time she got through.

"Professor Rekke," said a voice on the telephone, or at least that's what she thought she heard. But it must have said: "Professor Rekke's assistant," or something like that, because it wasn't him at all, rather some young guy, probably a student. He told her in English that the professor was busy, but of course he'd call back "as soon as he could". She didn't believe a word of it. His voice sounded hesitant and protective, and she was sick and tired of it all, pissed off with the lot of them, condescending snobs and idiot cops alike.

"You were so happy just a moment ago, weren't you?"

She jumped. Jonas Beijer had come over and was standing slightly too close to her. He smelled of horses and was dishevelled and hollow-eyed, as if he hadn't slept much. But his smile was as big as ever, and for a brief moment she wanted to tell him everything. Jonas was the only member of the team on her side, even if he didn't admit that in front of the others.

"What? . . . No, I'm OK," she said.

"Have you got hold of Rekke?" he said.

"No, but I don't care."

"Yeah, right," he answered, rolling his eyes. "But I'm not so sure it's necessary anyway," he said. "I spoke to the prosecutor."

"What did he say?"

Jonas paused for effect.

"Come on," she said.

"He's not going to file charges. He no longer thinks it holds together."

Her unease from the conversation with Rekke's assistant was vanquished in a second and she glanced at Jonas, thinking she'd get to see his broad smile again. But he looked serious, as if this were bad news – and of course for the team as a whole it was. It would be a huge embarrassment if it transpired they had gone all out after the wrong guy.

"That's fantastic," she said.

Jonas shushed her.

"Don't look so fucking pleased. Get out of here before Fransson finds out!"

She sidled past the others, her expression not giving away how she felt, and it was only when she was out in the corridor that she pumped her fist. So that was that, she thought, trying to picture how Beppe would react. But pretty soon she had other things to think about. Lucas, her brother, messaged to say he wanted to see her, and she smiled. Maybe this was just what she needed.

See you at Mamá's in half an hour, she wrote back.

EIGHT

When he was little, Lucas had run straight through a glass door. Since then, he'd had a pale scar running from one eyebrow up his forehead. Micaela had always thought the scar suited him. But sometimes it scared her. Sometimes, from a distance, she thought she saw something violent in his body, something only just kept in check. The impression always vanished when she got closer.

He had a wonderful, crooked smile, and he often gave her gifts – mostly clothes she never wore. He was always saying he was proud of her. There was an energy in him that she was drawn to.

"Hi there."

He was standing outside and waved her over. Before them loomed the green-clad block of flats in which they had grown up, with its white external walkways and square windows, and she walked towards him past the playground and the benches. It was a while before she had him to herself. People kept coming by and Lucas shook their hands and exchanged a few words with them. He could have been a politician on the campaign trail.

"I've missed you. Want to take a stroll?" he said once they were alone.

"Aren't we going to visit Mamá?"

"She doesn't need to hear everything."

They walked up Trondheimsgatan through the greenery and towards the centre of Husby. Market traders were out hawking their wares, but there weren't many people about. The sun was burning her neck. Further away by the car park, a police car pulled in.

"It's good to see you," he said. "I bumped into your old Swedish teacher yesterday. She thought you'd become a lawyer or doctor or something."

"Sorry to disappoint her."

"Nah, being on the murder squad is way more cool. But I've heard the cops are treating you like shit."

She looked into his big brown eyes.

"Who said that?"

He put an arm around her.

"No-one in particular. But you know, I have my contacts. Is there anything I can do?"

"It's not that bad," she said.

"That Fransson guy is a moron."

"A little, maybe."

She pictured the chief inspector's heavy body as he rushed off towards the watch department at NK.

"They say you think Beppe is innocent."

She shuddered, and was tempted to tell him what Jonas Beijer had said. But that would be inconceivable.

"More than ever," she said.

"And the others don't agree?"

"They will," she said, and tried to change the subject by asking whether he was still working as a bouncer at Sophie's.

He didn't seem to want to discuss it. Instead, he nodded at Héctor Pérez, one of his younger friends, who was standing outside the launderette having a smoke.

"There's a lot of chat about that referee."

"Would be strange if there wasn't," she said.

Lucas waved disparagingly at Héctor, who seemed to want to come over and talk.

"I've heard he was afraid."

Down by the Tunnelbana station, Micaela glimpsed a colleague in uniform, Filippa Gran, who was looking at her inquisitively, and she wondered for a moment whether to greet her.

"Who did you hear that from?"

He spread out his arms in the way she'd seen him do a thousand times before.

"You can't take the bloody piss out of me," she said. "This is the most important thing I've ever done."

"I'm not taking the piss."

She glowered at him in irritation.

"What is it he was supposed to have been afraid of, then?"

"I saw that report on TV," he said. "It was like he was inflating his ego to hide how shit-scared he was. Because there is some shit in his past, I promise you that."

"So you've become the worst psychologist ever."

"I've always been the worst psychologist ever."

She glanced at him sceptically, and he grinned back.

"I suppose we'll have to bring you in for questioning," she said.

Lucas put his arm around her again. She shook herself free.

"I can try and find out more. There are a lot of sick rumours going around."

She looked at him and became convinced he was just trying to make himself sound important. Throughout her childhood, Lucas had pretended to know things and generally behaved in a mysterious way, as if he possessed some great secret.

"Please," she said.

"We could help each other, you and me."

Of course they could. But she didn't like his tone and wondered whether Lucas was playing some kind of game with her. She thought about Rekke and what he had been about to say about Kabir's injuries.

*

Two days later, she was summoned to Carl Fransson's office. She couldn't help feeling a little expectant, a little hopeful, but really she had no idea why she was there. There was something in the air, and she straightened her back as she entered the room. Fransson was wearing a long-sleeved AIK jersey that strained over his belly. Lying on the desk was a bunch of tulips.

"Alright?" he said in a tone that was more easy-going than usual, and she replied in the same way and asked whether he'd been able to fix his wristwatch. Fransson muttered that it had been sent to Switzerland. It was going to be six weeks before it was ready.

"Rough," she said.

"Swiss precision craftsmanship. Can only be repaired on site."

"What did you want to talk about?" she asked.

Fransson hesitated.

"About your brother," he said.

She flinched.

"I'm guessing you mean Lucas," she said.

"What do you make of him?"

"I'm not quite sure what to say," she said awkwardly. "I don't think he's doing anything stupid anymore. He's got a job as a bouncer in the city centre. And he has a very law-abiding girlfriend who's doing a degree in marketing."

Fransson fidgeted, and seemed to have difficulty looking her in the eye.

"We, on the contrary, think he's branching out again."

"I haven't heard anything about that."

And she really hadn't. In fact, her mother and Simón had reassured her that Lucas was steering clear of bad company.

"But you're close, right?" he said.

"We were when we were younger, after my father died. But we don't see each other that much anymore."

"Yet you were strolling through Husby, arm in arm, only a couple of days ago."

So Filippa had found it necessary to report that, she thought to herself.

"What's this about?" she said, remembering that Lucas seemed to be keeping pretty good tabs on Fransson. He'd called him a moron. Was there some personal beef between them?

"We've been receiving some pretty worrying information about him, and we'd like your help."

"In what way?" she said, feeling her facial muscles tighten.

"We want you to keep your eyes peeled. It's not that you need to push him, or even snoop. We don't want you to make him suspicious – just listen and see whether you can find out anything."

"So you want me to infiltrate my own family?"

"Sort of – yes."

"How can you even ask me that?"

"Because sometimes, Micaela, we have to pick sides."

"You know which side I'm on."

"Of course. But sometimes we have to make more proactive choices. What do you say?"

She had no idea what to say. Everything was spinning inside her head, and it wasn't just Lucas who appeared there in a thousand guises. It was the murder inquiry too, and that old man in the green jacket with the limp, and the sense that something crucial was right there in front of her very eyes.

"I don't believe it," she said. "I just want to concentrate on the investigation."

"Well, that's it, see," Fransson said. "We're going to be making changes to the team."

"OK, that's good, I suppose," she said cautiously.

"And you're out."

"What?"

She grasped the armrest of her chair.

"You're out – unless you . . ."

"Unless I what?"

"Really show that you want to stay," he said, and then she didn't want to understand, she pushed the words away. Even so, her thoughts clarified into an uncomfortable question.

"So you're saying that I can stay if I set up my brother?" she said.

"We want you to offer us something extra."

"I was the only one who saw we were on the wrong track!"

"Just because there are no charges, it doesn't necessarily mean we were wrong. But it's true that we need to think outside the box, and that means we need a gang that's welded together – it's as simple as that."

"A gang of blokes?"

"Don't play the woman card, Micaela. It's beneath you."

"You can't do this to me."

"I can, actually, and as I said, we're giving you an opportunity to stay on the team. In fact, I consider it generous given the circumstances."

"What circumstances are those?"

"Your difficulty cooperating, among others," he said, leaving her fumbling for words. She felt she needed a comeback – nothing aggressive, something factual and incisive that demonstrated how unfair the whole situation was. After all, she was the only one on the team who hadn't been staring down a dark tunnel.

But no matter how hard she tried, she felt nothing, only blank and drained.

"I don't know," she muttered lamely and stood up.

"Leaving already?" he said.

"I need air," she said, heading into the corridor, down the stairs and out into the sunshine on Sundbybergsvägen.

A red cabriolet drove past and a guy in a cap and sunglasses waved at her. She gave him the finger and hoped he'd stop and kick off. But he kept on driving, and she decided to go home.

NINE

Late September, 2003

She never did take up Fransson's offer and was reassigned to the youth outreach department. With more time on her hands, she enrolled on the basic law course offered by Stockholm University and kept abreast of the murder inquiry as best she could. This much she knew: no major progress was being made. Since Solna District Court had released Giuseppe Costa, the team had got nowhere, and the more time passed, the more she let it go.

She busied herself with work and her studies, and every now and then she'd tag along with Vanessa to pubs and clubs. On one such evening when they'd had an early drink, she found herself strolling alone through Sturegallerian shopping mall. It was a quarter past eight, and further down on Stureplan she caught sight of a guy she vaguely recognised from the personal-protection detail at the Security Service.

His name was Albin, she couldn't remember his surname, and he was burly and blond with pronounced cheekbones and small, vigilant eyes. He was standing outside the entrance to the Sturehof restaurant, and she could tell from his body language that he was on duty. She nodded curtly before glancing into the restaurant to see who he was protecting. At first she spotted no-one special. Then she jumped.

Inside was Mats Kleeberger, the foreign minister. He was sitting right by the window with three other men, and that surprised her. It was no longer common for high-ranking politicians to be out and about in public. But there was Kleeberger – the most authoritarian luminary in the government. He wore a white shirt and a pair of mahogany-coloured spectacles that he had pushed up onto his forehead, and she could tell immediately from his expression and gestures that he was talking about something that engaged him.

He radiated the same absolute self-confidence as he did on television – the suggestion that he understood the world a little better than others. There was something about his charisma, or perhaps it was his elegance, that made other politicians seem provincial and lost.

She found herself bewitched by the scene. But pretty soon she realised that it was not in fact Kleeberger who fascinated her. A tall man in a black shirt was sitting diagonally opposite him, and unlike the others around the table he seemed bored – as if the foreign minister were no more than an awkward child.

It was the man's left leg, a leg that twitched nervously under the table, a bounce that she had seen before. The man was Hans Rekke, and she was seized by the impulse to run inside and ask all the questions she had been puzzling over. But naturally she remained outside the window, understanding more clearly why he hadn't answered her emails or returned her calls.

There was no room for someone like her in his world, especially not if he sat there bored even in the presence of the foreign minister – as if he wanted to move on to something more important in this instance too.

"Idiot," she murmured to herself, without really knowing who she was referring to, and just then something happened inside the restaurant. Rekke appeared to interrupt Kleeberger. Kleeberger responded by looking ashamed, and this left her floored. She had never seen anyone embarrass Kleeberger like that. As she left she uttered an obscenity. It was so . . . unfair.

Life was unfair. She had to fight, struggle, butt her way forward. Doors were shut in her face all the time, while he had everything: a carefree ability to speak his mind, respect even in government circles, wealth, a happy family – total fucking harmony, no doubt – even if sometimes he had to put up with dumb cops and tedious civil servants. But that probably wasn't so bad either. It gave him a chance to demonstrate his superiority. He could go to hell.

For the hundredth time she thought about their visit to the big house in Djursholm. It had been degrading, of course, an intellectual execution. Yet there had been an element of triumph there too – a feeling that Rekke had somehow given her satisfaction for all the times the rest of them had looked down on her. And she couldn't forget her glee and amazement when the crown on Fransson's watch had fallen off.

It was such a magical moment that not even Rekke, with his nonchalance and his silence over the summer, could kill it. When she reached Biblioteksgatan she began to smile, despite herself. Rekke was doubtless an arrogant arsehole. But she could not dismiss him for that. Rather, the glow around him was only enhanced by his indifference towards Kleeberger. Not that she would ever admit that to anyone, not even Vanessa. She pushed it out of her mind and continued on towards Kungsträdgården and the entrance to the Tunnelbana on Arsenalsgatan.

What was her name again? Martin Falkegren couldn't remember. But for some reason he followed her.

It was his wife's fault, in a way. Hanna had raced off to the hospital where she worked as an orthopaedic surgeon, and had left him alone, out on the town. A short while later he found himself on Stureplan, unsure whether to take a cab home or head off on his own adventures. And as his gaze roamed, looking for inspiration, he caught sight of his young Chilean colleague.

She'd certainly spruced herself up a bit. She was wearing a pair of tight jeans that showed off her arse, but her top was way too baggy and her fringe was still hanging down over her eyebrows. A young woman ought not to hide herself like that, he thought to himself, resolving to go over and engage her in small talk. Just then he noticed her body tense, as if she were about to launch herself at someone. But nothing happened. Nothing except that her shoulders shook, and then she vanished towards Biblioteksgatan. Instinctively, he took a few steps in her direction. Was he really going to follow her? Yes, why not, he thought. It was just a whim, a little madness. By the time he saw her crossing the square at Norrmalmstorg, he'd convinced himself that he really ought to speak to her.

He didn't know how much she still knew about the investigation, or how much had seeped out generally, so he decided to fish a little, and perhaps also . . . now that his wife was gone for the night . . . He allowed his gaze to wander over her body again.

"Well, hello there," he said.

She turned around, obviously surprised, possibly even nervous, and he liked that, and for a second he searched for other signs of respect, subservience. But as before he saw something ambivalent in her that he couldn't put his finger on.

"Hello," she said.

"I just wanted to have a word," he said, smiling his friendliest smile. "Are you happy with the way your work's going?"

She hesitated.

"I am, thanks," she said.

"I hope you weren't disappointed to be taken off the inquiry?"

Her expression clouded and he was convinced that she was furious, but she seemed determined not to admit it.

"It wasn't a problem. I like my new job," she said.

"Are you still in touch with the team?"

"I speak to Jonas Beijer sometimes. But I haven't heard from him for a while. I don't suppose there's much to tell either," she said, which provoked him, even though he was no longer involved with the murder.

There was an unpleasantness there that could flare up out of nowhere; he always took it personally when an investigation was criticised.

"There's this and that," he said. "Have you heard they're trying to identify the old man who walked past the pitch during the fight? They've put in a huge amount of work."

"Oh, is that right?" she said. "They weren't all that interested in him when I was involved."

"No?" he said unsympathetically. "Well, it's a hot lead now. They're getting help from American intelligence in Kabul."

"Jonas told me things weren't that easy with the Americans."

"Everything takes time down there. Goes without saying."

She seemed to consider this.

"Can I ask you something?"

"By all means. Whatever you like," he said, imagining that he would offer a long and somewhat fatherly response, possibly over a glass of wine somewhere nearby.

He glanced briefly at her hips.

"Have you considered calling Professor Rekke again?" she said, ruining the atmosphere in a second.

"No, it hasn't been necessary," he said.

"He saw things clearly."

"*Claritas, claritas*, as he always says."

Martin Falkegren tried to sound relaxed, though what he wanted to do was to spit out the words, to ram them down her throat. *Not everything is as straightforward as you believe, little girl*, he wanted to say. But he realised that would be a mistake, and decided to bring the conversation to a close.

"There was something in particular about Kabir's old injuries," she said.

"Exactly, yes, that might have been the case. But Rekke didn't always see as much as he thought he did. Anyway . . ."

"Yes?" she said.

"I've got to dash. It was lovely bumping into you," he said, shaking her hand and brushing her shoulder.

He jumped into a taxi and on the drive home he remembered the call from Rekke. Bloody liar, he thought to himself. Thinks he can throw around any accusation he likes just because he has his millions and his fancy degree. Falkegren felt proud not to have passed on the information like some goddamned gossip-monger.

He had quite simply taken responsibility and demonstrated leadership.

He dearly hoped the Americans would demolish Hans Rekke once and for all.

Micaela didn't get off at Kista. She went on to Husby, hoping to have a chat with her mother. But when she reached the area outside the block of flats, she glimpsed a familiar figure in a grey jacket. The figure was heading towards the wooded area beside Järvafältet.

"Lucas!" she shouted.

He didn't seem to hear, and she carried on towards the entrance and the lift, reflecting on her encounter with Falkegren. She couldn't make sense of it. Why had he approached her, and why had he acted so strange when she'd mentioned Rekke? Not long ago, Falkegren had admired the professor and irritated them all with his posturing and praise. Now he seemed uncomfortably affected by the name. Perhaps not so peculiar given what had happened on the investigation, but still . . . she had the impression there was more to it.

Lucas reappeared in her consciousness, and a moment later she turned on her heel and followed him to the wooded area.

It wasn't exactly the nicest place in Husby. Some of the drug-dealing had moved there, and she knew that Simón, her other brother, was often there in the evenings looking for drugs or whatever, a bit of company, a little drama. But now she could see no-one at all. The woods were deserted. The wind had begun to pick up. The leaves were already yellow, and rubbish and beer cans were scattered among them on the ground.

Through a gap between the trees she looked up at the grey-green block of flats and her mother's window on the third floor, and suddenly felt that she didn't want to be here but instead up there with her, drinking tea and gossiping about Rekke and Kleeberger, and hearing her mother say something at once naive and critical: "My God, what fine folk you run into. But don't imagine for one second that you can trust them."

The wind rustled in the trees. The atmosphere was threatening, elusive, and she took a couple of steps towards the footpath and the lamp post below. Then she heard a sound. It was hard to make out, a whimpering almost, and she might have dismissed it as an animal.

Concentrating intensely she heard it again, and now it sounded like a terrified person who didn't dare scream but was instead panting quietly. She stood there for a second, completely still. Then she spun around and peered into the woods in the direction of the noise.

She could just make out two men fighting, or rather . . . only one of them was fighting, and the other was Lucas. He seemed to be readying himself for something terrible. She was drawn closer – afraid she would be discovered but unable to look away. The next moment Lucas wrenched a pistol from his waistband and pressed it against the other man's Adam's apple. She realised that what frightened her most was not the threat itself, the muzzle pressed against the throat. It was how practised and natural his movement was, and while she couldn't hear what they said, she realised that the other one, a dark-skinned guy of eighteen or nineteen, would do anything for Lucas after that. The boy panted out a few helpless words as he fell to the ground, and Lucas vanished. She stood there for a short while as if paralysed, wondering whether she should approach. But when eventually she roused herself, he got up and ran off in the opposite direction and she was left alone, her body shaking.

Slowly, she began to walk towards the Tunnelbana station, and she noticed to her surprise that she was limping slightly. It was her damn hip again, her war wound as Vanessa used to call it. But by the time she reached the plaza, she had forgotten about it.

The memory of what she had just seen pounded through her, and for a long time she was determined to call Lucas and give him a piece of her mind. But then she started to see her life in a whole new light. Memories that had been beautiful or at least innocent were darkened and distorted, and she became increasingly furious. She decided to get in touch with Fransson and tell him what she had seen. If the result was a return to the murder inquiry, then so be it.

TEN

The next morning, when eight o'clock finally arrived, she called the chief inspector. But when he answered she hung up. She couldn't do it, not just because it felt harder than she'd expected to go behind Lucas's back. The knowledge that she had something personal to gain from it sullied the decision, and why should she give Fransson anything? In what way had he earned it?

She sat down in the kitchen and poured a cup of tea, wondering whether she should contact the organised-crime unit. But no, they wouldn't trust her. Instead, she ought to . . . what? Conduct some kind of investigation? That would be the rational thing to do.

She went into the living room, logged onto the computer and looked up Lucas's name. She didn't get a single hit, which didn't surprise her. On impulse, she instead entered *Rekke* into the search engine, mostly as a distraction, a flight from the thoughts gnawing at her.

A picture appeared of a man resembling the professor, but a little bigger, heavier, thinner-haired, a man whom she vaguely recognised, and whose eyes looked untrustworthy. The man was called Magnus Rekke. He was Hans Rekke's brother, but more importantly he was Undersecretary of State for Foreign Affairs – the right-hand man of Foreign Minister Kleeberger. That probably explained the dinner at Sturehof, and just to forget about Lucas for a while she read on. There was quite a bit.

Magnus Rekke was described as an *éminence grise*. It was said that he had increased his influence after 9/11. "Without Magnus, we would never have obtained so much superior intelligence," as Kleeberger put it. But apparently not everyone was as thrilled. "Magnus Rekke runs the CIA's errands like a schoolboy" was what one columnist had written in *Aftonbladet*. A string of pundits on both the right and the left had demanded his departure while simultaneously expressing a degree of admiration.

Magnus Rekke spoke English, German and French, as well as Chinese and Arabic, and he had got his doctorate in International Relations at Christ Church, Oxford. He was said to have an extensive network of contacts. He was even reputed to know Tony Blair and Condoleezza Rice, and to have connections with intelligence agencies around the world.

Magnus was described as very smart and well read, sometimes as cunning and often as "independent" – with no party affiliation. He had inherited a fortune from his father, a Norwegian shipping magnate called Harald Rekke, who had died when his sons were young. Magnus's mother was Elisabeth, née von Bülow, a former piano instructor at the Universität für Musik und darstellende Kunst in Vienna.

The article mentioned in passing that his little brother, Hans, had been a promising concert pianist who had trained at Juilliard in New York. But it didn't say why he had quit as a pianist, or even that he was now a professor at Stanford. All it said was that the sons had been expected from an early age to perform at a high level. Nothing else was good enough in their home. But it wasn't the titles that mattered, let alone the money – of which there was already a surplus; it was the ability to achieve something great or beautiful.

"We were to rise above our peers and think a little bigger than everyone else. Otherwise we were inadequate."

In an old picture of the audience thronging outside the auditorium before a concert given by the ageing pianist Arthur Rubinstein at the Stockholm Concert Hall, the brothers were standing close together

68

with amused smiles. They were young there, perhaps only in their twenties. Wearing debonair suits with pocket squares and shirts open at the collar, they seemed remarkably unaffected by the camera, as if they were more interested by other things in the sea of people than the photographer. In their very indifference to the flash photography Micaela thought she sensed their entire damned childhood of privilege. Only those spoiled by the spotlight from an early age could be so nonchalant in that setting, she thought to herself.

Then her thoughts returned to Lucas with renewed vigour. The photo had driven home the pain of her own situation. It wasn't just the weapon that he'd drawn and pressed against the young guy's Adam's apple. Once again, the events of her life – big and small – were cast in a new light, and she felt an intense sense of unease, as if her past was being rewritten. She pushed the feeling away and set off for work, and throughout the journey kept it at a distance, as though it were dangerous even to recall it. Instead of Lucas she thought about Rekke and his twitching left leg, as she would often do in the months that followed.

She became a little obsessed. She read all his books and academic articles, and sometimes when her colleagues said something dumb or unclear, she wondered secretly what Rekke would have said. What errors would he identify in their thinking and conclusions? On occasion, she would dream that they worked together. But it was only a dream.

No-one could be further from him than she was.

2004

ELEVEN

April 3, 2004

"Kiss me then," he said. "Be a little wild."

It was late and noisy, and she was out with Vanessa again, for the third or fourth time in a month. She hadn't gone wild exactly, but it had been fun and she seemed to have acquired an air of glamour thanks to Vanessa. Life was always throbbing around her.

Men flocked to Vanessa in the city-centre pubs and clubs – mostly guys from the suburbs, people they'd grown up with, but also businessmen, sporty guys, all sorts, even Mario Costa, who had put in an appearance and was standing about a millimetre away from her. Mario had just been bought by Marseille, the French team, and there was a buzz around him. He was the tearaway and the star. He scored goals and got into all kinds of trouble, and no matter how he behaved he could never get shot of the story about his old man and Jamal Kabir. It was like part of his body, accentuating the slightly dangerous streak in him. He was eighteen now, tall and muscular, wearing a tight black Nike T-shirt and a baseball cap at an angle. He came towards them just like Beppe back in the day, like he owned the place.

He hadn't seen her at first. Like everyone else, he was interested in Vanessa. But eventually he had turned towards her, and then she realised he didn't just move like Beppe. He got drunk like Beppe too.

"Hi there," he said.

"Hi," she said.

"Long time. I guess last time was . . . when you questioned me. When you asked whether Papá ever hit me."

"Might've been," she said.

"He's fucking grateful."

"I didn't do much."

"He's fucking grateful," he repeated.

"How's he doing?"

"He had to move. They were talking so much shit about him. I bought a flat for him."

"I know," she said.

"So why haven't you caught the killer?"

"It's nothing to do with me anymore."

"So why haven't you caught the killer?" he said, as if it were necessary to repeat everything.

"Because they're idiots."

"But you arrested another bloke, right? An Arab?"

"It was the wrong guy."

"My old man's still fucking grateful," he said, and it was then he leaned forwards, well, down – he was two heads taller than she was – and kissed her.

It wasn't wholly unpleasant, and she might even have enjoyed it if he hadn't been such a snotty little brat. But there was something so ridiculous about his face, as if he was making her an incredibly generous offer or paying her back for what she had done for Beppe. Curiously, she ended up thinking about Jojje Moreno. Any excitement or amusement was replaced with sudden discomfort.

She pushed him harder than she'd intended, and he was so hammered that he staggered backwards, crashing into his friend – a stocky, overweight guy with slicked-back hair and a gap between his front teeth who almost tumbled to the floor.

"What are you playing at?" he said.

"Oh, s'nothing," said Mario, staggering to his feet.

"Who's that bitch?"

"It's her, Vargas, the one I was talking about. The chick who investigated that ref's murder. She's OK."

"The fuck?" said the friend, turning towards Micaela.

"The fuck what?" she said.

"You should check out the ref. I heard he was dealing hash and shit."

"Exactly, wasn't there some shit about Afghanistan – isn't that what your lot thinks now?" Mario said, turning towards her again with a new, confused expression in his eyes, as if he really wanted to know and had completely forgotten that he had tried to snog her.

"I don't know what they think," she said, beating a retreat.

Some guy clutching three beers bumped into her and splashed her top, which made her swear out loud. Not just about Mario and his friend. She was thinking about the investigation. How the hell could they have fired her from the team? She'd carried on investigating juvenile theft in Husby, Rinkeby and Akalla, and even though her clean-up rate was higher than anyone else's in the unit, she couldn't get bigger cases. It didn't matter that she was twice as good as the others. She wasn't allowed in from the cold – unless she stabbed her brother in the back.

She blotted her top dry and wandered about inside Spy Bar looking for something to settle herself down – a smile, a flirtatious look, anything. But she soon tired of it and fetched her jacket and left.

After a grey and windy winter, it had finally got warmer, but her legs were freezing. Her tights had begun to ladder and it was 1.48 a.m., later than she had thought. She was worried she'd miss the final Tunnelbana home, so she ran to the station at Östermalmstorg with her head down, oblivious to the world around her.

She made it in time – the train was due in four minutes. She looked around. It was rowdy down here, full of people, most of them inebriated. Right next to her a gang of teenagers was having a kick-about with a beer can. They were yelling and waving their arms. There was something combustible about them, she thought, as if their joy might give way to anger at any second. But she was too tired to care.

She disappeared into her own thoughts, which turned to Lucas, as they often did. She had never confronted him about what she had seen in the woods, but a chill had grown between them. A woman coughed not far from her. Just as she'd thought, the lads in front of her were starting to get aggressive. "What are you looking at?" one of them said to an older bloke in a blazer standing nearby, and for a moment she considered stepping between them.

It never happened. She caught sight of something else, nothing remarkable, not at all, just a tall man in a dark-blue coat and a grey hat further up the platform. He was clearly pissed too. He was swaying. But he wasn't bothering anyone. He was just standing there on his own leaning vaguely forwards. Nevertheless, something about him put her on her guard, and perhaps fascinated her too, and it was only through sheer willpower that she redirected her gaze from him to the lads. It felt like it would only take a look, a word, for a fight to break out.

"Stop it, calm down," she said, and they turned towards her.

Someone kicked the beer can again and it rattled off onto the tracks while another member of the gang hissed: "Watch yourself, bitch." He even took a step closer to her, and for a moment she could feel his breath on her. She turned her back on him.

Her gaze was drawn again to the man further up the platform and it struck her: something wasn't right about his movements. It wasn't his unsteadiness. It was that his swaying seemed deliberate, and now there was a light coming from the tunnel beyond. The rails sang. The train was approaching. Then she realised the man was going to jump. She began to run before she'd even thought about it.

On her way, she crashed into the guy in front of her but didn't notice as he hit the deck and swore loudly. She rushed on shouting "Jesus Christ, no!", and when the man didn't reply or even react, she was

76

convinced she was too late. It was over, pointless. She was sure of it. Nevertheless, she ran on, blindly and wildly, and her father swam into her thoughts. For a moment, the man and her father merged into one and in that moment – in that microsecond – she lunged forward and she remembered afterwards how she had flown across the platform and hit something with violent force and been thrown backwards.

Her temples and cheek were burning diabolically as the carriages rattled past. She couldn't understand what had happened. Her head was pounding, and she couldn't see clearly. Red and yellow spots danced before her eyes. She was lying on something soft, a body, she realised, a stomach covered in fabric, and then she looked up and saw that the body was alive.

A man with a sharply chiselled face was looking back at her – simultaneously surprised and confused, as if he couldn't understand why he wasn't dead, and she tried to grasp the situation herself. What had happened? She had quite clearly saved the man. But why did it feel so weird, and why was she suddenly so angry?

"What the hell are you playing at?" she screamed.

"I . . ." said the man.

"Do you have any idea what you're doing?" she roared.

After all, this was a man who had decided to end it all. But neither her rage nor her confusion abated. Something was wrong, she could feel it. Presumably she was in shock. Her eyesight was flickering. She was in indescribable pain, and all she wanted to do was shut her eyes and disappear. Still, she got to her knees, shaking her head in an attempt to see more clearly, and was struck anew by the man's face.

It was incongruous. It was as if it belonged to someone else in some other place, and suddenly, or gradually – it was hard to tell – she understood: the man was Hans Rekke. Sharp as a knife, bloody Rekke, whom she'd thought was busy living the most perfect life in the world.

"It's you?" she stammered.

"What . . . no," he said idiotically.

"It is you."

"Who?"

"Hans Rekke?"

"Yes," he mumbled. "What happened?"

"I saved you," she said, and he could have said any number of things in response.

He could have thanked her or upbraided her for preventing him from taking that irrevocable step. Instead, he stared at her with eyes filled with desperation. Then he reached forward like a small child reaching for its mother. There was something so pitiable and helpless in that gesture that she felt a surge of contempt, as if her admiration for him had transformed in a second.

"I would have liked . . ."

"To die, right?"

"Wh . . . yes . . . perhaps."

"How the hell could you?"

"I'm so sorry. I have inconvenienced you," he said, to which she didn't reply. There were no words.

She stood up, took his hands and pulled him up. But he was heavier than she had expected, and they tumbled against each other again, now standing by the track and the train in a mad embrace, and for a second she was reminded how she had dreamed in a moment of weakness of pressing herself against him. But definitely not like this – as if she were holding a drowned body – and it was then that she realised they weren't alone.

The whole platform had gathered around them to watch the spectacle, and naturally the lads who'd been making a scene were there too. They were at the front of the cluster with their posturing and drunken gazes. She wanted to tell them to go to hell. But at that moment, she heard a voice saying loudly as if to itself:

"Oh my God, oh my God."

It was a man in his thirties with anxious blue eyes, wearing a dark-blue jacket.

"Are you alright?" he asked.

She looked at the man in irritation.

"I'm not really sure. Who are you?"

"I'm the train driver. I saw something flutter by and heard a bang. I was convinced that . . ."

He didn't complete his sentence, and she wondered whether the bang he had mentioned might have been her head striking the train. But her priority was to get away from the lot of them. She explained with all the authority she could muster that she was a police officer and that she would take care of the man. She was quite alright, she lied. Then she turned around and spotted something on the platform behind them. It was the grey hat that Rekke had been wearing. She picked it up, put it on him and dragged him towards the escalator. For a long time she said nothing. It was a struggle to keep him upright and she was still trying to understand what had just happened.

TWELVE

Someone tapped her shoulder and Vanessa turned around to see Mario Costa standing there. He was a local celebrity, a professional footballer, but he looked dumb as fuck, drunk and pushy. She was sick of hammered little boys, sick of people tugging at her elbow, pestering her.

"Where'd she go?" Mario said.

"Who?"

"Micaela."

"Don't ask me. I don't think she liked you trying to hit on her."

"I was gonna say something to her."

"So you had to throw yourself at her."

He smiled with such confusion and puzzlement that for a moment she felt sorry for him and took a step closer. He looked as if he wanted to say something important.

"What were you going to say to her?"

"I was gonna talk about the murder. They arrested some eighty-year-old bloke, right? But they released him."

"Micaela mentioned something like that."

"No-one could believe a codger like that had done it."

"Seems reasonable."

"Or it was the wrong bloke, I dunno. But that wasn't what I was gonna say. My dad saw another guy too, younger, although the cops don't believe him."

"Why don't they believe him?"

"Because he thought of it, like, now. You know what he's like."

She pictured Beppe staggering across the plaza in Husby and yelling at people to move.

"I know what he's like," she said.

Mario looked at her with a pleading expression.

"Was Micaela angry then?"

"I don't think Micaela was fucking pleased. You can't pick up girls by falling on them."

"Meh, I was just gonna talk. My dad is pissed off with them for not solving it, you must get that, and that bloke he saw, he was dodgy, right," he slurred, and Vanessa took a closer look at him.

He looked completely lost with his glistening, squinting eyes, and it struck her that the murder must have been tormenting both him and his father for a long time now. On the other hand, a professional football contract abroad was pretty good compensation. She gave him a quick hug and decided to do something more fun with the evening. But then Mario grabbed hold of her arm and said he was going to hire a private detective. She thought to herself that he might be pretty exciting in about ten years when he was sober and loaded. As she left, she heard him shout:

"Aren't you coming to my leaving party with the team?"

"Sure," she said. "When is it?"

"On Monday. Or Tuesday. For fuck's sake, I can't remember what the place is called," he said, which Vanessa found unsurprising. She wondered whether to down a few shots and get hammered too.

But then she thought of Micaela and decided to give her a ring.

When they emerged into the chill, Micaela looked at Rekke in astonishment. She was searching for traces of something dreadful, signs of an illness eating him from within. But in that moment, not far from

Östermalmstorg, he looked like a handsome gent out for a night-time stroll. What did he have to despair about?

His face was just as chiselled and hawk-like as it had been before, and she guessed the coat was cashmere. His shoes were polished and looked handmade, and his hat was a little old-fashioned and stylish – eccentric even – as if he wanted to make an impression on people. His movements still expressed the same aristocratic nonchalance she'd seen out at Djursholm, the one that had awakened her longing for another world. But his eyes were wild. There was a storm raging inside them.

"We need to call your family," she said.

He looked at her in confusion.

"My family?"

"Your wife, your brother, your daughter – someone who can take care of you."

"No, no, absolutely not."

"Then I'm taking you to the emergency psych ward. You need medical attention."

"Please," he said. "I don't live far from here. Just take me home. I promise not to do anything stupid."

"I don't trust you," she said, and he nodded as if he understood in spite of everything.

"No, of course. Why would you?"

"So you've moved from Djursholm?"

"What . . . yes, exactly."

"I was there last summer. You were helping us with the Jamal Kabir murder."

"I was?" he said.

Didn't the idiot even remember that?

"You dismissed our entire investigation."

"I apologise," he mumbled.

"You were right – on every single point."

"I doubt that."

"I admired you," she said, and at that he looked at her with his anxious blue eyes and something ignited within. He made a movement with his hand as if he wanted to stroke her cheek on the side of her face that was screaming with pain. But then he withdrew his hand and looked thoughtful, as if he were facing a new and difficult problem.

"You . . ." he said.

"Yes, me," she said.

"I remember your questions."

"What's happened to you?" she said.

"What can I say?"

"Well, something, for starters."

"I broke. I've always been broken."

"So nothing specific? Some form of catastrophe?"

"I would have liked a catastrophe."

"How can you say that?"

"I'd guess that people like me always long for a catastrophe. Something exterior to correlate with the interior."

"I'm so bloody disappointed in you."

"I am sad, of course. But please, take me home, if I just get some sleep then maybe . . ."

"OK," she said. "I'll come with you. But if you try to kill yourself again then I'll kill you," she said, and something new happened to his face. Not necessarily something good, but still a sign that he was becoming conscious of more than what was storming around his head.

"That was almost funny," he said.

"Almost," she muttered, and they walked on. For a while he seemed to want to say something to lighten the oppressive, anxious atmosphere, but step by step, the blood seemed to drain from his body.

He leaned on her more heavily and the wind blew. It began to rain, and further down Riddargatan she pressed the hat down onto his head and it was as if she were pressing his whole body down. For Christ's sake, she thought. Get a grip. They plodded on. She almost had to drag him along, and now and then she would look around at the closed restaurants and shops.

"Is it far?" she said.

He mumbled as they continued through the district until they reached a yellowish stone building on Grevgatan, down towards the water and Strandvägen. There he stopped outside a front door with a confused look in his eyes.

He tapped the numbers on the keypad at random – he didn't seem to remember the code – and then he pressed a button on the entryphone under the name Hansson. After some time it crackled to life and a sleepy woman's voice was audible from the speaker.

"Yes? Hello?"

"It's Hans," he said. "I can't get in."

"Good grief," said the voice, "I'll come down," and it didn't take long for a woman in slippers, wearing a black coat over her nightdress, to appear in the stairwell.

She was perhaps sixty-five, slight in figure, with small, nervous eyes and a pointy chin that jutted out like a little rock ledge on her face. Her hands trembled as she opened the door and stared at Rekke.

"My dear! We've been so worried. What have you been up to?"

"I'll explain, I promise. But I need to sleep," he muttered, walking inside. The woman turned to Micaela.

"What did he do?"

"He tried to take his own life," she said. "He needs medical attention."

The woman stood stock-still for a while as if taking in the words. Then she began to pummel her fists against Rekke's back and shoulders, shouting:

"How can you? How can you do that to us all?"

"I'm sorry. I'm hopeless," he said, without even seeming to notice the blows – except that he crouched – and then the woman stopped hitting him and turned to Micaela again.

"Do you hear that? Hopeless, he calls himself. But do you know what he actually is? A genius – no less. He sees things."

"I know. I met him—" Micaela said, but the woman continued:

"But what does he do? He puts himself down, and it's not the first time either. In Helsinki . . ." Her voice trailed off as she seemed to think of something else. "My God, we need to watch over him tonight," she said, desperation in her gaze. "We really must. We can't leave him for a second."

Then she shook her head again, and muttered to herself, and Micaela wondered whether she was up to dealing with a person in this state. She didn't think so.

"I'll come in and look after him," she said. "I'm a police officer. I'm used to emergencies." The woman eventually agreed to it, especially once she and Micaela had exchanged phone numbers and Micaela had promised to get in touch if anything happened.

The woman escorted them to the lift and pressed the button for the sixth floor. She closed the gate behind them and shouted: "Dearest Hans, you mustn't, you mustn't," and all manner of other commands that were soon audible only as stifled shouts from below as they slowly rose through the building.

It wasn't just Rekke who was all in. Micaela was black and blue and punch-drunk with a ringing in her ears. She needed to sit down. She needed to collapse into a bed. But she needed to take care of Rekke. At first she thought it would be fine in spite of everything.

In a robotic state he pushed aside the lift door and walked through a vaulted hallway with murals to a front door – the only one on that floor – with the name Rekke on the letterbox. They stepped into a large apartment with drawn drapes.

She had never seen anything like it. Ahead of them towered a studio-loft window some three or four metres in height, and there were rooms and corridors visible in all directions. Hanging on the walls were dark or brilliantly coloured paintings in heavy gilt frames. The parquet floor was covered in Persian rugs and everywhere there were books – stacked on the shelves, on the tables and on the floor – together with reports and print-outs in English, German and French. The furniture appeared to have been positioned at random, and in front of the huge window there was a black grand piano that seemed to her sad and lonely. Yet there was a kind of mournful charm to the place that appealed to her.

Rekke picked up pace. She just managed to catch up and get a foot in the door before he could shut himself into a large bathroom with a Middle Eastern mosaic on the floor. For a moment he stood looking lost in front of the mirror over the basin and then he opened the cabinet behind it.

"What are you doing?" she said.

"I need something to get me to sleep."

She glanced at the shelves: there was a bloody pharmacy in there, and she knew enough about pills to know that it didn't look good.

The cabinet contained uppers and downers, benzo, opiates, Ritalin, morphine, the whole shebang, and when he grabbed a yellow tub she slapped it out of his hand and pressed him against the wall.

"Oi," she said with aggression, as if she'd arrested a criminal.

"Yes . . ." he muttered.

"No somethings to get you to sleep. I'm going to chuck out every single pill and keep an eye on you all night. But then you need to find a different nurse. Got it?"

"What . . . yes . . . of course. You've already done more than enough," he said, putting his hand into his trouser pocket as if he wanted to tip her, and she was tempted to shout, *You rich, spoiled bastard.*

But she kept her calm and tried to see the situation more clearly. What should she do with the pills? Or the knives in the kitchen for that matter, or the windows that could be opened and jumped out of? She didn't know, because it was surely just like with Simón or any self-destructive idiot – whatever you did, where there was a will to destroy themselves, there was a way. She would just have to live with that.

"Even if I'm forbidden, my nurse – my highly temporary nurse – ought to take some painkillers. That was a nasty bang you had," he said in a voice that sounded momentarily good-humoured. But she wasn't going to be taken in.

"Where do you sleep?"

"I'll be happy to show you."

"Good," she said, and they passed through a series of rooms that alternated between high and low ceilings, between overstuffed and empty, before reaching a large bedroom with blue walls.

It shrieked of anxiety. The bottom sheet on the bed was loose and rolled up as if he'd attempted to wring the sweat out of it. Clothes and even more books were strewn all over the floor, and on the nightstand were mugs and glasses and two boxes of Nitrazepam. She quickly tidied these away and hid them in a cabinet in the adjacent room. She also adjusted the sheet and plumped the pillows.

Then she went over to the window facing the rooftops and took hold of a leather armchair – a classic English piece – that stood beneath an oil painting of a pale boy playing a flute in a different century.

"Can you help me?"

He nodded and together they carried the armchair so that it was blocking the exit.

"This is where I intend to sit all night and watch you," she said, and he smiled in resignation.

He undressed haphazardly and she caught a glimpse of his sinewy body. It still looked like it belonged to a runner – middle distance – and that bothered her too. She would have liked him more if he had become droopy and bloated. But he had been and clearly remained a physically magnificent specimen. What did he have to be sad about?

"I can't believe I looked up to you," she said.

"*Major e longinquo reverentia,*" he mumbled as if speaking to himself.

"What?" she said.

"When viewed from a distance, everything is beautiful."

She reflected on that for a second, then averted her gaze as Hans Rekke crept into bed, pulled the duvet over himself and looked across the rooftops with his anxious blue eyes.

Jonas Beijer awoke, frightened by a dream or a sound, and for a moment he had no idea where he was. But he was of course at home on Swedenborgsgatan, and lying beside him on her stomach was his wife, Linda, breathing softly and gently. He listened for sounds in the rest of the flat. Had one of the boys woken up? It didn't sound like it, and there was silence out in the street. Was it morning already? He didn't bother to check. The red numbers on the digital clock made him feel uncomfortable at night, as if they were counting down to something horrible and irrevocable. He turned over.

But he was completely unable to fall back to sleep, so he went into the kitchen to get something to eat. It was a terrible habit he'd picked up, of stuffing his face with sweets at night. It must be the job, or so he guessed, the stress of all those investigations just lying there waiting for him – above all, the Kabir case. He knew better than anyone else that they were failing on that.

He took a bar of Marabou chocolate from the fridge, ripped the wrapper off and feverishly ate every square. Afterwards he felt ashamed, more because of the murder inquiry than the chocolate, and as he returned to the bedroom he swore at his chiefs and the Americans in Kabul. It was as if they didn't want to understand.

He curled up as far from his wife as he could get but was still unable to drift off. On the contrary, he got even more worked up and pretty soon Micaela appeared in his thoughts. He often thought about her during his wakeful nights. He was tempted to call her and ask whether she wanted to meet up, but that would be madness.

*

Her head was on fire both inside and out, and time after time she relived the moment when she had lunged forwards across the platform. She saw herself flying towards him, and she wondered whether she hadn't already at that point sensed that it was him. But it didn't matter, surely? Here she was now, following all her attempts at making contact, at his home, in his bedroom, in circumstances that had been impossible to anticipate.

She listened to his breathing. It was heavy and irregular. He was clearly far from falling asleep.

"How are you feeling?"

"What can I say?" he muttered. "I need my drugs, my anaesthetics. But I'm guessing I've surrendered my right to complain. I've taken note of the fact that my nurse is strict," he said, in a voice that once again verged on ironic, and surely that had to be a good sign, she thought to herself.

"You sound better," she said.

"I don't know about that," he said. "But I assume that proximity to death can give us a little life in return."

"How could you be so stupid?"

"I should think it's beyond explanation," he said.

"You might like to try."

His eyes glowed in the darkness, and she had the feeling that he was withdrawing into himself, searching for words.

"Well, I would say then that depression has its phases," he said. "At times it simply hums through your arteries, a semitone too low, and shuts you out from the world. All the voices and laughter you hear on the other side exist only as reminders of everything that you are incapable of, and that's bad enough. But slowly, depression retunes itself and raises the volume. It begins to scream in red, unbearable tones, and then you reach a point where you no longer want to be a part of it."

"And that's where you were?"

"That's where I was. But then someone came flying through the air, and I hope I will soon thank you for that and even mean it."

"That's not necessary," she said.

"Oh no, it's necessary. It was a great act."

"Do you remember when we visited you that day?" she said.

"I remember," he said.

"I had a boss called Fransson. You were able to tell straight away that he'd been at the firing range that morning."

"I think I see things when I'm in my manic spells. Most of it's just invented by my brain. Nonsense."

"But you were right."

"Well, perhaps. But he was something of an open book, was he not?"

"I don't know about that," she said.

Rekke sat up in bed, pulled the duvet around his body and looked at her with his anxious eyes, which now seemed a little clearer.

"He . . ." he began.

"Yes?"

"He had a red callous between his thumb and forefinger left by the trigger and trigger guard. He grasped his forearm, flexed his wrist towards him and curled his fingers into his palm. A classic exercise he must have learned from his physiotherapist."

"Which means?"

"That he was suffering from tennis elbow, a common injury in sports with substantial static load, and one that is exacerbated by training. I could tell from his body that he was hardly a tennis player. On the contrary, his eyes had that glare common to people who hunt."

"You also knew the crown on his watch was going to fall off."

"Did I?"

"He had an IWC Schaffhausen – you admired it," she said.

"Ah yes. But surely that was obvious? There was a gap between the watch and the crown, and it was clear from the sheen and the scratches on the outer layer that it had taken a knock. He was also turning it so recklessly, as if he were transferring all his suppressed neurosis onto the poor crown. Things could only go badly."

"Surely you realise that it's remarkable to make those kinds of observations from just a quick glance?"

"Not really, no."

"You said you had a manic spell."

"My wife thought so. I crashed shortly afterwards at a conference at Stanford."

"Crashed?"

"I became overbearing, mad. I slated a couple of studies everyone else was lauding. I offered advice no-one had asked for, drew conclusions no-one wanted to hear. Then I thought I could see straight through some classified slush I'd been sent, and one morning when I woke up it all came back to haunt me. The mania was replaced by self-contempt. I could barely get out of bed."

"Was that why you didn't answer my emails or calls?"

"I guess so. I apologise," he said.

"But you seemed fine a few months later."

"Did I?"

"I saw you at Sturehof with Kleeberger."

"I can't imagine that made me feel any better."

"You seemed more bored than broken."

"Kleeberger's folly may perhaps have lent lustre to my own life. That's the gift of mediocrity to us."

"Do you even get how infuriating you are?"

"Perhaps not."

"You're lying there like a wreck and still brushing aside the brightest star in the government like you're some bloody king."

"Is that so dreadful?"

"It is for me. You don't realise how much you've had for free."

"Perhaps not."

"Well then. Go to sleep."

"I looked at you too, out at the house."

"And what did you see?"

"I saw aptitude – and self-censorship."

"That's the dumbest shit I've ever heard."

"Well, perhaps. But I also saw a darkness that appeared promising."

"In what way?"

"It wasn't inward-looking like my own. I thought you might put it to good use."

"Doing what?"

"Tearing yourself free."

"From what?"

"The net that captures us all and seeks to drag us to shore."

"And you were being so wise just a minute ago."

"And now I'm an idiot?"

"Yes."

"You're probably right."

"Well, good night."

"Good night, Micaela."

"You remember my name."

"Apparently."

She was convinced she wouldn't sleep a wink, and on several occasions she felt an intense desire to speak to him again. But she could tell from his breathing that he was falling asleep and for a long time she sat there in the armchair while morning arrived outside with the sound of cars on Strandvägen. Once, she quietly crept away to the toilet. The whole right side of her face had swollen up. It looked like the aftermath of a terrible beating, and she felt alienated by her reflection.

"I'm at Hans Rekke's," she said aloud to herself without really knowing why.

The whole situation was incomprehensible. She walked slowly back to the bedroom and curled up in the leather armchair with her arms around her legs. As a clock on the wall ticked, she thought not only about Rekke but also about his wife. What had happened to her and the mansion, and what exactly was this place?

Shortly after that she must have fallen asleep, and she didn't notice Rekke climbing over her and striding out into the apartment. She woke up not long after with a feeling of doom. The whole apartment was rumbling and she became convinced they were under attack.

THIRTEEN

She leaped up and ran, disorientated, around the apartment. She found him in the living room, at the grand piano beside the huge window. He was sitting there in a black, unbuttoned shirt, playing the most disquieting piece she'd ever heard. It was if he were beating back his anxiety. She stared in amazement at his hands rushing over the keys. He played like a god.

Nevertheless she was gripped by unease, and it wasn't just because of the fury contained in the music. It was his face. It was pale and tense, the cheekbones sharply visible. He looked like he was once again about to throw himself in front of a train, and for a long time she stood there entranced, watching him, until he slammed his fists recklessly into the keys and slumped over the piano.

"My God," she said.

He jumped in terror, as if he had been in a completely different reality.

"Yes . . . sorry. Did I wake you?"

"Is there anyone you didn't?"

"No, perhaps not," he said.

"What was that?"

"Prokofiev."

It didn't mean anything to her.

"Sounded like the end of the world."

"I should think that was the intention."

"But the world's still here."

He shrugged and then she looked more closely at him – at his shoulders, his back, his entire body wound tight, at everything she recognised from the day before. But there was something new about him. His eyes were glazed, cloudy, just like Simón's in the evenings in Husby, and then she understood. He'd taken something.

"What have you put inside yourself?"

"You can see," he said with a sad smile. "You've got an eye for detail too."

"What have you taken?"

"Two or three opiates, benzodiazepines, a dash of antipsychotics, and my pointless antidepressants."

"For Christ's sake."

He turned away from her and did up a couple of shirt buttons. "I enjoyed talking last night."

"I'm happy to hear it."

"But it wasn't as uplifting to wake up."

"So you had to do drugs and play the end of the world on the piano."

"Apparently."

"What's the name of the piece?"

"Prokofiev's piano concerto number two."

"Is there anything special about it?"

"I suppose there is," he said.

"What?"

"Prokofiev had just begun writing it when he received news that his friend Maximilian Schmidthof had shot himself, and it left its mark on the composition. I was obsessed with it when I was younger."

"I can imagine why," she said.

"And it didn't do any harm that Mamma hated it, and I was never allowed to perform it. I played it in secret. Schmidthof was a pianist too. It's said he shot himself because he realised he would never be good enough – not as good as Prokofiev."

"Did you see yourself in that?"

"I saw myself in the piece."

"What was it your mother hated?"

"She hated it when I became weak on our tours. She was my impresario from hell."

He looked out of the window.

"When was this?" she said.

"When I'd graduated from Juilliard and just wanted to escape it all."

"I understand," she said, though she didn't really, and perhaps he perceived the uncertainty in her eyes.

He raised his right hand to her cheek, then lowered it again.

"I'm sorry about your face."

"It's OK."

"So the wretches kicked you off the murder inquiry," he said.

She smiled.

"Yes," she said. "Have you been following the case?"

"Not really. But they arrested another person, didn't they?"

"They got the wrong guy. An Iraqi with an alibi."

"Who were they looking for?"

"Another old man, almost eighty, with a slight limp, stooping, bald, thin lips. He walked past Kabir on the touchline just after the match."

"Doesn't really sound like a murderer."

"No," she said. "But Kabir quite clearly reacted to him. It was you who drew our attention to that."

"I remember."

She hesitated, fumbling for words.

"But you never returned my emails or calls."

He looked down at his hands.

"I'm sorry."

"I thought you didn't want anything to do with someone like me."

He looked at her quizzically.

"Someone like you?" he said.

"A girl from the hood."

"I wish I met more like you – if there are any."

She tried to take this in. She felt a sudden need to change the subject.

"There was something I wanted to ask about," she said. "Something I've been thinking about for a long time."

"Pray tell," he said with a friendly smile.

"In Djursholm . . ." she began, suddenly unsure how to word it.

"Yes?" he said.

"You said that something didn't make sense about the old injuries on Kabir's body. You said it as if it indicated something. But you never finished what you were saying."

A hint of unease flashed across his face, and he looked down at the keys as if he wanted to start playing again.

"I remember."

"What were you about to say?"

Rekke shifted his head anxiously. It was obvious that he was troubled.

"I can't say," he said.

"What?"

"I can't say," he repeated. "I'm sorry."

"What do you mean?"

"It's just how it is, I'm afraid," he said, and she wanted to shout at him. But she didn't have time.

The doorbell rang. There was ringing and knocking, and in that moment Rekke's expression was transformed yet again and he looked at her with pleading eyes.

"Can you open the door?"

Why the hell was *she* supposed to open it?

"Do it yourself."

"I beg you."

"Yes, yes," she said, heading for the door but regretting it immediately. "If you play."

"Why should I play?"

"So that I know you're not getting up to any mischief. Preferably something happier if you please," she said.

He muttered a little, then began a gay and lively piece with bright trebles that danced through the apartment as she headed to the door.

Julia Rekke didn't go home to Djursholm very often these days. For the most part, she stayed at her boyfriend Christian's on Storgatan, and more often than not she slept in too late and let the days just slip by. But this morning, only ten minutes earlier, she had been woken by Mrs Hansson and had rushed here in a panic. She knocked harder.

A young woman who looked like she'd been hit by a bus opened the door. Half her face was an alarming rainbow landscape, and what on earth was she wearing? A glittery black top that stank of beer and a cheap short skirt. She looked trashy, Julia thought, as if she had come from the worst kind of party, and Julia most definitely didn't want to think about what her father had done with her.

"What's happened?" she said.

She didn't wait for the answer. She became aware of the music, Liszt's "La Campanella". Why the hell was he playing that? He hated the piece. He regarded it as a high-kicking circus act and associated it with his mother. She ran past the woman into the living room and saw her father sitting at the grand in a partially buttoned black shirt, and for a moment he seemed better – not as broken as yesterday. But when he turned towards her with shiny eyes, her heart sank again.

"Hello, my treasure," he said. "How are you?"

"Mrs Hansson says you tried to kill yourself."

Her voice was filled with subdued rage.

"What . . . no, absolutely not."

He looked down at his legs.

"Why would she make up something like that?"

"Mrs Hansson is, of course, wonderful, but she imagines things when she's excited."

"Nobody just imagines that kind of thing."

"Oh, they most certainly do. You should have seen me yesterday. Drunk as a teenager. Awfully embarrassing, and I probably muttered a few words she misinterpreted."

He stood up to embrace her and at first all she wanted to do was kick and punch him, but then she hugged him back, and mumbled:

"You can't, Pappa. You can't."

"I'm not going to," he said. "And I'm feeling better now. Micaela has been helping me."

"Her face is completely blue."

"I'm OK," said Micaela, who'd just come into the room.

"OK might be overdoing it," Rekke said. "I'm guessing she's got concussion, and of course that's my fault. I fell and she took the blow on my behalf. Nothing less than a heroic effort, and now she's got something of a Janus face looking both backwards to the past and forwards to the spring. Would you be a dear to both her and me, and prepare a little breakfast for the two of you? I bet you didn't have time to eat, did you? Mrs Hansson has probably filled my fridge. I love you, my treasure. But I need to rest. I'm going to sleep."

"No, you need to talk to me."

"I will, but first I'm going to take a closer look at something."

"You said you were going to sleep."

"To sleep and to read a bit. Perhaps you'd like to help me into bed and pass me my computer. I see Christian still hasn't shaved off his frightful beard."

"Can you give your bloody observations a rest?" she said, touching her cheek.

"Yes, yes, of course. Sorry."

When Julia entered the kitchen, the woman was putting away a wine bottle that had been on the dining table. She then wiped down the draining board and put the mugs and glasses in the dishwasher with lightning speed. Her movements were unusually efficient, and for a moment Julia wondered whether the woman might be a past cleaner of theirs that her father had picked up for some inconceivable reason – well, not that inconceivable, actually.

There was something attractive about her – Julia acknowledged this reluctantly. Not attractive in a way that would appeal to the rest of her family, to be honest – especially not Farmor – but nevertheless, the woman radiated a kind of repressed explosivity, and unlike Mamma and so many other women she knew, she had curves.

But no – she pushed that to one side – she refused to believe the woman was a lover. Not that she really knew Pappa in that way, but surely he wouldn't go out in that state on a Saturday night and drag someone home. Maybe the woman – Micaela, wasn't it? – really had helped him in a critical situation. It was just that she seemed so familiar, and there was such a special atmosphere between them, something simultaneously close and irritable. Julia smiled her best smile like the well-brought-up daughter she was.

"Mrs Hansson makes a good muesli," she said, "and I'm guessing there's Turkish yoghurt and berries in the fridge. Pappa's also got a decent espresso machine. So what do you say, shall we eat some breakfast and get to the bottom of what's happened?"

Micaela nodded and together they laid the table and set out the yoghurt, muesli, juice, white bread that Mrs Hansson had baked the day before, cheese, cucumber and tomatoes. Then they made a cappuccino each and sat there in silence as they ate.

"What exactly happened yesterday?" Julia eventually said.

"He was drunk," Micaela said. "I was afraid he was going to fall onto the tracks."

"Mrs Hansson mentioned a suicide attempt?"

"I suppose that's what she assumed," said Micaela. "He's very depressed, isn't he?"

"Yes," she said. "Worse than ever."

"What's up with him?"

Julia looked at the woman. Didn't she know?

"He's a manic depressive," she said abruptly. "Sometimes he verges on psychotic."

"Has he been like that for long?"

"How much has he told you?"

"Not much. He briefly mentioned his youth and his tours with his mother."

"Has he started banging on about that again?"

The other woman nodded and drank from her cup. She poured yoghurt into her bowl and sprinkled muesli, raisins and blueberries on top.

Why the hell was she so familiar? Julia combed her memory.

"Can I ask how you met?"

"I was out last night," Micaela said, "and happened to see him swaying on the platform at Östermalmstorg."

Julia looked at her suspiciously.

"What business did he have being there in the middle of the night?"

"I don't know."

"Am I supposed to believe that?"

"You should."

"Because that's what'll reassure me most, right?"

"Because it's the truth. What's happened to him?"

Julia fell silent and looked to the hallway diagonally to the right, and then back to the woman, Micaela, and spotted something she hadn't seen before. A gaze that made her forget the bruises and the trashy party clothes, a look that was . . . how to put it . . . sharp, perhaps, focused, as if she saw far more than she let on.

"Depression has happened to him," she said.

"And he doesn't live with your mother any longer. Are they getting divorced?"

Julia was quiet. She didn't know what to say.

"I suppose they are," she said.

"I'm sorry."

"Oh well," she said, as if she didn't care. "It didn't exactly help, him losing his job and his green card."

Micaela looked at her attentively.

"Why did he lose them?"

Shut your trap now, Julia thought to herself. Don't muck things up even more for him. But perhaps she wanted to muck things up a little. Take her revenge, even. Revenge for him once again putting the whole family in a state of emergency and keeping them awake at night.

"I'm not supposed to know," she said.

"But you do know."

Julia cut a slice of cheese and made a sandwich.

"Yes, I think so," she said.

"Can you tell me?"

"I'm pretty sure that he was given confidential assignments and that he fell out with his employers. There was a serious conflict."

"About?"

"I don't know any more than that," she said, thinking to herself that she'd said enough, at least for now, and for a while there was an awkward silence.

"He's good at getting into conflict, isn't he?"

Julia smiled hesitantly and sipped her cappuccino.

"I suppose he is."

Micaela smiled hesitantly back.

"Although he's actually afraid of conflict," Julia said, gripped by a sudden desire to talk, or at least to discuss anything except what had happened in the USA.

"I can't imagine that."

"Oh yes, he wants to be kind and polite, it's his nature in a way. He was brought up to say witty things and make people happy. But he can't help himself. When he sees shortcomings or emptiness, he just coughs it up."

"Is he usually right?"

Julia smiled at the question and poured a glass of juice.

"If you'd asked me that a year or so ago, I would have said: *Yes, always.* He's my father. He's the most intelligent person on earth. But now . . . no, afraid not, sometimes he's borderline hallucinatory. I've heard him be more wrong than anyone else I know."

"I was raised in Husby," the woman said suddenly.

"In Husby?"

Julia looked at her with renewed interest.

"Yes," Micaela said. "People wouldn't have got him there – the man with everything, who let it crumble away."

"I don't think people get it much more in Östermalm. We're the only ones who understand him in our own crazy way."

"Who's we?"

"The Rekkes. It fits perfectly with our family mythology."

"You have a family mythology?"

"Oh yes. Pappa is the role model and that's why we're all obsessed with him. He's a true Rekke: highly intelligent, and independent of course, but also overly sensitive and self-critical, and he has his black dogs."

"Black dogs?"

"Depressive episodes. We stole the expression from Churchill. Pappa is the chosen one, as Magnus – my uncle – usually says."

"Why would he be that?"

"It's a long story."

"I'd be happy to hear it," Micaela said, and in that moment Julia was sure that they'd met before, perhaps even in dramatic circumstances not so long ago.

But she couldn't understand where, and once again she stared at Micaela's bruises. It must have been one hell of a blow.

"Pappa stood out from the beginning," she said. "They say that when he was two or three he was so moved by Beethoven's string quartets that he was reduced to tears. They discovered that he had perfect pitch, and everything came easily to him. My grandmother, his mother, who herself had been a promising pianist, resolved to make a genius out of him. She quit her job as a teacher in Vienna. She decided the piano was his future. He had to practise eight, ten hours a day. He never went to school."

"How did that go?"

"It was the kind of set-up that the family are so good at. We always get around the rules, find loopholes. Magnus was sent to boarding school in Switzerland – Le Rosey – and Farmor arranged for Pappa to have tutors instead, to make sure that nothing got in the way of music. Farmor was very particular about that, and who could say no to her? You should see her. She gets people to stand to attention. She raises you up and casts you down with a single glance. Do you have any idea what it means to a little child when a person like that dedicates all their efforts, all their energy, to you? It's impossible to defend yourself, and Pappa was never strong enough for her."

"The impresario from hell is what he called her."

"But that was later, when he'd come to his senses and realised that music wasn't good for him."

"In what way?"

"When he was a child, the piano was the only place where he didn't have to suppress his emotions. I suppose that's why he was so badly afflicted. The big classical pieces were like storms for him, and he didn't have much objection to storms. But he wanted to know what was moving through the gusts of wind."

"And music didn't allow him to do that?"

"No, not always. He was shaken up without understanding what was shaking him up, and he couldn't stand it. He fell, got told off, hurt himself, got smacked. He could handle it as long as he understood what was happening. But the music didn't make things plain, he said. It lacked *claritas*. That was why from early on he preferred the logic of a story – a series of events."

"Wasn't he allowed stories?"

"Not if they disrupted his rehearsals. Farmor often hid his books and didn't let him watch the whodunits on TV that he loved – *Columbo* and all those others. It became her way of punishing him. Of course, it didn't help. Stories and films only became more attractive to him, and when he was nine or ten he had an epiphany."

Micaela didn't say that she didn't know what an epiphany was. She didn't say much at all. She had a headache, and was still annoyed that Rekke hadn't wanted to say what he'd seen in the autopsy photos. But she was flattered by Julia's attention, and she allowed herself to be drawn in. She forgot her annoyance and instead stared at her, amazed.

With her big blue eyes and her curly, strawberry-blonde hair, Julia was as beautiful as Vanessa. She was also completely different, not just because she was upper class and rich and all the rest of it. She spoke about her father as if she were convinced that everyone was as interested in him as she was. It was both arrogant and alluring.

"It might not sound so very remarkable," she said, "but for him, it was a revolution. They lived in Vienna at the time, in the Innere Stadt, and you know, it was just him and Farmor and the servants in the house. Farfar was away and died not long after. Magnus was at boarding school in Switzerland and Pappa was sitting at the piano practising some dreadfully dull piece. He couldn't stand it. He needed a break, and he was desperately longing for it to be eight o'clock. At eight o'clock there was some crime series on that he loved. But after they'd eaten dinner and Farmor had heard him play, all she said was, 'No, not good enough. No television tonight.' He shouted that it wasn't fair. Farmor said it was – 'You haven't practised properly' – and there was nothing else he could say. There was never any point with Farmor. Yet the words continued to sting him and a few days later he found some sad German philosophy book that claimed we often use words without understanding what they mean. Fair was one example. There were different types of fairness, it said. There was a principle of fairness based on merit and performance. But there was also a fairness based on need, à la Marx. Every single person should get what they need. What was more, everyone should get the same."

"I understand," Micaela said.

"Quite; it's nothing remarkable. But in that moment, he realised that Farmor had never explained the word. She had simply hit him with an unclear concept. You might think he'd be even angrier about that, but on the contrary, it made him happy."

"Why?"

"Because he understood what had felt wrong, and even more so because he realised what he was actually looking for. Music was dark, it stirred up emotions that couldn't be explained. Whereas logic, philosophy, semantics, phenomenology and all those other subjects a person can pick apart and make deductions about. In no time he learned it all. He became obsessed with clarity. He wanted to dedicate himself to what could be deduced and found out, and one day he read about a palaeontologist called Cuvier."

"Cuvier?"

"Right, Georges Cuvier. He was around in the late eighteenth and early nineteenth centuries. And you know, back then, they still believed that God had created the world in six days and that all the animals that were alive had always been around on Earth. If they discovered any fossils that didn't fit that story, they would find a way to explain it. But Cuvier didn't accept it, and when he examined some bones from Holland, he claimed they came from a species that no longer existed. He called it the mammoth. Later on, when he discovered more extinct species, he concluded that there must have been epochs with completely different flora and fauna. Based on a few old bone fragments, Cuvier rewrote history, and that was mind-blowing for Pappa. The idea that a few insignificant-looking objects could uncover lost worlds."

"You can understand why," Micaela said.

"Yes, and afterwards he began to say he was going to be a researcher. Or preferably a detective. I'm going to study the small things and find the big ones, he said. Anyway, you get it. A detective! Farmor thought it sounded like something out of a cheap novel. She told him it was out of the question."

"But then he ended up being a bit of a detective anyway."

"I suppose he did."

Micaela peered out into the hall, and remembered her own father and his advice: always go back to the source – to what preceded the interpretations that laid themselves like a filter over developments. Was that where her own longing for the truth had been born? Or was it . . . She pictured Lucas before her; she saw him drawing his weapon in the woods.

"We visited you last summer," she said.

Julia started.

"Who's we?"

"We were working on a murder inquiry."

"You're a cop?"

"It was me and three male colleagues. You were playing the violin and your mother interrupted you."

Julia was looking at her in shock.

"That was you?"

"What do you mean?"

"I remember you very well. I remember the way Pappa looked at you."

Micaela didn't want to know how Rekke had looked at her.

"Your father brought the whole investigation crashing down to earth. We'd been building a castle in the air."

"And you got angry, right?"

"Well, my boss got angry."

"I remember," she said. "Mamma was really annoyed. She can't stand it when Pappa insults people with his truths."

"I think we probably needed to hear them."

"I realised that afterwards. But at the time I didn't know anything. It was just another of Pappa's secret assignments that we weren't allowed to talk about, but that was why it interested me so much."

Julia leaned over the breakfast table, and suddenly she didn't just look like a sophisticated upper-class girl. There was defiance on her face.

"I eavesdropped on you."

"I saw you."

"I remember, and I guess I didn't get much of it," Julia said. "But I realised you were talking about that football referee that was killed and then I was fascinated. It was almost as though I was in a movie. But it's the commotion afterwards that I remember best."

"What commotion?"

Julia looked like she was in possession of a big secret and enjoying it.

"After you left, Pappa lost it. He was really worked up."

"He was?" said Micaela, remembering what she'd glimpsed when she'd turned around that day: Rekke and his wife disappearing, entwined, into the house.

She remembered the feeling that it had all been a footnote for him, a halt en route to something more important.

"I thought it was just another day at the office for him," she said.

"No, no, not at all. Pappa spent ages pacing back and forth, as if he was in a trance. I heard him muttering. Then he went up to his study and stayed there for hours. I crept up on him two or three times and each time he was sitting there looking at the same thing."

"At what?"

"The body. The injuries on the body, and I don't know what else, but it seemed as if he were comparing them with something. He had other documents out and was staring at them and some marks on the wrists.

I remember it pretty well. He swore, grabbed his phone and dialled, and it only took me half a second to realise he was talking to Magnus."

"His brother at the Ministry for Foreign Affairs."

"Exactly. He has a particular tone of voice with Magnus. He doesn't speak as quickly to anyone else, and I couldn't quite follow what he was saying. But it was definitely the football referee that they were talking about, and there was no doubt that Magnus was familiar with the case."

"Do you remember more specifically what they talked about?"

"I remember one thing."

"What?"

"Prison of Darkness."

"Prison of Darkness?"

"Exactly. And it made me think."

Micaela leaned across the table. She resisted the urge to take Julia by the hand.

"What does it mean?" she asked.

"I'm not certain, but I think it was the prison where the referee was tortured."

Micaela tried to process this, and put it together with what she knew about Kabir's life.

"Was it the Taliban?" she asked.

Julia hesitated and bit her lip. She looked defiant again.

"Come on," Micaela said with sudden fervour. "Tell me."

FOURTEEN

Jonas Beijer had never been unfaithful to his wife, not really. But there were days when he longed for an affair, an adventure that might get his heart pounding a little. His sons were squabbling in the kitchen. Linda shouted: "I don't care whose fault it was, just stop it."

He couldn't take any more. Wasn't Sunday meant to be a day of rest? These days, he spent his weekends longing for Monday – not that work was much better, but at least it was a kind of normality, a more peaceful failure.

It had been almost ten months since Kabir had been murdered, and the investigation had lost momentum. Perhaps that was no surprise, but no-one else on the team seemed to realise that anything was awry. Falkegren, that smarmy moron, had banged on with his "The Americans will help us, I know them" schtick and initially it had seemed promising.

Representatives from the CIA and American Military Police in Kabul had called and spoken to them at length. But what exactly had they found out? Not much at all. It was only when he'd contacted the local police in the city on his own initiative that he'd realised Kabir hadn't just been a great player who knew how to organise a football tournament. He was possibly a raving lunatic too.

Ought he to go into the kitchen and help his wife? Pah, it could wait. He was about to drive Samuel to the stables. He went into the bedroom, sat down on the bed and leafed through his black contacts book. But he couldn't find anyone he wanted to call – least of all any potential lovers – and then he thought about Micaela again and the glow she'd had during the investigation. It had been as if he was willing to stretch himself and work harder at the mere sight of her walking by. Hadn't life become much more boring around the time she left?

The door flew open. Linda came in and yelled at him for sitting there idly.

Julia drank the last of her cappuccino and stared into Micaela's black, impetuous eyes.

Was she really going to tell her?

She really shouldn't.

She ought to keep her trap shut and change the subject and say that she'd probably misunderstood. But that was precisely why it was so tempting to talk. Perhaps she did want revenge on her father for being such a self-absorbed idiot that he'd let his depression take over everything else. She smiled at Micaela. I'm not as much of a goody-goody as you think I am, she thought to herself.

"It was an American prison," she said.

Micaela gave her a blank look.

"What?"

"It was one of the CIA's black sites."

"You must be joking."

"No, I promise. It was one of those facilities they set up after 9/11 to detain suspected terrorists."

Micaela looked still more shocked and Julia wondered nervously if she'd said too much, but she also felt the thrill of power. Had she known something that not even the murder inquiry had been aware of?

"That's what he said, and it made Magnus nervous. I heard how Pappa was pushing him."

Micaela shook her head in agitation.

"Surely the Americans can't torture people," she said.

"I think . . ." Julia said, but she didn't know what to say.

"I mean . . ." Micaela said indignantly, "Kabir was completely ruined. He had marks from chains on his wrists as if he'd been in some old prison hole. According to the autopsy report, there were indications he'd been subjected to sexual assault. He'd had his jaw smashed in."

Julia looked at the grim concentration on Micaela's face and wondered what exactly she'd set in motion. But still . . . she wished she had more to say to keep that angry glow in Micaela's eyes alive.

"I remember Pappa was furious," she said.

"Why the hell didn't he say anything to us then?"

Micaela seized hold of her hand, and Julia wished she could go to her father and ask his advice. But that would only give her away. She also had an urge to smoke a joint.

"I think he's signed some NDAs," she said defensively.

Micaela looked at her in revulsion, as if it were all her fault, and Julia recoiled.

"Surely he can't obstruct a murder investigation for that," Micaela spluttered.

"I'm convinced . . ." Julia said, but couldn't finish her sentence.

Micaela stood up. Julia watched her, fascinated by the sudden decisiveness in her body language.

"What are you going to do?" she said.

"I have to speak to him."

"Wait . . . he might be sleeping."

That made no difference. Micaela careered off with a new single-mindedness in her movements – and with a rising sense of trepidation, Julia followed.

Hans Rekke was propped up in bed and had inserted the disk with the old recording from Grimsta IP. He leaned forward, his eyes narrowed, each time Jamal Kabir appeared in shot. How had Kabir's movements failed to fascinate him previously? The gestures had seemed so alien, but also, paradoxically, so familiar, like an echo from a world that had been close to him, and that was why he hadn't said a word about it. He had suspected it was his mania leading him astray.

But now . . . now that he had sunk into the mire, what did he see? The same thing? Perhaps. But mostly nothing. His gaze was dead and the only question clear in his mind was: had he once run like those players on the pitch? Had he once celebrated or been infuriated over nothing – a ball being fired into the goal, a cross hitting its mark, a penalty not awarded? It didn't feel like it. It seemed as if he had lived a life excluded from the things which troubled and delighted everyone else.

He took a few anxious breaths and listened to the traffic and tried to determine whether the frequency of the cars passing by outside could tell him what they were or what the time was. But no . . . the city was mute. Everything was mute and buzzing all at once. But wait . . .

Footsteps were approaching, decisive steps. Were they limping? Yes, slightly. Every second step landed a little harder on the floor. Ba dam, it went. Ba dam. Had he heard that back at Djursholm? He didn't think so; it had to be something temporary and almost imperceptible. Now she was visible in the doorway and he let his gaze sweep over her from her eyes down to the ladders in her tights.

"Your hip," he said.

"What about it?" she asked, and he realised at once: he'd upset her.

It wasn't a new injury from the night before, but an old poorly healed fracture that she thought was no longer noticeable. Perhaps it even represented a trauma. Her hand went down to her left side in a practised movement, force of habit, no doubt, she probably didn't notice since she was . . . he could see it clearly now . . . furious.

"Never mind," he said. "Is there something I can help you with?"

"Listen to her."

It was Julia who had appeared behind her.

"I'm listening," he said.

"Was Jamal Kabir in an American prison in Kabul?"

He closed his eyes and thought: So the idiot hadn't said anything about it then? He longed to be far away, asleep.

"I can't say anything," he said.

"Of course you bloody can. I already know," Julia said.

"Do you?" he said.

"I overheard your call to Magnus that time."

He opened his eyes and thought: What do I care, and what do I have to lose? Nothing.

"Yes, yes, well . . . he was inside," he said.

"Why the hell weren't we informed?" Micaela hissed.

"Because no-one knew about it then – apart from certain individuals in the American administration and a couple of people here at the Ministry for Foreign Affairs. I don't suppose they thought it necessary to tell you when everything indicated that it was just an act of madness committed by a drunk football dad."

"This is insane."

"No," he said. "It's true."

"How were we supposed to do our jobs if we didn't have all the facts?"

"Naturally, that was also my view. That was why I called your assistant commissioner, Martin Falkegren, and informed him. But it would appear that he kept that information to himself."

"Bloody hell."

"I'm sorry."

"But clearly the Americans informed you."

"No, no, absolutely not. They denied the suggestion and threatened me in the most enchanting manner."

"Well then, how did you find out?"

"*Mortui vivos docent.*"

"What?"

"The dead teach the living."

"What are you talking about?"

He took a deep breath and thought: Time to bend or break. Time for them to find out what I've been doing, what kind of dark knowledge I possess and have been forced to keep quiet about.

Rekke put his laptop on the nightstand and looked at them with a gradually clearing gaze. His dry lips were moving soundlessly, as if he were trying out a few silent words to himself.

"In January 2000, I was given a chair at Stanford," he said. "I suppose it was largely my work on intuition that gave rise to the appointment. But what I've written on interrogation techniques during times of war also played a role, and piqued interest both at the university and with the CIA."

"*War and the Art of Telling the Truth*," Micaela said. "I've read the book."

"You have, have you? May God forgive me my trespasses. But that, plus a couple of things I did for the San Francisco Police Department gave me a reputation for understanding confessions," he said. "I was regarded as a great expert on the matter. After 9/11 . . . I'm sure you can guess . . . the sky came tumbling down somewhat on the intelligence organisations. The CIA was crying out for expertise, and I was deluged with witness statements – most of them from Guantanamo Bay."

"Terrorist interrogations?" Micaela said.

Rekke smiled mournfully to himself.

"Yes, some of them really were terrorists. But most of the interviews were so preposterous that I was unable to say anything about them unless I knew more about the context. It was . . . how to put it . . . like hearing an out-of-tune singing voice without understanding whether it was from a lack of talent or from the person being throttled, and after several rows and some to-ing and fro-ing, I was given more information. I learned about what was so beautifully referred to as 'enhanced interrogation'."

"What's that?"

"A euphemism for torture, something that began with President Bush defining terrorist suspects as illegal combatants, which meant they could circumvent the Geneva Convention and the country's own anti-torture laws. Of course, I knew that. But I had no idea about the extent and wasn't imaginative enough to envisage the escalation that inevitably occurs when we discard our own fundamental principles."

"What escalation do you mean?"

"The gradual normalisation and intensification. I have to say that I was astounded. On the other hand, I learned a great deal about the subject: mostly about white torture, as they refer to it – loud noises, strong lighting around the clock, disruption of sleep, extreme cold and darkness. But also classic abuse, waterboarding and sexual humiliation – anal penetration, insertion of fluids in the rectum. All pretty beastly, but at the same time, it was – how should I put it? – characteristic."

"How?"

"The interrogators all seemed to have had the same training, and I learned to recognise the methods and patterns, the very culture you might say. The approaches differed. But there was always a common denominator – a method that went back to a few underlying documents, and that came to interest me. I was already well read in the subject, and of course I knew that torture has its own cultural peculiarities, its own fingerprints. Not only can you trace the perpetrator, but you can also trace the context he is operating in. The ideology behind it leaves its traces on the tortured body."

Rekke reached for a glass on the nightstand – it was empty, but he still drank from it, even though he was only swallowing air. Micaela wondered whether she should fetch him something to drink. But she brushed the thought aside and said impatiently:

"In what way?"

"The Taliban, for instance, were amused from early on by show trials," he said. "As you know, they filled football stadiums and executed and maimed people in front of an audience. Thus their methods became more spectacular. They used whips, nails hammered into hands, amputations, while the Americans . . . well, it goes without saying . . . saw

116

themselves as a great democracy that doesn't torture its prisoners. Hence American torture was more discreet, designed to be invisible. Pretty early on I thought the marks on Kabir's body – especially the frostbite on his chest – felt more like the CIA than Mullah Omar, and that fitted with my original theory."

"Which was?"

"My dear Julia, would you be so good as to fetch me some water?" he said, lifting the glass from the nightstand again.

Julia grimaced theatrically and turned to Micaela.

"See what he's like?" she said. "Used to people running his errands all the time."

"Naturally I'm ashamed," he said.

"Then he's always ashamed."

Julia went to the kitchen and returned with a bottle of Ramlösa mineral water that she poured for him. He drank it greedily, and looked at Micaela with the same melancholy as before.

"You said that it fitted with your original theory," she said.

"I couldn't make Kabir's story add up, and I didn't think anyone else had managed to either," he said. "I understood enough about the paranoia at the time to know that the intelligence services would never have left a guy like that in peace. I became convinced that he'd been interrogated inside out – if not here, then elsewhere. That was why I was reading the records from the Migration Agency and why I went through the autopsy report five – ten – times, and slowly I became certain of my case. The guy had been in one of the CIA's prisons."

"And that was why you called Magnus afterwards," Julia said.

"Yes. I guessed that Magnus was aware of the case, not just because it must have been a sensitive foreign policy issue. The scars on Kabir's right wrist gave me the jitters. Do you remember them, Micaela?"

"Of course," she said. "I just mentioned them. Faint, pale impressions from a heavy chain."

"Exactly, and those marks seemed to be whispering something to me. They felt like a clue from a crime scene that I'd previously overlooked, and I knew instinctively that they were associated with the frostbite damage. So I looked around. I became quite obsessed with it, and eventually I realised. I'd seen similar scars and frostbite on another dead man."

"Who?"

"A prisoner called Gulman Ghazali. They chained him up, naked from the waist down, in an ice-cold room. Ghazali complained that he was so cold he couldn't think. Then they decided to push him even harder. They drenched him in cold water and made sure he couldn't sleep. On November 20, 2002, he was found frozen to death in his cell with the same scars on his wrist that Kabir had."

"My God."

"Quite. He was at a black site north of Kabul, code named the Salt Pit or Cobalt. But since the best-known method of torture there is to keep prisoners in complete darkness, the inmates have a different name for the place."

"Prison of Darkness," said Micaela.

"Or Dark Prison," he said. "I've also seen the name Music Prison too. The interrogators play hard rock or hip hop at top volume around the clock in the cells. It drives the prisoners crazy. For them, it's never night or day – it's just a black abyss of nothingness. Often they're bound or chained to the ground so that they can't walk or sit."

"And the USA is doing this?"

"Yes, I'm afraid so."

She thought about it. It wasn't that she was under any illusions about the CIA – not after what her father had told her. But still . . .

"It's insane," she said.

"Quite. But what I was going to say was that Magnus reluctantly confirmed to me that Kabir had been in the same prison. It became a rather poisonous story. You know . . ." Rekke hesitated and gave a small smile of resignation, "Magnus is pretty much up to his ears in this too."

"In what way?"

"He approved the rendition of Swedes suspected of terrorism out of the country to be tortured on foreign soil on behalf of the CIA. That's why he's being such a pitbull over this, and when we met at Sturehof that time that you saw us, Micaela, he was being rather childishly threatening."

"I see," she said, hardly listening now.

In front of her she saw Kabir, freezing and chained up in a pitch-black room far away in Kabul. She had pictured a similar scenario before, but not with the CIA as the tormentors.

"It's political dynamite, isn't it?"

"You might say that. There are a lot of people besides Magnus who are doing everything they can to ensure it doesn't get out."

She shivered, but at that same moment she was struck by another thought.

"So Kabir was a suspected terrorist rather than a popular hero."

"Yes, apparently," Rekke said.

He peered up towards the painting of the boy and his flute on the wall.

"But we'll have to assume he was innocent, given that he was released," he said.

"Yes, I suppose so."

"Although I've got to say I wonder about that too."

"Why's that?"

"It's usually impossible to get people out of there – regardless of their guilt."

"So what's your conclusion?" Micaela said.

"My conclusion . . ." he said slowly, ". . . is that Kabir had an unexpected ally. But also . . ."

"What?"

"Many enemies."

"Why do you say that?"

Because apparently I still believe I can draw conclusions about people, Rekke thought to himself.

"Because I'm talking," he said. "Because all I'm doing is talking."

FIFTEEN

Micaela looked at him and shook her head. How could he see so much in so little, in a couple of pale scars, and a few discolorations to the skin on his chest and thighs?

She stared into Rekke's eyes as if the answer to why he saw so clearly would be found there in the dull glow of his gaze. But she noticed something else: she was becoming increasingly agitated. Not as a result of gaining insight into something politically dirty. Rather, it was the revelation that crucial information had been concealed from them that made her heart pound.

"You've turned everything upside down," she said.

"You should have been told sooner. I never imagined that your assistant commissioner would keep the information to himself. But I was naive."

"I want to strangle him."

"Then I think you'll have to strangle many others while you're at it. Kleeberger and my dear brother for starters."

She took a step closer to the bed.

"Surely withholding information from a murder inquiry is an offence," she said.

He squinted at her and put his hand to his brow. He looked completely exhausted, as if the exposition had demanded all his strength.

"Without doubt they were taking a risk when they kept it secret from you."

"So why did they do that?"

He looked down at the duvet.

"If we start with Falkegren, someone must have given him the impression that my observations were false. But if we go further back, then we can only assume the CIA didn't want it to come out that they tortured people."

"For Christ's sake, they can't derail a police investigation just because of that," she said.

"I think they can do worse," he said. "But you're right, there must be another reason. After all, they did release Kabir from their prison, and compelled the Ministry for Foreign Affairs to welcome him in Sweden. That's a pretty big deal. I'm guessing there's something else buried here."

"Aren't you going to find out what it is then?" she said, more harshly than she had intended. "For example, by speaking to your brother again."

Rekke hesitated. Then he shook his head, closed his eyes and sank even deeper into the bed.

"I think Magnus has already said more than he should."

"And you're satisfied with that," she hissed.

He opened his eyes and looked guilty for a moment.

"Once upon a time I might not have been. But now . . . I'm no longer someone to be trusted."

Micaela felt the blood coursing through her veins.

"You just showed that you actually are."

"No, no," he said.

"What do you mean 'no, no'? You realised from just a few scars that he'd been in prison."

"Those were old conclusions – my gaze now is dead. I'm sorry to disappoint you."

He turned towards Julia.

"To disappoint you both. But now I must sleep. Would you be so kind as to turn off the light?"

Micaela stood there as her thoughts buzzed around. What should she do? She ought to shake Rekke back to life, to get him to pull himself together, but at the same time she wanted to get out of here and take immediate action.

"I'm going to try and find out more and get you up to speed," she said.

"You are?" he said in a tired voice. "Of course, that's a kind thought, but I think—"

"Is your phone number the same?" she interrupted.

He held out his arms as if he wasn't quite sure. She settled for that and left, but got no further than the hall. She ran back. The room was already dark, apart from the faint light seeping past the curtains. Julia was leaning over him, adjusting his pillows.

"Can you stay with him today?"

"Not really," Julia said.

"No-one needs to stay with me," Rekke mumbled, as if already asleep.

"I'll call Mrs Hansson."

"No, no, I'll stay," Julia said.

"Good. I'm off. I'll be in touch."

"That would be most gratifying," Rekke said in a voice that barely seemed conscious of itself.

She took the lift downstairs and emerged onto the street. The sky was a clear blue. There was a wind blowing off the water. Feeling strong and decisive, she decided to call Jonas Beijer.

But her resolve was short-lived; it began to dissipate with the realisation that she didn't like the sunshine. It felt like needles in her eyes. It pressed against her temples and cheeks. She was unsure whether she'd be able to make it to the Tunnelbana station. Should she turn around? No, no. She didn't want to go crawling back.

Call Lucas, she thought to herself, and ended up standing there with the phone in her hand. Of course, he was the last person she ought to call. Things weren't the way they'd been before. I'll fix it, I'll just pull myself together, she thought, staggering off, but pretty soon she began to fade.

She sank to her knees and once again the whole drama in the Tunnelbana station flickered before her, and she sat there on the pavement, gasping for breath. A voice said:

"Are you alright, dear?"

A middle-aged lady in a bright-blue coat was looking down at her with kind, empathetic eyes. To Micaela, it felt like a new needle thrust into her body: no-one in Östermalm was allowed to feel sorry for her, and she stood up on unsteady legs and muttered to the woman like an angry child:

"I'll be fine. I just . . ."

She didn't finish the sentence, instead staggering off and taking a left onto Riddargatan. But eventually she could go no further. Her head was splitting, and she leaned against a building wall, breathing heavily. At that moment, her phone vibrated in her pocket. She hoped it was her mother or Vanessa. It was Lucas.

"You called," he said.

"No, no," she managed to stammer. "Pocket-dialled, maybe."

"You sound like shit."

"I'm OK."

"I don't believe that. Where are you?"

She definitely didn't intend to tell him. Nevertheless, she stammered out her location and heard the triumph in his voice.

"I'm coming. I'll take care of you, *hermanita*."

Julia was still in the room. Her father's eyes shone with a faint glow in the darkness. What was up with him? A few minutes ago he'd seemed like he was back. But now . . . she crept over to the bedroom window, tugged aside the curtains and looked down towards the inner courtyard. Why couldn't he pull himself together? He had something to cling on to now.

"You don't seem able to sleep," she said.

"Pardon, what did you say?"

Sweat was glistening on his brow.

"Nothing," she said.

She looked down at his hands.

"I was thinking about that prison," she said.

"Aren't there more fun things to think about?"

"I wondered what it was like there."

"I shouldn't have told you."

"What do you think it was like?"

"I don't know," he said. "But one prisoner described it as a darkness without words, a nameless horror, and I remember thinking about that."

"What did you conclude?"

"Nothing, I think."

"You should look at the investigation again. It'd do you good."

She could tell that the challenge made him uncomfortable.

"I think the police can manage just fine on their own," he said.

"It doesn't exactly seem like it."

"Julia, won't you please leave me in peace for a while?"

She thought about Micaela's footsteps disappearing off, the way she moved with such incredible purpose.

"Why was the referee in that prison?"

His jaw tensed.

"Why?" she repeated.

"He was suspected of collaboration with the Taliban."

"What sort of collaboration?"

"Magnus didn't want to say."

"And you just forgot about it?"

"Apparently."

"Because you got depressed, right?" she said.

"I'm guessing so."

"Well think about it now," she said.

But all he did was close his eyes, as if he wanted to disappear inside himself again – to his own Prison of Darkness.

In a darkness without words. A nameless horror. Was that what he was in? He recognised how grandiose it was to compare himself with the prisoners being tortured. Yet it was as if he envied them.

He envied them the tangibility of their suffering: the chains, the cold, the blows, the music pounding for real and not just as an atonal howl inside his head. But above all, he envied them for the simple solution to their suffering – freedom. Their torment would end if they were set free, while his darkness belonged to his body, to the very depths of his gaze.

"Of course you're right," he said to Julia. "I ought . . ." But he got no further.

He saw the train rushing towards him. He remembered his body tensing, and the currents of air from the tunnel. He remembered the voice in his head: *Do it, don't hesitate.* But also other things: steps approaching, clattering, a focused tread, as if two fateful forces were moving towards him from two different directions.

"I'm going to the kitchen to study or something," Julia said.

He looked up at her and tried to untangle himself from the flood of memories and dark associations that were occupying his retinas, and he felt it more than ever: Julia shouldn't have to see him like this. She ought to be occupied with being young and happy, and he fumbled for a response – any would do.

"How are your studies going?"

"Not great," she said.

"Are you still studying the Renaissance?"

"What?"

"Are you still doing the Renaissance?"

"My God, what a relevant question for this moment."

"Well, quite," he said, trying to smile while he switched on the reading lamp. "On the money, I suppose. Won't you help your father out then and tell him what he ought to ask about?"

"He should tell me what he did yesterday."

"He got drunk, just as he said."

"And pulled a cop from Husby."

"I didn't pull anyone."

"Did you sleep with her?"

"I most certainly did not."

"Or is she an old lover? I remember when she visited us."

"No, no, she was just kind and helped me."

"Wouldn't surprise me if she were a protest against Farmor."

"What on earth are you talking about?"

"Wouldn't it be the perfect way to taunt her – getting together with some girl from the hood? Farmor would have a heart attack at the very thought."

"Enough, sweetheart, enough. I beg you. But perhaps you're right. I should look again at the investigation," he said, reaching for his computer on the nightstand.

But when he perched it on his stomach, it felt threatening and alien, so he got up instead, resolved to engage with the tasks of daily life – like a good patient, in spite of it all. He went into the bathroom and even more diligently resisted the temptation to pop more pills.

Instead, he showered under cold water as a kind of mortification. He shaved, brushed his teeth, combed his hair – all the things that in good times were merely moments of irritation, getting between him and the things he wanted to get to grips with right away, but which now felt like small mountains that he was climbing. Added to that was the need to button up his shirt, pull on his jeans and a blue cashmere sweater before he went into the kitchen.

The plan was to have an espresso, just like anyone else on a Sunday morning, and to read the papers, and to get his daughter to believe that her pappa was a more or less normal father.

Lucas came in his Audi and honked at her, and she swore to herself. Why did she need to play along with this charade? But he was here now and once she'd got into the car, she said thank you. Like a good sister. But she couldn't stand the way he looked at her. She closed her eyes and tried to signal that she didn't feel up to talking.

"Who did this?" he said, pointing to her cheek, clearly agitated and doing his *no-one touches my sister* thing.

Nevertheless, she had the feeling that he was pleased he'd been allowed to pick her up and play the knight in shining armour. His hair was cut short, and he wore a blue shirt and a black nylon jacket. There was something neat, stylish even, about his person, which didn't conceal an underlying aggression. They drove through Vasastan and across the Sankt Eriksbron bridge.

"Hang on," she said. "Where are you going? I want to go home."

"I'm taking you to Natali," he said, and although she tried to protest she eventually relented.

Natali had been his girlfriend for almost a year, and she lived in her own co-op flat down by Kungsholmstorg, where Lucas usually went when he wasn't hanging out in Husby and Akalla. Like a true gentleman, he opened the car door when they arrived and helped her up the stairs to the lift. Natali met them at the door with a troubled expression.

Natali was as cute as a doll, wearing a floral dress that would have been more suitable for a summer's day, and, as ever, she looked startlingly proper and Swedish with her blonde hair and her friendly smile. It was as if she were part of Lucas's efforts to climb the social ladder.

"Oh baby," she said. "What's happened to you?"

"She's been on an adventure to Östermalm," Lucas said, putting Micaela on the sofa by the balcony.

He laid a blanket over her and gave her a glass of water and two painkillers that she didn't take. Then he sat down opposite her in a red armchair, and it was clear how curious he was. He fiddled with his keyring. Coming from the kitchen was the sound of "You Raise Me Up" by Josh Groban.

"So you don't want to go to hospital and let someone take a look at that?" he said.

"No," she said.

"And there's no-one you'd like me to have a word with?"

She looked anxiously at him.

"Dear God, no."

"Good," he said. "I'm listening, *hermanita*."

It was as if he understood it better than she did, because it wasn't just that she'd wanted to be rescued when she'd stood there faffing with her phone. She'd wanted to talk, maybe even work.

"I bumped into Mario Costa last night," she said.

She saw a sudden excitement in Lucas's eyes, and wondered whether he was hoping that it had been Mario who had given her those bruises on her face. A worthy opponent.

"So what did *he* say?"

"He was pissed."

"Aren't professional footballers meant to stay sober?"

"I don't think he really cares."

"He's going to screw up his contract with Marseille, I swear."

"He asked about Kabir," she said.

Lucas stopped fiddling with his keys.

"Are you back on the investigation?" he said.

"That investigation is pretty much dead in the water."

"So you're not back."

"I'm just a little interested in it again. You said there was talk about Kabir being scared."

Lucas looked towards the kitchen.

"Was there something in particular you heard?" she said.

He looked thoughtful at that.

"There was some talk that he was in a funk about people trying to find him after that TV report."

Micaela made to sit up. Lucas carefully pushed her down and adjusted her blanket.

"Easy. No rapid movements."

"Who was going to find him?"

He looked at her with that crooked smile that always seemed to suggest he knew something no-one else did, but which might just as easily be a tactic he used to unsettle people.

"Why don't you ask that TV reporter – Tove – the one who did the report?"

"Tove Lehmann. She's been questioned several times."

"She might have more to say now. Someone said she didn't take to your colleagues."

"OK," she said. "Maybe I will."

"You look like shit."

"Yeah, I feel pretty lousy," she said, and it was true.

A new wave of nausea swept over her. She glanced up at Lucas looking at her with something resembling affection, then she closed her eyes and disappeared.

SIXTEEN

Lucas looked at her face, black and blue with a pallor underneath, and thought: What a fighter she is. It doesn't matter how many blows she takes. She just grits her teeth and keeps going without a word of complaint. It was true that she was a bitch on occasion. But he'd always been proud of her, and had even loved accompanying her to the termly reviews with her teachers at school.

The teachers perked up when they saw her, and you could see why. No-one picked things up as easily, and her work rate was something else. It was like magic. You gave her something and, bish bash bosh, it was done. There was often no need even to ask, it just happened.

Her pupils were still moving restlessly. Her jaw was thrust out as it always was when she was frustrated. What's happened? he thought to himself. Who's been mean to you?

"Micaela," he whispered, caressing her hair and her unblemished cheek.

He wanted a smile in return, acknowledgement of his kindness. But she merely grimaced in her sleep and he wondered yet again why she had been so strange and chilly of late. She froze at the very sight of him, and he was reminded of that day in the plaza, the summer after she and Vanessa had graduated from sixth form. He hadn't seen her for a long time then either. She was wearing the white dress he'd bought for her graduation day, and she was tossing an orange up and down. She was radiant, he thought, and he walked towards her expectantly. But when she turned around she didn't look at him the way he'd hoped. The happy, easy-going part of her vanished.

"What is it?" he said.

"I'm going to be a police officer," she replied, before heading into the Tunnelbana station with a new defiance in her stride.

He'd returned to that incident often in recent months, perhaps because deep down he knew that it was one thing with Fransson and those other bozos in the police, but if his sister turned against him he wouldn't stand a chance. He smiled at that thought for a moment.

"Fighter," he said, looking down at her hands resting on her stomach above the grey blanket.

He stroked her injured cheek as far as her throat, and felt a sudden desire to press down, lightly to leave a slight mark, or hard to erase that independence he had discovered far too late.

While Julia made yet another cappuccino in the kitchen, she remembered that day in September before Pappa had gone to Stanford for the last time.

She had just started her Art History degree at Stockholm University but was still living at home in Djursholm. Things were tense between her parents – well, things were tense with Mamma, who couldn't stand Pappa's indifference to everything that was important in her world: dinners, the house, the beautiful facade. "You're going to crash again, and I can't bear it!" she had yelled from upstairs that morning, and Pappa had replied: "No, no, sorry, of course not. Is there something I can do for you, sweetheart?"

There was a feeling of anxiety in the house, and not long afterwards that man Charles had come to visit – the one who looked like a high-ranking general, with his neat white beard. She'd always had the impression that Charles admired Pappa. But on that occasion, the conversation was irritable, no matter how much Mamma tried to lighten the mood. Pappa was brusque and took Charles up to his study. When they came back down again, Julia heard Charles say:

"I understand you, Hans. But don't forget that these guys are monsters."

"Do you know the worst thing about monsters?" her father replied. "They make monsters of us."

It was nothing, really, just one of those quips he sometimes delivered. But then when it all crumbled and Pappa was kicked out of Stanford and the USA, Julia wondered whether those words had in fact been the beginning of his fall. She had never really understood him. Now, for example, he'd got out of bed and dressed, as if he wanted to show that life was continuing as normal. But then he'd slumped forward over the kitchen table, frozen into his cataleptic trance as Mamma used to put it, and she was tempted to pummel his back with her hands. Instead, she went towards him with her cappuccino and put a hand on his neck.

"What are you thinking about?"

He shuddered, as if waking back to life.

"I'm not sure," he said.

"I really think you ought to call Magnus and push him on that football referee."

"He's not going to tell me anything."

She looked at her father encouragingly.

"I don't know how you can say that."

"Why not?"

"Because you're the great interrogation expert. You're supposed to be able to prise information out of a stone wall."

He turned his gaze to her.

"Me? Who can't even ask his daughter about her boyfriend?"

He was trying to sound tender and make light of it, but the effort it required shone through.

"Well, why don't you give him a ring and fuck with him a bit?" she said. "It might cheer you up."

He smiled tranquilly, as if he didn't think the idea completely lacked merit, or as if he recognised that he had nothing to lose: things couldn't get worse.

When Micaela woke up, it was half past one in the afternoon and Natali was sitting in Lucas's place, smiling at her. She had spruced herself up since Micaela had fallen asleep: she'd applied lipstick and mascara, as well as changing into a dress that was darker and more restrained. It looked like she was posing. She had her legs crossed and her upper body slightly twisted. Her figure was enviable, you had to give her that.

"Hi," she said. "How are you feeling?"

Micaela looked around the room. Through the window she could see dark clouds scudding across the sky. There were pigeons sitting on the balcony, motionless, as if they had been petrified into statues.

"OK," she said.

The headache spread across her brow.

"That was quite a thump you got."

"I suppose so."

"What happened?"

"I fell. Where's Lucas?"

"He had to head. But seriously . . . we're worried about you."

She looked at Natali again. The girl seemed nervous.

"You know you always have a friend in us," Natali said. "If anything's happened, you can always come here. Lucas misses you."

"He doesn't have to," she said. "I'm here now."

"But it's been ages since we all got together. So I thought maybe you'd heard something or whatever."

Micaela sat up on the sofa.

"At work, you mean?"

"I mean generally."

She thought about the weapon that Lucas had drawn in the woods.

"What do you think I might have heard?" she said.

"Oh, you know," Natali said awkwardly. "I've dreamed about you and me becoming friends. Kind of like sisters."

Come on, Micaela thought. Come on.

"Lucas never talks about your childhood," she said. "But I'd really like to hear about it. You and him were close as anything. Took care of everything and stuff."

"I'll tell you sometime," she said curtly, standing up.

Micaela headed for the bathroom. She wanted to get out of there. Natali trailed behind her like a lost dog, and in the hallway she took her hand. Their eyes met with unexpected intensity.

"Do you know what Lucas says?" she said.

"No."

"He says that you were always the good one, while he always ended up in fights and lots of trouble, but that it ought to be the other way around."

"Why's that?"

"Because he longs for order and calm, while deep down you've always wanted to break the rules and cause chaos. You're like your dad, he says. What you really want is to defy and protest."

Micaela remembered her father's refrain about a person's duty to stand up against injustice and all that. She said:

"He's talking shit. I'm Miss Goody Two Shoes."

"I think . . ." Natali began.

But Micaela patted her kindly on the head and went into the bathroom, where she splashed cold water on her face and tried to conceal the bruise on her cheek with a little of Natali's make-up. Before she left, she hugged Natali with exaggerated warmth as if they really were friends or sisters.

She felt cold and sick, and did her best to avoid people's looks. Up on Hantverkargatan, she rejected yet another call from Vanessa and called Jonas Beijer, surprised at how pleased he sounded.

*

The telephone rang. It was his mother again – third time today – and he let it ring. It wasn't about him, the less loved one. It was about Hans. Everything was always about Hans, and now, since Hans had sunk into acute depression, a state of emergency prevailed in the family. Nothing else seemed important.

The beloved son had to be rescued. Magnus was sick to the teeth of it. He went into the kitchen and, although it was still quite early, he poured a glass of beer up to the brim and sat down on the red sofa with its views of Oscarskyrkan and knocked back his drink. Once the alcohol reached his head, he felt a little better and even smiled at the whole affair. Not that he rejoiced in the misfortunes of others. Not really.

He himself bore some guilt for the course of events. Still, something in him wanted to say: *What did I tell you?* It could only have gone badly. The whole analysis team had been bewitched, and they'd given Hans far too much without ever suspecting that he never just did his job and kept his mouth shut. He always had to proclaim his truths and this time it wasn't exactly innocent information he possessed.

Why couldn't he have kept quiet?

When the first warnings arrived, Hans had merely shrugged and moved on to other assignments. He was engaged by everyone back then. But of course, his mania wore off and the paralysis descended – the depression too – and it was then, they now knew, that he'd spoken to Maureen Hamilton at the *Washington Post*. No-one really believed he'd divulged anything important. If he had, it would have been in the paper. But the fear that he was going to talk grew, and Magnus might have contributed to that worry. He had whispered into Charles Bruckner's ear, and after that they'd set about Hans in all their paranoia and intrusiveness. It was no surprise, really, that he'd caved.

Magnus looked at the time. It was Sunday. He was expecting a call from the French foreign minister about the War on Terror. His basic principle was that it was always better for him – rather than Kleeberger – to take that kind of call. Maybe he should have another beer? He liked being gently tipsy when talking to these dignitaries. It made him more nimble in his thinking. Yes, why not, if he was being honest? He headed for the kitchen. The telephone rang again. Monsieur Chevalier already? No, no, it was Hans, His Majesty himself, and Magnus noticed right away from his breathing that he wasn't exactly happy, but he wasn't dejected either.

"You sound better," he said.

"You, on the other hand, have been drinking."

"I have not. To what do I owe the honour?"

"Jamal Kabir who was murdered in Grimsta. There was something you didn't tell me about his application for asylum."

Magnus stiffened and ran his hand through his hair. Easy now, he thought to himself.

"I told you every single thing," he said.

"Then you're not as omniscient as I've always believed you to be. The story doesn't add up."

"Why doesn't it add up?"

"There's some embarrassment, isn't there? Some form of deal or agreement with the CIA?"

"I don't intend to discuss this with you, and most certainly not on an unsecured line."

"Surely they're not so impertinent as to tap people's phones?"

"Very funny."

"Is that the second or third beer you're on?"

"Mamma says you're not answering when she calls. She's beside herself."

"Poor thing."

"She thinks you're going to jump off a bridge or something. She's started bleating on about your breakdown in Helsinki again."

"She needn't worry about that."

"About what?"

"About anything."

"So you're back on this old chestnut again. Don't you have anything better to do?"

"I'd very much like to speak to the maestro. You'll have to set up a meeting."

"He knows no more than I do."

"Rather less, I should say. But he's got a more amenable personality."

"For goodness' sake, you can't have an audience with Kleeberger any old time you fancy. I promise you, there's nothing – not at the level you're imagining, anyway. It's just your illness speaking."

Hans fell silent and that was a good sign, Magnus told himself.

"OK," he eventually said. "I'll add my bipolarism as a factor into the equation. But perhaps . . ."

"What?"

"You should do that too. See me as something of a risk factor."

"For goodness' sake, Hans."

"Thank you, brother dearest."

Magnus hung up and swore to himself and downed his second beer. His good mood was ruined, which was the last thing he needed ahead of a call as important as this one with Monsieur Chevalier. To hell with you, Hans – and Kabir? Why are you looking at Kabir of all people? Just recently you sounded half dead. But now . . . what happened?

He intended to find out right away. He stood there for a while with the telephone in his hand, planning to call Kleeberger, but decided instead to go straight to the source.

"Don't play with me, Hans," he muttered. "Don't play with me."

Jonas Beijer had just got home from the stables with Samuel when Micaela called. "Hello," he said, instantly animated, remembering that he had thought about her during the night.

But he couldn't admit to that. He was about to ask her how she was when he realised she sounded strange. Then she said something even stranger. He must have misheard. He set down his bag in the kitchen and told Samuel he was on a work call. He went into the bedroom and shut the door.

"What are you talking about?" he said.

"The Americans tortured Kabir."

"No, no," he replied. "It was the Taliban. You know that."

"That was a lie," she said. "Can we meet?"

He was eager to see her, had been longing for it. But he couldn't think straight. Had the Americans really chained up Kabir and tortured him?

"The Americans don't do that," he said.

"Can we meet at that café near yours?"

"You're not drunk are you? You sound . . ."

"We were kept in the dark," she interrupted, and that made him want to snap at her to cut the bullshit.

At the same time, something was shifting, as if part of him didn't want to reject what she was saying. There was a logic to it, wasn't there? The Americans in Kabul had been so bloody evasive, as if they were indeed hiding something.

"Who is claiming this?" he said.

"It's been confirmed by the Ministry for Foreign Affairs, and Falkegren has been aware of it since last summer," she said, and he didn't reply to that – it was more than he could take in.

He heard himself saying that he'd be happy to see her in half an hour at his regular.

"I'd very much like to speak to the maestro. You'll have to set up a meeting."

His interpreter, Maria Ekselius, was translating the call for him, and Charles Bruckner muttered to himself. It was a Sunday, he was in sweaty workout clothes and his calf was starting to cramp. He wasn't supposed to be here at all. But he'd been over-ambitious with his routine again: "your way of dealing with your fear of death" as his wife put it. He hadn't settled for jogging around Djurgården; he'd come here instead, and had been mid-session in the gym when he'd suddenly been interrupted.

Like most agents of his generation – he had just turned fifty-eight – Charles Bruckner had been trained to take part in the Cold War. Early on he'd been assigned to counter-espionage with postings to Berlin, then Moscow. After the fall of Communism, he'd been at a loss like so many others, and in the absence of any better option he'd applied to the Middle East counter-terrorism department and ended up in Khartoum. He'd felt like the wrong man in the wrong place. But after 9/11, he thanked his lucky stars. In Khartoum there had been a Saudi on the run who had fought in Afghanistan. He'd learned a bit about this man, who was called Osama Bin Laden, and in no time at all Charles had come to be seen as an agent with unique insider knowledge.

He rose through the ranks and formed ties with a series of external experts. In spite of that, here he was just a few years later in a retirement posting in Stockholm. Not on account of any mistakes he'd made, but because his wife had grown tired of his hours, his comings and goings, and declared that it was her turn to call the shots. So they moved to Sweden when Charlotte had been appointed visiting professor at the School of Architecture in Stockholm. On occasion he cursed this turn of events, but at least he had more time to work out. And now some modest excitement had come his way.

Peter McDonnell from his old team at Langley had called to say they'd captured a call from "your professor, your reliable genius". The gibe did not escape Charles. He had run to find his interpreter, Maria, and listened to the call and now he was looking at her quizzically and muttering that it was strange. It was barely comprehensible, truth be told. As recently as the day before they had all been convinced that tapping Rekke's phone was pointless. He represented no threat. He barely touched his computer, replied only monosyllabically on the phone and seemed run down and suicidal. But now, all of a sudden, he wanted to meet the foreign minister.

"Why the hell does he want to do that?" Charles said.

"Surely it isn't that remarkable? Aren't they close?" Maria said defensively, as if she felt accused.

"Not anymore," he said, putting his tracksuit top back on. He headed into the corridor without even saying goodbye.

After just a few metres he changed his mind and considered going back. Maria was the one who knew the language, after all. But no, he continued on – he needed to work out how serious this was. It could turn into a veritable crisis if things went south.

The Associated Press had published a lengthy report on Abu Ghraib. The article hadn't garnered much attention. People probably understood that it wasn't possible to use ordinary interrogation techniques on these guys. But the facts in circulation were troubling. If Rekke with his insights and his turn of phrase started talking now that journalists had scented blood, it would be bad. Still, Charles Bruckner couldn't believe it – not really. Hans was a man of honour. At any rate Charles had missed him.

"*Claritas*, Charles, don't you see where that leads?"

He smiled at the memory as he hurried across the underground car park and unlocked his Ford – a black diplomatic vehicle. The car was slightly too conspicuous for his tastes, but it had its merits and engendered a certain respect. As soon as he'd emerged from the embassy his phone rang. More people needing him urgently, so it seemed.

"Magnus," he said. "How are you?"

"I am not at ease, nor am I quiet. How's Charlotte?"

"Top notch. I'm just missing the warmth back home."

"But spring's on its way. Stockholm does spring well."

"Not until July," he said, pulling onto Gärdesgatan and wondering how long it would take Magnus to come to the point.

"I'm a bit worried about my brother," he said.

Not long at all, apparently.

"Oh, why's that?" Charles replied innocently.

"He's digging into the old Kabir case again, and I don't want him to end up in trouble."

"Family comes first, huh?" he said, only a little sarcastically. "What can I do for you?"

"I thought you might remind him that it isn't such a smart idea, given the legal ramifications."

"Isn't it better if you tell him yourself?"

"I was thinking we'd go for a pincer movement."

Charles pulled onto Oxenstiernsgatan and wondered what courses of actions were open to him. Should he pay Hans a visit?

"What got him riled up?" he asked.

"He must have seen something. I'm looking into it."

"What's he after?" Charles said.

"I'm guessing he just wants to know. He can't stand things being unsolved. It's some kind of itch for him."

"I know," Charles said, resolving to swing by right now, not necessarily for a chat but simply to make his presence felt.

He made a U-turn and drove back up towards Grevgatan, thinking about the professor's clear blue eyes that always saw more than they should – both in this world and in other, alternate universes.

Micaela shouldn't have come. She ought to have gone home and slept and got rid of the headache. But here she was at Jonas's regular haunt on Mariatorget, squinting at him with tormented eyes.

"I'll run you to hospital," he said. "You're turning bluer by the second."

"Don't worry about it," she said.

He seemed fuddled and smelled of horse. He was wearing a black leather jacket and white T-shirt as if he had been clubbing. It looked like he'd slept badly.

"At least tell me what's happened," he said. "Surely you haven't been slapped about?"

"I was just clumsy."

"But you've come straight here from a party, right?"

She looked down at her skirt and her top that smelled of beer and could tell that the damn clothes hadn't even been good at Spy Bar.

"Kinda," she said, wanting to hide inside an extra-large jumper like she did at work, and perhaps he noticed that. He put a hand on hers and muttered that he really ought to get out more himself.

But then he turned serious again.

"And after that you walked into a door."

She removed his hand.

"Something like that."

"How did that happen?"

"It just did."

"My God, Micaela. Don't you know how crazy you sounded over the phone?"

She did, and wondered how much more to say.

"But you didn't seem that shocked by what I told you."

He shook his head.

"I'm as shocked as anything." He paused. "I just refuse to believe that torturing people like some medieval—"

"The CIA changed their interrogation methods after 9/11," Micaela interrupted.

"I read something about that," he said. "But for Christ's sake . . . leaving people in total darkness and letting them freeze to death?"

"I gather things gradually got out of control."

"I don't know," he said. "Why would Falkegren have kept us in the dark about it?"

"I expect he had his reasons."

Jonas shook his head again. Outside on Sankt Paulsgatan there was a yellow bin lorry taking on rubbish.

"Well, OK then," he said. "It doesn't sound completely unlikely."

143

She looked out towards the bin lorry and felt nauseous.

"Why do you say that?" she said.

"Everything's been so goddamn slow."

He fell silent, as if he was asking himself how much he should say. But she didn't doubt for a second that he intended to talk. He looked far too guilty to keep his trap shut.

"In what way?" she said.

"We had no reason to doubt that the Taliban tortured Jamal Kabir. There were medical certificates and the Migration Agency considered it confirmed. But the American representatives in Kabul we spoke to hummed and hawed and didn't give us anything concrete, so I turned to the local police and that didn't go much better. But, eventually, they faxed us a document that turned everything upside down."

"What did it say?"

"That Kabir worked for the Taliban – off and on," he said. "He was loosely tied to one of their ministries."

She stared at him in astonishment.

"Which ministry?"

"One with a foul name. The Department for the Promotion of Virtue and Prevention of Vice."

"What did he do for them?"

"Apparently he beat up people who broke the Taliban's rules – well, some of their rules anyway."

"He was meant to be a popular hero."

"The Migration Agency did an awful job."

"We did an awful job."

"Yes, perhaps," he said, gazing across the café. "Not that our perception of him was wrong, really. He was incredibly resourceful and almost everyone has good things to say about him. It's just that . . . something doesn't add up. Many say that he hated the Taliban regime. Yet he was a close friend of Mullah Zakaria – one of their leaders."

"The one who was shot in Copenhagen?"

144

"That's him, and that's something we looked into as well – whether they'd been in touch after the fall of the regime. But the interesting thing is the outburst Kabir had. We've all heard about the insane rules the regime created. You couldn't do anything, couldn't read, couldn't watch films or TV, couldn't listen to or play music, you couldn't even have canaries in the house – and women, well, you know all that. They were locked up and deprived of their rights. We thought Kabir was against all this insanity. Now we're wondering whether there might be a motive here. An assault he committed, say, for which someone wanted revenge."

"But you didn't find anything."

"Nothing big, nothing serious, mostly vandalism to be honest. But it's still dodgy. You know what? In the spring of 1997 the Taliban began a big persecution of musicians – especially those who had been educated by the Russians during the Soviet occupation in the 1980s."

"OK," she said.

"Music was considered to lead to loose morals. Instruments and cassettes and gramophone records were smashed up from day one after the Taliban came to power."

"I know," she said.

"But while musicians were generally regarded as criminals, it was worst for those who'd played Western classical music and collaborated with the blasphemous, anti-Muslim communists. Several of them disappeared or were murdered that spring."

Micaela leaned forward and tried to shake off the headache and nausea.

"You mean that Kabir . . ."

"No, no, I don't mean that. We've got nothing to suggest he committed acts of violence."

"But . . ."

"He smashed up instruments, including a violin and a clarinet. It was as if he went mad."

"That sounds insane," she said.

"Yes, a little," said Jonas. "But we can't get any further than that."

She blinked her eyes and tried to think clearly. But the headache only got worse, and when she looked towards the bin lorry outside it swam in and out of focus.

"You don't have a name?" she said. "Anyone I can speak to?"

She felt a hand against her neck and looked into Jonas's troubled face.

"Do you know what?" he said. "I think I will take you to hospital."

"No, no. I asked for a name."

"Don't start on this. You'll only drive Fransson up the wall."

"A name."

"Emma Gulwal," he said. "She was one of the musicians in Kabul that Kabir attacked. He smashed up her clarinet and went raving mad. Gulwal is in Berlin now. You can find her via international directory enquiries. But please, don't do anything now. If what you say about the CIA is true then I promise to try and bring you back onto the investigation."

"Oh great," she said, removing his hand from her neck and writing down the name on a napkin.

They sat in silence for a while.

"OK," he said. "You won't let me take you to hospital. But let me ask something else instead: was it Rekke you spoke to?"

She looked out at the square.

"Why do you ask?" she said.

Jonas looked at the square too, then turned back to her with sudden agitation.

"Because it feels like it. Falkegren . . ."

"Yes?"

"That moron called me just after the district court released Costa," he said. "I don't remember what he wanted. He was mostly confused, I reckon, about all the crap we'd got in the press. But I told him we wanted to engage Rekke again. You know, I might have complimented him on sending the files to the professor in the first place. I guess I thought he'd be flattered."

"But he wasn't, right?" Micaela said.

Jonas looked amused, as if he'd been reminded of something funny. Then he stood up to fetch more tea and Micaela stayed seated, thoughtful and nauseous, and rejected another call from Vanessa.

SEVENTEEN

Did he really want to meet Kleeberger? Did he even care about the investigation? Not anymore. Presumably, he had just wanted to prove to himself – or perhaps to Julia – that he could still take the initiative.

He listened for sounds from the apartment, waiting for her footsteps, and now he heard her. She looked curious. He averted his gaze.

"What did Magnus say?" she asked.

"He was mostly irritated," he replied, standing up.

He looked at her again, proudly, but also with a sense of alienation – as if at that moment he realised that she had become an entirely independent person without his having noticed.

"I really think it would do you some good to take a look at it," she said.

"Yes, perhaps," he replied. "But first I'm going to go to bed. Aren't you going to head off and make something of your Sunday?"

"Do you know what you once said to me?"

"No, what did I say?"

"That which is kept secret is distorted. Like a plant bending under a cover."

"Did I express myself that poetically?"

"You said that the darkness not only conceals, it also transforms. Corrupts."

"So the moral is . . ."

"That you should find out what Magnus is hiding from you," she said. "You can't just lie there being introspective."

No, that wasn't a good thing, he thought to himself. *Horror vacui.* Nothing is worse than the void within us. On the other hand, it was no different looking out at the world. The same darkness was everywhere. But he really ought to pull himself together for Julia's sake. First he needed to . . . He went into the bathroom and rifled through his medicine cabinet, wondering what to take. What a miserable life I've ended up with, he thought. What a hopeless father she's got.

He was once again reminded of the train rushing towards him in the tunnel and the clattering footsteps approaching at the same time. Two forces tugging at him, and fighting over him – like God and the Devil. Nonsense, he thought. Melodramatic drivel. He shut the cabinet, indecisive, anxious.

But the thought didn't disappear, and he pictured Micaela's eyes, looking at him as if he had disappointed her. He thought about all the suppressed power in her body. Aloud, he said:

"I don't give a damn."

"What?" Julia called out.

"Nothing," he said.

Then he went to his desk in his study and the blasted Rodin statue of the girl curtseying that he had once bought because he thought she resembled him as a boy, but which now gave the impression that the girl spent all day dancing for him. He really ought to declutter in here and put her in the attic. Leave her to curtsey in peace and dream of a better life.

Didn't he have the Kabir files somewhere? He'd found the CD from the football match that morning, but the rest . . . he didn't quite remember what was on the computer and what had come as print-outs.

He searched for the investigation among his confidential files and pulled up some of it. Why not take a look? In the past, nothing had healed him like the challenge of an unresolved crime. He would approach each one with a dark sense that he would uncover something new about himself if only he found the answer. But now, with all that red screeching in his head, with all his incapacity, no, it was a torment. Like playing the piano with broken fingers.

Nevertheless, he skipped absent-mindedly between witness statements, autopsy photos, the crime scene report, all without finding any focus whatsoever. All he saw was his own darkness.

When he looked at Kabir lying in the woods in Grimsta, the crown of his head crushed and his arms crossed over his chest, he thought he saw himself in an alternative reality in which he'd been permitted to take that step onto the Tunnelbana tracks.

He enlarged the pictures on the computer and that helped him to see through the mist of associations and memories that had laid themselves over the photographs, and then he was drawn into it again, as if Kabir's dead body was slowly bringing him back to life.

What happened to you, poor devil? he thought. And what did you do to deserve such an ending?

Jonas Beijer drank his tea, maintaining an amused smile. The bin lorry outside was now very close by and Micaela put her hand to her brow. The headache was like a membrane between her and the world. She really ought to go home.

"We tried to reach him ourselves," Jonas said. "Even Fransson was in on the idea. But we never got hold of him. He didn't return our calls or emails, and that was why I asked Falkegren. I thought he might have a channel to him that we didn't. But when I started talking about the professor, he was evasive and changed the subject. I weaselled it out of him at last. I demanded that he speak plainly, and it came out."

"What came out?"

"He'd been contacted by the American embassy."

Micaela looked at him searchingly, and squinted to suppress the headache.

"Why?"

"He knew some bigwig there who warned him against engaging Rekke in any matter tied to American interests in Iraq and Afghanistan, since the professor reportedly had his own agenda on those issues."

"What's that supposed to mean?" she said.

"I took it to mean that the Americans were afraid of Rekke, and I said as much. But then it was Falkegren who took it badly. He said it was nothing more than good advice and what was more, he said, Rekke was psychologically unstable. He'd been working on an investigation in San Francisco and was kicked out for coming up with crazy conclusions."

"What crazy conclusions?"

"Apparently he saw himself in the assailant and mixed up his own experiences with those of others. But I can't say I believed it. Falkegren mostly seemed to be throwing that around to boost his case, and now . . . well, Jesus."

"What?" she said, putting a hand to her cheek.

"Now you have to wonder whether the one thing is tied to the other."

"You do," she said.

Jonas looked down at the table. Then he looked up at her with the same troubled expression as before.

"I'll have to look into it," he said. "I'll make sure Falkegren finds out that Rekke's alive and kicking. But my God, Micaela . . . you look like you're about to faint."

She squinted again and tried to concentrate on the thousand and one questions that were cropping up in her head.

"What about the old man who walked by?" she said.

"We arrested the wrong guy, you know that. He was the same age, and the witnesses were pretty certain. But he had a clear-as-day alibi. No connection whatsoever. But look . . . I really do mean it. If you don't want to go to hospital I can run you home."

She was tempted by the offer.

"I'll manage," she said.

"I'm not so sure," he said. "You didn't answer my question. Is it Hans Rekke that you spoke to?"

"No, we don't exactly move in the same circles."

Then she hugged Jonas for slightly too long and vanished up Swedenborgsgatan without staggering or stumbling. But within minutes her strength deserted her and she could barely make it down into the Tunnelbana station.

What was he playing at? Perhaps it was just a way of self-medicating. A substitute for the morphine and the benzodiazepines. But he was pretending to be Jamal Kabir. He even imagined he was dead like Kabir, lying in the woods in Grimsta with his head crushed and flies buzzing around the wound. He got up.

Or rather, he imagined Kabir getting up, the blood and dirt vanishing from his head and throat, going backwards in time and space and coming to life again, through the woods, out onto Gulddragargränd, into the football stadium. Eventually, he was standing there just in front of Costa, watching the whole ruckus with a collected expression, until he caught sight of something – an old man in a green jacket, as Micaela had described – who made him grimace almost imperceptibly.

Afterwards, he left the pitch and headed once again back towards his death. The rain had paused, they knew that, it was just drizzling. It was about to start lashing down, and he guessed that Kabir had been agitated and probably afraid, too. Is someone following me? He must have thought that. According to witnesses, he pulled out his mobile. Was he thinking about contacting someone to ask for help?

Instead, he cut off into the woods and there he must have kept listening for footsteps. He was shaken. His attention must have been heightened. He could hardly have missed a person approaching. He must have turned around and seen his attacker, and either been reassured or told him to get lost, vamoose, then carried on, proud and defiant. It could have been like that, and then came the first blow to the back of the head with a sharp little rock that might have been no bigger than something that could be concealed in the hand.

The assault continued – if not frenziedly then methodically and unendingly. Someone struck and struck long after Kabir was dead, and it was hardly the ideal way to kill. It would have been easier to use a proper weapon, a knife for instance. What did it mean that the murderer had used a stone? Was that the first or best thing to hand? Or was there intent behind it?

In any event, the murderer could hardly have been familiar with the territory. There was no way to know that the crime would occur precisely there, and the assailant would have been bloodied and messy afterwards. He must have sought out a stream, a puddle to wash his hands in, and changed into something he had brought in a bag, probably a rucksack – because otherwise surely he would have been noticed by passers-by? Unless there was a car waiting for him down on Gulddragargränd.

Rekke visualised a whole series of scenarios and became absorbed by them – alternative realities that divided into even more worlds. But he quickly realised he was daydreaming rather than analysing, and that was a sign that he lacked information.

He looked once again at the pictures of the body in the woods. Then he enlarged the adjacent terrain, bit by bit, not to clear his gaze of the detritus floating around in his head but to truly scrutinise the ground. The doorbell rang. He didn't pay it any heed. He saw something yellow in the dirt and disorder beside Kabir's neck – a flower, he guessed. Nothing disturbing, not at all, but he must have missed it the first time.

It was barely visible. It was concealed by blood and soil. Yet somehow it shone like a small flame, a glimmer of beauty amid all the horror, and perhaps – although it was almost impossible to see – it was slightly too flat and lifeless to belong to the vegetation. Might it have been pressed? Could someone have put it there? He didn't think so – not really.

But still his attention remained glued to it. Was it some kind of iris? Perhaps. The flower was yellow and violet, and the leaves were sword-like. He went online and looked up irises and was on the verge of packing it in – there were far too many species – when he caught sight of an image of *Iris darwasica*. Could that be it? No, not quite, barely at all, actually. What on earth was he doing? It was presumably some kind of conceited desire for significant details. Give up, he thought. Go to bed. Outside, Mrs Hansson was talking to Julia.

"I didn't want to worry him," she said.

That made him smile, perhaps because he couldn't think of what would worry him. For want of anything else, he continued staring at the irises. The flowers seemed to be sneering at him in their colour and splendour. As if they existed merely to remind him how difficult his own life was. There was a knock on the door. He ignored it. He caught sight of another species that seemed a better match. *Iris afghanica* was its name. That didn't sound like something that grew in the Grimsta woods. *Afghanica* . . . He hastily read on. It was an alpine species, apparently, discovered and first catalogued in 1964 on a mountainside north of Kabul. Another knock, and he made a note.

"Come in," he said.

The door opened and Mrs Hansson looked at him with an unconcerned expression in spite of everything. It was unlikely that anything remarkable had happened, he thought.

"What are you doing?" she said.

"I'm working, I suppose you might say," he said.

"But that's fantastic, isn't it? Julia says you've been in here for hours."

"I hardly think it's been that long."

"Are you back up and running?"

"In a way. Perhaps."

"That makes me so happy, Hans."

"It's gratifying to be able to surprise you with so little. But you were worried about something."

"No, and I'm sure it's nothing to do with you."

"But?"

"That diplomatic car with its horrible tinted windows is outside again."

"Oh, really?" he said. "I thought it had abandoned me."

"Don't joke. I've never liked it, you know that. There are people in it just waiting and watching," she said, and he thought about the time they had rushed up to him in the street at Stanford and pulled him into their car.

It had been so dramatic he'd almost laughed. But somehow, it had taken hold of his body. He felt it now when Mrs Hansson was talking about that confounded diplomatic car that could hardly have any purpose other than to annoy him and increase his claustrophobia. He wasn't worth watching. All he did was sit here staring into himself. Though was that true? He'd spoken to Magnus and run searches on the computer. Perhaps that was connected to the car?

"I ought to get encryption," he muttered.

"What did you say?"

"Nothing. But what would I do without you, Sigrid? You see and hear everything."

"I'm worried about you, Hans."

"There's no need for that. Not in the slightest, goodness me. I'm better now, as you can tell," he said, standing up, determined to deal with the matter at once.

Perhaps he could go downstairs and speak to them. It was not impossible that it was Charles Bruckner himself who wished to remind him of his existence. But instead he went to the bathroom, opened the medicine cabinet and heard the siren song emerging from the tunnel and the train.

EIGHTEEN

When Micaela eventually got home, she staggered into the bedroom and collapsed into bed still in her clothes. She was convinced she would fall asleep immediately. But her heart was pounding too fast, and she sat up panting. I have to calm down, she thought. I need to slow my breathing. But it was impossible. It struck her that it might not have been such a good idea to talk to Jonas.

Perhaps she had put Rekke at risk. But no, she had to prioritise the murder inquiry, even if the murder inquiry wasn't exactly prioritising her. She got up from the bed. The room swayed and she staggered into the kitchen and touched her breast pocket. There was something inside it: a napkin on which she'd written two words, and it took a second before she realised what they were. It was the name Jonas had mentioned: Emma Gulwal, the woman whose clarinet Kabir had smashed to pieces in Kabul.

She opened the fridge and drank feverishly from a bottle of juice. That was strange, wasn't it? Why did a football referee spend his free time smashing up instruments? Why would a man who fought for the right to play football in an Islamic country engage with the prevention of vice? She went into the living room and sat down at her desk – an IKEA leaf bolted to the wall. There had to be something in that, she thought to herself. Someone who demolished musical instruments – regardless of the consequences, as Jonas had put it – had to be capable of other things too.

She switched on her computer, and as ever it took an eternity before it was up and running. It just seemed to sit there spluttering away. But once she'd finally got it going, she went to Google, searched for the name Emma Gulwal and found herself looking at a woman with round glasses and a pageboy haircut. Gulwal looked a little stern, or at any rate single-minded, with those distinctive eyebrows and narrow, squinting eyes. Further down the page was a picture of her in front of an orchestra on a large stage. It looked professional. But Gulwal seemed to have quit as a musician and was now a nurse in Berlin. Should she contact her? Of course she shouldn't. She felt like shit. She should take a shower and go back to bed. But she didn't get far before Jonas Beijer called.

"I just wanted to check that you got home alright," he said.

"I'm checking out that Emma Gulwal you mentioned."

"Give it a rest," he said. "You need to lie down in a darkened room. Have you got some painkillers?"

"I don't take painkillers. But I am wondering why Kabir was so hostile towards music."

There was a pause, then Jonas said:

"A lot of people over there were. It was a legacy from Wahhabism in Saudi Arabia – but I guess you know that? The Saudis banned music in 1978. Khomeini did the same in Iran in 1979. It was regarded as the Devil's temptation."

"But Kabir doesn't seem to have been an extremist otherwise."

"He definitely seems to have been an opportunist. He did whatever it took to keep going with his football. Perhaps he wanted to show his pal Mullah Zakaria that he was a true believer."

She thought about Jonas's suggestion of lying in a darkened room. It was a pretty good one.

"Isn't it also strange," she said, "that he was friends with the Mullah of all people? It doesn't tally with the image of him as the friendly football guy."

"No, not really."

"And smashing up instruments," she said. "That sounds like more than just opportunism."

"Perhaps there was a class dimension – straightforward class hatred?"

"In what way?"

"The musicians he attacked were all from the old, upper echelons of Kabul society with ties to the West."

Micaela headed for bed.

"Didn't you say that musicians were murdered as well?"

"Or they vanished."

She lay down on her back.

"There's nothing particular you've been looking at?" she said.

"Not really. Although that spring – April 1997 – there was a case we took an interest in. A female violinist was shot in the back of the head in the middle of the night while playing in her basement. The woman was a good friend of Emma Gulwal's. They'd studied together at the Soviet college in Kabul in the eighties. But there's nothing to suggest that Kabir was involved in the murder."

She closed her eyes.

"How can you be sure?"

"I don't think we're sure of anything much," he said. "But it seems clear that the woman knew her killer. By all accounts, she let him in of her own volition and showed him her violin, which was hidden in the basement. And it wasn't a murder ordered by the Taliban. It adhered to their style of persecution, but it wasn't on the agenda. We've got no evidence that the woman and Kabir ever met – quite the contrary, in fact. She was an upper-class prima donna. He was a motorbike mechanic from a small village outside Kandahar."

"I see," Micaela said, pulling the duvet over her body. "What do you actually have then?"

"We've got some loose threads, and lately Costa – of all people – has resurfaced to tell us he thinks he saw a mysterious man at Grimsta. But his testimony is so weak and cloudy that we don't have much to go on."

"Sounds like you've done a pretty lousy job."

Jonas sighed down the line.

"It's been tough going."

"There may be an explanation for that."

He was silent for a moment.

"Do you think the Americans have been lying to our faces?"

"It's possible."

"That would just devastate Falkegren, if he really . . ."

He didn't seem able to find the words and she was about to say that they had to find out why Kabir had ended up in the Prison of Darkness. Then she thought to herself that it might be better raised with Rekke.

"I felt kind of the same way," she said.

"I'll look into it first thing tomorrow."

Once again she thought she should have kept her trap shut, at least for the time being.

"OK," she said. "I'm going to sleep now."

"Sounds sensible to me. Take care."

She pulled the duvet over her head and tried to think clearly. She didn't have much success. She lay curled in the foetal position as a lightning sequence of snapshots flashed through her thoughts. Then she must have fallen asleep. She only vaguely heard the phone ringing. In her dreams, the ringing became screeching alarm clocks that kept going for hours. She woke with a start and only then did she realise what had woken her. Was it the phone again or noise in the square outside? No, there was hammering on the door.

Someone wanted to come in.

It was half past eight on Monday morning and Rekke was fully dressed. That surprised him. He was sitting at the kitchen table without knowing how he had got there. The walk from his bed was a blank, and not the only one, either. Admittedly, he had a few chaotic memories from the night. But they were memories he would have preferred to forget.

These included him lying on the bathroom floor and trying to throw up. Otherwise, the last twelve hours were nothing but a fog, and it wasn't much better now that he was sitting slumped with his head in his hands trying to grasp what had happened. Just recently he had been up playing the piano and going through an old murder investigation. But that had been nothing more than a brief detour – one that was barely real – and he was back at square one: full of hopelessness and paralysis, which was to be expected. Why should he suddenly be restored to normality?

He straightened his back as best he could and looked down at his hands stretched out before him on the table. The hands looked alien and spider-like. It surprised him that they obeyed when he tapped out the first bars from Beethoven's *Appassionata* on the tabletop. There was a smell of coffee beans. Behind him he could hear the hall clock ticking and footsteps drawing nearer. He raised his gaze, squinting. Mrs Hansson was standing in front of him.

"Good grief, Hans. You shouldn't be up."

"No, perhaps not. But here I am," he said breezily.

"Do you have any memory of what happened yesterday?"

"Oh yes, I naturally remember your great kindness, and that I was not altogether capable of acknowledging it. I apologise for that. Thank you, dearest Sigrid . . ."

"You were in a dreadful state," she said. "You went to sleep in your clothes."

"That explains matters. I was wondering what sort of absurd morning attire this was." He smiled as best he could.

"Don't joke like that. I've been desperately worried."

"No, of course not. I shan't joke. I don't feel like much of a joker. So I shall obey your advice. I retreat. I capitulate to the circumstances," he said in the same artificial, drawling voice, before staggering into the bathroom and downing another handful of pills.

Then he tottered to the bed and collapsed just like Kabir in the grove of trees with his arms folded over his chest; he felt a heavy, anxious darkness draw across him like a wave from the sea.

"*De profundis clamavi ad te, Domine,*" he mumbled, not entirely joking.

"That's the most insane thing I ever heard," said Vanessa. "What did you do then?"

"I went home with him."

"And he was as rich as anything."

"It was a massive flat at any rate, and books everywhere."

"Weren't you kinda into him before?"

"I just, like, thought he had it all."

It was ten past eight in the morning. But the day was already upside down. She had fallen asleep again in the afternoon and woken up at four in the morning. Vanessa had been lying next to her in bed, and at first that had been incomprehensible. Then she remembered that Vanessa had knocked on the door and that she had eventually dragged herself out of bed and let her in and encountered a storm of accusations. Vanessa had called "about seven hundred times" and been "as worried as my fucking mother". Apparently the outcome had been Vanessa sleeping over.

"What did you do then? I will lose my mind if you slept together."

"Enough already," she said. "He'd tried to kill himself. It wasn't exactly sexy time."

"So what did you do?"

She regretted even mentioning it. It felt wrong.

They were sitting in the kitchen opposite one another. Outside, the sun was shining, or perhaps it was the kitchen light reflected against the window. She wasn't quite sure. The headache was still a membrane between her and the world, and if she wanted anything at all – other than to go back to bed – it was to better understand what Kabir had done for the Taliban. But she hadn't learned anything from the random searches she'd done that morning, apart from discovering that Emma Gulwal, whose clarinet he had smashed to pieces, had studied at something known as the Soviet–Afghan Friendship University for Classical Music.

"I still think we should go to casualty," Vanessa said.

"I've got to work."

"You definitely shouldn't be working. What is it you keep looking at?"

Micaela glanced up from the computer.

"I'm working on that football referee."

Vanessa started.

"Is it because of him? Rekke?"

Micaela fidgeted.

"I've found out a few things, is all," she said.

"Like what?"

"I think the murder of the ref may have been revenge for some shit he did in Afghanistan."

"I thought he was a good guy."

"I thought so too. But what do we know?"

"Yes, what do we know?" Vanessa said, laughing for some reason, but when Micaela didn't laugh as well she reiterated that they ought to go to hospital.

Micaela wasn't really listening. She continued to wonder why Kabir had attacked musicians. She couldn't make it add up – but then she didn't understand the Taliban at all. She shut down the computer, stood up and stumbled. The sun's rays made her feel sick.

"Shit," Vanessa said, standing up to help.

"It's OK."

"You're totally not OK."

"Meh," Micaela said, shaking herself free from Vanessa's arms and heading for the bathroom.

It's not that bloody bad, she thought to herself. Her eyes were bloodshot and her cheek looked insane. But she was going to fix that. She covered the bruise with concealer and went back out. Vanessa had settled down in the living room and switched on the TV. Some bearded expert was on the TV4 breakfast show saying that more than a year had passed without any chemical weapons being uncovered in Iraq. "The whole situation is deeply worrying," the expert explained. "The whole region has been destabilised. It's as if they have opened Pandora's box."

"That war is so nuts," said Micaela. "They were supposed to fight terror, but in practice they've created three times the number of terrorists."

"What?" Vanessa said.

"Haven't they learned anything from their old mistakes?"

"You back to talking about Pinochet and the CIA again?"

"I mean in general."

"You need to chill out. I'm banning you from going to work."

"I need to check something."

Vanessa let out a deep sigh.

"You're crazy."

"Don't you have customers?"

"Elena can deal with them."

Elena was the woman Vanessa shared her hairdressing salon with.

"I saw Lucas yesterday too," Micaela said.

Vanessa looked up, interested – she and Lucas had always been close.

"What did he say?"

"He said the ref was scared of something."

"Fuck me, you keep banging on about that guy."

"They've made such a fucking hash of the investigation."

"But surely there's no rush? Let's rent a video instead."

"I'm too restless."

"You should speak to Beppe."

"Why should I speak to him?"

"Because Mario said that he's begun to remember new things about the murder."

"I heard that."

"You've got too much slap on your cheek."

"Yes, yes," she said, grabbing a spare set of keys from the bureau in the hallway and chucking them onto the coffee table in front of Vanessa.

She set off for work, but before she had even reached the Tunnelbana she was contemplating going back. How many days off sick had she had in her life? None that she could remember, and she'd have liked to watch a film, or just sleep for a day and get rid of that headache. But she carried on, as if she had some inescapable duty to fulfil.

NINETEEN

Jonas didn't say a word to Chief Inspector Fransson, who was his immediate superior. He made an appointment with Assistant Commissioner Martin Falkegren instead, without saying what it was about. Falkegren's secretary had replied: "No chance, he doesn't have time." But in the end she had given him fifteen minutes at ten o'clock.

Now it was five to ten and Jonas was still sitting at his desk in the open-plan office. He saw Micaela pass by. She didn't seem to be feeling much better today, and he was struck by the impulse to bound up and hug her. But another part of him was angry.

Her entire black-and-blue determined existence reminded him of their failure in the investigation. He stood up and got grumpily into the lift, then pressed the button for the ninth floor. I'm going to give that smarmy git a talking to, he thought to himself. I'll show him. But when he arrived, his courage faltered and he was no longer sure that he believed Micaela.

Had the Americans put Kabir in chains and more or less left him to freeze to death? And had the Ministry for Foreign Affairs really covered it up, sabotaged a Swedish murder inquiry and to cap it off let in a probable terrorist? The absurdity of it all gave him pause. He stopped outside Falkegren's door and knocked more discreetly than he had intended.

The door flew open and the assistant commissioner received him with a moment's uncertainty. Then a big smile beamed across his face.

"Jonas," he said. "What a pleasure. I've heard a lot of good things about you lately."

"I don't know about that," he said, embarrassed. "I mostly feel inadequate."

"Isn't that what characterises a good police officer? Constant self-doubt."

In that case I must be incredible, Jonas thought – but he said nothing. He merely sat down and looked at Falkegren and wondered whether the assistant commissioner hadn't understood what the purpose of his visit was. Perhaps the flattery was just a tactic, an attempt to disarm him? But no, he couldn't reasonably know. He was wearing jeans and a freshly ironed blue shirt and he proffered a bowl of Finnish liquorice.

Jonas shook his head.

"What can I do for you?" Falkegren said.

"I've been looking over the Kabir case all morning."

"Haven't you put that one behind you? Don't we have enough issues on our home turf?"

Jonas took a small fistful of liquorice after all.

"It happened on home soil," he said.

"You know what I mean."

"Not really," he said. "But I heard some quite sensational stuff yesterday."

Martin Falkegren looked at him sharply.

"And what was that?"

Jonas finished chewing on the liquorice. He thought Falkegren seemed a little nervous now.

"That Kabir had supposedly been in American captivity in Kabul and gravely tortured. I heard that you'd been told the same thing, but much earlier – last summer."

Martin Falkegren made a movement with his mouth that was hard to interpret. He opened a desk drawer and closed it again.

"Yes, that's correct," he said a little officiously.

"And?"

Martin Falkegren straightened his back in a blatant attempt to appear as self-assured and complacent as before.

"Naturally I took it very seriously. But I was able to rule it out pretty quickly. I've got good sources in that area."

"You have a contact at the American embassy?" Jonas said.

"Exactly, someone with a complete overview, and we were able to dismiss the information as left-wing propaganda. The USA is quite rightly hard on its terrorist suspects, but they don't torture people like that."

"It would have been better had we been able to check the details ourselves."

Falkegren shook his head and made a nervous gesture with his tongue.

"Why would I burden you with false information? Surely you had plenty of other things to be getting on with?"

Jonas tried to summon some authority.

"Yes, of course, but if it isn't false then it's extremely serious, isn't it? That turns our entire investigation on its head."

"But it so happens that it *is* false," Falkegren said.

"Perhaps, but yesterday I heard – admittedly second-hand – that the information had been confirmed by the Ministry for Foreign Affairs."

Martin Falkegren flinched.

"I shouldn't think so," he said, clearly troubled.

"I'm sure you acted in good faith," Jonas said, more defensively than he would have liked.

"I most certainly did. The information bears no relation to reality."

"I'd still like to know how much you knew, and what it was you heard. Was it Hans Rekke who contacted you?"

Falkegren assumed an injured expression.

"That man isn't credible," he said.

"You've said that."

"But it's become even clearer now. Did you know that he was deemed a security risk and deported from the USA?"

"Really?" Jonas said, uncertain again. "I'd have to verify that with Foreign Affairs."

"No, no. Better that I do that. I know the undersecretary."

"You mean Rekke's brother?"

"Yes, exactly. It's a rather delicate situation."

Jonas nodded without telling him that he had already submitted his query to Kleeberger's secretary.

"Excellent, then we're in agreement," Falkegren said.

"I'm not so sure. There's one more thing. I think we should bring Vargas back onto the investigation."

"What . . . Why?"

Falkegren barely seemed aware of what he had said. He appeared to be lost in anxious thought, and Jonas resolved to raise it with Fransson instead.

Micaela was sitting at her desk wondering whether she ought to get to work for appearances' sake. But she had difficulty focusing. In the distance, she saw Jonas Beijer emerging from the lifts. He looked frustrated.

She got up and started towards the stairs. Then her phone rang.

"Hello, is that Micaela?" said a voice at the other end.

"Yes," she said.

"This is Sigrid Hansson. I'm worried about Hans."

"What's happened?" Micaela said, turning around to check whether anyone was listening.

"He's popped a lot of pills. I don't think he's in acute danger. But he's out cold and I'm here keeping an eye on him."

"Bloody hell," she said, beginning to head down the stairs.

"It was amazing how you inspired him. He was up and working yesterday. You got him going again."

Micaela remembered Rekke lying in bed with that faint glow in his eyes.

"Unless it was proximity to death that brought him back to life."

"What do you mean?"

"Those were his own words," she said.

"Well, I don't believe it. You've met before, haven't you? Worked on one of his cases. I could tell at once that you were good for him."

"I don't know about that."

"Oh no, I can feel that kind of thing. When he's depressed, he can't stand anyone. But you ignited a spark in him."

"Didn't you say he'd got worse again?"

"Yes, I'm afraid so. But it's partly my fault. I told him about that awful diplomatic car out in the street. You see, I think he's being watched again."

"Watched?" Micaela said, perturbed.

"Yes, really, and I'm not crazy or paranoid. That car has been here before. Just after he moved in, it would turn up at all hours, and it was clear that it reminded him of something dreadful that happened in America."

"What would that be?"

"I suspect he's in possession of secrets they're worried about. I think they want to show that they're watching him. That's why I can't help asking . . . I gather you live alone."

Micaela started.

"How did you gather that?"

"I asked Hans. Don't be upset. It wasn't my intention to poke around in your business. But I thought you might visit him again and maybe even . . ."

"What?"

Phone to her ear, Micaela exited the police station and wondered whether to head into town.

"Nothing," Mrs Hansson said. "But you have to understand, it's been heart-rending to see him over the last few months. He's barely moved from his bed. But then, all of a sudden, like I said, when you were here yesterday, he became a little more active. It was wonderful to see."

"I'm glad," she said.

"And that's why I was going to say –" she hesitated briefly – ". . . that you're most welcome to consider his apartment as a second home. Please visit whenever you like – right away preferably, if I'm honest."

Micaela came to a halt, gripped by a feeling she didn't entirely understand. It was part irritation – *Don't you tell me what to do* – but also astonishment. She had sought him out so desperately and been convinced that he didn't have time for people like her. Now she was being asked to visit him as often as she could.

"I'll look in later today," she said. "There's something I wanted to discuss with him."

"That would be wonderful. I'm sure I'll manage for the time being." Mrs Hansson sounded disappointed, as if she had been hoping for more.

"How do you and Hans Rekke know each other?" Micaela said, mostly to change the subject.

"I've been helping the family for half a century now. I've seen the boys grow up and I've remained close to Hans – especially since he collapsed at the concert in Helsinki."

"What happened?"

"It was all going to pot. He broke down after the performance . . . and was standing on a balcony. On the balustrade, in fact. He didn't give any more concerts after that."

"No?" Micaela said, not knowing what to say.

"But sometimes I wonder whether things are actually worse now. It's all happened so quickly. He had to leave the USA. He got divorced."

"Why did he get divorced?"

"I think it was Lovisa who couldn't cope. She's –" Mrs Hansson hesitated – ". . . not at all like Hans. On the surface, she's perfect, and she's wealthy too, pretty as a picture, from a fine family with a long lineage, well educated, and cultivated, interested in music. But . . ."

"Yes?" said Micaela.

"If I may say so, she's a little too fixated on the exterior, the beautiful facade, while Hans – as I'm sure you've noticed – lives in his own world. He seeks out stimuli for his anxious thoughts, and that drove Lovisa crazy. I think Hans made her into a perfectionist. As if she wanted to compensate for him."

"Really?"

"Goodness gracious yes, you should see their house out in Djursholm. You can imagine how it went when Lovisa invited her socialite friends around. Hans was so bored he would pace back and forth, or, worse, come out with observations no-one had asked for."

"I can imagine," Micaela said.

"And Lovisa herself – my goodness I'm being indiscreet . . . She started seeing other men, and I don't suppose I blame her. Hans isn't an easy person. But when she and Magnus ganged up, that was crossing a line . . ."

"You mean Lovisa and Hans's brother . . . ?"

"No, no, I don't mean that, not really, I'm just talking. What I was going to say was that all of a sudden Hans needed a place to live, and he wasn't exactly in the right state of mind to look for one himself. So I tipped him off about the attic apartment one floor up from me that hadn't sold because it's so . . . how should I put it . . . meandering. Hans bought it sight unseen."

"That's strange," Micaela said.

"Not at all – he's like that, and as you can tell, I'm very pleased to have him close by. To begin with he was in a fairly good state. Then it was as if a demon possessed him. I could feel it from a distance. As if he were secreting poison. He'd spend all day in bed in a state of semi-paralysis and I called everyone I could think of, his friends, his family, his doctor – his good doctor, that is. He's got a bad doctor too. Apologies for my frankness. Where was I? Yes, Hans got worse and now . . . now that awful car is here again . . . I'm beginning to worry, and not just that he might do himself harm."

"Also that someone else might do it, right?"

"I don't know. I really don't know. I'm probably getting worked up over nothing. At any rate, it wouldn't do any harm to have a police officer in the house."

"I'll come by as soon as I can," Micaela said.

She ended the call and went down into the Tunnelbana. She continued onto the platform under the vaulted, red-painted ceiling. The sign said the train was due in six minutes, so she took the opportunity to call the SVT switchboard.

She asked to speak to Tove Lehmann the reporter, just as Lucas had suggested.

Tove Lehmann explained rather reluctantly that she could meet her in an hour's time in the canteen at the television centre.

Sigrid Hansson shook her head and wondered what had possessed her. She didn't even know the girl. Yet here she was, already dreaming that Micaela would move in and help get Hans back on his feet. That was strange, surely? But something about Micaela reassured her, as if things would work out in her presence. She helped herself to a small piece of Swiss chocolate from the larder, opened the fridge and poured herself a glass of sparkling water.

She went back into the bedroom and noticed immediately from his pallor that Hans had deteriorated. Just as before, he was lying on his stomach, fully dressed, his arms under his chest. But his breathing was more laboured now, and his forehead and cheeks were an ashen grey. She swore aloud and rushed forward.

"Hans, wake up," she said, shaking him.

She got no response, not even a grunt, no movement, nothing. He was just lying there, comatose, his mouth open and eyes closed, so she slapped him. That didn't help. What she wanted to do was shout and scream, and call Dr Richter right away, but first – she knew this – she had to be resourceful and act quickly. It was an emergency.

"Hans," she said loudly. "You have to drink something. You look parched."

But when she tried to get him to drink a little Ramlösa, the water ran down his lips and chin, and in the end she splashed the remains of her glass over his face – out of desperation and anger. How could he be such an idiot?

That didn't help either, so she picked up her phone to call Dr Richter, although something made her hesitate. She didn't know what at first. Then she realised – she could hear footsteps in the stairwell. The lock rattled.

Someone was coming in with their own set of keys. It had to be Julia. No, the steps were heavier, male. Now they came to a halt, and she ought to have called out and asked who it was, but she was frightened.

There was something not right about those footsteps. Surely no-one stopped like that, deadly silent, after entering someone's apartment? Something was wrong. She was certain of it and she listened for a noise from the rest of the flat. All she could make out clearly at that moment was the ticking of the gilded pendulum on the wall-mounted clock, and that only reinforced her sense of unease, and then she realised: she had to do something. The footsteps sounded again, focused, decisive, and she called out:

"Hello? Who's there?"

She got no answer. God help her. The steps continued and she shook Hans's shoulders, still seeing no sign of life in him.

"Wake up," she said. "Wake up, there's someone here."

TWENTY

"I liked Kabir," she said. "I still like him."

"What do you mean, still?"

"He was a hero before, right? But now he's a bit suspect, isn't he? That's what you all think?"

Tove Lehmann was probably one hundred and eighty-five centimetres tall. She looked like the swimmer she had once been, broad-shouldered with long legs, but what stood out at that moment was the injured expression on her face. She had come down to the canteen with an aura about her, greeting people as if it she was bestowing her grace upon them. Tove had risen to presenter and expert commentator for elite swimming competitions, and it had moulded her body language and given her a film-star smile. But when she sat down beside Micaela, she transformed in a second. Her eyes flashed with irritation.

"Thanks for agreeing to meet me," Micaela said.

"I thought you'd dropped the case."

"Murders don't get dropped so easily."

"I meant dropped me. Not that I've been counting, but I think I've apologised around ten times."

Micaela decided to lay her cards on the table.

"I'm not involved in the investigation any longer."

Tove looked at her in surprise.

"Then what are you doing here?"

"I've received new information. I want to check a few things."

"I've said everything I have to say."

"But not to me. What was it you apologised for?"

"Nothing."

"Come on. Didn't you just say you liked him?"

"What's that got to do with it?"

"Isn't it a good thing if we do what we can to catch his killer?"

Tove hesitated and appeared to gather her thoughts.

"I didn't tell you everything, OK? And that was stupid. Sorry," she said just as acidly.

"What did you leave out?"

"That he called me the day after the TV report aired."

"Why did he do that?"

"He said he was worried. He hadn't realised it would be such a big deal, and I felt a little sorry for him and I was off that day. So I asked him whether we could grab a coffee or a drink. Then we met at Löwenbräu – my local on Fridhemsplan."

"How was he then?"

Tove Lehmann stared across the canteen and appeared not to know whether she should say anything or not. She looked tormented. Her eyes flickered. This was quite clearly a memory she was reluctant to return to.

"He was wearing sunglasses and a hat, as if he wanted to hide, and he was definitely nervous."

"In what way?"

"Well, not in a suspicious way or anything. More in a cute way, as if he were shy."

"Did he speak good English?"

"Yes, actually. I'd noticed that during filming. But we'd already booked an interpreter, and he was dead set on doing his bit in Pashto."

"What did he say?"

"That he was an idiot for talking so much in the report. That he didn't know what had got into him. But it was because of me, he said. I was amazing. I looked like an Amazon queen and so on, and for a while I thought he was hitting on me – in his slightly clumsy, shy way. But then I realised that he was actually after something else entirely."

"What?"

"He didn't want the report to be re-aired or distributed to other countries."

"Why not?"

"I should think you have a better idea than I do. He was worried about something."

"Did you get a sense of what?"

"I guess the Taliban? They'd just tortured him and stuff."

"Or maybe he was one of them?"

Tove looked at her sceptically.

"Oh come on," she said.

"Why is that so unlikely?"

Tove thought for a moment.

"He didn't act like a fanatic. For example, he was a pretty enthusiastic drinker."

So you got pissed together, Micaela thought, and you kept that secret from us. But she hid her anger. She didn't want to put Tove on the defensive again, so she smiled in amusement as if it were no more than an entertaining snippet.

"What did he drink?"

"Beer to start with, and then he wanted vodka. It didn't feel like the first time he'd ordered it either."

"What did you talk about?"

Tove Lehmann became absorbed in her thoughts and weighed her words carefully.

"All sorts. How he was finding Sweden and so on. Then we talked football, of course – favourite players and all that, and he told me about buying his referee's uniform at a market in Kabul. The uniform was from the fifties or something. He loved it because it was so retro. He was really . . . quite something, and he knew things that made me do a double take."

"Like what?"

"He'd read Dostoevsky and stuff, or at least he claimed he had. But then he got a bit hazy and began talking about awful things he'd seen in Afghanistan. There was the president who was strung up by the Taliban from a set of traffic lights and had his cock cut off. And there was a woman they shot in the back of the head. He'd been forced to witness the execution."

Micaela was reminded of the murder of the violinist that Jonas had told her about, but she knew that the Taliban had also shot women at public executions and commanded people to come and watch. She'd watched a terrible video clip from Ghazi Stadium in Kabul.

"Why do you think he told you that?"

"I don't know," Tove said. "He was pretty drunk and I don't remember everything he said. But it was as if he'd been standing close by. The woman was so thin, he said. He'd seen her shoulder blades under her blouse."

"Blouse?"

"Well, burka. I don't remember. But I do remember that he looked at me with incredible intensity as he talked about it. As if it was really deep-rooted inside him."

"Why didn't you tell us about this?"

Tove Lehmann stared across the canteen and looked once again like she wanted to flee.

"Because he called again a few days after our meeting and was pissed off."

"Why?"

"Because the report had re-aired on the breakfast bulletins, and AFP had used parts of the interview in a piece on football under the Taliban regime. The story ran in fifteen countries or something."

"So you didn't manage to stop it spreading?"

"Once our reports are broadcast we don't have much control over them."

"Did you say that to him too?"

Tove looked down at her hands.

"Perhaps not straight up."

"So he was disappointed."

"He said they were going to come after him. He shouted that I'd tricked him and all sorts of stupid shit, and I retorted: 'If you're so scared of them, why did you talk to us in the first place?' He hung up. That was the last time I heard from him."

"And then he was murdered."

Tove stared out of the window, her jaw tensed.

"And you were worried you'd lured his enemies here, so you kept quiet about your meeting?" Micaela said.

"What was I supposed to do? Go back in some bloody time machine and put it all right?"

Micaela looked at her with a forgiving expression.

"If it's any consolation, I can tell you that we were the ones who fucked up the investigation, not you," she said.

"Thanks."

"You're welcome."

"Can I ask what you did to your face?" Tove said.

"I fell."

"Looks like you should be at home today."

"You don't mean that," Micaela said. "That woman who was shot in the back of the head. Did Kabir say anything else about her?"

"No," she said. "But now, with hindsight . . . I don't know."

Micaela leaned forward.

"What?" she said.

"I felt like he got excited talking about her. He had *Schadenfreude* in his eyes, as my father would have said."

*

Footsteps were approaching and Sigrid saw the contours of a man in the doorway. She was so afraid that it took her a moment to recognise him.

"Dear God, Magnus, you frightened me," she said, tempted to snap at him that he should have knocked or at least responded to her shouts.

But she didn't. Something in his gaze and his way of leaning forward meant that she couldn't relax. Magnus was wearing a double-breasted suit and a red tie, and his eyes were roving restlessly around as if searching for something. He appeared to have put on weight since she'd last seen him, which reinforced the bulldozer look of his body.

"What the hell's going on?" he said.

"What the hell's going on with *you*?" was what she wanted to say.

"Your brother is in a bad way," she said instead.

"Oh no," Magnus said, running to the bed. He raised Hans's eyelids and gave him a few slaps, which made Hans whimper. He even muttered a couple of confused sentences.

"There's no need to worry about him. He'll soon be on his feet."

"I still think we ought to call Dr Richter," Sigrid said.

"Oh, let him sleep. But what's all this circus?"

"What do you mean?" she said.

"He was being defiant and trying to provoke me, and now he's lying here drugged up," he said.

"He's depressed again – you know that, Magnus."

"Of course, yes. But he usually sticks to one state at a time," he said in a voice she perceived as cold. She was tempted to ask whether he had anything to do with the diplomatic car outside, and perhaps he noticed that.

He patted her on the shoulder and said how fortunate it was that Hans had her.

"You're a rock, Sigrid. Go and make him some coffee and I'll take a look around. I'd like to see how he's getting on."

He left the room with his forward-leaning, aggressive gait, and for a moment she didn't know what to do. But then she followed him and realised that he was looking for something particular.

"I can't wrap my head around this monstrosity of a flat, it's a complete labyrinth," he said.

"What are you looking for?"

"His study."

"It's on the left, but . . ."

She never finished the sentence. Magnus rushed into the room and over to the desk and began rifling through his brother's papers with an impatient, irritated energy, and she could feel it in her gut: it was wrong, he couldn't be permitted to do that.

"I really don't think . . ." she began.

"*Iris afghanica*," Magnus read aloud from a notepad on the table. "Is he engaged in some botanical study?"

"Magnus, please . . ." she said.

"Do you have the password to his computer?"

"I must ask you to leave."

"Oh come, we have no secrets from each other," he said, completely unaffected by her words, switching on the computer.

She wondered whether she ought to kindly but firmly drag him out of there. Just then she heard footsteps shuffling nearer, and the words:

"I would actually say that we have nothing but secrets that we keep from each other. It's only occasionally that we lift the veil of secrecy a little and behave honestly."

"Hans . . ." she said, turning around. "You shouldn't be up," and it was true.

He looked awful, covered in sweat, and groggy, his hair sticky and plastered to one temple. He was struggling to keep upright. He leaned against the door frame, out of breath. But he had at least got up and that had to mean the situation wasn't acute.

"So in other words, Magnus, out," he said.

"Yes, yes, of course. I was just worried when you started going on about Kabir again. Haven't you got enough enemies already?"

"I'm collecting them. Out," Hans hissed, and for a moment it felt as if the brothers wanted to set about each other.

But then Magnus smiled – albeit not warmly – and turned to Sigrid.

"You see, there's no need to worry about him."

He patted Hans kindly on the back and left the room. It could almost have been touching.

Hans offered a wry smile in response, as if for a second he had been amused rather than angry, and she remembered scenes from their childhood when they had squabbled in the same way and made up in an instant . . . But on this occasion their reconciliation was superficial. The unspoken threats lingered in the air.

Magnus scrutinised his brother's movements and appeared to be weighing up how to proceed.

"Naturally you may do whatever you please," he said.

"Generous of you," Hans said.

"But I become concerned when your inquiries spread more or less directly to the Solna police."

Hans looked at his brother in surprise, as if he hadn't understood, or perhaps the blood had just drained from him.

"What do you mean?" he said.

"I just took a call from Assistant Commissioner Falkegren, who sounded very agitated and wondered whether it was true that we had confirmed your conclusions about Kabir's torture-related injuries."

Hans didn't reply. Instead, he returned to the living room. But then he staggered, and Magnus hurried over and led him to the sofa. Hans was panting heavily and closed his eyes when he sank down, as if his outburst had demanded all his strength. Magnus observed him with caution.

"Do you know why the assistant commissioner has suddenly woken up and has the heebie-jeebies?" he said.

"Perhaps because you've concealed the truth."

"It's not that simple – you know that."

"Especially when you're inclined to bow down before the superior force," Hans muttered.

"You don't know the whole story," Magnus snapped. "But we're more than happy to resolve it for you. Kleeberger can see you today at three o'clock."

Hans put a hand to his brow.

"I don't know if I'm up to it."

"Then why don't you forget about the whole thing and book yourself into rehab?"

"Yes, perhaps."

Sigrid noted that Magnus seemed satisfied with the reply, even if he did his best to pretend otherwise.

"It would hardly stimulate you anyway."

"No, perhaps not."

"What on earth sent you back to the case in the first place?" Magnus said casually, and that made Sigrid pay attention, because even if she didn't understand what it was all about, she realised two things in that moment. The first was that the answer to Magnus's question was Micaela – she was the one who had got Hans to return to some form of investigation. The second was that Magnus was hiding something and didn't want Hans rooting around. Normally she'd be certain that Hans had noticed that much sooner than she had, but now she couldn't be sure, and she was worried he was going to say too much.

"I think Hans needs to rest," she said.

"Don't get involved in this, Sigrid. You wouldn't understand."

Magnus turned towards his brother.

"Who is it you've spoken to?"

"I met someone on the Tunnelbana," Hans said, as if he sensed nothing amiss, or was no longer entirely present.

"On the Tunnelbana?"

"Quite. I am always trying new forms of amusement."

He squinted towards the big window and perhaps he smiled, which ought to have been a good sign, she thought.

"And who was that?"

"I must have been under the influence then too," he said languidly. "I don't quite remember."

"Don't talk drivel."

"Not at all, I'm a serious man, as ever. But I am sure you will be pleased to hear that I cannot deal with Kleeberger today. You'll have to keep your power intrigues to yourselves."

"Wise decision," Magnus said, looking far too satisfied, which made Sigrid want to shout at Hans: *Don't give in now, meet Kleeberger, corner them both.*

But it was probably just a primal longing for revenge since Magnus had frightened her so, and in any event she had nothing to do with it. She escorted Magnus out of the apartment.

Micaela left the television centre and thought about Kabir. What kind of person was he really? She still didn't know, and her headache wasn't dissipating either. She regretted not having stayed at home with Vanessa. She shouldn't pretend she was so strong all the time. Frankly it was absurd to think she'd succeed in something that the others on the team had failed at.

They were filming further down Oxenstiernsgatan. She passed them on the opposite side of the street, and continued towards Strandvägen. It was April. But there was no feeling of spring in the air. The sky was dark and she pulled her coat around her body. Over by the Djurgården Bridge she thought she glimpsed Julia. But she was probably mistaken. From a distance, all young women out here resembled Julia, she thought to herself. Pale, beautiful, well dressed. What must it have been like growing up as Rekke's daughter?

Were you afraid of not being up to scratch, of disappointing him?

Or did you take it for granted that the brilliance would be there, as part of the privilege you were born with? Micaela allowed her thoughts to wander back and forth until they stopped at the Prison of Darkness – which sounded like something from an evil fairy tale.

The details about the prison did more than just turn the investigation upside down. They also changed her way of seeing Kabir. Torture had always been particularly charged for her. Her father had been tortured in Chile. It had shaped his personality, and perhaps for this reason she had felt for Kabir at once. She had thought that he – just like Papá – had been tormented for his beliefs. But now . . . now he had brought with him some of the darkness of the prison. Hadn't he?

He had still been tortured. Perhaps even more severely than they had first thought. Nevertheless, two images collided in her consciousness: Kabir the victim and Kabir the credible assailant for something unmentionable that had happened in Kabul. It was best not to speculate, at least not until she had spoken to Rekke. She wasn't far from his apartment now.

Should she go straight up, or call first? Neither felt quite right. She was eager to tell him what Jonas Beijer had said. Her body was tense with expectation. But the old feelings of inferiority also returned. Why was she so silly? She pushed away the memory of Rekke in Djursholm, and saw him instead on the platform in the Tunnelbana.

That gave her a little strength, so she called him. He didn't pick up, of course, and she wondered whether to go home after all. But then Rekke called back, and she jumped ever so slightly.

"Hello," she said.

"How are you feeling?"

He sounded tired.

"OK," she said. "You sound tired."

"It's fine."

"I've got new information."

"That's good," he said, as if he didn't care at all, or wasn't even listening. She wondered whether she ought to leave him alone, but she decided just to come out with it.

"Kabir, he—"

"Where are you?" he interjected.

"Close by."

"Come up then," he said.

His speech was a little slurred, but she didn't give that much thought. Instead, she turned onto Grevgatan and went up to the yellow door under the sign that read 2B.

TWENTY-ONE

Martin Falkegren was sitting at his desk feeling a hint of panic. Was it really the Americans who had tortured Kabir? Had Professor Rekke been right after all?

It had almost seemed that way when he'd spoken to Hans Rekke's brother. Was it all going to come back to slap them in the face? It was bad enough when they had released Giuseppe Costa, and now what could he expect? A new gauntlet to be run in the press . . .

He pushed that away and thought about Rekke, and when he'd seen him lecture at the university. There had been such a buzz around him, and Falkegren had been so proud when he'd managed to involve him in the investigation. What a brainwave, he'd thought at the time. What a smart move.

But then . . . how things had changed.

Charles Bruckner at the American embassy – with whom he'd recently become acquainted, by coincidence, or so he hoped – had called him and said the professor wasn't to be trusted, and like the idiot he was he'd allowed himself to be persuaded. But now . . . bloody hell . . . he couldn't help wondering whether Bruckner had exploited him and lied to his face.

No, no . . . Falkegren refused to believe that. Surely the Americans hadn't chained the ref up and tortured him like barbarians. Surely that wasn't possible?

But then again . . . He needed to act. He ate the final piece of liquorice in the bowl on his desk and called Fransson, who picked up after one ring and said it was a good thing he was calling.

"Why is it good?"

"Because we're considering bringing Vargas back onto the Kabir investigation," he said.

Falkegren remembered that Jonas Beijer had said something about that, and tried to deduce whether it was related to the new information.

"Over my dead body," he said. "Isn't her brother some kind of gangster?"

"Yes, broadly speaking," said Fransson. "But the Kabir investigation needs new energy, and she seems to have turned up something new."

"Oh really," Falkegren said, ill at ease.

"And she's digging regardless."

"What do you mean by that?"

"I've just had a call from Tove Lehmann – you remember, the reporter who did the piece on Kabir on TV. Vargas has spoken to her on her own initiative."

"Surely we shouldn't reward her for that?"

"Perhaps not. But I think it may be worth keeping her close at this stage."

Falkegren tried to marshal his thoughts – it felt like there was a storm in his head.

"Was it Jonas who made the suggestion?"

Fransson hesitated.

"It was."

"Did he mention he'd spoken to me?"

"I don't think so."

That was for the best, Falkegren thought to himself. He resolved to call Magnus Rekke again and get him to speak plainly.

*

Micaela turned around. She had the impression someone was watching her. But all she saw was a young man standing in the next doorway, staring down towards the water. It's probably nothing, she thought, before taking the lift upstairs. Mrs Hansson met her at the door. She was on the phone and mimed that Rekke was in bed. Micaela took off her coat and went through the living room with its parquet floor, past the grand piano. It still felt like entering a strange and forbidden world, and she remembered her father and all the books they'd had in the house back when he was still with them, but which Lucas had got rid of – as if he wanted to demonstrate that he had taken over.

"Hi, hello, can I come in?" she called out when she was almost at the bedroom.

"Please do," Rekke said, and once again she felt the desire to tell him what she had heard.

But her expectations died when she saw him. He was sitting up in bed, fully dressed. Everything about him was wilted and pale, and he could barely keep his eyes open. He had looked better standing on the platform edge.

"Good evening," he said.

"It's barely good afternoon."

"Yes, quite," he muttered. "How's your headache?"

"It suddenly got better when I saw you."

"Then I've already succeeded in something."

"What have you done?" she said.

"Been imprudent."

"I should have thrown out your pills. Perhaps I'll do that now."

Rekke smiled weakly. His lips moved as if forming an amusing retort, but nothing came out. His face crumpled and with a trembling hand he wiped sweat from his brow.

"You need to pull yourself together," she said, with a fervour that surprised her.

"I agree," he said.

"Mrs Hansson says they've started watching you. That there's been some dodgy car outside."

"That's not entirely surprising."

She looked at him: he looked spent, and she wondered how to word what she had to say.

"I have new information," she said, pausing in the hope that he would ask what it was.

"So you said," he mumbled, looking as if he wished she would just go.

"Kabir was actually in league with the Taliban."

"Oh really?" he said politely.

"He was good friends with Mullah Zakaria – you know, that stateless Egyptian who was one of the senior Taliban commanders. The one who was shot last year in Copenhagen by the Danish Security and Intelligence Service."

Rekke nodded, and she was certain she'd got his attention at last. But he merely closed his eyes and frowned.

"I'm sorry. I must rest. Perhaps we can talk again tomorrow," he said, which made her want to shout at him.

But it wouldn't help. She sank back into the brown armchair, wondering whether she should wait for him to wake up or whether she ought just to head home. She didn't feel like doing anything. She felt very alone. She had been so looking forward to talking to him, hoping that he would once again see something that no-one else had spotted.

But now he was lying there with a tormented expression, looking like Simón and other junkies she'd met while on duty, and it wasn't like when she'd been on the platform. All her old admiration had vanished. Instead of a brilliant academic and truth-teller, she saw a wreck, unable to pull himself together, and for a while she just sat there while her thoughts flickered.

She heard him sigh and turn over. To break the silence, she said:

"He persecuted musicians. He destroyed their instruments."

Rekke opened his eyes and looked up at the ceiling.

"What?" he said.

"Kabir destroyed instruments including a clarinet and a violin in fits of rage," she said, and he turned slowly towards her.

Then he closed his eyes again and breathed heavily and she thought: It's not worth talking to him. In the distance on Strandvägen an ambulance wailed. The bedroom windows rattled in the wind. She stood up to leave, or perhaps go to the kitchen and see whether Mrs Hansson was off the phone yet.

But just then, when she was half turned away, he jerked. His eyes were moving under his eyelids as if he were dreaming or watching something, and his body had stiffened, as if his exhaustion had been replaced by a great tension. He made a sudden sweeping gesture with his right hand that felt oddly familiar and reminded her of the gracious movements in a dance.

"What was that?" she asked.

"Can you help me?" he said. "I need . . ."

He reached forward with a hand and she pulled him upright.

"What?" she asked. "What do you need?"

"Something to clear the fog. I need to think," he said, staggering towards the bathroom.

Carl Fransson wanted to run upstairs to the assistant commissioner and cause a scene. But he felt too heavy for such drastic action – he really did need to lose weight. He needed to do all sorts of things. Although it would have to be later this summer. Right now he had his hands full, and in front of him he had Jonas Beijer, who was making his head ache. The whole damn thing was insane.

"How the hell could he keep something like that from us?" he said.

Jonas Beijer shrugged.

"It was denied by a source at the American embassy, and perhaps he didn't believe it himself either. He thinks highly of the USA."

Fransson grew even angrier.

"It's verging on criminal," he snapped.

"It's pretty bad."

"What do we do now?"

"We check out whether it's true, for starters. But I can't get hold of anyone at Foreign Affairs who knows."

"Then how was Vargas aware of this?"

Jonas looked like he could say but didn't want to, which irritated Fransson.

"I knew Kabir was some sort of terrorist," he muttered.

"Did you?" said Jonas.

"From the word go," he said, and if that wasn't entirely accurate, it wasn't entirely inaccurate either.

He'd been sceptical of Kabir even when everyone else had been praising him, and the more they had worked on the investigation, the more he had been proved right. There was still much they didn't know, but it had been a challenge getting hold of information from over there. It wasn't just the language and the phone connections and the whole languid Kabuli bureaucracy. There was something fishy too – some kind of resistance.

"We shouldn't have trusted the Americans in Kabul as much as we did," Jonas said.

"But what were we supposed to do?" Fransson said angrily. "The local police are completely corrupt."

"I'm not so sure."

"Hmm, well, run along and see whether you can get this madness confirmed," he snapped, and for some reason Lovisa Rekke sprang to mind.

She often appeared in his thoughts when he felt at his most vulnerable, as if her entire existence reminded him of what he couldn't have, and for safety's sake he told Jonas Beijer to get a move on.

*

Rekke opened the medicine cabinet in the bathroom and wondered what to take. He needed an upper. He desperately needed his thoughts to clear.

He rifled through the cabinet and eventually settled for a jar of Attentin, swallowing a fistful – it was over the top, but this was something he needed to try to understand.

He found Micaela on the sofa by the piano. She looked at once worried and curious, and he did his best to walk in a straight line. He sat down in the armchair opposite her and scrutinised her bruises.

"So Kabir smashed musical instruments," he said.

"In violent outbursts, apparently."

"On his own?"

"No, he seems to have been involved in the Taliban's persecution of musicians. He was loosely tied to one of their ministries."

He thought for a while.

"You mentioned a clarinet and a violin. They're not particularly common instruments over there."

She looked at him intently – almost hopefully.

"It happened in the spring of 1997. The Taliban were conducting a witch-hunt against people who played Western classical music and who had been educated by the Russians," she said. "There were murders too, according to my colleague, including that of a gifted violinist."

"That's interesting," he said, closing his eyes.

Rekke appeared to have entered a trance-like state. His body was tensed and his eyes moved beneath his eyelids again. Was he having a seizure? Micaela had a feeling he might be. But then he opened his eyes and began to tap his left leg.

"What is it?" she said.

He turned to her.

"How should I put this to avoid sounding mad? I took an early interest in Kabir's movements on the pitch."

"We all did. They were unusual."

"They *were* unusual. But I saw something more specific. Or in any case I did for a while. Then I dismissed it as projection – a sign of *déformation professionnelle.*"

"What?" she said.

"I thought my old profession was distorting my vision. When I'm manic, my outward gaze can be rather like looking in the mirror. I see my own reality in others."

"So what was it you saw in Kabir's movements?"

"I saw a technique that seemed to have been transplanted from one world to another. But above all I saw myself at Juilliard. I saw what I never quite mastered."

"And what is that?"

"The rising movement for the crescendo, the soft one for the diminuendo. I thought I saw the passionate short one for staccato, the long sweep for legato. I thought I saw the grandiosity of one who initiates and silences," he said.

"What are you trying to say?"

"That there were times when Kabir's hands moved in a way that felt practised, seemingly retained in his body, as if he had rehearsed them for hours, days, years – not to referee but to stand before an orchestra. I had a sense that Kabir had been a conductor. Or at least that he had dreamed of being one and trained for it. I thought I discerned something Russian in his technique. Traits from Musin and Belinsky."

"That sounds . . . strange."

"Yes," he said thoughtfully. "Not what you would expect of a motorcycle mechanic from a small village outside Kandahar."

"And you still believe it?"

"I believe that I may not be completely insane."

She shivered in the same way she had when Rekke spoke about Kabir's injuries.

"So you're saying," she said, "that this hatred of music was perhaps once . . ."

"Love?" Rekke said.

"What should we do?"

"We should look more closely at that persecution of musicians and understand why Kabir was part of it. Didn't you say that a violinist had been murdered?"

"Yes," she said.

"Then let's find out more about that, and identify the people who played Western classical music in Kabul during the Soviet occupation."

She looked over towards the grand piano and smiled to herself, as if she had just regained something she hadn't even realised she had lost.

TWENTY-TWO

Micaela went into the kitchen to think. She remembered when she had first noticed Kabir's movements on the pitch.

It had been during her first week on the investigation. As was often the case, she hadn't been given anything concrete. She spent most of her time waiting to run errands or run quick checks for the others. This meant she was secretly able to take the initiative herself and get lost in things that might not be important but that interested her in the moment.

On one of those mornings she had been watching the Bromma-pojkarna match footage from Grimsta, mostly to see Beppe run into the penalty area in a mad frenzy towards the end, but also to study events on the pitch, and it had been then that she had started staring at Kabir. She didn't know at first what it was that fascinated her, and he only rarely appeared in shot. But after a while, she realised that his sad facial expression wasn't the only noteworthy thing about him: his movements were distinctive too. Not just because they were unusually jerky. There was something about their timing.

"Kabir gesticulates weirdly," she had said to Jonas Beijer when he walked past.

Jonas had smiled wryly.

"I know," he said. "Like a mini Napoleon."

She hadn't thought Napoleon was a good description. Rather, the movements had looked simultaneously agitated, exaggerated and undulating, like caresses, as if Kabir was not only refereeing the match but also imagining that he was commanding the game itself. Come on, come on, his hands seemed to say as the teams reset. Forward, forward, he would wave as the players attacked.

Afterwards, she had raised it with Fransson. "Yes," he'd said. "It's a bit unusual, but nothing to worry about. We all gesticulate differently," and naturally that was true. Nevertheless, it had remained with her, not as something significant, but she had still pondered it and thought that the movements reinforced Kabir's authority. But a conductor . . . was that even possible?

"How sure are you?" she said when she returned from the kitchen with a glass of water.

Rekke had his head buried in his hands. Outside, the wind was striking the studio window.

"How sure are you that he used to be a conductor?" she repeated.

He slumped a little more.

"Not sure at all," he said. "As I said, I'm not to be trusted any longer."

"But then again," he continued, as if to placate her, "once you've formulated a thought like that, details keep cropping up to support it. The light begins to fall in a new way."

"You mean, that's what's happening now?"

"Yes, a little, in spite of everything. And I think I need to take another look at those autopsy photos."

"What do you want to look at there?"

"I'm going to leave that unsaid for the time being. But I can say this much: if he really was a conductor, or at least trained to be one, then he must have played something too. No-one becomes a conductor without first mastering an instrument, and back in the day I often, or at least believed myself able to . . ."

His voice tailed off and he put his hands to his brow.

"What did you believe you were able to do?"

"Nothing. Not really," he said.

He appeared to oscillate between resignation and hopefulness, and she was seized by an impulse to grab him hard by the wrists, or to shake him like a rag doll.

"I suppose we should check it out anyway," she said. "You said we should look into the circles that played classical music during the Soviet occupation."

"Yes," he said, "and perhaps that starting point is a good one after all."

"How do you mean?"

"Afghanistan has an entirely different musical heritage," he said. "They have different traditions and different types of instruments. Classical music over there almost always refers to Hindustani classical music from northern India."

"What else do you have to say on the matter?"

He winked and put a hand to his chest.

"That it's something completely different. While our classical music might have five hundred years of history, this is a tradition that goes back three thousand years and is closely associated with religion. Hindustani music has twelve semitones, just like Western music. But the distance between them isn't the same, and the musicians make no distinction between minor and major keys. They have no chords or parts, and the melody is often improvised."

"OK," she said. "And what does that mean for us?"

"That almost all classical musicians over there are adherents to the Hindustani tradition. The people who played the clarinet or violin as per the Western model and conducted the way that Kabir appeared to must have been a fairly limited group. I don't imagine that there was any higher education available to them except under Soviet auspices."

"So you mean our search will be limited?"

"Without doubt, and I believe that those who grew up playing Western classical music must have grown up with some form of British or European influence."

She fell silent and tried to think clearly. Were they on a wild goose chase, or might Rekke's theories be right? She didn't know. But *if* they were true then Kabir must have been a completely different person from the man they'd believed him to be, and he would very probably have had another name too.

She was reminded of what Tove Lehmann had said. Kabir had spoken good English and claimed to have read Russian writers. What was more . . . She felt a surge of excitement.

"Can I ask something completely different?" she said.

He nodded.

"Of course," he said.

"*Schadenfreude*," she said. "What does that mean?"

He looked at her in surprise, as if it were not at all what he had been expecting.

"It's a German expression," he replied. "From *Schaden*, harm, and *Freude*, joy. I've always preferred the Swedish word *skadeglädje*. Why do you ask?"

"I spoke to Tove Lehmann, the reporter who did that piece for *Sportspegeln* on TV. Kabir told her about a woman he had seen shot in Kabul. Tove said that he had an air of *schadenfreude* about him."

"It's unusual for young people to use that word," Rekke said.

"I think Tove has a German father."

"Yes, of course."

"But what do you think?"

"Hmm," he said. "I don't know. But we all tend to feel some degree of *schadenfreude* when we see a stranger having a bad time of it. We feel it instinctively: thank God it's not me. And sometimes we perk up when a little drama enters our lives. Those feelings are often experienced in parallel with other, more sympathetic traits."

"But in this case it seemed to be more than that."

"Hmm. Well, there are other explanations too."

"Like what?"

Rekke's hand nervously brushed across his hair.

"We're not always straightforward or noble. Sometimes when we see someone we don't like suffering, it strengthens our unity with our own. It confirms our values and status as a group, and validates our outlook on life. Sort of like a lynch mob: people closing ranks to punish someone for their outsiderdom."

"I understand," she said.

"Other times, we have a feeling that life metes out its own justice. That those who do us harm or have generally been swines get their just deserts, affording us a sense of revenge. And we may feel an evolutionary advantage when a competitor or rival is afflicted. We experience joy at advancing our own position in the herd at the expense of someone else."

"Unpleasant."

"But human."

"To some extent."

"Sometimes it can be downright sadism."

"I'm mostly asking," she said, "because the execution that Kabir described to Tove Lehmann resembled the murder of the violinist that I mentioned."

Rekke looked at her with deep concentration.

"That's interesting. What was the violinist's name?"

Micaela felt a pang of shame.

"I don't know," she said. "But I'll find out."

She pulled out her Nokia and fired off a text to Jonas Beijer. She received a reply immediately. *Latifa Sarwani*, he wrote. *Shot 1997 in Kabul. Should be able to get you back onto investigation. Fransson coming round to it.*

Coming round to it might have been pushing it.

Vargas unsettled him, and he didn't trust her – some chick from Husby with criminals for siblings. That was the last person on earth he wanted to be lectured by. But Fransson was smart enough to realise they needed help, and Vargas seemed to have her channels. What was more, he could make a fresh attempt at getting her to open up about her brother. There was a knock on the door. What now? It was Beijer again. Of course.

"What do you want this time?" he said.

"I've got confirmation from Foreign Affairs," Jonas said.

"What have they confirmed?"

"Kabir really was tortured by the CIA. He was in that prison no-one knows about. The Salt Pit or the Prison of Darkness, as the prisoners called it."

"For Christ's sake," Fransson said.

"And worst of all . . . do you know what's worst of all?" Jonas said.

"I really do not."

"The CIA has more dirt on him that we don't know about."

Fransson couldn't deal with this any longer. He couldn't stand the whole circus around this investigation, and the feeling of never truly being in control or knowing anything.

"What's that?"

"I've no idea. But if they tortured him that much, they must have found out something, and just recently . . ."

Jonas hesitated and sat down on Fransson's visitor's chair again, fidgeting anxiously.

"Yes?"

"I'm pretty certain that Micaela is holed up with Rekke somewhere."

"Why would she be?"

"Because I got that impression when I saw her."

"How the hell did they find each other?"

"I've no idea. But I think they've got material that we don't have access to."

"It seems like they might."

"And it feels like there's more than that stuff about the CIA and torture."

"What makes you say that?"

"A couple of minutes ago I got a text from Micaela. She wanted the name of the violinist who was shot in her basement in Kabul."

"What does she want that for? We know that Kabir had nothing to do with it."

"Yes, we know that," Jonas said, but he didn't look as certain as Fransson had hoped. Fransson thought about Lovisa Rekke again, and the violin being played in that big house in Djursholm.

For a moment it was as if he understood why people wanted to smash what was beyond their reach. But he pushed that thought aside and told Jonas he had work to be getting on with.

They went to his study and searched online for the name. There wasn't much, but there was a bit, including a sort of fan page. Rekke clicked on it and very, very slowly a picture began to appear on the screen. At first only her hair was visible – charcoal black and extended like wings – and then the forehead and eyes. Wow, Micaela thought to herself. Wow.

The eyes were big, dark, heavily made up and fiery. She thought there was something defiant there, something wild, as if the woman wanted to say: *You won't put me down. You won't be the master of me.* Not surprising, really, that the Taliban had killed her, Micaela thought. The woman looked as if she could get just about anyone to lose their composure. But that was a stupidly spineless thought, and she felt ashamed for having it. She couldn't help wondering, however, what feelings a person like that aroused in men who wanted to lock up and hide women.

Micaela was transfixed. The woman was beautiful. Not a traditional beauty, admittedly. The nose and eyes were disproportionately large. But she was radiant. Her lips were plump, covered in red lipstick and slightly parted, and in her left hand she held a violin raised towards the ceiling in a dramatic movement. It looked as if she had just given a violent toss of her head. That would explain why her hair was flaring outwards.

"How old do you think she is in the photo?" Micaela said.

Rekke turned to her.

"Seventeen perhaps."

"Not older?"

"She's playing the role of an experienced woman. I would guess it's a stage persona."

He scrolled down the page and found other photos, almost all taken when she was young, and although she looked different in each one, she displayed the same defiant and passionate radiance in all of them. There were captions underneath in Arabic – or perhaps it was Pashto. Here and there they found information in English and links to articles and even – with a warning above it – a photograph of her dead. She was wearing a green hijab and a dark-brown blouse, and was lying in a small basement chamber next to a toppled chair with blood pouring from her head.

Micaela thought Rekke would stop at that photo. But he hurried onwards, and together they gained an overview of Latifa Sarwani's life. She had been born in February 1968 in Kabul and had died – shot in the head in the same city – on the night of April 3, 1997, in the middle of the Taliban witch hunt against musicians.

There was, however, nothing to suggest that the murder had been ordered by the regime – as Jonas Beijer had pointed out – even if it was likely to have been tied to the persecution. The regime didn't appear to have investigated the murderer either, instead regarding it as a consequence of her crime against Allah and his Prophet. The only thing that seemed certain was that Latifa must have known her killer. She had clearly opened the door to him in the middle of the night and brought him down to the basement where she kept her violin, her eighteenth-century Gagliano, hidden under some planks of wood.

Since the chair found toppled had been lifted forward from its position by the wall, it was assumed that Latifa had been sitting on it and playing by night, especially since her violin was lying beside her corpse, trampled and crushed to pieces. According to a report in *The*

Guardian she had been shot at close range with an old Soviet pistol called a Tokarev.

Latifa had been identified as a prodigy from an early age, and at sixteen she had won a place at the Moscow Conservatory. But when the Soviets withdrew their troops from Afghanistan and the cultural partnership between the two countries was terminated, she had been forced to return to Kabul. There was no information about what had happened to her in the following years, but her life must have changed drastically.

During the Soviet occupation, there had been many opportunities for a violinist to perform and play. But by 1992, under the rule of President Rabbani, female musicians had been prohibited from practising their craft. Latifa's career must have more or less died, and then – Micaela tried to imagine it – the Taliban had seized power, and what had previously been prohibited became downright dangerous. Above all for a woman who was both a musician and someone who had collaborated with the godless communists.

"Why didn't she leave the country?" she said.

"You have to wonder," said Rekke. "What do you think? Should we listen?"

Under one of the childhood photos there was an audio link and when she nodded, Rekke clicked on it and leaned back. He still looked exhausted: covered in a cold sweat, and pale, his eyes cloudy and squinting and fixed grimly on the bronze statue of a girl curtseying. But he appeared not to see it; he seemed completely lost within himself. The sound of a melancholy violin sliced through the room, affecting Micaela at once.

Latifa played as if her life depended on it, and Micaela couldn't help thinking of the piece as a lament for what had happened to Latifa herself, as if she were grieving for her own death many years in advance. Before long she was lost in the music. She was gripped by a feeling that something that had irrevocably disappeared had been brought to life, and not until the music stopped did she say:

"What is she playing?"

Rekke looked as if he were still not entirely present.

"The adagio in Bruch's violin concerto," he replied.

"It's pretty, isn't it?"

"It's beautiful," he said. "Expressive and filled with temperament. But also a little careless."

"Careless?"

"That is no perfectionist playing. Rather, a woman who believes in herself and dares to play slipshod. She isn't particularly masterful or well drilled. She is aware of her ability, and she isn't afraid of big emotional movements. Yes, it's beautiful. But also a little melodramatic. She hasn't faced great sorrows yet, I would guess – although she is doing a good job of pretending. She is theatrically gifted, as I sensed from the pictures. A finisher and boundary crosser. Not altogether easy to control, I suspect."

"And you can hear all that?"

He shrugged.

"I believe I hear it, at any rate. But with violinists it can be a bit tricky. Sometimes you hear a clear personality in their music but still get it wrong. What you hear is something that is only there when they are holding their instrument and is otherwise invisible. You perceive something which remains concealed as a tiny, secret passion in their heart. But here . . . what should I say? I discern hints of Russian schooling, as expected, but also . . . no Westerner would slip between notes like that. You can hear quite clearly the influence of qawwali and Hindustani. I dare say she held the room like a queen."

"Have you any idea how insane it is when you make those kinds of observations after hearing one single piece?"

"Perhaps, yes. But then again, I talk a lot, and it's not really what I'm thinking about."

"What is then?" she said.

"I'm wondering whether we oughtn't to take a closer look at her and the others who played Western classical music in Kabul at that time. Perhaps Kabir might crop up somewhere there in one shape or another – unless I'm quite mistaken."

"Do you have a way in?" she said.

"Yes, actually," he said, checking his watch.

He stood up with a shudder and began to walk as if he was suddenly in a hurry. Then he turned on his heel and looked at her with unexpected intensity.

"Do you know something?" he said. "You've given me a little of my life back."

She was bewildered.

"It's almost becoming a habit," she said.

He raised his hand as if to stroke her hair, but withdrew it.

"My brother was here today," he said. "He'd organised a meeting for me. But I didn't think that I'd be up to it."

"But now you are, aren't you?"

"Yes, perhaps," he said. "But first I have to . . ."

He shook his head and vanished towards the bathroom, and she was fairly certain he was going to root through his medicine cabinet. But this time she didn't try to stop him, perhaps because he had shown a little spirit.

When he returned, his cheeks and hair were damp – as if he had splashed water on his face. His eyes were narrowed and he muttered that he needed to make a call. "Excuse me," he said. Shortly afterwards, she heard him talking in the kitchen. His voice was irritable. "Yes, yes, I'll keep it brief," he said.

When he returned, he explained that he had reinstated his meeting but that he would only have ten minutes – fifteen tops. That would have to do, he said. He offered no further explanation. Instead he went into the living room and sat down at the grand piano, completely still, as if seeking inspiration or lost in his thoughts again.

His hands began to move across the keys. Initially it sounded nothing more than anxious and strange, as if he were playing it wrongly. But then there was a fumbling melody, perhaps the same as the one in the Bruch piece, although Micaela wasn't sure. The melody vanished just as quickly as it had begun, and was replaced by a completely different fragment of sound. It was – she couldn't explain it any better – as if he were searching for something amid the notes.

TWENTY-THREE

Julia heard him from the lift. He was extemporising, jumping between notes and set pieces. It sounded as if he were lost and looking for a way out. She became even more worried.

Those words about suicide that Mrs Hansson had been tossing around and that he and Micaela had dismissed had come back to her and kept her awake. Fucking Pappa. He could be wonderful and sharp as a knife and see her more clearly than anyone else in the whole world, but other times, like now, he was a wreck and let people exploit him.

Magnus had been there snooping, so she'd heard, and that made her crazy, because while Magnus might play the world's best friend, he was actually so full of jealousy he was splitting down the sides. She was convinced of it and she didn't doubt for even a second that, given the chance, he would crush Pappa. She took a deep breath and stepped through the door. Mrs Hansson met her in the hall looking rather satisfied.

"What's happening?" Julia said, pointing to the living room and the grand piano.

"I'm not quite sure. Micaela's here," Mrs Hansson told her, as if that were quite normal, and Julia muttered:

"Fuck me, they're tight all of a sudden."

Heading into the living room, she remembered she'd just smoked a joint. She stopped, took a couple of pieces of peppermint gum from her trouser pocket and chewed them frantically. She continued to the grand piano, nodding to Micaela, then placed a hand on her father's back and heard him sniff.

She was certain he would give her away. But when he stopped playing and turned towards her, it looked as if he were in a completely different world.

"What are you doing?" she said.

"I'm thinking, I suppose."

She backed away a little to be safe.

"Mrs Hansson says that Magnus has been here snooping."

"He did me the courtesy of stopping by and showing a certain interest."

"Can't you drop the irony for once?"

"I'll try. What time is it?"

"Quarter to three," she said irritably.

"Then I must dash."

"Where are you going?"

"He's got a meeting," Micaela said, now standing beside her and seeming rather tense.

"How come you're suddenly off to a meeting?"

"I want to get some answers."

She looked at him again, at the matted hair and the sweat glistening on his brow.

"Then you have to shower," she said.

"I don't have time to shower."

"Then you'll have to change. You look a mess."

He glanced down at his hands and his trousers.

"Perhaps a little. Fetch me a decent jacket and my overcoat. I'm sure that will do."

"To go with that shirt?"

"To go with anything."

"You appear to have slept in it."

"I did sleep in it."

"Who are you meeting?"

"Kleeberger."

"You're going to meet Kleeberger?" Micaela said with surprise, looking even tenser. "Isn't that risky?" she said. "Given that . . ."

"No, no," he said. "I'm just going to see whether I can get him and Magnus to come clean."

"About the football ref?" Julia said.

"Exactly. You wanted to get me going. But . . . sorry, would you mind hurrying? I just had the most peculiar thought and lost my sense of time and space."

Julia dashed to his wardrobe. She tugged at a speckled blue jacket that definitely didn't suit the Ministry for Foreign Affairs and a grey, more austere spring overcoat, and returned to the study where her father and Micaela had obviously been talking about Kleeberger. Both fell silent when she entered, and neither of them said a word while she helped him into his clothes and adjusted his hair.

"There we are. Now you're verging on respectable again."

"Verging on respectable will do nicely," he said.

"But you still look like you're drugged."

"I think he just tried to even it out with an upper," Micaela said.

"Jesus Christ, Pappa."

"Which reminds me, have you been smoking a joint?" asked Rekke.

"Most definitely not."

"You should quit."

"You're one to talk," she snapped, and he shuddered as if he were truly considering the words.

Then he shook his head and said: "*Alea iacta est.*" He kissed her on the cheek, nodded to Micaela and left the flat not entirely steadily. Julia stood in silence, lost in her own thoughts. She turned to Micaela.

"So the meeting is about the Prison of Darkness?"

"I think so," said Micaela.

"Magnus is a snake."

"I'll bear that in mind."

"Pappa had a peculiar thought, he said."

"You might say that."

"What was it?"

Micaela didn't reply, not at first. Then she said, as if trying to avoid the question:

"You said that he can be more wrong than anyone else you know."

"Did I?"

Julia was annoyed at Micaela for changing the subject, and resentful that her father and Micaela had got so close in no time at all, and she wondered whether to even bother answering. But then again, sometimes Pappa just said stuff – trying out something far-fetched or off the wall. Sometimes you couldn't tell whether he was serious or joking, while at other times he seemed almost hallucinatory in his conclusions.

"He can go off the rails," she said. "He can even seem completely stupid. I think his brain has trouble with a lack of order."

"So he creates his own order."

"He sees patterns where there are none. He adds one and one and gets three. What did he say?"

Micaela hesitated and ran her hand through her hair. She seemed to be considering how much she should say.

"He . . ." she began.

Julia tensed, desperate to know. But just then Micaela's phone rang and when Micaela saw who it was, her body language changed. Julia took an involuntary step back.

"I've got to take this," Micaela said. "See you later."

"Sure," Julia said, feeling uneasy.

Not just because Micaela's gaze had darkened. She realised she was afraid that Magnus and Kleeberger would set some kind of trap for her father, and perhaps Micaela too, if she had been dragged into this. For a second, she wondered whether to warn her, but by then Micaela had already gone.

Rekke felt sluggish in body and soul. He didn't know whether Kleeberger and Magnus were seeing him because they were scared or because they regarded him as harmless. He would know soon enough. There was a wind blowing off the water as he walked down Strandvägen. I saw something in Kabir's technique, he had said. Was it nonsense or was it real? He didn't know. What had recently seemed so clear appeared once again cloudy and dreamlike. As if he had regressed.

As a little boy, he had often sat at dinners or concerts trying to work out what kind of lives the people next to him led. He examined their hands, clothes, faces, gestures, manners, and for the most part he made rational observations. But sometimes he began to fantasise, and afterwards he was never quite sure when the real or possible world had slipped into fiction, and perhaps that was what had happened now. Perhaps he had found a connection that only existed in his world of impressions, a wished-for trail that not only seemed to lead him forward in the investigation but also back to the painful moments in his own life. Maybe he was going mad again?

But did it matter? The main thing was that something had been ignited within him. The world had drawn him back into it.

A car honked further along. The traffic was heavy. He looked down and thought about Micaela again and her eyes and the clattering sound of her footsteps on the Tunnelbana platform.

You have to pull yourself together, she'd said.

He had to . . .

A loud sound cut through the city. A drill, he realised. Hammering at the asphalt. Anxiety was permeating his body. Perhaps the amphetamines were kicking in.

He turned around. Was someone following him? Nonsense, he muttered. Just paranoia. He reached Kungsträdgården and continued towards the opera and Gustav Adolfs torg. Then he received a text. He hated texts, hated having to press a button for every damn letter. But Magnus had apparently learned the art and even wasted his words.

For goodness' sake you better not be late.

Rekke didn't bother replying, but he did pick up his pace.

It wasn't Lucas who had called. It was Simón, and Micaela really had no desire to speak to him. But she had been overcome with unease. Simón never called nowadays unless he absolutely had to, and according to Mamá he was looking worse than ever. She called back as soon as she was out on the street.

"What do you want?" she said.

"Do I always have to want something?"

He sounded hoarse.

"You can talk about the weather if you like. But I can tell right now that something's up."

"Lucas thinks someone's knocked you about."

"No-one's knocked me about."

"Says your whole face is black and blue."

"It's healed," she lied.

"He wonders why you're back on that football ref again."

"Why should he care?"

"He cares about everything all the time, don't he?"

"What's he after?"

"Maybe it's not so easy for him, having a cop for a sister."

She stopped at the crossroads with Riddargatan.

"So he asked you to go fishing."

Simón didn't answer.

"Where are you?" she said.

"What's that?"

"We should meet."

"I'm in Husby. At Mustafa's."

"Then I'll see you outside the flats in forty," she said, hanging up so that he couldn't quibble.

Not that she really thought he would tell her anything of value. But it couldn't hurt to see him, and if nothing else she could pop up to see her mother.

On the way to Karlaplan, she wondered if she should withdraw some cash for him, although he'd probably got more than enough out of Lucas. She passed Oscarskyrkan and pulled out her phone again. Should she call Jonas? She dialled. He didn't answer, and she was disappointed. But why should he be sitting there waiting for her calls?

She increased her pace – the wind was blowing hard and it felt more like November than April. In the distance she heard sirens – faraway shrieks – which seemed to start up again the moment they died out. But then it wasn't sirens anymore – it was her phone making a noise that blended into the sounds of the city.

"Hello," she said.

"You were right about the prison," Jonas said. "I think I can get you back onto the investigation now."

"What does Fransson say?"

"He's got other things on his plate. The whole place is ripe for revolt," he said. "Even the National Police Commissioner is involved. He's calling the foreign minister."

She thought about Rekke on his way to Foreign Affairs and Kleeberger, then pushed that aside and closed her eyes. She had contributed a crucial element.

"Look, Micaela. Please be honest with me. It was Rekke who whispered into your ear, right?" he said.

She hesitated, staring at Narvavägen.

"Yes," she said.

"How did you meet?"

"I'll tell you later."

It was his turn to hesitate.

"We could grab a beer."

"We could."

He seemed satisfied with the answer.

"May I ask why you wanted the name of the violinist?"

"We wondered . . ." she said, choosing her words carefully.

"What did you wonder?"

"Whether Kabir was a classical musician too."

Jonas was silent, maybe from surprise.

"Are you mad?" he said.

"It's just one line of inquiry," she said defensively.

"How did you come up with that? Because he smashed up some instruments?"

Was she supposed to say that it was because of his movements on the pitch? No, she thought. That sounded ridiculous.

"Have you had any indication of that yourselves?"

He fell silent again.

"I don't know what to say. To be honest, the thought hadn't even occurred to me."

"So no signs that he knew anything about scales and chords?"

"Definitely not."

She paused outside the Tunnelbana station at Karlaplan.

"And Kabir didn't know Latifa Sarwani," she said.

"No, I told you. They were from completely separate worlds."

"They might still have met?"

"Of course. But we really have looked into it. They didn't have anything to do with each other – not in Kabul or anywhere else in Afghanistan."

"Maybe they met abroad? Sarwani studied in Moscow."

"But he didn't. He was a bloody motorcycle mechanic."

He was. She thought about this for a while and wondered whether Rekke might not be mad after all.

"He was a linguist," she said.

"He was better at English than we thought, that's true."

"Couldn't he have been better at other things too?"

"He could have been. But we haven't got any further."

"It seemed as if he hated music."

"Perhaps."

"And that hatred must have come from somewhere?"

"Hate isn't always explicable."

She thought about that.

"I'm just saying you might have missed something."

"Of course we've bloody missed something. Otherwise we would have solved this, wouldn't we?"

"True," she said, surprised by his sudden anger. "Let's talk later. I'm about to head down into the Tunnelbana."

"Let's," he said. "Sorry I lost it. I look forward to that beer."

"Get me back onto the investigation first."

"I'll do my best."

"And tell Fransson that this time it's got to be unconditional."

"OK . . ." he said quizzically.

She hung up, descended the stairs to the turnstiles and made her way onto the platform.

TWENTY-FOUR

Mats Kleeberger, Minister for Foreign Affairs, surveyed his large office and glanced with dissatisfaction into the mirror above the fireplace with its marble surround. Hadn't he said that the Kabir case was a boil that would burst sooner or later?

Beyond the window loomed the royal palace and parliament. He stared vacantly towards them and swore. He couldn't believe he had conceded. But then again, it had been because of the terrorist attacks. Everything had been black and white since 9/11, and he wasn't exactly alone in giving in to the pressure. Few of his European colleagues had been able to resist. What will we do to fight terrorism? Whatever it takes, they had replied like obedient soldiers. But it was easy to be wise with the benefit of hindsight. There had been such a sense of urgency that it seemed reasonable not to be too fussy, and he wanted to say to Rekke: "Would it have been better if we had been blown to bits?"

He checked his wristwatch and thought that Hans ought to be here by now. He'd said he was coming right away, and surely it wasn't that far from Grevgatan? Bloody man. Hans's father used to say: *Some people have a willingness to stay quiet, while others can't stop talking* – and that was how it had been for a long time with Hans. Kleeberger came to life under Hans's penetrating gaze – Rekke seemed to see right through him before he'd had time to utter a word.

But then . . . Hans had changed and stopped considering things in political terms. He just spoke his awful truths and it was hardly surprising that he began to be regarded as dangerous. So reckless, thought Kleeberger, so rash. He really wanted – he wasn't exaggerating – to knock him about and scare him into silence.

Surely that shouldn't be so difficult? It was possible to get to him in all sorts of ways now. But it was tricky to pin Hans down, even when he was depressed. And then, of course, there was Magnus. Kleeberger couldn't manage without him. But Magnus was always a sly fox and frankly Kleeberger wasn't sure whether he was for or against his brother. Probably both . . . he wanted to corner him and rescue him all at once.

There was a knock on the door.

"Professor Rekke is here now," said his secretary. Kleeberger straightened his back and assumed an expression he thought radiated authority and empathy.

It was not the usual Hans Rekke who entered, rather a pale and very tired man in a wrinkled shirt and a jacket . . . good grief . . . Was this some kind of joke? He looked like a harlequin – and his hair! Couldn't he have run a comb through it?

"Take a seat, my dear chap," he said.

Rekke sat down in the yellow armchair in front of the desk and wiped a bead of sweat from his brow. His eyes flickered across the gilded walls. His hand was trembling. Things looked promising.

"Sorry to say this, Hans, but you seem tired."

"I've seen better days," he said with a forced smile and Kleeberger almost felt sorry for him.

Only with an effort was Hans able to raise his head and look at him.

"But I'm glad you're in fine form," Rekke said. "You're still playing tennis regularly, I see."

"Oh, you can tell?"

"From your brachioradialis. More prominent in your right arm, although you play a two-handed backhand, don't you?"

217

"That's right. I was inspired by Björn Borg back in the seventies. But let's get to the point. I'm afraid I don't have much time."

Rekke nodded and Kleeberger pressed the intercom button.

Magnus stepped in with a folder in his hand. Kleeberger glanced at him to gauge how agitated he was, but Magnus exhibited nothing but his usual urbanity. He seemed ready for battle, while his brother seemed ever more slumped and listless, with his glazed eyes. This is going to go well, he told himself.

"So you've started already?" Magnus said.

"Your brother was just admiring my tennis muscles."

"Oh yes, he's always been fascinated by bodies."

"Anyway," Kleeberger said, turning back to Hans, "Magnus says you need help."

Hans put a hand to his forehead, looking troubled, and repositioned himself on the chair.

"Yes, quite. I find myself a little puzzled," he said.

"Aren't we all?" Kleeberger replied generously.

"But I should think it's a bit worse in the case of Hans," Magnus said, taking a seat beside his brother.

"I heard that," Kleeberger said. "Our American friends are apparently squabbling with you, although I don't understand why. Could you tell me?"

Hans fidgeted as if he were not especially keen to explain and Magnus took over.

"It began with a guy in Guantanamo, because he'd been called by his uncle on Osama Bin Laden's satellite phone. Suspicious, of course. But the guy seemed to know nothing about al-Qaeda. Then suddenly he knew everything. Charles Bruckner at the CIA – who was based in Langley at the time – wanted Hans to take a look at the interrogation transcripts."

"And what were your conclusions?" Kleeberger said, turning to Rekke.

"Hans concluded that the chap hadn't said what he knew but what he thought he needed to say to avoid torture," Magnus said.

"Oh dear," said Kleeberger. "Not good."

"After that, the CIA started hurling more interrogation transcripts at him, so that Hans could detect what was true and false about them, and Hans became increasingly . . . how should I put this? Confused. Is that the right word, Hans? Or simply angry?"

Rekke shrugged.

"Well, it doesn't matter. The important thing is he cited a number of studies that showed that violence is not a good way of obtaining information, especially not when the interrogators are unsure of the suspects' guilt, or what they are looking for in the first place. Of course, Hans understood that it can be tempting in troubled times to make the interrogation itself part of the punishment. But following moral impulses rather than empirical knowledge is rarely intellectually fruitful, he said."

"Surely they ought to have been able to take that."

"They took it very well at first," Magnus said. "But step by step, he pushed it further. He said he'd never heard a worse cacophony of contradictory and coerced voices, and that the whole approach was not only a failure but counterproductive. Instead of crushing the enemy, more enemies were being created, and he warned them that it would have disastrous consequences for the perception of America if it got out."

"I see," Kleeberger said.

"But above all," Magnus said, "he made it clear that the CIA were in danger of failing to spot what was truly serious when they were swamped with such an extraordinary volume of subpar information."

Rekke looked at his brother as if Magnus was talking nothing but nonsense.

"And matters were hardly improved when he contacted the *Washington Post*," Magnus said.

"Ah yes, I heard something about that," Kleeberger said.

"I might add that the *Washington Post* contacted *me*," said Hans.

"Perhaps they did," Magnus said, "and I don't think you gave the journalist any more than a couple of general home truths. But nevertheless . . . our friends in the CIA were concerned and resolved to discredit you – before you discredited them by letting all hell break loose in the press. Would you say that's a good summary, Hans?"

"Not especially," he said.

"Oh well, perhaps not. But I think I captured a little of the truth."

"Are you going to let all hell break loose in my ministry?" Kleeberger said with a cautious smile.

Hans didn't smile back. He chose to look down, instead, at his long hands. Kleeberger still felt that it boded well. There was no trace of Hans's old spirit, none of the usual luminescence.

"I don't think I have that power."

"So you're not wondering whether to follow the law or your conscience?" he said in deliberate provocation.

"I'm not sure what either of them say. My ambitions are more modest. I just want a little information," Hans said.

"About Kabir?" Magnus said.

"Indeed," he said, and Kleeberger looked at Magnus with an expression that said: *Say it now, ram it down his throat.*

"I just spoke to Bruckner," Magnus said.

"I'm glad to hear you remain close during a crisis," Hans said.

"Charles pointed out quite firmly that your non-disclosure agreement says you cannot exploit in any future inquiries knowledge acquired while working for the CIA."

"Isn't it the case that you risk the wrath of the law if you do?" said Kleeberger. "You might even be extradited to the USA."

"I'm not so sure about that," Hans said with a calm that made Kleeberger a little nervous after all. "*Leges sine moribus vanae.*"

"Laws without morals are useless," Magnus translated.

"Furthermore, we are in a twilight zone where the law and political power are not as separate as we might hope, and that is why – in spite of everything – I am convinced that you will help me," Rekke said.

"Why should we do that?"

"Because it is in your interest to do so. It is no more complicated than that. Allow me briefly to recount the case."

"That really isn't necessary."

"I shall do so anyway," Hans said, seeming all of a sudden to grow in stature.

Or perhaps grow was the wrong word – it felt as if the old Hans had returned, one who self-consciously, almost against his will, gave his version of the truth. Kleeberger cast another anxious glance at Magnus.

"On August 22, 2002, a man arrives in Sweden under the name of Jamal Kabir," Hans said. "However, his real name, we may infer, is something else entirely. He arrives straight from a secret prison to the north of Kabul with the code name Cobalt or Salt Pit, where he was tortured using cold and darkness and loud music."

"Well?" said Magnus impatiently, biting his lip. At that moment, Kleeberger had the uncomfortable thought that the brothers both knew something he didn't. But he pushed it aside.

"That's strange in itself, isn't it?" Hans said. "How often are captives released from that kind of facility and generously flown to a new location?"

"Not often."

"But the really interesting thing is that the Migration Agency and the police were not informed."

"The police bloody well were informed," Kleeberger said with sudden vehemence, not just because he had taken care to ensure the details reached the police top brass, but because he realised that was what might be particularly sensitive if the story were to leak.

"*I* informed Falkegren," Rekke said drily. "But the information was never passed down the organisation."

"That's hardly our fault."

"I should think it is," Rekke said. "Someone must have denied the facts given to Falkegren. He would hardly have dared keep quiet about them otherwise."

Magnus nodded as if he knew exactly who had denied what, and that made Kleeberger even more uneasy.

"Well," he said irritably. "Continue."

"Not telling the police everything when they embark upon a murder inquiry is scandalous, and I shall return to that," Rekke said. "But first I want to talk a little about the underlying logic. Why were you so reluctant to say what you knew? The answer is, one assumes, that you were under pressure. The Americans didn't want it to come out that they had tortured a man like that, and risk the discovery of a secret prison. Of course, that is what happened. But I don't think it's enough of a motive."

Kleeberger crossed his arms over his stomach.

"No?" he said.

"No. There must have been some kind of agreement too. I don't know what, so you can relax on that count."

Thank goodness, Kleeberger thought to himself. Good.

"But naturally I have my theories. I know, for instance, that several Taliban leaders in Kabul were never apprehended, and that there are not even photos of some of them. I can imagine that Kabir's task in Sweden was to identify some of them. Mullah Zakaria was in Norsborg for a time before fleeing to Copenhagen, where he was shot. But that makes little difference and it is not what interests me at present."

"What does interest you then?"

"The cover-up itself."

Kleeberger looked anxiously again at Magnus.

"In what way?" he said.

"How should I begin? We don't know why Kabir was murdered. But it seems probable that one reason it happened was no outsiders were allowed to know there was a threat against him."

"I think—" Kleeberger began.

"First and foremost," Hans continued, "it perverted the police inquiry. An innocent man was arrested and remanded as a result of the inadequate information in the detectives' possession. In the meantime, the killer was given a head start. One might deduce from this that those who allowed Kabir to enter the country didn't want the murder to be solved, since the solution would cast them in a bad light."

"Where are you going with this?" Kleeberger said.

"I would like a small exchange of services, just as you must have agreed with the CIA."

"Well, spit it out."

"I will refrain from letting all hell break loose, as Magnus so beautifully phrased it, if you tell me what Kabir did as a member of the Taliban regime and why he ended up in the Salt Pit. I simply want to know why there were grounds to kill him."

"Why would we know that?"

"Because you must have received a file or part of a file from the CIA. Otherwise you wouldn't have let him into the country."

Mats Kleeberger cast a quizzical glance at Magnus and there was silence for a while in the room. Then there was laughter. It was Magnus, who all of a sudden seemed amused.

"OK," he said.

"OK what?" Kleeberger said uncertainly.

"I think it's just as well we give him what he wants. He won't give up otherwise," Magnus said.

"Is it really safe . . . ?" Kleeberger said before stopping himself. He felt weak.

"I looked up the flower you were researching," Magnus said, as if he hadn't heard his hesitation.

"Which flower are we talking about?" said Kleeberger.

"*Iris afghanica*. It grows in the mountains around Kabul. A tenacious, beautiful little flower. It's regarded as a symbol of resistance." Magnus turned to Rekke. "Is it related to the murder?"

"I don't know. But I think there was a reason to kill Kabir," Hans said absently, and Kleeberger felt a need to resume authority.

"Yes, yes," he said brusquely, standing up. "You win, at least for now. My congratulations. But I have no intention of handing over classified papers to you willy-nilly. I'm going to have our lawyer take a look at it, then Magnus can pop round with whatever we can give you tomorrow morning."

"Splendid," said Hans, also standing up.

He shook their hands and left with unexpected haste. Mats Kleeberger clenched his fists under the desk, unsure whether from fear or because he wanted to strike back with all his might.

TWENTY-FIVE

Simón didn't show up, and no matter how much she rang around, she was unable to get hold of him. Mustafa éven denied that Simón had ever been at his. Pretty soon she gave up and took the lift up to her mother's. She followed the walkway that her mother ought to have moved away from long ago and rang the doorbell.

Her mother opened the door, wearing a bohemian dress splashed with red and green flowers. She looked like a hippy again, her black and white hair worn down and a little dishevelled, and Micaela was about to ask "What are you doing?" when her mother's eyes opened wide.

"What have you done to yourself?" she said.

"What do you mean, 'done'?"

"Your cheek."

"It looks worse than it is. Have you started painting again?"

"Why would I have started painting?" her mother said, beckoning her inside with big, exaggerated gestures.

"Because you're wearing that," Micaela said, pointing at her dress. It wasn't uncommon for her mother to wear clothes like this, but it usually happened when she got out her oil paints and wanted to travel back to the happy hippy days of the Allende era.

"What . . . no. Just some togs I'm trying out. You must be hungry."

Micaela took a seat on the leather sofa in the living room and was about to say that she wasn't hungry when her mother took a detour to the kitchen and returned with empanadas and yerba mate.

"Thanks, Mamá. It really isn't necessary. You look like you've had better nights' sleep."

"Pah, who sleeps these days?"

Micaela picked up the blanket that lay on the sofa and draped it over herself, then stared at her mother's dress. It really looked like she was about to start yelling *peace and love* all over again.

"I went to see Simón. He never showed."

"He didn't turn up? Does he ever? He turns me grey," her mother said, tugging at her hair to demonstrate. "But for God's sake tell me – surely you haven't been beaten up?"

Micaela shook her head.

"I just fell. I was out partying with Vanessa."

"I can't understand why you don't find yourself a husband instead," her mother said out of nowhere.

"So if I had a husband he would have been there to catch me?"

Her mother looked at her as if wondering what exactly she meant by that.

"If you had a husband, you wouldn't have been running around with Vanessa. That girl is far too beautiful for her own good. Do you know what your father said?"

"What did Papá say?" she said, pleased that they were already on the way to changing the subject.

"He said that beautiful girls get lazy."

"Why should they get lazy?"

"Because they never have to make an effort. But people like us . . ."

"Thanks, Mamá!"

"You're much sweeter than you think, darling. But people like us who don't realise how wonderful we are, we struggle constantly and take nothing for granted."

"And my God, isn't it going well . . . ?"

"What's that supposed to mean? Things are going very well for you. But you have to stop brushing your fringe down. You look like you want to hide."

"Now you sound like Lucas."

"Is that such a bad thing?"

Micaela sighed. "Don't you have anything fun to tell me? Some gossip. Something other than the fact that you've become a hippy again."

"I've never liked that word, you know that. One thing I can tell you: everyone will be gossiping about you and your face. Although . . ." her mother said, suddenly animated, "do you know who's back in the bar in Husby?"

"Who?"

"Beppe. He's back as if nothing happened. He's sitting there all puffed up and bragging about Mario. Carlos was just here and he told me."

Micaela thought about that. She removed the blanket and folded it up.

"You know what, Mamá? I'm going to go and say hi to him."

Her mother looked at her with the same expression of horror she'd worn at the door a little earlier.

"What are you talking about?"

"We haven't seen each other since he was on remand."

Her mother looked offended.

"For goodness' sake, you just arrived. Aren't you at least going to finish your mate?"

Micaela stood up.

"Sorry."

"So you'd rather spend time with that drunk than your own mother," she said.

"I'm taking another look at the murder inquiry."

"But since when has Beppe had anything worthwhile to say? All he does is lie."

"He was treated unfairly."

"You're worse than Simón," her mother said. "You just come and go. Lucas is better. He always takes the time."

"Yes, yes," she said, hugging her mother again.

In the hallway, she got out her wallet and left three one-hundred-krona notes on the bureau by the front door. Then she took the lift down and wandered into the yard. It had got colder and cloudier, she noticed as she strolled past the green and white blocks of flats with their external walkways and satellite dishes.

She walked along Edvard Griegsgången towards the centre of Husby – *town* as they used to refer to it back in the day, even though *town* wasn't much more than a plaza and a few shops. Everywhere she looked she recognised people. There were a lot of new faces, too, but even they probably knew she was a cop. She could see it in their eyes. She picked up a small piece of broken glass in front of the entrance to the Tunnelbana station and eyeballed a group of lads sitting on the green benches over by the Ica supermarket, smirking at her.

"Everything alright?" she said.

"Yep, everything alright. Just got a bit of business with your bro," said the tallest of them, a guy by the name of Fadi.

"Take care you don't get conned."

"Don't worry, I've got my stuff under control," he said, patting his trouser pockets and looking around stupidly at his friends. She forced herself to smile back at them and continued over to the bar. There was a dull glow from within. She took a deep breath as if seeing Beppe again took some effort.

But the place was almost deserted, and she became convinced that he'd already gone or never actually been there. She nodded to Yusuf, who was polishing some glasses, and was about to leave when she heard a yell.

"Micaela!"

She turned around and saw him. He was sitting in the furthest corner with Amir and was staring cheerfully at her. She barely recognised him. He was far too dressed up and far too not-drunk, even if he wasn't actually sober. He wore a brown suit, and had just had a haircut and shave. There was a cut on his upper lip and his cheeks were as bloodshot as usual, but he looked unexpectedly well.

"Beppe," she said. "Welcome back."

"Sometimes the man must return to the place," he said with a grin. "Come and take a seat. You know Amir, don't you? We're heading out to celebrate Mario's transfer. The club's invited us."

She sat down and looked at him, trying to determine whether he was as happy as he looked. It must have been nothing short of hell for him. Half of Husby still thought he was guilty. Micaela knew that *murderer* had been scrawled on his door before he'd packed up and moved to Kristineberg.

"You look good," she said.

He held out his arms and puffed out his ribcage as if to confirm her words.

"You know," he said to Amir, "without Micaela I wouldn't be sitting here today."

"Of course you would. We had nothing on you. We were morons."

"But not you," he said. "You fought for me." He bent forward to hug her.

Then he shuddered and glowered at her cheek.

"What happened to you?" he said.

"Fell," she said. "Come on, let's go for a walk."

He looked at her as if he didn't understand, and looked a little worried too.

"We've just ordered the next round," he said.

She looked into his glassy eyes.

"Surely it's no good you arriving drunk at the party?"

"Who said anything about getting drunk?"

"Sorry, Amir, we'll be back soon."

Beppe nodded and stood up reluctantly. On the way out he whispered into her ear: "You trying to pin some shit on me?"

"Nope, not at all."

He appeared thoughtful.

"I heard you bumped into Mario. Did he embarrass himself?"

"He was nothing but sweet," she said.

They went outside to the plaza and she could feel it right away – they were attracting attention. People were whispering behind their backs and Beppe was reacting to it just like before. He puffed himself up and strutted like a cowboy with his arms swinging at his sides.

"You see them staring?" he said. "They think you're going to arrest me."

She smiled at them all to show that she and Beppe were nothing more than two old friends taking a walk.

"Ignore them," she said. "Be proud instead. It's amazing news about Mario."

He perked up and took a step closer to her and it was impossible not to be reminded of the brutal force in Beppe's body, which had once seemed to point to his guilt.

"I pushed Mario to be the best. You must remember that, right? Every day we'd be out there doing shooting and dribbling. Come bloody rain or shine. Sometimes snow up to our knees."

"I remember," she said, although she couldn't recollect a single occasion she'd seen them playing together – let alone in winter.

"He's going to be a global superstar."

"I bet," she said.

"We did it together, him and me. Do you know what I always told him?"

"What did you always tell him, Beppe?"

"Never stop fighting. Never ever."

"Those must have been valuable words of wisdom."

"It's about the psyche," he said, pointing to his forehead. "The psyche."

She smiled at him and was inclined to say something about his own psyche. But she resisted the temptation.

"Let's head down to the football pitch," she said. "Maybe you can show me what you did."

He nodded and they strolled towards the church and the mosque. When a gang of young men stared at them with curiosity and looked like they wanted to approach, she signalled to them that they were busy. She remembered being in the courtyard outside the flats when she first heard about the murder: the agitation in the air, the shining faces, the voices talking over each other. *Schadenfreude*, she thought to herself.

"Bloody hell," he said. "I'm glad to see you. You know . . . for a while it felt like I was screwed. I almost started believing I had done it."

"I'm sorry," she said.

"On the contrary, you're my hero. How's Lucas?"

"Same old," she said.

"He's a bit of a gangster, isn't he?"

"I don't think it's that bad really," she said.

He stopped and looked thoughtful again. It felt as if he, just like Mario at Spy Bar, wanted to do something for her as a form of repayment.

"Do you remember asking me about Simón's rap that we sang together outside the flats?"

"Of course," she said.

"I remembered something about it."

She looked at him curiously.

"What?"

"We sang about your old man and the whole catastrophe."

"I think I remember something like that," she said.

"I remember one line," he said.

"Which line?"

"*My brother wanted to take over. So he made a manoeuvre.*"

She took in the words.

"Was that supposed to be a reference to Lucas?"

"Who else?"

"Everyone always thinks the worst of him," she said.

"What? No . . . I don't," he said. "I remember the way he took care of you. No-one dared touch you because of him. You were practically queen of Husby for a while."

"Most definitely not," she said. "I heard you'd started remembering more from Grimsta."

"What . . . ?" he said. "Yes, maybe. But it's mostly Mario who's making a thing out of it. The cops . . ."

He grimaced.

"What about them?"

"Oh nothing. But I've got a therapist these days."

She looked at him in surprise. She didn't know anyone in therapy, and if she had tried to guess who might start going, it would definitely not have been Beppe.

"I was given a lady to go and see after my time inside," he said. "To manage my anger."

"I suppose that's good."

"I couldn't stand it. The bitch seemed to think I was guilty. After a while, though, it felt good, and I realised I'd never really dug into it. I'd mostly been fighting back in the interrogations."

"And then you remembered that you'd seen someone."

"I realised I saw someone up on Gulddragargränd."

"Who was that then?"

He looked at her with his cloudy eyes as if he wasn't sure that he believed it himself.

"It's all so dim," he said. "You almost know this better than me."

"I don't know about that. But you were drunk and had fallen into a ditch."

"I was like a walking puddle, and I'd got onto the road and seen that brat who IDed me."

"Filip Grundström," she said.

"And it was raining and blowing a gale and I tried calling Mario to see where he was. But my phone was soaked and I couldn't switch it on and I swore and carried on. Then the road goes around another bend, right, and I saw a guy who couldn't walk straight, y'know. As if he was drunk too."

"What guy was that?"

"I'm not sure. It was all a mess and I had a sore elbow and I just wanted to get home. It wasn't like I was thinking it was important to remember stuff. But there were a few things I noticed all the same."

"Like what?"

"He was young and strong-looking and he was heading away on the road towards Vällingby."

"Young, you say?"

"Well, not old. It definitely wasn't that wrinkled old man they kept banging on about."

"That's interesting," she said. "Do you remember anything else?"

"He kept brushing himself down, as if there was rubbish stuck to him, and I think he was mumbling something, almost as if he was singing. There was something fishy about him."

"But you didn't see his face?"

"No, just his back. He was wearing a rucksack – a grey rucksack – and had some kind of tattoo on his neck."

"What kind of tattoo?"

"Or it might have been dirt. I don't know."

He perked up, suddenly happy, and she wanted to snap at him: *What's so funny about you not remembering?*

"Over there," he said.

"What?"

"That's where Mario and I practised shooting and dribbling."

He pointed towards the football pitch in the valley beyond the fence, and for a moment she barely understood what she was looking at. She was still in the rain on Gulddragargränd.

"Are you sure you weren't down the pub?" she said.

"Jesus, Micaela, you saw it with your own eyes."

"You were pretty fucked up back then, you do remember that, right?" she said.

He looked hurt.

"Enough already," he said. "I promise you . . . I made that boy. Mario knows it. 'Thanks, Papá,' is what he says to me, 'for being so tough and straight with me.'"

"Sure, Beppe. I'm sure that's true. At any rate, the last time I saw him, he reminded me of you."

"Did he?"

"Definitely. The same staggering charm."

"Micaela, you're pretty, you are," he said. He was drunker than she'd realised.

"Thanks," she said irritably.

"Haven't you found yourself a husband yet?" he said, sounding just like her mother. "Someone to take care of you?"

"No. Have you?" she said, wondering whether to call Rekke and find out how he'd got on with Kleeberger. She had misgivings about that meeting, but she tried to ignore them.

Rekke left the Ministry for Foreign Affairs and was walking home again, so absorbed in his thoughts that he didn't see the car with diplomatic plates slowly rolling along behind him on Kungsträdgårdsgatan. Which was why he had no idea that Charles Bruckner and his colleague Henry Lamar were contemplating dragging him into the car and scaring the living daylights out of him.

He was far removed from the city he was walking through. But that did not mean his inner world was any sharper. He felt drugged and heavy, and wondered about dropping the whole thing until he had recovered.

But something important was evading him – something right in front of his face that kept dodging out of sight. He headed up towards

Hamngatan and Nybroplan and was almost hit by a tram. A car honked too, in warning. He thought about Kabir and his waving on the pitch. No doubt under the surface there was a completely different story. But was it what he thought it was? The fact that he had seen something of himself in Kabir's story had served as a warning sign, but then again . . . Viktor, he thought. Good old Viktor. Might he be able to help? He searched his contacts and sent a text message.

Viktor Malikov was – at least when he'd last been in touch – a professor of harmony at the Moscow Conservatory, where Latifa Sarwani from Kabul had studied. But Viktor had appeared in his thoughts for another reason. They were at Juilliard together, only seventeen at the time, and one night they'd been drinking wine at the King's Theatre with the Brooklyn Philharmonic. Even back then Viktor had got drunk the second he had the chance. He'd been a defector and dissident ever since he'd been invited to play in Leonard Bernstein's world youth orchestra, and he strained his nerves looking for KGB agents on every street corner. He was constantly complaining of some real or imagined ailment.

But at least he whined with style. Like all good hypochondriacs, he was well read on the topic of his illnesses, full of anecdotes about famous people afflicted by the same things he had. That night there had been something wrong with his back and shoulders. "I'm starting to grow into that damn piano," he'd said. "I'm just as edgy."

Rekke liked the idea that all the hours of practice left their mark on the body, and soon he took to guessing what instrument people played even before they had taken their seats in the orchestra. He searched manically for callouses on the hands, traces of resin, pressure marks on the skin, scars, small muscles that had been worked hard, cuts on fingertips, trumpet lips, everything possible, even deducing the status of the musicians in the group from their posture and gaze.

This had developed into something of an art form and now, as he walked home through the city thinking about Kabir and his body language, he was certain of one thing. Not that the guy had been a conductor, but that he hadn't.

The gestures felt too strained and theatrical to be professional. But they were nonetheless the motions of a conductor, the dream of a conductor's movements. Somewhere underneath the surface was palpable ambition, and if that were true then the guy – as he'd told Micaela – must also have played a musical instrument. No-one could seriously dream of becoming a conductor unless they played hour after hour, year after year. But which instrument? Up on Strandvägen, he saw that Viktor had already replied.

Brother. What a delight to hear from you. Has it been a hundred years or only ten?

Rekke didn't like the forced tone. He wanted to keep things objective. At the same time, the words focused him, as if the very fact that he had sent a message through his phone and received a response was a sign that he was up and running and had overcome his listlessness.

He ducked into Grevgatan, pleased that he remembered the entry code, still not noticing the diplomatic car gliding down the street behind him. He took the lift upstairs and once again pictured Micaela's gaze, her black eyes that had judged him so harshly, as if he had deprived her of a great and beautiful illusion.

"You have to pull yourself together," she'd said.

I really do have to bloody pull myself together, he thought.

The lift seemed to be running more slowly than usual, which gave him time to think. He wanted to move forward – not just away and down into forgetfulness – and he made a drastic decision, maybe because of that feeling of urgency, or maybe because he looked godawful in the mirror inside the lift, but probably because of Micaela and Julia.

When he entered the apartment, he went straight to the medicine cabinet. He took out his pills and ampoules and jars and threw them into a plastic bag, and before he could change his mind he went out onto the landing and put it down the rubbish chute. When he went back inside he met Mrs Hansson. Good Lord, was he destined never to be left alone?

"Sorry, Hans. How are you feeling?"

"I threw my pills in the bin," he said.

She looked as if she didn't know whether that was good or bad news. But then she smiled.

"She's good for you, isn't she? That girl?"

"Which girl?"

"Micaela, of course."

"Yes, perhaps," he said.

"You're alike in some ways, do you know that?"

"Dearest Sigrid, we're not at all alike. She is young and strong."

"And so are you. You're just imagining that you're weak."

"Of course, of course," he said.

"And she's had her knocks in life. Even I can see that."

"That may be."

"You mustn't ask . . ."

He wasn't listening properly as he headed for the kitchen and wondered whether it might be best to start drinking instead. But he wasn't up to that either. Mrs Hansson was standing behind him again.

"Don't be angry with me," she said, "but you really must eat something. You're so wrapped up in yourself that you forget to eat."

"You're quite right," he said, reaching for the fruit bowl on the bar.

"Hans, that's a lemon."

"What . . . yes . . . exactly," he said. "My favourite. We strong young men regard the lemon as the new orange."

"I'll cook you dinner."

"You'll do no such thing. Go downstairs and rest," he said. He went to his study, sat down at the computer and pulled up the autopsy photos of Kabir.

He grimaced again as if it were him lying there, powerless, his skull crushed. But soon his head cleared and it was as if he had returned to a devastated landscape he had seen before – in another time. A better time, when his gaze registered more than it did now, and for a long time he sat there, staring at the old injuries that had once upon a time led him to the Prison of Darkness. Then he focused on the hands.

They were a worker's hands, those of a mechanic, stained with oil. There was dirt, small scars, scratches, but also . . . He enlarged the photos, stared at the fingertips and saw the very faint, almost invisible lines running diagonally from the papillae. But he wasn't sure how to interpret them. The space between the lines was too large, and he shook his head. It didn't make sense. Perhaps there was nothing there.

It was like looking for footprints in the sand. Like searching for something that had been washed away by the waves many times over.

He stood up and muttered inaudibly. A couple of phrases from Beethoven's *Grosse Fuge* rose in his head, perhaps as a worrying accompaniment to the autopsy photos, or perhaps . . . He froze as an idea struck him. He went online to try to find something to compare it against.

He found nothing, and remained uncertain. Nevertheless, he felt a sudden, intensifying lust for life, as if a door had opened onto another world. He wrote a hasty response to Viktor Malikov. "*Claritas, claritas,*" he mumbled.

TWENTY-SIX

She had made pasta with tomato sauce. Outside, rain was falling even though the sky was clearer now. It looked like it was going to be a fine evening. She sat in the kitchen eating while thinking about what Rekke had said about Kabir's movements. The observation made nothing clearer, yet it was mind-blowing, and she thought she ought to call Jonas Beijer. But she didn't want to bother him if they were weighing up whether to let her back onto the investigation.

She went into the living room, turned on the computer and pulled up the photos of Latifa Sarwani. Once again she was drawn to Latifa's eyes, which had an almost hypnotic allure. She wondered whether Kabir had looked into those eyes, and, if so, what he had felt.

Had he loved her and been disappointed? Or had he felt ignored and wanted to destroy the thing he could not have? It was impossible to know, or not yet, and perhaps it had nothing to do with the story. But on the other hand . . . She pulled up the picture of Latifa's corpse, which had been incongruously posted on the site, and saw the toppled chair and the curled body on the floor with the hand reaching towards the crushed violin.

Next to it were loose pieces that must have flown off when the violin had been smashed, and small clumps of earth or soil. A river of blood had pumped from the back of her head, which was shrouded in a dark-brown shawl. It was hard to grasp that this was the same person whose eyes stared so defiantly and proudly out of the other photos. But then again, the face wasn't visible in the picture – only the bony body, the legs, the hips, the narrow neck and the back with the shoulder blades visible through the blouse. The shoulder blades . . . She thought about Tove Lehmann. Could it have been Latifa that Kabir had told her about?

The phone rang. It was Lucas. He was at his kindest and wanted to know whether she was feeling better. She told him she was, and was reminded of what Beppe had said about Simón's lyrics. But it would only upset Lucas if she brought it up, she thought to herself, especially now that he was in a good mood. So she chatted with him about everything and nothing. Then she thanked him for helping her and that made him a little more cautious and he asked why she'd got so interested in Kabir again. She said she'd met a professor who had given her new information about the murder. She regretted it at once.

"Is it him? Rekke?" he said.

She started.

"How do you know about him?"

"There was some chat about him a while back. Isn't he rich?" he said.

She said she didn't know and explained that she was tired and that she still had a headache. He said he understood. He would look in on her in the morning. She'd prefer he didn't, she mumbled. But by then he'd already hung up. *Bloody Vanessa*. She must have been the one who'd blabbed. She'd never stopped being impressed by Lucas. And she always talked too much. But six months ago, when Micaela had been talking about Rekke, none of them had had a clue that his name would be sensitive information. It probably didn't matter, she reflected, and in the absence of anything else to do she returned to the photos of Latifa Sarwani. But once again she was interrupted. When the phone rang this time, it was Jonas Beijer. He sounded agitated.

*

Rekke was in his study, wondering whether they had tapped his phone. He guessed they had, and thought about asking to borrow Mrs Hansson's phone. No, he didn't want to get her mixed up in this. Instead he looked at the autopsy photos again, at the almost imperceptible lines on Kabir's hands and fingertips. Could he be right? He thought so – so he sent an email to Viktor Malikov in Moscow:

How are you getting on these days?

He received a reply immediately – as if Viktor had been sitting by the computer waiting.

What does one say to a man who sees through all phrases and is regarded as capable of uncovering the Devil himself?

He wrote back, his own prose a little strained too:

One merely provides him with a few doctored facts. He is easily pleased.

Viktor was again quick to answer.

I begin to regret returning to the fatherland. Doesn't look like it's going to be much of a democracy this time around either. But I have remarried – a ballerina – have four children, and I no longer play very often, except when I must while teaching. However, I am not excessively bitter. I read a lot and drink a lot, and naturally I am in constant pain in various places. But on occasion I do find that I miss you. I heard a whisper that you lost your job.

I think the job is still there, he replied. *But they kicked me out of the country and gagged me.*

Oh dear. What happened?

Can I call? he wrote.

You most certainly should.

Rekke was quiet for a while, wondering whether to send a message to the CIA as part of their discussion if they were indeed tapping his phone. But eventually he dialled and took a deep breath as he prepared to put on a little social theatre.

Not that Viktor wasn't aware of his depressive self, but it usually helped if he adjusted to Viktor's boisterous charm.

"It's wonderful to hear your voice," Viktor said. "But what are you telling me? They kicked you out of America?"

"It's not all bad," he said. "I'm getting by. I just struggle to keep my mouth shut on occasion."

"I know, old friend. I know."

"Do you remember when we tried to guess which instruments musicians played?"

"I do," Viktor said.

"I have returned to the discipline. But first I require a little information."

"Speak, speak. I am at once intrigued."

Rekke took a deep breath and said:

"I want to learn more about the Afghan musicians who studied within the Soviet education system during the 1980s. I am seeking a man who later called himself Jamal Kabir. But it may be easier if we begin with a woman who I guess the older among you will remember. Sasha Belinsky will almost certainly remember her."

"Sasha is going gaga."

"With a little luck, you may still be able to get the memories out of him. The woman studied at the conservatory from 1985 to 1988. Highly gifted. Somewhat dramatically predisposed. Knew her value and provoked strong emotions, I would imagine. She was called Latifa Sarwani and she came from Kabul."

"What happened to her?"

"She was shot in the back of the head in Kabul on April 4, 1997, at a time when musicians were being persecuted and subjected to serious harassment by the Taliban regime."

"My God, I should have known you would bring me a detective story. Wasn't that always what you did?" Viktor said.

Rekke smiled reluctantly.

"I may have done. But I would like to know as much as possible about her and would like to identify those associated with her from her home country."

"Are you looking for anyone in particular?"

"Isn't one always in a detective story?"

"Of course."

"It's a man, as I said, very young at the time, the same age as Sarwani or a little younger, sharp features, dark hair, powerful build, fairly short. I'll send some photos and a brief description, but I have no name. At least not one I believe to be genuine."

"What did he play?"

"He played . . ." he began, before deciding to wait. "I'm not sure."

"That doesn't sound like my Rekke."

"Your Rekke is gone."

"I can't imagine that."

"You're too kind, Viktor. But I believe this man had serious ambitions to become a conductor."

"A star too?"

"I'm not so sure. Rather, I see something grandiose in him, and signs of self-aggrandisement. But perhaps I should be careful in what I say."

"For goodness' sake don't be. Please, speculate as much as you like. That was always such a riot with you."

Rekke smiled again and felt a sudden desire to reel off his theories. But he resisted the temptation.

"I haven't got enough to go on," he said. "Dare I hope that you'll hurry?"

"I'll do my best. You've brought colour to my day."

Afterwards, when they had rung off, Rekke closed the autopsy photos and wondered whether he should search the apartment to see if there were some pills hiding anywhere. If not, he would have to call his old pusher, Freddie.

Had Kabir been a classical musician too? Micaela's words had sounded crazy at first. But then the idea had taken hold and Jonas Beijer had become increasingly uncertain. Small things began to come back to him, small things he hadn't reflected upon, but which now appeared in a different light.

This included the interview with Emma Gulwal, the clarinettist. He had questioned her personally in Berlin and remembered how she had initially received him with hostility. That had passed quickly. He had interpreted it as the discomfort many felt speaking to the police.

The evening he wanted information about, the evening when she had been visited by three representatives of the religious police in Kabul, had been March 24, 1997, quite late. Her two children had been in bed for hours, she said. The atmosphere in the city was increasingly turbulent, and she had jumped with fright when they stormed in. She had been relieved, however, when she'd seen that one of them was Kabir. Jonas asked why. She had heard good things about Kabir, so she claimed. He was a more moderate force; he was involved in football. He made beautiful things too. So she had almost immediately produced her clarinet from the wardrobe and given it to him "so that they didn't have to turn the whole house upside down".

"I was hardly in a position to play, and he promised to take care of it," she had said, and it sounded logical, Jonas thought.

It was the kind of atmosphere that made people do whatever it took to avoid harm to themselves or being taken away, and at first, she said, things had looked hopeful. Kabir had caressed the clarinet and raised it up, "almost as if he wanted to play it". Then he had transformed in a second. His eyes had darkened and he had smashed the instrument against the door frame "as if he wanted to avenge his whole life". Those were the words that now came back to Jonas. It was those words that made him call Micaela as soon as he was back home on Swedenborgsgatan and had locked himself in the bedroom so that he didn't have to deal with Linda and the boys.

"How are you feeling?" he said.

"Good," she said. "Have you got something to tell me?"

"Not yet," he said. "But don't worry, I won't stop until I've got you back on the team. What I wanted to say is . . . bloody hell . . . I'm almost ashamed to say it."

"What are you ashamed about?"

"We haven't covered ourselves in glory. Sometimes I wonder whether we've allowed ourselves to be demoralised."

"How do you mean?"

He felt an inner resistance, but also a compulsive need to put it into words.

"We felt it the whole time, ever since we released Costa, that the top brass weren't prioritising the investigation, and we let that affect us. Perhaps it was also because they were so slow over there, and the Americans who were meant to help us never really gave us anything that was much use. Somehow it felt good not to have to grapple with all that."

"But what was it you wanted to say?"

"Perhaps you have a point about Kabir's possible background in music."

He sensed her interest pick up.

"Why do you say that?"

"Because I've started to think that Emma Gulwal had known Kabir for a long time, and because he behaved strangely with her clarinet."

He told her what Emma had said, and there was a small silence before Micaela said:

"Why would she keep quiet about knowing him before?"

"I don't know," he said. "I don't know. Why don't we get that beer right now and talk about it?"

"I've got too much of a headache," she said, and while he knew it was probably the truth, he took it personally.

Afterwards, he sat down with the investigation file and read until half past one in the morning.

*

It was a sleepless night. Rekke had expected nothing else. But he felt strengthened by having survived the witching hour, even if he had long known that the first day of abstinence was nothing. Only on the seventh or eighth day would the full storm descend. But he tried not to think about that. He went out running on Djurgården, and returned home such a wreck that he barely felt the anxious tremors in his body. Instead, he crouched in the shower, panting. Afterwards, he dressed in a pale-blue shirt and grey suit, and sat down in his study to check his email. Viktor had sent him something at 2.48 in the morning, photographs it seemed, and an exhortation to call *as soon as possible, but only after nine and once I've had some coffee because I've been drinking wine and vodka all bloody night for your sake.*

Rekke checked his wristwatch and added an hour. It was twenty past eight in Moscow – almost nine, in other words. He dialled and after five rings was met with a grunt.

"What is it?" Viktor asked in Russian.

"You wake up and I'll look through your pictures for the time being," he said, peering at what he had received.

They were mostly portraits of third-year students at the Moscow Conservatory in the autumn of 1987, and it didn't take long for him to find Latifa. She stared at him from the second row up, on the right-hand side, and looked more or less as he had become accustomed to seeing her: beautiful and proud, with disproportionately large eyes and a gaze that offered no apology. But perhaps – he looked more closely – there was also something there that he hadn't seen in the childhood photos from Kabul. A sidelong and slightly anxious air that made her harder to read.

"*Gospodi!* Is it already nine o'clock?" Viktor said.

"By and large, yes. Who were you drinking with?"

"Belinsky. He's still got it. He may be half-senile at times, but he drinks like there's no tomorrow. He claims to have conducted you when you played Ravel in Bern."

"Oh, what awful memories, although without Sasha I wouldn't have survived. Did you come up with anything?"

"Far too much. Belinsky wouldn't stop talking about your violinist. Sounds as though he was in love with her. Hugely gifted, he said. Often went at it so hard she almost cracked up, and bordering on pretentious. But sometimes it was as if time stopped, he said. Belinsky teared up when he spoke about her. 'They shot the best of all my pupils,' he said. 'What does that say about our time?'"

"One does wonder."

"Played like an angel, he said. Mostly Brahms, Sibelius, Paganini. Rehearsed constantly. But she wasn't some good little girl, for all that. She had one hell of a temper. Slammed doors and started rows. She was always the centre of attention, he said, and there was always gossip about her – a lot of shit. People were jealous, thought she was a diva and overrated. There are cynics who say it's no surprise she was shot dead. Belinsky himself can't comprehend how anyone – even the Taliban – could silence her. He thought she would overcome everything."

"Did you find any other Afghan musicians in her circle?"

"Go up three rows in the photo and a little to the right. There's one Darman Dirani. Do you see him?"

Rekke saw him. A young man – perhaps nineteen or twenty – with dark, curly hair, small eyes, a big, crooked nose and something bashful in his gaze. The man wore a black shirt buttoned up to the neck and round spectacles.

"Darman was a compatriot and the same age. Another violinist," Viktor said. "He and Latifa arrived at the conservatory at the same time and had been close friends since their early teens. They had the same teacher in Kabul, and may have been a couple at one time – I don't know for sure. But Darman can't have had an easy time of it. Look at the other photo I sent you, from their string quartet. Can you see the way he's looking at her? Admiringly, right? But also uncertainly, almost self-effacing. Darman loved her with all his heart, and Latifa loved him – not quite as much."

"Is he alive?"

"He lives in Cologne these days."

"In Cologne," Rekke muttered.

"Yes. He's a second violinist in the Gürzenich Orchestra. I'm convinced he'd be worth speaking to. Apparently he always had his eye on her. Always followed her with his gaze. But here's what's really interesting."

Rekke looked again at the class photo of Latifa and tried to understand what had changed about her. It was, he thought, as if something had already been taken from her.

"Was she unwell?" he said.

Viktor, who had been about to say something else, struggled to adjust.

"What? Yes, exactly . . . there were early suspicions of epilepsy, it seems. She had a seizure while playing in a masterclass. But what I was going to say was that Latifa and Darman Dirani came from a college in Kabul with the somewhat awkward name of Soviet–Afghan Friendship University for Classical Music," he said. "The college was run by Elena Drugov. Do you know of her?"

"Not at all."

"No, and why would you? She was a former cellist and conductor from Novosibirsk. But above all she was a missionary, an impassioned soul. I don't think the party even had to give the order to her to go to Kabul. She went of her own accord and set up her school. But you may understand the thinking. The war was to be won not only with weapons, but also through culture and Marxism–Leninism. The school was never that popular – nothing Soviet was popular in Kabul – but still a surprising number of pupils attended, including from abroad – possibly committed communists. Most of them, though, were young people who just wanted the chance to play Western composers and develop as musicians. In a fairly short time, the school managed to gain a good reputation and it was known that Elena had a healthy budget for stipends. She could send her best students to the USSR, usually to us at the conservatory. No-one else had the opportunities that Latifa and Darman did, but many – well, quite a lot – were given the chance to play for a briefer period and benefit from qualified teaching in Moscow. This is where it gets a little weird."

"In what way?"

"Several of those scholarship recipients later disappeared during the Taliban regime. One of them, Latifa, was found shot dead in her home. But others seemed to vanish into thin air, never to be seen again."

"Interesting," he said.

"Of course, they were at risk," Viktor said. "They had been in league with the Soviets. They were practitioners of something that had been banned by the regime and was associated with the West. But I still think it seems suspicious. Musicians were persecuted in Afghanistan – I've read up a bit about that. Their instruments were smashed, and they were harassed, whipped. Sometimes they were even killed."

"But it wasn't common."

"No, and there are too many of them from Elena Drugov's school. It's statistically troubling, in my view."

Rekke fell silent and digested what he'd heard. Mrs Hansson was standing a little nervously nearby, as if she wanted to say something. A jolt in his chest made its way into his heart. He thought about Latifa Sarwani and managed to forget about Mrs Hansson, who left self-consciously.

"These Kabuli scholarship students," he said. "Is there a list of them?"

"I have the names."

"Very good. You're a rock, Viktor. Is Elena Drugov still alive?"

"She died of cancer in August 2001. But towards the end of her life, she is said to have worried that someone meant to harm her old pupils."

"That's interesting. And that picture I sent of the football referee – no-one recognised him?" he said.

"Ah, yes . . . I forgot to say. Belinsky took the photo home last night. He said it made him dizzy."

"Because the man seemed familiar?"

"I'm not sure we should take it that way. All he said was there was something odd about the picture. But perhaps it was because of the peculiar costume the guy was wearing."

"Do tell Sasha that I think the guy played the viola. It might help him to remember," Rekke said.

Viktor laughed.

"So you've worked out what he played after all. I knew it."

"I did a couple of minor studies, but I'm not certain."

"Aren't you breathing a little heavily, by the by?"

"I shouldn't think so. But you've done a splendid job, Viktor. I'll be in touch soon."

"Surely you're not hanging up already? We've barely said hello."

"I'm hanging up. Sleep it off and we'll talk later," Rekke said, ending the call.

He was struggling not to pant. His body was also shuddering, as if it had received a shock, and he muttered to himself: "What is this nonsense? Some kind of self-torment?"

He phoned Freddie Nilsson – he didn't have time for bloody cold turkey – but there was no answer. Mrs Hansson came into the room again and said that Micaela was on her way, so he decided to postpone his relapse for a little while.

He scrutinised the class photo of Latifa again. He was finding it hard to focus, but eventually he saw what had bothered him earlier. It was Latifa's left eye: something there had shone once but did so no longer.

Micaela slept for ten hours and woke at eight o'clock on Tuesday with a feeling of release. Outside, a timely spring rain was falling, and she lay on her back with her hands on her stomach while the preceding evening returned to her. Then she understood why the morning felt hopeful.

The headache was gone and they had taken another step forward in the murder inquiry. It was as if she had regained what she had lost, and she wondered what to do. Should she call Vanessa and scold her for running her mouth? No, she thought, it didn't much matter if Lucas knew who she had met. And it could have been someone from the police who had leaked it. Instead she allowed her thoughts to wander. She was reminded of what Jonas Beijer had said about Emma Gulwal: that Kabir had caressed her clarinet lovingly, "almost as if he wanted to play it", but that a moment later he had gone mad and smashed it against a door frame "as if he wanted to avenge his whole life".

It didn't have to mean a thing. But it didn't contradict the idea that Kabir had been a classical musician. She got up, went to the bathroom and listened to the notes chiming in her head. It was the adagio from the Bruch piece, and she hummed to herself as she pondered whether she really would get back onto the investigation. She would just have to wait and see. But in any event, she wanted to work on the murder today. She examined the bruising in the mirror. It felt better but didn't look good, and that was for the best, she thought to herself. Before she had time to hesitate and feel dutiful, she called in sick.

"I feel like crap," she said.

Her boss didn't skip a beat. He said: "Yes, my God, I can understand why," which was exactly what a skiving police officer wanted to hear. Afterwards, she glowered at herself in the mirror and wondered: What does Rekke think of me? How does he see me? Who am I to him?

The questions didn't do her much good. They simply made her find fault with herself. She tried brushing her fringe back and leaving her forehead clear like everyone said she should, and it was better – she admitted that. But she didn't intend to humour them. She really needed to get a haircut. Her hair came down to her shoulders and her eyes looked . . . how to put it? . . . too serious. She pretended to laugh, and acted as if she were a model, striking a few idiotic poses. Fortunately, she was interrupted by her phone ringing. It was Mrs Hansson, apologetic about disturbing her.

"What's happened?" Micaela asked.

"He's thrown out his pills and not slept a wink. I heard him wandering around all night up there."

"Was that such a good idea?" she said.

"Of course it wasn't. He'll probably have the most awful withdrawal symptoms. But it still suggests a little progress. You've worked wonders with him, Micaela. Won't you come here before he manages to get up to any more mischief?"

"Hmm," she said.

"Please?"

"I'm on my way," she said.

She still delayed her departure. She tried on one outfit after another, even high heels, although she settled for her customary jeans, hoodie and trainers, with no more and no less make-up than usual. But for the first time since Saturday, she felt a spring in her step. She ran down the stairs. Which was why she didn't hear the familiar footsteps on the floor below.

Charles Bruckner was sitting in his diplomatic car on Grevgatan. He was pretty sure they were going to take Rekke down again. There was no doubt that the professor was a risk factor. They should head up there right away and grab him. But . . . Charles wanted to keep a cool head and see whether he could establish further grounds for such a move. As ever, he had to wait for the right moment.

Sometimes Charles missed his old life. He hadn't been involved in a major operation since they gunned down Gamal Zakaria in Copenhagen, after Hassan Barozai – or Kabir as he usually called him – had come through with information, proving that it hadn't been a mistake to let him go.

Well, Charles had never really thought it was. Only amid the current excitement had he started to have doubts. In the scheme of things, it was nothing unusual: they had released a small crook to get to a bigger one. It was the logic of war. Granted, they didn't know for sure what Kabir had got up to in Kabul. They hadn't managed to break him completely during interrogation. There were question marks and concerns, because no-one – least of all the Swedish foreign ministry – wanted to be seen to have let a murderer and terrorist into the country.

That wouldn't look good, especially not with thunder rumbling on the horizon. Both CBS and *The New Yorker* were about to publish compromising details. Nothing new, not really. The AP had published a long article in November the year before, but still . . . it was troubling. There would be photographs of Arabs with hoods over their heads and electrodes attached to their bodies, of naked men on leads or tied up in unnatural positions, sometimes with faeces on their bodies, sometimes lying naked in heaps on top of each other while American soldiers stood beside them, grinning and with their thumbs up for the camera. It would do damage, no doubt about that.

But still . . . it could be blamed on a few bad apples. None of it had been ordered from on high. These were deviations and those responsible would be punished. Nothing was said about the overarching strategy, which meant it would be devastating if information now emerged about the Salt Pit. The phone rang. It was Henry Lamar at the embassy.

"How's it going?" Henry said.

"Rekke is expecting a female visitor," Charles said. "Someone named Micaela; we're looking into who she is. They're going to discuss the violinist, Sarwani, who was shot in Kabul in April 1997. Rekke has been searching for information about her."

"Did Kabir have anything to do with her?" Henry said.

"I hope not," Charles said. "But . . ." He stared up the length of Grevgatan. "Can I call you back? I see something."

He saw a young woman on the pavement on the opposite side of the street. She might very well be Micaela. The voice that had spoken on Sigrid Hansson's mobile had sounded young and a little uncertain, and the girl over there was barely thirty and a Latina. She might not be beautiful, but her restless black eyes were interesting. She had a large bruise on her cheek and there was something guarded and intense in her demeanour.

Beside her was a slightly older man, similar in appearance – possibly a relative: dark, temperamental-looking, with a scar running down his forehead. A criminal, Charles thought. A high-ranking criminal. He felt a twinge of anxiety when he saw her reaction to his car and realised they must be on their way to Rekke's. There was something simultaneously professional and nervous about her expression, as if she knew exactly what he was up to.

He pulled out his phone and called Henry Lamar, telling him he had to identify this Micaela right away and put eyes on her. But he didn't get any further than that, because he realised something was brewing between the man and the woman. They looked tense. He got the feeling that the situation was about to explode.

TWENTY-SEVEN

For a man like Rekke, there were many pitfalls in a murder investigation. One was that a clue might interest him too much, not because it was important to the solution but because it awakened something within him, and at times he wondered whether that was the case with Latifa Sarwani.

He was increasingly convinced that her murder and Kabir's were connected. He had made several small observations during the night that had persuaded him. What was more, Viktor had given him a piece of the jigsaw, nothing remarkable in itself, but nevertheless . . . He was examining a recent photo of Darman Dirani, Latifa's close friend at the Moscow Conservatory. Dirani looked more distinguished than he had in his youth. He was now thirty-nine years old, and none of that bashful uncertainty remained in his eyes. Instead he looked proud and a little conceited. Unlike Latifa Sarwani, he had completed his education and made his way to Europe, which had been a wise move.

While the oxygen had slowly been removed from Latifa's life in Kabul, Dirani had built a career in Europe and was now a second violinist in the Gürzenich Orchestra in Cologne, which was no small achievement. But would Rekke be up to talking to him? The prospect didn't appeal – nothing appealed – but he couldn't give in now. So he took a deep breath and dialled the number. After two or three rings, a broken-sounding voice, a little wheezy, answered.

"Darman Dirani."

"I hope I'm not bothering you," he said in German. "My name is Hans Rekke."

"The pianist?"

"That was some time ago."

"It's still an honour. Why did you stop?"

"I wasn't in the right frame of mind for it towards the end, and there was the matter of a small incident that befell me in Helsinki."

"I remember hearing something about that."

"Most gratifying to be remembered. But nowadays I am a psychologist and am sometimes engaged as a consultant in criminal investigations. For example, I worked on the murder investigation of a countryman of yours, Jamal Kabir, in Stockholm."

"Is that so?" Dirani said, now more reserved.

"You may have heard about the murder?"

"Yes, in passing."

"That's splendid," Rekke said. "But what really interests me is the Taliban's war on music. It affected many people you knew, did it not?"

"Yes, it did."

"You former pupils of Professor Drugov's college seem to have fared particularly badly, I believe?"

"We weren't just seen as musicians. We were regarded as traitors to our country and blasphemous opponents to Islam."

Rekke fell silent and pretended to consider this.

"And no-one met with a more terrible demise than your friend Latifa?"

"No," he said. "It was indescribable."

Rekke changed tack.

"It's difficult, isn't it – from our Western vantage point – to understand the Taliban? The desire to destroy what is such a joy to others? But still . . . many of those young men received no education other than in madrasas that taught literal Islam and a nostalgia for the seventh century.

They hardly took the time to get to know their enemy, to understand what they wanted to crush with their holy rage."

"No," Dirani said. "They were barbarians."

"But the person Latifa admitted to her home on the night of April 3, 1997, seems, on the contrary, to have been intimate with her world."

"Why do you say that?"

"She showed the murderer her violin, which she and her father had carefully hidden in the basement."

"Could it not have been under duress?"

"Absolutely," said Rekke. "But she also appears to have played for the killer. Not only do the positions of the violin and her body suggest that she was holding the instrument when she was shot, but I read last night on Al Jazeera that violin music was heard coming from the house that night. A neighbour described it as beautiful and melancholy, and I know, I know, Sarwani may have played under duress. But nevertheless . . . the murderer wanted to hear it. He took that risk, so he must have been interested. Perhaps he even longed to hear it."

"So what are you getting at?"

"That perhaps it was more than just religious fanaticism that killed Latifa Sarwani, perhaps it was also . . ."

He paused deliberately. At the same time, a shiver passed through his body.

"What?" Dirani said.

"I thought you might be able to help me there. It feels like the killer may have been someone with knowledge of your old school."

"It's possible, of course."

"But you don't have any suggestions?"

"Suggestions about what?"

"People from your circle who might have been capable of something like this."

Dirani took offence at that.

"No, definitely not. If I had, I would have said so long ago."

Rekke shivered again. Should he go down to the bin store and see whether his pills were still down there? Only with great effort did he manage to say:

"You and Latifa were close, were you not?"

"In the eighties, yes."

"But not later on?"

"We tried to stay in touch, but it was hard given the distance. For a time, some friends and I were working to try to get her out of the country. But in the end it was as if she no longer wanted to leave. She was very depressed and unwell in the final years."

"That's sad to hear. I saw that she had married."

"It was a forced marriage. It was impossible to be a single woman under the Taliban. But her father paid the man to stay away."

"So who was closest to her in her final years?"

"Her father and her brother Taisir, although she and Taisir had their disagreements."

"What kind of disagreements?"

"Taisir was more conservative than his father, and never took to this arrangement with her marriage."

"He must have been in her shadow all his life."

"I should think so."

"Who else did Latifa see?"

"Not many people. She remained isolated and would stay in bed, at least in the final period. She lost weight and her hair fell out. She was in a very bad way."

"It must have been a considerable risk keeping the violin hidden in the house," Rekke said.

"Where else would she have kept it?" Dirani said. "It was the most valuable possession the family had."

"A Gagliano, I believe?"

"Yes, made by Nicolò Gagliano in the late eighteenth century."

"And it was hidden under two planks of wood in the basement?"

"Mohammad, her father, would occasionally retrieve it and maintain it. But otherwise they kept it hidden in the cellar. They told everyone they had sold it in Europe."

Rekke got up to take yet another pointless tour of the apartment to see whether any morphine tablets might appear in some hidey-hole.

"I looked at the photograph of Latifa's body," he said.

"Oh, really?"

"And I wondered who took that picture," he said, while turning over the cushions on the living room sofa to see whether any pills had fallen between them. "It didn't seem to be part of a crime scene investigation."

"Mohammad, her father, took it – despite being in shock. He realised the Taliban wouldn't do much to solve the crime. He wanted to document it."

Rekke returned to his bedroom.

"To secure evidence?"

"He wanted justice."

Rekke bent down and looked under the bed. Surely that must be something . . . for Christ's sake, no, it was a raisin. How had a raisin ended up there?

"Of course," he said. "Did you love Latifa?"

The question seemed to take Dirani by surprise.

"We all loved her in one way or another," he said. "I know there aren't many recordings of her left, but you should have heard her. The way she played made you want to offer thanks to Allah."

"But she could be hard work too, couldn't she? Demanding, sure of her talent, a classic soloist?"

"She was easy to forgive."

"So you don't think she might have formed enemies as a result of her personality?"

"I suppose it's possible."

"But then again, there's no-one particular you have in mind, no-one you encountered during your education?"

"I've thought about that a great deal, but as I said, no . . . no-one who could have taken it this far."

"You said that you all loved her in one way or another?"

"She had that gift."

"Perhaps it was the other way around then: that one of the people who loved her killed her."

"I have difficulty believing that."

"Yet it's not completely illogical, is it?"

"How do you mean?"

"It takes great passion to want to destroy. Do you share that view?"

"It can."

"But more than anything, all those of you who loved her must have wanted to know who killed her."

"Of course."

"And what did you conclude?"

"Only that the person ultimately responsible must have been Mullah Zakaria. He was the one who whipped up hatred of musicians, and of women like her. Sometimes he didn't even have to use his own forces. He got people to take the law into their own hands."

"So there was no doubt about the threat?"

"No."

"And yet . . ."

"What?"

"Latifa was left alone that last night."

"She was sick of having her father and brother constantly in the house. She wanted her own life."

"Perhaps she wanted to be alone with someone else on that particular night?"

"I doubt it. She was in complete isolation towards the end."

Rekke spoke as calmly as he could.

"But there's something you're not saying, isn't there?"

Dirani was quiet.

"How do you mean?" he said.

"I mean that I hear the silences."

"You can hear them?"

"It's a different kind of musicality, I suppose," Rekke said. "But then I think about the coincidences in the account."

"Which coincidences?"

"You and Latifa's brother now live in the same city."

Dirani let out an insulted sigh.

"When you are in exile, you stay close to your countrymen."

"Did Latifa damage her optic nerve in Moscow?" Rekke said.

Dirani seemed surprised.

"How could you know that?"

"An eye that is no longer as strong is visible. It's a bit like a mirror no-one looks at."

"Really?" Dirani said uncertainly. "But yes . . . Latifa had an epileptic seizure in her final year in the USSR, and hit the back of her head. It was one of the reasons why she didn't complete her training, even though Professor Belinsky could have made arrangements."

Rekke looked at his inbox and saw that he had received a new email from Viktor in Moscow. It appeared to be a list. He sent it to the printer.

"One more thing," he said. "There were other students from Kabul who came to the conservatory too, so I heard. Pupils on shorter scholarships."

"Yes. I often felt sorry for them."

"How so?"

"They received very little guidance and were rarely up to scratch. They were just part of the political game."

"I have a list of six of them here – six young Afghans who came to the conservatory for a brief period while you were there. Would you mind looking at the names and seeing what you remember?"

"I suppose I could. But now I need to dash. I've got rehearsals."

"What are you rehearsing?" Rekke said.

"Dvořák."

"Ninth symphony?"

"Exactly, pandering to the audience, I suppose."

"Not at all. There's a fantastic molto vivace. Well, I'm sure we'll be in touch again."

"Perhaps," said Darman Dirani, as Rekke was struck by a sudden desire to reacquaint himself with Cologne.

Micaela wasn't surprised to see Lucas by the main door – he had visited her before in the mornings without any reason. He just wants to see how I'm feeling, she tried to persuade herself.

"Hi," she said, examining his face.

She didn't like his smile or his gait. He was tense and his shirt was too tight across his chest. His eyes seemed cold, or at least calculating, and the scar slicing down his forehead was more mobile than usual, as if it had come alive. Something was definitely up. Regardless, she pretended to be pleasantly surprised.

"It's nice to be visited," she said.

"Nice as anything," he said.

She was already late, she said. She needed to rush.

"Are you going to work?" he asked, and, idiot that she was, she hesitated for a second too long.

"I'm off to town."

"Then I'll tag along," he said, and together they hurried out of the rain and into the Tunnelbana station.

As always at that time of day, two worlds collided down there: those who lived in Kista and were setting out, and those who were stumbling off the trains on their way to their blue-chip tech jobs in Science City. The ones going somewhere, and the ones who had been left behind, as Micaela had once dramatically put it. Lucas drew her in to him. She couldn't read him. He smelled of aftershave.

"I think Mamá's started painting again," she said.

He wasn't interested. Instead he commented on her appearance as they got onto the train, adding: "Are you wearing perfume?"

She shook her head.

"I think it's your eau de cologne – it's strong enough for the two of us," she said.

He didn't seem to like the comment.

"What do you want?" she said.

"You going to Östermalm again?"

"Yup."

"I don't think he's good for you," he said, and she racked her brains in the hope that he might mean anyone other than Rekke.

"What do you mean?" she said.

"I think he's getting you to go through a lot of shit that's not good for you."

She felt a wave of resentment.

"I can go through whatever I like."

He took her by the wrists.

"You've got to understand how it looks to me. You meet some rich bloke in Östermalm and come back black and blue."

"That had nothing to do with him," she said, withdrawing her hand.

After that, they sat in silence in their seats. When the train pulled into the central station where she was meant to change onto the Ropsten service, she wondered whether to wait until the very last moment before getting off. But she decided to calm the atmosphere, so she thanked him for his consideration and promised to be careful. She got up and so did he. *Leave me alone!* was what she wanted to hiss, but she said nothing.

"I just care about you," Lucas said.

"I know. But can't we meet up later instead?"

"I'll come a bit further with you," he said, which was why they got onto another Tunnelbana train together.

His eyes were kinder now, more relaxed, and it was only when they got off the train and walked down towards Strandvägen from Karlaplan that she really got worried.

"Thanks," she said. "I can manage from here."

"Of course you can," he said, but he made no effort to leave her, and she was overcome by an impulse to shove him. Instead, she thought to herself: He'll never come with me the whole way. He's not that stupid. But he displayed no signs of leaving, and on Riddargatan, around where he'd picked her up last time, she decided to change direction and lead him away from Rekke. Of course, there was no fooling him.

"Doesn't he live on Grevgatan?" he said in an ominous voice, and she realised that Lucas had checked Rekke out, or at least knew his address.

"You need to get out of here now," she said. "You can't do this to me."

"I'll come with you to the door," he said, and she thought: Fine, but not a step further.

They walked down the length of Grevgatan and it was then that she spotted the diplomatic car with its tinted windows and started. Of course Lucas noticed.

"You seem tense," he said.

"I'm tense because you're meddling."

Lucas shook his head as if he didn't believe her, looked at the diplomatic car and said he would come up to say hello.

"Over my dead body you will," she said, tempted to slap him.

But that would have been madness. Instead, entering into an alternative reality, she thought, It'll be fine. Perhaps Lucas will even be impressed. He definitely won't want to stay. He'll feel lost up there with all the books and paintings. Together they went inside, and as she stood in the lift with her brother, she had a feeling that something was about to go very awry.

TWENTY-EIGHT

"I'm sorry," she said in the doorway. "But my brother wanted to say hello."

Rekke was clutching a piece of paper and seemed lost in himself. But he smiled the moment he spotted Lucas and proffered his hand.

"What a delight," he said. "Do come in. I'm Hans Rekke."

There was warmth in his voice, the wretched naturalness of the upper classes, she thought, and of course Lucas took it well. He was also a professional when it came to greetings: he introduced himself and looked through the door into the apartment with curiosity, uttering some nonchalant phrases, as if he was always visiting homes like this.

"What a pleasure to become acquainted with other members of the family," Rekke said. "May I offer you breakfast? Personally, I'm as hungry as a wolf."

"I'm not staying. I just wanted to say that Micaela is important to me. If anything happens to her . . ."

He trailed off and for a brief moment Micaela thought she recognised his body language from the woods in Husby, and she was afraid that he would do something violent – that he might even draw a weapon.

"Quite, quite," Rekke said. "I do understand. There are three of you siblings, are there not? And you are the eldest? Growing up, you were the man of the house and took care of your little sister?"

"I still take care of her."

Rekke took a step closer, and although he was still smiling, his body language had changed. He seemed alert. His arms were tensed.

"Of course, that's as it should be," he said. "But on the other hand, you take care of others too, don't you? You're a man of responsibility."

"Maybe," Lucas said.

"Don't be shy. You have authority – it is a valuable and sometimes hazardous gift."

"I do what I must."

"I don't doubt that," Rekke said, staring sternly into his eyes, the ghost of a smile still present on his lips. "I'm impressed."

"By what?"

"Your ability to speak without words."

"I just thought it'd be a good idea for us to meet," Lucas said.

"It was a pleasure. But surely you aren't leaving already?"

Lucas looked around again, then cast a hasty, stern look at Micaela.

"You seem to have got the message, Professor."

"It has been received. I do hope we meet again," Rekke said with a broad smile. He shivered once more.

Something flared up and died down just as quickly. But perhaps it was nothing, because the next moment they shook hands and Rekke offered to accompany Lucas to the lift. He was gone longer than he should have been, and it was only when he returned that Micaela realised how nervous she had been. It was as if she wanted to collapse into bed or onto the sofa, and she took a deep breath while Rekke scrutinised her. *Don't look at me like that*, she wanted to scream.

Instead she said:

"Lucas can seem cocky, but he's OK. He's just looking out for me."

Rekke continued to look at her with concentration.

"He's exciting," he said. "But your pupils are constricted."

"Wh-what?"

"May I feel your hand?"

"Absolutely not," she said, heading into the living room, where she flopped onto the sofa by the grand piano and closed her eyes.

She heard Rekke sit down opposite her, and she was tempted to say more – first and foremost to explain why she had ended up bringing Lucas to the apartment. But she didn't have time to say anything. There was a knock at the door and Mrs Hansson stepped in, saying she didn't want to disturb them. It was possible that Micaela just had the jitters, but she couldn't help wondering whether Mrs Hansson had bumped into Lucas downstairs and been worried.

"I thought I'd have a drink," Rekke said. "Would you care to join me?"

Micaela looked at him with incomprehension.

"Didn't we just discuss breakfast?"

"True," he said. "I must apologise. My withdrawal symptoms distort the temporal dimension."

She looked at him suspiciously.

"Or perhaps you think it's me who needs a drink?" she said.

"I think . . ." he said, but didn't finish his sentence, and that was just as well, because she reluctantly admitted he had a point. She desperately wanted some alcohol, no matter how far below the yardarm the sun remained.

"Do you have beer?" she said.

"I've got a couple of Heinekens, unless my awful brother drank them."

"That'll do."

"Sigrid, my dear, I apologise for running you ragged, but would you fetch a couple of cold pilsners for Micaela and me?"

Micaela couldn't understand why he didn't fetch the beers himself if he felt obliged to apologise for his request.

Don't be so quick to make a diagnosis, Rekke thought to himself. You've allowed yourself to be deceived before. But there in the brother's dark eyes he thought he had seen narcissism, psychopathy, Machiavellianism. The dark triad in full. He felt as though he'd glimpsed a pure and black wickedness, a pit of ice-cold calculations, and somewhere deep down he knew: Micaela had seen the same thing and lived with it, but didn't dare admit it.

He remembered when he had seen her for the first time in Djursholm. His eyes had been drawn to her. It was as if she shouldered a heavy burden, but also as if that burden hadn't broken her but on the contrary had made her strong, as if she had drawn strength from the trauma. There was something oddly attractive about it, he thought. A kind of antithesis to his own flight into depression.

"How are you feeling?"

She had almost finished her beer.

"Good."

He guessed she always said that.

"How about you?" she asked.

"The way I deserve to feel, I suppose. But I think our investigation is becoming increasingly interesting."

She leaned forward.

"So you still believe he was a classical musician?"

"Yes. And I believe the murders of Latifa Sarwani and Kabir are connected."

She looked at him in concentration and once again he was drawn to the darkness in her eyes and to the restrained power in her body. *You know your brother is deadly*, he wanted to say. But he kept quiet.

Instead, he recounted his conversations with Viktor and Darman Dirani. Afterwards they sat in silence, finishing their beer.

"Do you think Kabir and Sarwani might have played together?" she said.

"I would say it's not improbable."

"Is there something new you've spotted?"

He nodded and glanced over to the grand.

"I've studied his hands," he said. He pictured Kabir's fingertips before him. "There was dried oil, furrows, small wounds. Indications that he was a motorcycle mechanic – just as he said."

"That doesn't exactly sound like a conductor in tails and cufflinks."

"No," he said. "But the interesting thing is that there were traces of something else. When I scrutinised his fingertips, I discerned pale scratches running diagonally to the papillae."

"What do you think that means?"

"I took it to mean that those fingers had been pressed against strings for such a long time that scars had formed."

"What kind of strings?"

"My initial thought was those of a violin," he said. "I've seen those kinds of lines on many violinists. But then I was unsure. I didn't think the scratches were small enough, so I thought of something coarser, such as a cello. But I ruled out the cello too, since I saw – or believed I saw – skin changes following long-term, regular pressure against the neck. Then I began to . . ."

He hesitated and wondered again whether he was right.

"What did you begin to do?" she said.

"I began to think about the *altfiol* – the viola," he said. "For a moment, I believed it all made sense."

"What made sense?"

Her shoulders tensed and her eyes narrowed as if she were expecting some kind of breakthrough, and perhaps that was what it was. If he were right, then Kabir would definitely be traceable.

"The viola is coarser," he said, looking down at his own hands. "The fretboard is larger. The strings are longer, and more separated. It takes more weight and force to play, and that makes it likely that the marks will remain long afterwards. And there's something else, which may be even more speculative, but which seems to fit."

"Which is?"

He felt a wave of anxiety pass through his body. He spoke slowly and hesitantly.

"I believe Kabir suffered a great disappointment or setback."

"He looked melancholy," she said.

"Yes," he said. "But I also sense something revanchist in his speech patterns. While I don't wish to be prejudiced towards the viola – I like the strident, slightly melancholy sound, and I have liked most violists that I have met – it is not an instrument you start out on or dream of playing. There's a stigma there."

"How come?"

He weighed his words, as if afraid that some violist might be eaves-dropping.

"It is an instrument given to those who are destined to be part of the background, playing the accompaniment or second part in string quartets. Most are assigned to it because they don't make the cut as violinists. It is not an instrument that is offered to those who are expected to become stars in the orchestra. Of course, many are satisfied with that, but perhaps not all. The violist is situated far from the conductor and the soloist, and it is also the instrument about which there are the most deprecating jokes."

"Such as?" she said.

He laughed a little sadly.

"I have suppressed most of them. But you know the kind of thing: why don't violists ever play hide and seek?"

"Why?"

"No-one bothers looking for them. Or: what's the difference between a pizza and a viola?"

"What?" she said.

"A pizza can feed a family of four."

He glanced over at the piano again.

"Not that anyone sensible takes those jokes seriously," he said. "But still . . . they're there, they leave their marks somewhere, and I think there may be history with two people such as Latifa and Kabir."

"How do you mean?"

"I mean that a person with that kind of radiance and talent, and a person like Kabir . . ." he said.

"Who wanted to shine but perhaps didn't manage to?"

"Yes, perhaps," he said, before going to fetch more beer from the kitchen.

TWENTY-NINE

October 1987, Building no. 1, 26 Malaya Gruzinskaya Street, Moscow

He woke with tears in his eyes and couldn't understand it. What's wrong with me? he thought. I never cry. But perhaps it wasn't so strange after all. He had been rehearsing day and night until his fingers were tender and calloused, and now he was finally here. It had been a dreadful strain.

In the pre-dawn gloom he could just make out the portraits of Tchaikovsky as a young man on the white walls. He had arrived here late the evening before and staggered into bed. His head ached. He wanted to go back to sleep, but he couldn't.

Tears were flowing. Have I dreamed something strange? he thought. But in that case it hadn't been anything sad, because he was smiling too, as if he were happy, which was why he closed his eyes in the hope of being able to return to the dream. Instead, he became more widely awake and realised that he could hear music. A solitary violin was being played in the distance, and he realised that it had never been a dream. It was the violin that had penetrated his sleep and so confused him.

Forget it, he thought. Go back to sleep and gather your strength. You'll need it. But the notes drew him out of bed. He fumbled for the light switch and put on a pair of trousers and a jumper. Then he crept into the corridor. He got lost straight away. All the doors looked the same and before long he didn't even know whether he had come from the left or the right. He staggered along, drunk on sleep, and eventually he stood before the room from which the music seemed to be emanating, and without knocking he opened the door and entered.

A young woman holding a violin stood next to an unmade bed, her black hair loose, tucked over her right shoulder. Her shoulder blades were moving beneath a thin white top. A forcefield seemed to radiate from her and he was enveloped by the music, which took him back in time to his mother's lullabies over the crib. He gasped. The woman turned around, at first afraid. Then, as if she immediately realised he was harmless, she continued to play, and she was so impossibly beautiful that he barely knew where she ended and the music began.

"Sorry," he mumbled.

"You're crying," she said in English as she stopped playing.

"No, no, absolutely not," he said, as he tried to come up with a good explanation.

But in that moment he realised: she was the one from Kabul. He had never met her before, not in real life. He had only seen pictures and heard stories. She was Professor Drugov's pride and joy.

She was the pride and joy of the whole school, in fact, and now here he was standing before her, lost, with tears in his eyes, and it didn't help that she began to play again and they were alone in her bedroom.

"You might have knocked," she said.

"What were you playing?" he replied in Pashto, still thrown.

She scrutinised him from head to toe.

"The 'Méditation' from Thaïs by Massenet. Did Elena send you here?"

"I remembered . . ." he stammered.

But he barely knew what he had remembered. It was as if he had been sleepwalking and had only now woken up, raw and naked, and when she stood up and offered him her hand, it was too much. He stumbled out of the room, paying no heed to her voice calling after him:

"Wait, wait."

*

273

When Rekke disappeared off towards the kitchen, Micaela remembered the palaeontologist Julia had mentioned, the one who sketched whole lost worlds from just a couple of bone fragments. Wasn't it kind of the same now? On the basis of a couple of scars on a man's fingers, Rekke was pointing her in an entirely new direction. And wasn't that how a criminal investigator worked too? It was in the little things that she was able to make out the big and the unpleasant. Perhaps that was why she had wanted to be a police officer, unless . . . She pictured Lucas, his gaze directed at Rekke. She pushed the thought aside.

Rekke returned and passed her another Heineken, then sat down in his armchair.

"Has your housekeeper left?" she said.

"Yes," he said. "She must feel reassured now that you're here. You've made a good impression."

"We servants have a natural bond."

"Am I such an appalling aristocrat?"

She fell silent and wanted to say: *Yes, my God, you really are. Look at the way you lean back in your armchair.*

"You've had the luxury of being able to be weak," she said.

"That's true, of course."

"Julia said that your family think it's somehow refined."

"I suppose we have made calamity something of a virtue."

"In ours, you had to be strong. Weak was the worst thing you could be. Lucas said that the one thing he couldn't stand was weak people."

Rekke looked troubled.

"That's pretty typical for . . ."

He stopped.

"For what?"

"Nothing," he said.

She looked angrily at him.

"You met Lucas for, like, two seconds, and you think you know something about him."

"You have a point, of course."

She wanted to change the subject.

"There's something I've been wondering," she said. "Emma Gulwal, the clarinettist, said she knew Kabir – but only for his football. Isn't that a little odd? If he really was a violist and the circle of people who played classical Western music in Afghanistan was small, wouldn't she and the other musicians he attacked have known full well who he was?"

"You would think so," he said.

"Perhaps he wasn't from Afghanistan."

He looked at her with his intense gaze.

"He could have been one of the many foreigners drawn to the Taliban movement – one of those who came to Kabul to join the struggle."

"Perhaps it was the war on music in particular that appealed to him," she said.

"Perhaps," he said, draining his beer.

His gaze wavered nervously and he crossed his hands over his chest.

"How are you feeling?" she said.

"The patient is longing for his drugs. But he'll manage."

"Why did you have to chuck all of them out in one go?"

"Out of the same recklessness that made me take them, I should think."

"You said you believed Darman Dirani was holding something back when you spoke on the phone?"

Rekke looked thoughtful.

"He wasn't sufficiently interested in the murder of the woman he had once loved. It was as if he already knew all there was to know."

"Sounds like we should take a closer look at him."

"Without doubt."

"And then . . ."

She leaned forward, feeling an urge to place a hand around Rekke's throat. She pushed the thought aside.

"Then there's Emma Gulwal," she said.

"What about her?"

"She described the way Kabir looked at her clarinet as loving, almost as if he wanted to play it. The next second he smashed it to pieces in a fury. It seemed like he wanted to avenge his life, she said."

"That's interesting," he said.

"How do you interpret it?"

He looked amused.

"Naturally I'm tempted to postulate something intriguing. Love and rage are such an old and unhappy pair of bedfellows. But I think I ought to wait before drawing my conclusions. We have a little more to establish first."

"Where should we begin?"

He reached towards the coffee table and picked up the sheet of paper he had been holding when she and Lucas had come through the door.

"Perhaps with this," he said.

"May I see it?"

He passed it to her, and for a while she sat there staring at it. It showed six names – six names, she gathered, from Elena Drugov's music college in Kabul, students who had benefited from brief scholarship visits to the Moscow Conservatory from 1985 to 1988.

"Emma Gulwal is here too," she said.

He nodded.

On the paper was written:

Emma Gulwal

Gedi Afridi

Jabroot Safi

Pazir Lohani

Hassan Barozai

Taara Jadun

"Shouldn't we see whether any of them know who Kabir actually was?" she said.

He fidgeted and put his hands to his chest again. He was about to say something but was unable to get the words out. Their phones rang – first hers, then his.

Professor Alexander Belinsky had helped to nurture several great violinists, but had harboured the greatest hopes for Latifa Sarwani. None of his pupils had moved him so much – and not only because he was infatuated with her. The way she had played had restored his faith in life.

"I dreamed of Latifa last night," he said. "Or this morning, to be precise."

"Indeed."

"You can't tempt an old man to drink like that. Not even if he is given the chance to become nostalgic and happy."

Viktor Malikov was sitting opposite him in his office at the conservatory, a patient smile on his face, although it was perhaps a little forced. He was unusually smartly dressed, in a grey tweed suit, and he held a black hat on his lap. It was also clear – thank goodness – that he'd drunk himself into a stupor too. His double chins were more visible than usual. His eyes looked red and shiny.

"You forget that I am malevolent," Viktor said. "A specialist in tempting old men to perdition. But in my defence, I could point out that you were on most vigorous form yesterday. What did you dream?"

"That I was running down a corridor, trying to stop her. I saw her

277

back grow smaller and smaller until she vanished from sight into the darkness."

"That's not difficult to interpret."

"Perhaps not," he said. "But I think constantly of her death."

"I can understand that."

"Do you know that she was playing in her basement in the middle of the night when she was shot?"

"You said that yesterday. Awful."

For a moment, Sasha pictured Latifa with astonishing clarity: she was sitting in his classroom and moving so rapidly that her hair flew, and of course she was disconcertingly beautiful. He could almost hear people tattling behind her back, jealous, covetous, admiring.

"Rekke asked me to tell you something else. The man in the photo that I gave you played the viola," Viktor said.

"In that costume?" Sasha said, in all seriousness.

He was confused and he had been ever since he had seen the picture of the young man standing on the football pitch in that peculiar black and white striped attire.

"I don't think he played the viola in that costume."

"No, of course not. How has Rekke reached that understanding?"

"I suppose it's just the kind of thing he understands."

Sasha remembered Hans sitting in his dressing room in Bern, shaking.

"Wouldn't it be better if he understood how to take care of himself instead?"

"Regrettably, I fear we must accept the full package when it comes to Rekke. But does it ring any bells?"

Sasha picked up the photo which he had brought to the conservatory to see whether anyone else recognised the man, and which was now lying on his much-too-cluttered desk. Surely the boy was familiar? He didn't think so, yet . . . He peered at it a little longer, trying to disregard the angular, injured jaw, and he suddenly saw the melancholic features of the man – something that wasn't necessarily in the photo but existed in his own head.

"I don't know," he said. "Perhaps."

Viktor lit up, as if his "perhaps" was actually promising, and this spurred Sasha to try to remember. The impression grew stronger. There was unhappiness in that man. Something unfortunate had happened to him, surely?

"Didn't you say the man waved his hands like a conductor?" he said.

"According to Rekke, yes."

"Strange."

"What is strange?"

"Waving like that on the football pitch. Weren't the players confused?"

"Yes, very. They all began to run in time."

"Really?"

"It was a joke, Sasha. A joke."

"I see," he said, embarrassed, but he quickly regained his composure and recalled a small, hunched-over figure coming into the classroom.

"I really do remember something," he said.

THIRTY

The sound of her phone ringing made Micaela jump. She thought it might be Lucas. But it was Jonas Beijer and he sounded excited, so she went into the hallway, watching Rekke depart in the opposite direction, also clutching his phone.

"I've got good news," Jonas said.

"What?"

"You're back on the investigation."

She expected to feel a tingle of joy. But on the contrary, she was worried, as if the news might sabotage something she already had.

"Is it a done deal?" she said.

"You'll have to do a handover," Jonas said, "and keep an eye on your old cases. It's been a long time since any of us were able to give this our full attention. But yes . . . We're dealing with the practical stuff, although there's one last thing."

"What?" she said.

"We want to hire Rekke too."

She nodded to herself.

"Good thinking."

"Do you know what his fees are?"

"No idea," she said. "But I'm sure he could be tempted. He might even need this."

Jonas fell silent and seemed to be thinking something through.

"You seem to know him very well all of a sudden."

"Yes, a little, I guess."

"Micaela . . ."

"Yes?"

"You haven't got together with him, have you?"

"Christ, no."

"That's quite the denial."

She grimaced.

"I'll ask him if he wants in," she said.

"And if he does, perhaps you could both show up first thing tomorrow for a review of the case. I'll lead it. Fransson would probably prefer to keep his distance."

"What does Falkegren say?"

Jonas fell silent again.

"He doesn't dare say much. Fransson is banging on about him being on the way out. But I think things will calm down."

"Why would they do that?"

"We've got the spark back in the investigation again. We all want to solve this now. How's that headache?"

"Better," she said, listening to Rekke pacing back and forth in the kitchen.

"Then I'll see you tomorrow," he said.

She closed her eyes.

"Yes," she said. "You will."

Jonas hesitated, then laughed.

"Fuck me, Micaela . . . You come tearing in from left field and upend everything."

She laughed too, but she was overcome by the news, and wanted to retreat to think it over. She wasn't fully aware of saying goodbye. All she knew was that she was standing there and trying to take it all in when Lucas appeared in her thoughts again: threatening, worrying, staring. In the kitchen she heard Rekke say:

"On the contrary, isn't it strange it's taken so long?"

She went back to the living room, feeling as though she needed to anchor her thoughts to something. Lying on the coffee table was a note. It was the list of Afghan students who had gone to the Moscow Conservatory in the eighties. Should she have another go? Why not? *Keep yourself busy*, a voice inside her said. Forget Lucas. But she needed a computer, so she sat down on the sofa to wait for Rekke.

Mirpur, Pakistan, 1977

He was a little boy playing football alone in the yard in front of the annexe where he and his family lived. His father was a chauffeur for the Lumley family who lived in the big colonial house next door. His mother was the housekeeper, and during the course of his brief life – he was eight years old – he had felt like a son in both homes. He loved nothing like he loved football.

It had been Stephen Lumley, the eldest son, who had taught him, and on this particular evening he was taking shots at the garage. Bang, it went, bang. He was in his own world. He was scoring in the World Cup final. He was Argentina's Mario Kempes. He was all sorts of people, and he could almost hear the sizzle of the stadium crowd. But eventually something broke through. Music, of course. The Lumleys always played music. "The house is afraid of silence," his father used to say, not without pungency.

"You must be able to listen to Allah too. To wait for His voice in the darkness."

Personally, he didn't care about Allah or music. He lived for football. He was a boy with just one thought at a time in his head, as his mother said, and yet he stopped for a brief while to listen, perhaps because it wasn't the gramophone or the daughters practising. It sounded like the television, and the television had always captivated him, not just because they didn't have one of their own. The Lumleys had a video player too, and sometimes the family would return home with films and recordings from England that gave him a glimpse of another, bigger world. So he eventually kicked the ball aside and rushed inside the house without even knocking, up the stairs and into the living room, where he greeted them all in a state of distraction.

"Hallo Hassan, have you been playing football?"

Then they seemed to forget about him, and he forgot them. He watched in amazement. On the television was a man with wild white hair whose black suit jacket was as long as a coat, waving his hands in front of a large orchestra, and at first Hassan didn't know which fascinated him most, the music or the man. But then he realised it was both of them: they were connected. He thought to himself: Magician, he must be a magician, and not just because the man held a baton in his right hand. Each time he made a big movement, something would happen in the music. It was as if he were conjuring the notes and merging into them, and afterwards, when he had finished, the audience exploded and the man turned around and bowed. People stood up to applaud, and shouted with tears in their eyes.

Hassan watched it, enchanted, as if there was something new and great about life that he now understood, and in the following days he thought of little else. He would often stand in the garden and wave a twig and pretend to lead an orchestra, and without him realising it, the Lumley family began to talk about him with new interest.

"On the contrary, isn't it strange it's taken so long?"

Charles Bruckner was having Rekke's call translated and he wished he could interrupt the conversation and snap: *That's easy for you to say now, you goddamn idiot.*

He calmed down a minute later and tried to look at it more soberly. A shitstorm was on its way and when it arrived the Rekke and Kabir problem would only be one small part of a far-wider-reaching chaos. According to his sources, it was a matter of days, perhaps hours, before *The New Yorker* and CBS published their reports about torture and humiliation at Abu Ghraib. It would cause great harm, and there was nothing he or anyone else could do about it.

They had to concentrate on shutting the mouths of Rekke and that cop. Her name was Vargas, and she was known to be effective and quick-witted, a good girl on the outside, but beneath the surface she was cunning, a pain in the arse and the sister – as Charles had guessed – of a hardened criminal who seemed to hate her relationship with Rekke. What gangster wouldn't?

But none of them could figure out how they'd come to know one another, except that they had probably established contact due to Vargas's earlier work on the murder inquiry. Charles felt uncomfortably certain that they were sharing information. In other words, the Rekke problem had doubled in size. But who had said it would be easy? They would just have to up the ante, he told himself, pick up the pace. The question was how and when. Charles heard Rekke end his call. His younger colleague, Henry Lamar, turned to him. Henry's gaze flickered around the room.

"What do we do?" he said.

"We bring them both in," Charles said. "Ride them hard."

Lamar regarded him with distaste.

"Doesn't that risk making matters worse?" he said.

"Not if we use force. You can't make an omelette without breaking eggs," he said, sounding absolutely certain of himself, though in fact he was fearful of what Rekke's countermove would be.

It was strange how openly Rekke was discussing things on the phone, as if he wanted to send them a message. Or was he just reckless – manic again? Charles hoped so.

Rekke eventually came back into the living room carrying another two beers. When Micaela declined, he seemed happy to drink them both himself.

"You look like you've received news," he said.

She didn't ask how he knew.

"I'm back on the investigation."

He raised his glass.

"Allow me to offer my congratulations . . ." he said, after a brief pause.

"Thank you," she said.

"I mean, congratulations to them. The team."

She smiled.

"They want you too."

"Well, I'll be damned."

His body shuddered with yet another jolt of withdrawal.

"They want to know what your fees are."

"Hmm, what do you think they should be?"

New drugs, she thought. New pills.

"I'd like you to have a free rein this time around," he said.

"But you're in?"

"I'll do my best."

She smiled and put a hand on his arm.

"Who did *you* speak to?" she said.

"My brother."

"Is he worried that this Kabir business is going to get out?"

"He's definitely worried, but he's also exhilarated, as ever, in advance of public uproar."

"You said something on the phone about it being strange it hadn't leaked earlier."

Rekke moved on to the next beer.

"It seems that we – by some freak of nature – have become a small part of a greater drama. The CIA's extensive use of torture and humiliation is about to come out. And all without my agency."

She leaned forward.

"How?"

"Dear old Seymour Hersh – the journalist famed for scooping the My Lai massacre in Vietnam – is about to publish a big piece in *The New Yorker.*"

"Really?" she said, with a feeling of the big wide world drawing her closer.

"But as far as Magnus is concerned, all that matters is how it affects him and the ministry. You know," Rekke said, "he and Kleeberger are already in it up to their necks. They've allowed suspects to be flown out of the country and tortured on foreign soil on behalf of the CIA. It's going to get them too."

She was silent.

"And when they let in Kabir, they let in a possible murderer and terrorist."

"I assume so," he said.

"Dodgy."

"Yes," he said, and she was silent for a little longer.

She stood up, went into the kitchen, walked over to the window overlooking Grevgatan, and peered out to see whether the diplomatic car was still there, or if anything else was brewing.

She saw nothing other than an old lady with a white dog walking along the pavement. When she returned to the living room, Rekke looked at her with a troubled expression.

"I'm sorry," he said.

"For what?"

"I don't know yet," he said.

She met his gaze and tried to shake off the sudden feeling of anxiety.

"You said that it shouldn't be that difficult to find Kabir's real identity if he really was a violist," she said.

"Precisely," he said.

"Why don't we get on with it and check that list your friend sent?"

He set down the beer bottle on the coffee table.

"How about we start tomorrow?" he said.

"Come on," she said.

"I need to pull myself together first."

He looked at her with unexpected fervour.

"Then I'll do it myself," she said, taking the list from the table and standing up again, hesitant, wondering if she ought to stay with him.

"Do you have a computer I can borrow?"

"Of course," he said, also standing up, seeming disappointed, or perhaps overcome by anxiety.

He looked over to the grand piano as if he wanted to play it again. Then he walked through the apartment and showed her to a room she had never seen before where there was yet another computer. He logged in for her and left her alone.

She looked around. There was of course a bookcase in here too, and a guest bed and a painting of a girl in a blue dress with a mandolin in her hand, but otherwise nothing of interest. She thought about Rekke and his eyes. And then she turned her gaze to the list of names:

Emma Gulwal
Gedi Afridi
Jabroot Safi
Pazir Lohani
Hassan Barozai
Taara Jadun

Who should she start with? She chose Gedi Afridi, and established fairly quickly that he was a music teacher and pianist who had been missing since March 1997, which was of interest. That was the spring when so many other musicians had been attacked in Kabul and the entire musical district of Kharabat had fallen silent. People had been imprisoned and whipped and instruments had been trampled and burned. Micaela wanted to start with someone she could talk to, if that were even possible without an interpreter.

She decided to leave Emma Gulwal until she had more, so she moved on to Jabroot Safi, which sounded like an unusual name. She got no hits at all, not even a trace of a person with that name, so then she moved on to Pazir Lohani, and there was something about him – for surely it was a him – but it was all in Pashto.

Hassan Barozai, however, turned up several hits, including some in English, but nothing seemed to indicate someone who might have spent a brief spell at the Moscow Conservatory. There was a Hassan Barozai who was a doctor of internal medicine, a Hassan Barozai who was a Pakistani army colonel, a Hassan Barozai who ran a business in Jalalabad – a company that delivered "digital and smart solutions" – and a couple of other hits she didn't understand, including something from Mirpur AJK, which she also believed to be a company. But nothing felt right, and eventually she gave up and wandered back to the living room, to find that Rekke was no longer there.

Sasha Belinsky was alone in his office, and it slowly began to come back to him – a dim memory, but clear enough for him to recall most of the incident. It must have been 1986, or perhaps 1987. Latifa had already established herself as a rising star. She was wearing something red, and looking towards a new pupil whom Sasha hadn't seen before. Her gaze was inquisitive, perhaps even lovelorn. That was probably why Belinsky remembered the pupil.

He remembered the boy as a reflection in her eyes, an image mirrored in her tensed body. But he also remembered the boy himself, a violist, and the proud and single-minded features of his face, which were reminiscent of the man in the referee's strip.

The pupil radiated something that made Sasha believe he too possessed great talent. The light in Latifa's eyes elevated his expectations.

They must have been in a masterclass. He remembered people playing, and that he eventually turned to the newcomer and asked him to perform something, and in that moment the lad had been transformed. He didn't look tough or proud anymore; rather, he was afraid, and for a brief moment he glanced at Latifa. There was clearly an understanding between them, and there was no doubt that Latifa wished him well.

For once, she wasn't preoccupied with herself. Instead, she was staring at the boy, and Sasha remembered that he had also tensed and nodded to Jelena, the piano accompanist. It was always a special moment when a pupil no-one had heard before played, so the classroom was both silent and a little reverent. But the nerves and anxiety were audible in his very first strokes on the viola – and instead of starting over and catching his breath, the boy continued. It only got worse.

He played lifelessly and edgily, perhaps even insincerely, and it was clear how much he was suffering, how Latifa was suffering, having seemingly prepared to shower him with compliments. But now that was no longer possible – not even with the greatest will in the world. Belinsky didn't know what had happened after that, and why would he? It hadn't been that bad, merely a failed performance, nothing more. But it had stayed with him, and he suddenly knew why. He had seen the boy again, and on that occasion the young man had been hammered and bloodied and muttering like a child that he wanted to go home.

Micaela found Rekke in his study, by the bronze statue. He was sitting at the computer, onto a bottle of red wine now. He turned around when she came in and looked at her absent-mindedly, as if he had been engrossed in other thoughts for a long time. But they seemed not to be related to the investigation.

"So your father was a historian. A specialist on the Incas," he said.

She nodded.

"His mother, my grandmother, was a Quechua – the descendants of the Incas."

"Marvellous," he said.

"I don't know about that," she said.

Rekke's gaze flickered anxiously from the computer to her, as if he didn't know what to do. Then he asked whether she had found anything. She shook her head and sat down next to him.

"I had difficulty focusing," she said.

"What happened to him?"

"My father? He died," she said tersely.

"I know that – I found an article," he said.

"Why are you asking?"

"I'm interested."

She wanted to shout at him to drop it.

"Have you heard any more from your friend in Moscow?" she said instead.

"No," he said. "It's not entirely clear how your father died, is it?"

"Let it go."

"How was it classified?"

"Suicide."

"But there are questions around it, aren't there? That fall from the walkway they wrote about, I don't quite understand it."

Speak to Simón, she thought. Speak to Lucas. But she said nothing. She merely stood up again and wondered whether she should get on with her list. Not only because she wanted to escape the conversation. There was something gnawing from within her. It was probably nothing. But she might as well take a look at it if Rekke was going to be so hopeless again.

"I'm going to check something," she said.

Kabul, January 1986

Elena Drugov wore a black suit that no longer quite fitted. She had gained weight. It was the stress, or so he guessed. She'd received death threats, and there had been gunfire in the neighbourhood. But she was still beautiful, despite being old. Old to him, at least. He was just seventeen years old. She was forty, had grey roots, smoked constantly and was always clutching a glass of vodka or whisky.

But she moved with such elegance, and he loved her movements when she was conducting, or like now when she was sitting in her chair with her arms splayed. Her grey eyes were at once hard and soft. It was hard to predict whether they would caress or wound.

"I'm proud of you, Hassan," she said, and he knew that she was.

It had been a year since he had arrived in Kabul, encouraged by Madam Bukhari, his violin teacher in Mirpur, and with a little cash in his pocket from the Lumleys – a small bursary, as they had described it. But it hadn't been easy. Using all means possible, his parents had tried to stop him from going. Communists are ungodly, his father had said. They're warlords. They're occupying Muslim soil. But from the very first moment he had heard about Drugov's conducting courses, he knew he had to go. He needed it in order to make the leap he had dreamed of, and while the money he'd been given didn't go far and he was sharing a room with three other pupils in the dormitory and he had been beaten to the ground while in the street on one occasion, it had all been worth it.

He had learned to read scores and realised he had a talent for it. Not only because he was analytical and quick-witted and could rapidly gain insight into both the details and the whole. He had leadership qualities. He could hold a room. People listened to him, even older ones. It was as if he were made to be a conductor. He was convinced of it, and no-one practised like he did. Forever practising. Twelve, fourteen hours a day. Of course Professor Drugov was proud. He was proud too. He had left everything else behind – even football. Elena couldn't have asked for a better pupil. Yet she was about to say "but". He could hear the secondary tone in her voice. He saw it in the wrinkles on her forehead, and in the way she stubbed her cigarette out in the blue ashtray.

"Thank you," he said.

"But you started a little late with the violin – as you know. You do not have the required technical skills," she said, and he wanted to protest. Or most of all, to get out the violin and show her at once that he could play like any other virtuoso.

It was just her, that damn bitch, who hadn't been listening properly.

But he knew that to protest would achieve nothing, and instead he stared at her while she bent down and picked up an instrument that she set on the desk. She said nothing. Neither of them said anything, and really there was no need to. They both knew what lay before them, beside the ashtray. It was a viola.

"I think the viola might suit you better," she said, and he didn't reply.

He stood up in silence, feeling like he'd been punched in the gut.

Micaela heard Rekke say a couple of words. But she was already too far away, heading for the room where she had just been using his computer. She pulled up the post about the Hassan Barozai who had something to do with Mirpur AJK. She had taken Mirpur AJK to be a company or a region, but it might just as well – it occurred to her – be a sports association. A football club. She entered the phrase into the search engine and pulled up nothing – just general information about the district of Mirpur in the Azad Kashmir region of Pakistan. But she didn't give in. She searched on and found a football team called FC Mirpur AJK. Could that have been what was meant?

The word had appeared in a text in Pashto – where only the names were written in English. Names and affiliations with things like Mirpur AJK, Baloch Quetta, Humma and WAPDA. She looked up the other names too and they were . . . A shiver ran down her spine. They were all football teams. Keep cool, calm down. It didn't have to mean anything, she thought to herself. Nothing at all. But it was worth investigating, surely?

Mirpur for starters. What was it? A town in north-western Pakistan, it transpired. Home to around one hundred thousand people. Many had emigrated from there to England in the fifties and sixties, apparently. Sometimes the town was known as Little England. There were reportedly many British products in the local shops, and widespread British influence. That was of interest, surely? According to Rekke, no-one would take up classical Western music in this part of the world without being subject to some form of European influence.

She called international directory inquiries and asked whether there were any Barozais in Mirpur. There were. There were four or five families by that name. Then she took a deep breath and tried someone called Fahmi Barozai. He didn't pick up, so she moved on to Yafir Barozai, a kind man who didn't seem to speak much English but was still keen to help.

"I am looking for a Hassan Barozai," she said, and the man replied with an imperceptible "Yes, yes" as if he actually knew of such a person in Mirpur.

He gave her a number that he reeled off in both English and French, and she was undeniably a little excited. Had she got it right? Then she calmed down. It couldn't be Kabir at any rate. He was dead and would hardly still have a telephone number in Pakistan. But perhaps it was the Barozai who had studied for a brief period at the Moscow Conservatory. If he'd also been related to a football club then surely it wasn't improbable that he knew Kabir? It was definitely worth checking. She dialled the number and heard the ringing on the line like distant foghorns. When she was about to give up, a woman's voice answered. She sounded old.

"Do you speak English?" Micaela said.

"Yes," said the voice. "What do you want?"

"I . . ." Micaela said, and hesitated. She decided to treat it like any other call in the line of duty.

"My name is Micaela Vargas," she said. "I'm calling from the Swedish police and I am looking for a Hassan Barozai. Is there anyone by that name there?"

"He's at the mosque," said the woman. "Why are you looking for him?"

"He may have information that is valuable to us."

"He's an old and God-fearing man."

"I don't doubt that. But I would still like—"

"You'll have to call later," the woman interjected.

"I'd be happy to."

An old and God-fearing man, she thought. It had to be the wrong person.

"So he's never taken an interest in classical Western music?"

"No."

"OK, well, sorry to have disturbed you."

"Very well," said the woman. "Was that all?"

"That was all. Thank you," she said, and hung up.

THIRTY-ONE

Viktor Malikov had just sat down to prepare for his lesson when Sasha Belinsky knocked on the door. Dear God, Viktor thought, what a wreck. If he had seemed like a relatively young man a day earlier, Sasha now looked a hundred years old. He was pale and trembling, and the bags under his eyes, which had been far from flattering for some time, were swollen, giving him a sickly look.

"Did you think of something?" Viktor said, letting Sasha take a seat.

Sasha's upper body shook as he sank onto the chair. He wiped sweat from his neck.

"I think so," he said. "You know . . ." He removed his glasses and wiped them with a white handkerchief. "I often wondered why Latifa bothered so many people."

"I don't suppose it was all that difficult to understand, really," Viktor said, letting Sasha catch his breath a little.

"No, perhaps not," Sasha said. "She was so gifted and beautiful that people were forced to bring her down to earth to put up with her. But there was something else. She shone – there was a kind of passion, I think, that permeated her whole personality. But she could also become lifeless, as if she had lost all interest in you or in the world at large, and when that happened it hurt."

"Where are you going with this?"

Sasha looked at him in confusion.

"I'm not quite sure. But we had a pupil for a brief period during the eighties. Just like Latifa, he came here thanks to our cultural exchange programme and Elena Drugov's efforts in Kabul."

"OK," said Viktor, suddenly attentive.

"Something had happened between him and Latifa is what I would say. She and he seemed to have an understanding – I would guess a romance. She looked at him in a way that almost made me jealous. What was it about that boy? I thought to myself. What a popinjay. I allowed him to play for us in a masterclass, and afterwards I actually had a guilty conscience about it. The situation got completely out of hand. The poor boy choked. It sounded dreadful. He played Bach's 'Fantasia Cromatica' – and afterwards . . ."

"Latifa didn't look at him in the same way."

"Not that she was unpleasant or careless. But it was noticeable that she was troubled by his company, and that he in turn avoided her and looked at her from a distance with something dark in his gaze."

"And you think this is the same guy as the one in the picture Rekke sent?" said Viktor.

Sasha thought about the man again and the feeling of having seen something tragic or sad written on his face.

"I have that impression," he said. "You see, a few days later the boy came to me. He seemed both shy and agitated at the same time, and he told me that he had seen me on television in the seventies."

"We all saw you on television in the seventies, Sasha. You were the grand eccentric with the crazy hair."

"Indeed, those were the days," he said, tugging at a few loose strands of hair on his head. "But for this young man, I apparently had some special significance. He said that I had made him want to be a conductor – well, more than that. He had changed his whole life after seeing a recording of me conducting Rachmaninov's second in London. It was a life-changing event for him in some way. He told me he rehearsed as much as possible. I'm a leader by nature, he said. A leader. I remember that in particular. The wild, lost boy that people avoided, standing there shouting that he was a leader."

"What did you do?" Viktor said.

"Gave him a few half-baked promises, I suppose. Promised to set up a small group that he could conduct. Something like that. Of course, it never happened. I began avoiding him too, and I'm sure I would have forgotten him had I not seen him one final time."

"What happened then?"

"I had stayed late at the school and was on my way home when I heard a commotion at the front door and stumbled that way. There was a man at the bottom of the steps. He was drunk and filthy, his forehead bloodied, and quite a few of us tried to help him. But when he came to, he merely tugged himself free and stared at us with a gaze I shall never forget. He looked like an outcast, like someone who had lost a terrible and decisive battle, and we all felt instinctively that we should leave him be. Shortly afterwards, he went back."

"To Afghanistan?"

"Or was it Pakistan? I don't remember," Sasha said, seeming for a moment abandoned and lonely too, as if he identified with the poor boy.

Micaela went to Rekke, who was sitting on the sofa by the piano with his hands crossed over his chest again. He didn't look very well, and he had almost emptied the wine bottle. But he still seemed to be deep in pained concentration.

"What are you doing?" she said.

He clearly hadn't heard her because he remained still, mumbling to himself.

"What are you doing?" she repeated.

"I . . . sorry," he said. "I was trying to gather my thoughts."

"Is it going well?"

He turned towards her and smiled.

"Perhaps," he said.

"That sounds promising."

"But I was also thinking about your father."

She wondered whether to tell him to shut up.

"You were eleven, weren't you?" he said.

Or should she merely return to the computer? But she stayed, and sat down on the sofa.

"And you were close to him?"

"Yes," she said.

"It says he was left deaf by the torture in Chile. Did you sign to each other?"

"We wrote notes," she said.

Rekke nodded. He didn't look particularly critical. But she still felt obliged to defend those notes that had formed her childhood.

"It was a bit roundabout. But it meant we had to think."

"I understand," he said.

She wanted to say more, despite everything.

"Sometimes it was still too slow, and then he would read my lips or speak in a voice that was either too loud or too quiet. But most often he would write."

"Because it felt more dignified?"

"He was a writing kind of man," she said, thinking of Simón.

Simón had never liked those notes. He was too restless and dyslexic for them and, just like Mamá, he preferred pictures to words, which was probably significant.

"What sorts of things did he write?" Rekke said.

"Jokes, everyday comments, compliments, small riddles, anything. But there was always a lot of politics. The world is unjust. But it's our duty to do something about it, and all that."

"Sounds like a good father."

"He was. But during his final autumn and winter something happened to him," she said. "Perhaps he ended up like you. We saw him retreat and become mute and stop bothering to read people's lips. Perhaps winter had something to do with it too. It was minus twenty that year, and windy, and he would often sit awake in the kitchen with books that I wonder whether he even read. One of those nights, or early one morning I suppose, my brother Simón staggered home – high and hammered. They started to argue. Their shouting woke me up. But I was stupid enough to stay in bed, and I thought Lucas would calm them down."

"So he got up?"

"He ran into the kitchen, and it was as if he had taken over. I heard him yell: 'Calm yourselves the fuck down and let us sleep.'"

"What happened?"

"I don't know," she said. "There was silence, and I must have fallen back asleep. When I woke it was colder, there was a draught from the front door, and I got up and found Lucas and Simón standing out on the walkway. I stared at their backs and saw them looking down at something. It was ice-cold, and I was shaking. Lucas turned around and told me to go back to bed. But I had to see. I leaned over, and there he was, lying on his stomach, his arms splayed. His hands were still moving, as if he was reaching for something, or as if he thought he was still falling, and then Mamá came running across the yard barefoot in just her nightie screaming, 'No, no.' Papá died that afternoon in the Karolinska."

Rekke laid his hand on hers.

"And it was classified as suicide?"

"There was no other explanation. Simón and Lucas had gone to bed after the fight, and they knew he had been deeply depressed. The fight with my brothers was seen as a trigger."

Rekke appeared thoughtful, and for a moment she was worried that he would say something that would turn her own convictions upside down.

"That pains me," he said.

Afterwards, they sat in silence and she allowed her thoughts to meander. The conversation with the old lady in Mirpur came back to her, but now it didn't seem idiotic or embarrassing. Now the woman's nervous and slightly nasal voice niggled at her, and she looked at Rekke, whose hand had a vice-like grip on his shoulder.

"I have a question."

"Pray tell," he said.

"If I were to ask you something . . . Anything at all. Something you weren't expecting in the slightest. Like . . ." She racked her brains. "Have you ever been a figure skater in Russia? How would you answer?"

"I would immediately begin to describe my fantastic pirouettes."

"I mean, how would normal people answer it?"

"I suppose most would say: 'What on earth makes you ask that?'"

"Exactly," she said. "Exactly."

He looked at her curiously and she thought about the somewhat uncomfortable telephone call, the feeling throughout that the woman wanted to hang up.

"What is it you've found?" he said.

"I'm not sure. But I need to make a call."

He nodded and she went back to the room with the computer again. Later she would remember how she had sat there for a long time, breathing. Then she had picked up the phone and dialled again, and this time the woman answered right away, as if she had been waiting.

"It's me again, from the Swedish police," she said.

"I can hear that," said the woman.

"It was your husband that we were talking about before, wasn't it?"

"Yes," she said.

"And he hasn't got anything to do with the football club in your town, has he? FC Mirpur AJK?"

"No," she said.

"Yet there is another Hassan Barozai who did."

There was silence on the line and Micaela heard heavy breathing, and some kind of clicking, perhaps fingers drumming.

"Our son played for the team as a boy."

Micaela took a deep breath.

"Really," she said.

"Later on he was their coach. He was very prominent."

"I see," Micaela said. "Was he sometimes a referee too?"

"Sometimes," said the woman.

Micaela felt a wave of excitement, and did her best to ensure it wasn't audible.

"Was he also interested in classical Western music?"

Yet more silence on the line.

"He played the violin," the woman said eventually. "He was very good. It was our English neighbours and employers, the Lumley family, who taught him. But later in life he distanced himself from that."

"Why did he do that?"

The woman hesitated, as if she didn't know what to say.

"He became like his father."

"So he began to see music as blasphemous?"

"He felt that it offended Allah and His Prophet, peace be upon him. It wasn't a time for joy, he said, but rather one for sorrow and gravity."

Micaela digested these words and concentrated on saying something that didn't destroy the vulnerable openness that had occurred.

"Was that the whole reason?" she said.

"Is more needed?"

"Perhaps not. But sometimes there is a trigger."

The woman fell silent again.

"They treated him unfairly."

"Who treated him unfairly?"

"The communists. They persecuted Muslims and turned against Allah."

"I don't doubt that," she said. "Was your son in Moscow?"

"Briefly, but he returned home a new person. We were most grateful for that."

"I understand," she said. "Where's your son now?"

Once again Micaela heard those heavy breaths down the line.

"He returned to Afghanistan."

"To the Taliban?"

"Yes," said the woman. "But he had nothing to do with terrorists. He was very considerate. He spread joy."

"Through his football?"

"Among other things."

"Did he die in Afghanistan?" she said.

"Yes," said the woman.

"I'm sorry to ask," she said, "but was a body ever returned to you for burial?"

The woman didn't reply. Once again the line was quiet, with only the woman's breathing audible, and Micaela wondered whether it was her place to tell her that her son hadn't died in Afghanistan at all, but had instead been murdered in distant Stockholm.

"Was he reported missing?" she said.

"Yes," said the woman. "But last summer we were notified by the American embassy that there was no longer any hope. But you still . . ."

She didn't finish the sentence.

"Who was it that called from the embassy?"

"I need to speak to my husband."

Micaela took a deep breath.

"I understand. I can call back later. But may I ask one final question?"

"One."

"Who else was your son close to in Mirpur? Who knows more about why he felt unfairly treated?"

"Madam Mariam Bukhari, his violin teacher. She loved him – we all did. He was a good person. He would never harm anyone."

"Has anyone claimed he did?"

"I must go."

"No, wait."

The woman hung up and Micaela realised that she hadn't secured a definitive identifying detail. She should have asked about the birthmark on Kabir's thigh, or emailed a photo. But she didn't want to call for a third time, and it wasn't really necessary either, she reflected. Kabir and Hassan Barozai from Mirpur had to be one and the same person. There was far too much overlap, and that meant . . . what? Just about anything, if she was honest. It was a major breakthrough – it had to be – and she could feel in her whole body the desire to go and tell Rekke. But she didn't get far.

The doorbell rang, and she jumped in fright.

Charles Bruckner was at the embassy listening in to Micaela's call, and he thought to himself: There goes my information advantage, or at least most of it. Now all that remained for Rekke and his Vargas was to work out the connections between Barozai and Gamal Zakaria. But they would probably make short work of that.

It was an association that could hardly be missed, although – and this was the awkward thing – his own knowledge didn't go much further, for the simple reason that there had been things that not even torture had been able to provide answers to.

Barozai had immediately, almost vengefully, told all he knew about Zakaria and his followers. But when it came to his own crimes there was something unmentionable there that not even physical suffering could lure out. So Charles did not know whether it had been Barozai who had shot Latifa Sarwani, or even how involved he had been in the war on music that had turned into such a dark madness in 1997.

On the other hand, he didn't much care, just as he didn't care about the poor mother in Mirpur. He had been the one who called her and told her that her son was dead: "We found his DNA following a terrorist attack in Kabul, and there is no body to bury." He had done it last summer to avoid unnecessary questions – his main responsibility was to seal things up and make sure nothing leaked. That was why he was now gathering a team to raid Rekke's apartment that evening or early the next morning. But at the moment he was waiting, even if that was becoming increasingly difficult. It was as if there were a fire within him, and he kept imagining that Rekke would find something unexpected that upended everything. Outside in the corridor, he heard footsteps coming towards him. He stood up and wondered whether he should tell Magnus, who was on his way to his brother, about that confounded Vargas. But he didn't want to divulge how closely they had been following developments. Instead, he went out to meet Henry Lamar, who was impatient to strike.

Micaela heard Rekke say hello and welcome someone. A man thanked him and asked whether he had been drinking. "Trying to deal with some withdrawal symptoms," Rekke replied. There was a familiar, almost teasing tone between the men.

"Do you have the Kabir file with you, or am I to be subjected to your liberal censorship?" Rekke said.

The brother, it had to be the brother – Magnus. He replied with a couple of words she didn't catch, but which included reserved laughter, at which she was stupid enough to get up, whether that was to hear better or just because she was restless and excited.

"Do you have a visitor?" said the brother, and there was silence for a while, as if Rekke didn't know what to say, and she thought she might as well make herself known.

It was a mistake. When she stepped across the threshold, she was looking straight at Magnus Rekke. Whereas his brother's gaze was curious, open – it was as if she only realised it at this moment – Magnus's held fleeting contempt. Magnus barely looked at her before dismissing her as nothing, which allowed her several seconds to examine him. He was a large man with an impressive stature, sharp narrow eyes, thick lips and a large nose that gave him a bear-like appearance. His gaze seemed to absorb his surroundings, as if he were wondering what he could grab.

"You have a cleaner?" he said.

Hans Rekke put an arm around his brother's shoulders. Magnus nervously lifted his hand to his neck and loosened his tie. Rekke touched his wristwatch.

"Dear Magnus, I believe you were here for around forty-three seconds before you managed to say something rude. This is Micaela," he said, gesturing towards her.

"Sorry," Magnus said. "I thought . . ."

"It matters not what you thought," Rekke said. "Apologise and admit you are a boor."

Magnus tore himself from Rekke's embrace and shook his head.

"I apologise, and naturally I am a boor. An incorrigible one at that."

He smiled at her, not exactly guiltily, but still as if he were making an effort.

"Sorry, I was a fool," he said, proffering a hand to her. "I was confused by your . . ."

He put a hand to her cheek, as if to show that he really hadn't missed her bruise, though it was hardly the best way to apologise. But she didn't care.

"It's OK," she said, shaking his hand.

"Are you sure? Nevertheless, I'm Magnus Rekke – the older and always untidier brother."

"My name's Micaela Vargas."

"Charmed," he said. "May I ask how you know each other?"

"We're colleagues," Rekke said.

Micaela felt a shiver of pleasure.

"Well, well. In which field?" Magnus said.

"I'm a police officer."

"Detective colleagues. I see."

"Something like that," Rekke said, extending his hand as if to indicate that they should all proceed to the living room.

But Magnus stopped, as if he had thought of something, and he scrutinised Micaela once more. Although he was smiling, he had a look of suspicion.

"You're not by any chance involved in the Kabir case, are you?" he said.

She hesitated for a moment, then nodded curtly. Magnus reacted immediately.

"My God, that explains things. So it was you who triggered this circus," he said.

Rekke ran a hand through his hair.

"If a circus is what we've got, Magnus, then you're entirely responsible for its organisation," he said, gesturing to them both to sit down on the sofa.

Magnus took a seat and shook his head while inspecting the wine bottle on the table.

"It's still rather thrilling," he said, "to grasp the chronology of the drama. Are you old friends, or did you meet recently?"

"We met recently as old friends," said Rekke. "But let us get to the point. What do you have to offer us from the file?"

"Perhaps it's better if I come back later."

"Not at all. We're all ears."

Magnus put a hand to his brow, seeming troubled again. He turned to Rekke.

"I gather that Micaela is investigating the murder and that you are working together, or whatever it is you do together. But come on, Hans. We had a deal. I must ask that Micaela leaves while we talk."

"Nonsense," Rekke said. "Out with it."

"So she's your Watson all of a sudden."

"More like my Virgil. My Sancho Panza. Out with it."

"Yes, yes, OK," Magnus said, as if he really were capitulating.

"Shall we begin for the sake of simplicity with Kabir's real name?"

Magnus looked around with a gaze that appeared to be genuinely uncertain.

"I don't have any other name. We were informed of the suspicions about his criminal activities, and obtained information about his network of contacts."

"Rubbish," Rekke said.

"No, no, I swear," said Magnus, suddenly agitated, at which Rekke looked unsure – perhaps not entirely certain that his brother was lying.

"So you were deceived too."

"I should have known," Magnus muttered. "But no, I promise I have no other name – nothing more than that he was prisoner twelve at the Salt Pit, arrested in December 2001, and released in August 2002. He was supposedly traumatised, but strong, so they said. No risk of violent tendencies, not an extremist. He had apparently abandoned his religious beliefs, and he was regarded as an important channel of information. He was reportedly in a position to lead the CIA to key figures in the Taliban who fled before the American invasion."

Rekke seemed lost in thought.

"Then we must find out his name for ourselves," he said.

Micaela leaned forward, and experienced once again the excitement she'd felt in the study.

"He was called Hassan Barozai and he came from Mirpur in Pakistan," she said, at which the brothers looked at her in astonishment.

"Really?" said Magnus, now nervous. "That's not information I'm in possession of."

"I just received confirmation from his mother. He left Mirpur in the nineties to join the Taliban. He used to play both football and the violin, and he studied in Kabul under Professor Drugov, as well as at the conservatory in Moscow for a brief spell."

Rekke drank the last of his wine and smiled at her, slightly covertly, with a look that she perceived as pride.

Proud of her.

"Bloody hell," Magnus said. "Is that definite?"

She nodded.

"I could strangle them. But Barozai, you say? A Pakistani. Doesn't sound altogether unlikely, given his idiom. What else do you know about him?"

"It wasn't supposed to be Micaela who did the talking, it was supposed to be you," Rekke said. "What did he do to catch the eye of the CIA?"

Magnus didn't look like he wanted to accept that the question had been directed at him. But eventually he said:

"I believe you have a good grasp of this from the inquiry."

"All we know for certain is that he was loosely tied to one of the Taliban's ministries and that he harassed musicians and smashed their instruments," Micaela said.

"Yes, yes, he didn't just love football, apparently, he also hated music. Rather rational in his puritanical perversion, don't you think, Hans?" Magnus said in an attempt to sound at ease. "I suppose you've already guessed it wasn't Kabir's actions that drew the interest of the CIA. It was his ties to Mullah Zakaria."

Rekke leaned forward and placed his hands together as if praying.

"Were they close?"

"Yes, apparently they went a long way back. They met in Pakistan, if I've understood correctly. Gamal Zakaria is a pretty interesting chap. Most definitely more than just a bumpkin who studied in Wahhabi madrasas. I don't know how much you know about him?"

"Educate me, brother dear," Rekke said.

"He was an Egyptian, and studied political science and law in Alexandria – a bit of a ladies' man, so I gather. Western influences until well into the seventies, politically on the left and flirted with communism. He was in a pop group that sang lyrics critical of society."

"So he was a musician too."

"Mostly a loudmouth, I think. But he was radicalised, and in the early eighties he participated in Islamist attacks on Copts in Cairo. I have no idea whether he had anything to do with the murder of Sadat. But he was one of hundreds arrested and tortured, and that seems to have been a turning point for him. During his torture, the Prophet Muhammad himself came to him, he said, and probably a lot of angels too, and urged him to drive the communists out of Afghanistan and to establish an Islamic state."

"So he joined the mujahedin?"

"Quite. He became a guerrilla soldier, highly charismatic, and was regarded as a unifying force. He was tall – 196 centimetres – and powerful, and he was injured several times. He had shrapnel wounds to his face, a bullet hole in his leg and another in the shoulder. It seems he made an impression. There was something of an Islamist Che Guevara about him."

"Yet there were few photos of him, is that right?" Rekke said.

"None at all, really, except for a couple of useless ones from his youth in Alexandria."

"Photos must have been taken when he was arrested," Micaela said.

"They disappeared or were deleted. But the interesting thing is that he travelled to Pakistan from time to time to recuperate, and it was apparently there that he met Kabir, although the circumstances around this encounter are unclear – at least to me."

"Was it Zakaria who recruited Kabir to the Taliban?" Micaela said.

"It seems so, and it was also Zakaria who helped him with the football tournaments in Kabul and defended him against all the people who wanted to ban football. But their relationship was not uncomplicated. Zakaria became increasingly violent, urged on by his young cadre, while Kabir seemed to be torn between two things."

"As if he wanted both to smash musical instruments to pieces and to play them," said Rekke.

"Yes, perhaps. By the time he ended up in the Salt Pit there wasn't much left of their friendship. Kabir made the most dreadful accusations and said that Zakaria had personally executed women who had been defenceless, on their knees. That he had enjoyed it. He said that it was Zakaria who was behind the disappearance and murder of so many Kabuli musicians at the time."

Rekke looked at Magnus in deep concentration.

"Were any of the women called Latifa Sarwani?"

"I'm afraid I don't know," he said. "But if I may guess, I believe something dramatic happened between them. Something on that level. At the Salt Pit, Kabir began saying he would do whatever it took to see Zakaria apprehended and killed."

"And the CIA took the bait," Rekke said.

"Yes, eventually. They desperately needed to placate public opinion on the home front with a scalp of that distinction, and they began to believe that Kabir was their chance to get to Zakaria. So they set him free with a GPS tracker and a bugged phone."

Rekke nodded and stared at a point beyond the grand piano, squinting.

"Why did Kabir end up in Sweden?"

"Because the trail led him here. To begin with, he was in Abbottabad in Pakistan. But later on he received a tip-off – supported by intelligence – that Zakaria had made his way to Sweden on a false passport and was hiding in the south-western suburbs of Stockholm. So the CIA decided to send Kabir here instead."

"And you welcomed him with open arms and lied rather convincingly for their sake?" said Rekke.

"We—"

"Or *you* specifically . . .?" Rekke interjected.

"Naturally I informed Kleeberger, and if I'm honest, what was I supposed to do? It was a vital operation – the Americans were applying pressure to us."

"But I'm sure you negotiated a splendid trade deal."

"Of course. I'm not stupid. But now, good God . . ."

"You're wondering whether they hid things from you."

"Exactly, yes. I'm furious. I'm going to have a drop, though I don't share your passion for Italian wines," he said.

He grasped Rekke's empty glass, poured the remainder of the bottle into it and took a gulp. Afterwards, they sat in silence and Micaela thought to herself: What double-dealing, what treachery, and for a couple of seconds she was convinced that she should say something. But Magnus's arrogant presence made her hesitate, and instead she sat in silence, as if thinking to herself.

"Yet Zakaria was shot in Copenhagen, rather than Stockholm."

"He was warned and fled the country in an old Volvo. But Kabir's tip-off was on the money. He did his duty before he met his fate."

"That must have been a very real consolation," Rekke said sarcastically, at which Magnus declared that he had to return to work before the whole affair exploded in his face.

THIRTY-TWO

Mirpur, Pakistan, 1993

For a long time, Hassan thought he would get over it, and even come to see it as part of life. "To grow up is to lose our dreams," as Claire Lumley had said when he returned to Mirpur. But naturally nothing was simple, and the events in Moscow often returned to him like body blows.

It could be as simple as a piece of Brahms or Tchaikovsky being played on the radio, or the very fact that a musician was referred to in an admiring tone in the newspaper. The slightest thing could tear open wounds, and in those moments he seemed not only to have lost a career as a conductor or violinist, but also to have lost his ability to find pleasure in music.

Nevertheless, life went on, and he returned to his football – now as a coach and referee. Now and then he would attend the mosque with his father and on one of those days a burly man with a long beard approached him. The man's arm was in a cast and he had shrapnel scars on his face. He had a slight limp too. Yet he made a powerful impression, and Hassan loved his smile. The smile made him feel seen, and after chatting about football – the man had watched him coaching the youth team – they got into issues of life and death in no time at all.

Gamal spoke with a fervour and dignity that Hassan had rarely encountered. Many of his views were extreme, but he had a self-assured authority, reminiscent of Elena Drugov's, and he spoke in a low voice as if each and every word were a secret. He often passed comment with restrained gravitas on what he saw before him. One day in Nangi Park they heard bhangra music playing from a balcony in the distance.

"Beautiful, isn't it?" Gamal said.

Hassan nodded.

"Although all that will be banned."

"Why?" asked Hassan.

"Because it leads us away from the only beauty that means anything."

Hassan argued robustly against this perspective, but afterwards came to understand.

There is a beauty, he thought, that shuts us out and gives rise to anger and hate. Not long afterwards as they strolled towards the lake, he told Gamal about Latifa. How he'd seen her playing beside her unmade bed in Moscow.

"It was as if I lost myself," he said.

"She turned your head, she was a slut," said Gamal, and although Hassan protested, and defended Latifa, the man's words alleviated some of the pain of his memories.

After that, it became a habit for him to walk with Gamal after he'd finished work for the day at the Honda garage on Allama Iqbal Road.

Martin Falkegren would have preferred to hang up immediately. He was furious with Charles Bruckner. He was convinced that Charles had lied to him and left him in the thick of it. Yet he was unable to bring himself to end the call.

"What do you want?" he said.

"I want to apologise," Charles said, which Falkegren didn't believe for one moment.

But it felt good to hear it, especially right now as he hastened towards his car to drive into the city centre for a meeting with the national police commissioner.

"That's not good enough," he said. "I'm going to run the gauntlet for your sake."

Charles paused, then said:

"It won't happen, Martin. We'll back you up, and you're going to be fully informed starting now."

Falkegren unlocked the car.

"Give me something. Show me that you mean it."

Charles paused again.

"Kabir's real name was Hassan Barozai. He was close friends with Mullah Zakaria, but ended up hating him. We and Foreign Affairs let Barozai into Sweden so he could help us to locate Zakaria. He was part of a secret operation – a successful operation."

Martin Falkegren nodded and started the engine.

"I'll inform the team," he said.

"Good," said Charles. "We'll give you more later. But there's one more thing."

Falkegren switched off the engine.

"What?" he said.

"There's this girl, Vargas, that you've put back onto the investigation. She has a brother . . ."

"Who's an out-and-out crook. You don't think we already know?" Martin Falkegren said.

"I know you have your eye on the ball," Charles said. "But I wanted to say that, according to our sources, they're closer than you think. Lucas Vargas has provided for the family more or less her whole life. She has to know where the money comes from."

Falkegren started the car again and pulled onto Sundbybergsvägen.

"What is it you're getting at?" he said.

"Nothing really," said Charles. "Nothing except that a lot can happen to a girl like that."

"Of course it can," he said, accelerating, exhilarated but also disturbed.

*

Micaela returned to the study, picturing Kabir's movements on the pitch. His gestures returned to her with renewed power, and at first she didn't really understand why. But then it struck her that there was a paradox there, wasn't there? If Kabir had abandoned music and considered it *haram*, why did his old movements reappear in his football? Were they subconscious, or had he transformed the role of referee into a replacement for what he had lost?

A sheet of A4 was lying in front of her on the desk. Rekke had written a couple of lines she hadn't noticed before. Curious, she tried to read them. The handwriting was so careless that it reminded her of stenography, but she thought she could make out the word *Obscuritas*. Yet more Latin, she guessed. *Obscuritas*. She let it sink in for a moment, then looked it up on the computer. She discovered that it meant darkness, or occasionally that which was obscure or unclear – withdrawn. Why had he written it? Was he making reference to his own darkness or was it . . . Her train of thought was interrupted.

She discovered that she had scribbled something herself on the same sheet of paper. *Madame Bukhari*. Madame Mariam Bukhari. The violin teacher whom the woman in Mirpur had mentioned. For a minute or two, she was lost in her own thoughts. Then she called international directory inquiries again.

Mariam Bukhari was now seventy years old, but still looked fifty, or so she often heard. She thought herself to be tall and elegant, even if she would have preferred fuller lips and a smaller nose. Her children used to say she walked as aggressively as a man, as if she were always on the way to an important meeting. Sometimes that hurt her. But she mostly took it as a compliment. She wanted to hurry and radiate authority, especially now that she had less to do. There was barely anyone who wanted to learn to play the violin or cello these days. They were new times.

The Lumleys had moved long ago, and the West was no longer rated as highly. Sometimes she felt like a relic of an old and forgotten age.

She sought to be active and keep herself occupied. Right now, she was in the kitchen preparing dinner while listening to the Mendelssohn violin concerto and humming to herself. The phone rang. She guessed it was her sister. They usually spoke just after lunch. But the call was long distance – the line was crackling. Someone very young introduced themselves as Vargas something-or-other from the Swedish police, which made her ill at ease, even though she knew she had done nothing to attract the attention of the law here at home or abroad.

"Do you speak English?" the officer asked.

"Yes," she said.

"And you were a violin teacher?"

That was hurtful.

"I *am* a violin teacher," she said.

"Then I've found the right person. It may sound strange for me to ask this after such a long time," the woman said, "but have you ever had a pupil by the name of Hassan Barozai?"

She started, and pictured Hassan's intense gaze.

"Oh yes," she said. "He was my pride and joy once upon a time, but then, of course, he changed. Why do you ask?"

"I'm investigating the circumstances around his death," said the woman, which made her wince again. But it was only logical, she thought, that they try to find out what had happened to the ones who had disappeared during the war. But why was the woman calling from Sweden?

"Why are you calling from Sweden?"

"I need information," the woman said, as if she hadn't heard her question. "You said that Hassan changed. Can you tell me about him?"

"He grew up with the Lumleys, one of the finer English families in town. The father, George, was from London. And he'd been a prominent violinist in his youth. He married a young girl from these parts in the sixties – a real beauty – and moved here when he secured the import rights for Honda."

"I see," said the woman.

"But more than anything, I think he'd have liked to be a musician. He played throughout his life, and he sent his daughters to learn with me. I thought they were a wonderful family, even if their son, Stephen, was a bit of a nuisance."

"And Hassan Barozai?" said the woman.

"He was the only child of Hassan Senior and Yalina, who both worked for the Lumleys. They lived in a small servants' house next door. Hassan was treated as a son by both families, which was lovely. But it also caused tension, and I believe that even as a young boy Hassan was torn between his father's rather strict world and the Lumleys' more permissive lifestyle."

"He played football, didn't he?"

"Incessantly, often on the Lumleys' old tennis court, which Stephen – the son – had converted into a football pitch. He'd be there for hours, and I've often thought about it – how Hassan would kick a ball around while the girls played the violin over in the house. It must have had an impact on him."

"Playing football to the sound of classical music?"

"Yes, exactly. The daughters, who practised constantly and were very accomplished, would often be on the veranda overlooking the court. Not that I think Hassan cared much to begin with. You know how boys never care about anything when they have their own thing. But all the same, one day he turned up and wanted to learn to play with me, even though he barely knew one end of the instrument from the other."

"Was he any good?"

Mariam Bukhari conjured up Hassan's serious face and tensed shoulders, the eyes looking up at her, hungry for praise.

"I don't believe I've ever seen such energy, such single-mindedness," she said. "Right from the beginning, he played as if it were life and death, which meant he made rapid progress. Incredible progress."

"He went to Kabul, to Elena Drugov's school, didn't he?"

"Exactly – he was just sixteen at the time. To be quite honest, I wasn't good enough for him. He needed more qualified teaching and I was in touch from time to time with Professor Drugov. When I told Hassan about it, he became very enthusiastic."

"It must have been a big deal, going to Kabul at just sixteen."

"It was. His father opposed it in every way he could."

"But Hassan still went?"

"He was desperate to develop. He was so ambitious, and when the Lumley family decided to support him financially, there was no stopping him. Then . . . I almost forgot. Professor Drugov offered courses in conducting. She had been a conductor herself, and Hassan was completely consumed by it."

"I guessed that," said the woman.

"Oh, really? I thought he did his best to suppress it later on."

"What happened to him?"

"The same thing that happens to many young men. He fell into the wrong company, and became increasingly extreme in his views. I saw hatred in him that frightened me, if I'm honest. It was as if he wanted revenge on everything he'd previously found beautiful."

"How did it begin?"

"I don't actually know. We had lost touch long before it happened. You might say that Drugov took over my role. She became his new hero."

"Drugov sent him to Moscow, didn't she?"

"Yes, exactly. And perhaps that was where he broke a little. I don't know. I'm guessing he was disappointed. But still . . ."

"Yes?" said the woman.

"At first he dealt with it well. I met him just after he'd returned home and been reconciled with his father. He had become the coach for the junior football team. He was full of energy and hopes for the future. But then he met that awful man."

"Which awful man would that be?"

"Gamal was his name. Gamal Zakaria."

"You mean . . . ?" said the woman, her voice suddenly eager.

"Yes, he was an Egyptian who went on to be a Taliban commander. Brutal, so I've heard. A ruthless individual, and sometimes I'm afraid that . . ."

She hesitated and rearranged some dishes on the draining board.

"What are you afraid of?"

"That Hassan got pulled into all that. I saw such darkness in his gaze towards the end, and sometimes I wondered whether he might harbour the same obsessive energy for destruction that he'd once had for playing. I hope he is with Allah now."

Rekke had said goodbye to his brother and was now on the phone in his study speaking to Viktor Malikov in Moscow. Without his realising it, his left leg had begun to twitch. On the computer, he was absent-mindedly running searches.

"Interesting," he said. "Do you know what happened next?"

"We've got a note that says Elena Drugov was worried about Barozai, and told Sasha off for being too hard on him. Although that's pretty much it. He disappeared off the school's radar."

Rekke remembered Belinsky's hand on his neck when he had been shaking in his dressing room in Bern.

"Was Sasha really that strict?"

"I have a hard time believing it," Viktor said. "And if I've got the story right, then no-one was harder on Barozai than Barozai himself. He mostly seems to have encountered polite silence."

"Of course, that can be bad enough."

"Although hardly a motive for murder," Viktor said.

Rekke turned his attention to the apartment, hoping to hear Micaela.

"There are motives for murder that have been stranger than that," he said. "Something big was taken from him. A door was closed. He wouldn't be the first person to set the world alight for something like that."

"Are you thinking of our little corporal who didn't get into art school in Vienna?"

"I was mostly thinking about what may have happened afterwards with such bitterness. What form did it take?"

"How do you mean?"

"I'm asking myself whether those emotions were displaced onto a religion that legitimised them. But you're right . . . it's pretty thin at this stage. Didn't you say that Sasha thought Sarwani and Barozai were romantically involved?"

"Yes. At first he thought so. Before Barozai began to play."

"Perhaps that's worth looking into," Rekke said thoughtfully.

"Perhaps it's a Mozart and Salieri story too? Barozai realised he'd never be able to play like Latifa and decided to seek revenge. Come on, don't try claiming that Pushkin made it all up and that Mozart and Salieri were actually just friends."

"Pushkin made it all up and Mozart and Salieri were actually just—"

"You know what I mean."

Rekke did understand. He had already had similar thoughts.

"I understand. Do pass on my thanks to Sasha. He's my hero. I'll be in touch," he said, sitting stock-still for a while, as if frozen.

Then he went online and sought out the picture of Latifa Sarwani's dead body which her father had incomprehensibly – or perhaps not so incomprehensibly – posted online, and an hour or more slipped by as he sat staring with no sense of time at the photograph, which was of surprisingly good quality.

He heard steps behind him. They belonged to Micaela, and he could see in her eyes that she had something to tell him too, and he thought once again about the train rushing out of the tunnel and her clattering footsteps coming from the other direction.

Kabul, Afghanistan, 1997

Hassan never forgot the liberation that the fit of rage brought with it: the dark anger, and the silence that followed. Equally, he remembered the music that returned afterwards, like a wave or a counterattack, and which sometimes appeared in his gestures and movements. It had begun almost immediately after the Taliban takeover of Kabul in the autumn of 1996.

He had tagged along with Gamal and his bodyguards to Kharabat, the music district of Kabul, and at first he had been shocked not by the Taliban's violence but by their indifference. They destroyed as if it were an absent-minded duty, a job that simply had to be done, and for a long time he could barely stand it. It hurt him when the tanburs and the zurnas were smashed against the walls and in the streets. But then one day . . . it must have been in December . . .

It had been cold and windy and he had accompanied them to the home of a man his own age who was said to be a writer and music teacher. The man lived in a large flat in the old town with his wife and his four children. He was a Sikh with a well-groomed beard and a red turban. He had received them at the door, not fearfully like so many others, or even angrily, but with contempt – an overt contempt that got under his skin. It was a beautiful home filled with books and paintings, and deep within it was a room with sitars mounted on the walls, which was where Gamal had gone straight away. For a brief moment he stood still as if admiring the instruments. Then he had taken one of them down – the most beautiful one, which was decorated with small white flowers – and had given it to Hassan.

"Smash it," he said. "It will please Allah."

It felt just as unthinkable as before. But then Hassan saw again the contempt in the Sikh's eyes. He heard him say: "No, not that one, it's a Sharma," and something happened.

The blood had gone to his head and he smashed the sitar against the wall, surprised by the anger welling up within him. He hadn't thought he had it in him. But he lost himself completely in the outburst, and afterwards he was surprised even more by the absence of shame. Rather than guilt, he was filled with relief, as if he had done away with a burden, and that was how it began – with a sitar, a 1954 Sharma.

After that, he would occasionally go on raids. It became a part of his life alongside the motorcycle garage and football, and on each occasion a little more of his resistance dissipated. He even longed to smash things. But then again, it wasn't his world. At first, he set about musicians from a completely different tradition from his own, which made it easier to hide behind Gamal's foot soldiers.

The people from Drugov's school felt completely different. It went against the grain in a different way, and it was a while before he dared approach them. Nevertheless, he was drawn to them, and one evening in the following year he and Gamal passed by the old presidential palace. It was a beautiful, cool evening, and surprisingly few people were out and about, although Gamal had his retinue of bodyguards and subordinates with him as he always did back then. In front of them on the pavement there was a dead dog – he remembered that later – but Gamal didn't see it. He raised his gaze and pointed to the Asamayi mountain.

"There," he said.

"What?"

"Up there in Deh Mazang is where your whore lives."

"Who?" he said.

"You know who I mean. She lives alone and in sin. It is rumoured that she plays by night and turns the heads of people. We're going to raid her."

Hassan – or Jamal as he had started calling himself – froze.

"Do you want me to come with you?" he said.

Gamal looked mockingly at him.

"I wanted you to have the opportunity to see her by yourself first. I give you my permission to do what is right. May Allah bless you."

"I don't know," he said.

"Don't hesitate now. This is your chance. But tell me when you're going. We have to protect you from her brother."

Hassan nodded and left with gritted teeth while feeling something new awaken in him – a desire for revenge. It was April 1, 1997, and two days passed before he dared approach her.

THIRTY-THREE

Rekke and Micaela were discussing the case when Mrs Hansson returned upstairs to cook them dinner. "Fish," she said. It was a char bought in the Östermalm market, cooked with white-wine sauce and celeriac purée. "Hans doesn't eat meat," she said. "He lives according to the principle that you can destroy yourself, but not the climate," she added, which made Hans fidget with embarrassment, mumbling that the unfortunate thing about self-destruction was that it still brought about other issues.

After that he had the sense to keep quiet and disappeared into his trance-like state. This left Micaela free to assuage her feelings of guilt at being waited on by helping Mrs Hansson with the dinner, all the while wondering whether Rekke had even noticed that he was once again being served by women.

"Delicious," she said to Mrs Hansson, who then retreated downstairs to her flat.

"Delicious," Rekke repeated, as if he had no idea what he was saying, and for a brief moment she stared at him as he ate.

"Do you even know what you're eating?" she said.

Hans looked at her in confusion.

"What . . . yes . . . more or less," he said.

"But you're mostly full of banalities, right? Things that roll off the tongue automatically – reflexively. *Thank you, thank you, sorry, sorry, delicious, splendid.*"

He peered at her in amusement.

"That's an interesting observation, and naturally you're right. They're rather like tics, aren't they? The injuries inflicted by a life of being spoiled. You, on the other hand –" he looked at her more closely – ". . . have waited upon others, haven't you? You've had spoiled brothers to deal with, and you've constantly staved off conflicts."

She shuddered.

"What makes you say that?"

"Because I see it in your quickness, in the efficiency of your movements, and your unconscious glances over your shoulder. You assumed responsibility at home from an early age, didn't you?"

"My mother did lots too," she said defensively.

He didn't comment on that, perhaps out of tactfulness or because he was absorbed again in other thoughts. But he was right. Mamá hadn't put in much of an appearance on the domestic scene since her father had died, and Lucas didn't see household chores as his responsibility.

"Were you thinking about Latifa Sarwani?" she said.

He looked at her again.

"No – you," he said.

She felt uncomfortable, but couldn't help asking:

"In what way?"

"I'm guessing that time is beginning to run out for us, and it worries me that I've brought you into this. I'm afraid they may be more desperate than I dared imagine."

"Are you talking about the CIA?"

He nodded.

"I shall do my best to strike back," he said.

"It'll be OK," she said hopefully.

"I hope so, and it ought to help that we've made such progress. We may even have caught a glimpse of the libretto itself," he said, in an attempt at cheerfulness.

She put down her cutlery.

"And what does that look like?"

"Hmm, well, to give it something of a three-act structure: a violist with grand ambitions has his dreams crushed in Moscow. He returns to his hometown in Pakistan and becomes friends with Gamal, who later becomes Mullah Zakaria in Kabul. Our hero starts a new life and assumes a new name. He transforms his love for music into something else entirely and manages to convince himself that what he had once seen as jealousy and bitterness was actually Allah's anger, and under that awful illusion he commits a terrible crime."

"But . . ."

"Perhaps it's a little too easy, and there are also parts that are untidy. That disrupt the dramaturgy."

"Like what?"

"He refereed football matches as if he still wanted to conduct, as you pointed out. I have difficulty believing he would still have had those scars on his fingers had he stopped playing that early."

"So you don't think he gave up on music after all?"

"I'm primarily wondering whether he killed Latifa Sarwani. Whether he had that much hate inside him."

She considered his words.

"But surely we first need to understand who took revenge on him?"

"Yes, we do," he said, then shook with withdrawal tremors. That irritated her.

Take your damn drugs so that you can solve this rather than talking drivel about the libretto was what she wanted to shout. Instead, she got up and cleared the dishes from the table – no doubt with the efficiency he had identified – and wondered whether he might help.

He didn't stir. She left to grapple with a thought that had been gnawing away at her for the last few hours. It related to Latifa Sarwani's father, Mohammad, who seemed to be the administrator of his daughter's online fan page.

Mohammad Sarwani was a women's doctor, a gynaecologist, born in 1925 but still practising – at least occasionally – in a clinic in Cologne. A photograph of him that she'd found online showed him to have kind eyes and a reassuring smile devoid of any smugness. His shoulders were slender and his dark hair thinning.

There was nothing distinctive or eye-catching about him, but she couldn't help thinking that his appearance matched the description of the old man who had been passing by the pitch at Grimsta after the game had finished.

Admittedly, it wasn't a conclusive match, and the description of the man in Grimsta as a decrepit little man was at odds with the quiet authority that Mohammad Sarwani radiated in the photo. But it was worth checking out, so she found the number for Niklas Jensen – the father who had seen the old man passing the pitch in his green coat.

Niklas was reluctant, just as he had been when they had last met.

"Are you at the computer?" she said.

He wasn't, but he could get to one "if necessary", and once he had, he complained that it wasn't working very well. "Sometimes I almost have to kick it to get it going," he said, "like an old banger," and she must have waited for ten minutes before he managed to pull up the link she had sent him.

"Well?" she said.

He was silent.

"No," he said. "It's not him."

"Are you sure?" she said.

"It's impossible to be sure of anything this long after the fact," he said.

"But if you look at the shoulders and the hair, and perhaps the eyes, it does feel quite similar to what you described."

"Perhaps," he said.

"And if he were to turn out to have a limp too . . ."

"I guess it's pretty close."

She got no further. He hung up irritably and she went back to the kitchen, to find that Rekke hadn't moved.

"We need to call Latifa Sarwani's father," she said.

Rekke didn't reply. He was lost in thought about the method of the murder: death by stoning, like in the old Abrahamic laws. It was as if the murder were simultaneously religious and ceremonial, yet also rash and indiscriminate. What wasn't he getting?

"What?" he said.

"We need to find out whether Mohammad Sarwani has a limp," she said. He looked at Micaela with sudden reserve, as if her appearance had reminded him of everything he ought to do, and he mumbled, "Oh, should we?" while wondering for the hundredth time whether there were any morphine tablets in the flat.

Kabul, April 3, 1997

An insight had begun to germinate within him: smashing instruments delivered a kick that passed increasingly rapidly. It was like a ball being pressed down into dark water: it always popped back up again. He resolved not to go to Latifa's again; he resolved to leave her alone, and he told Gamal this.

"It is never easy to serve Islam," Gamal said, "but in the end we receive our reward one thousandfold," and Hassan pretended to agree. But he also said, with unusual frankness, that he had felt small and like a failure when he had walked up to her house the day before. It was as if the days in Moscow had returned.

"Overcome it," said Gamal. "Go there tonight. Perhaps I shall come too."

They discussed it for a while, and before they parted, Gamal gave Hassan a pistol, an old Soviet Tokarev, just to be safe – so Gamal said. Hassan accepted the weapon hesitantly and put it in his nylon bag. He knew he should show more courage now that the times had changed, but every so often his courage deserted him and he felt weak.

That Thursday afternoon, he adjudicated a football match between two junior teams – Maiwand and Ordu – at the Ghazi Stadium. The stands were empty. The arena looked haunted. But the pitch was in good condition and the lines were freshly painted – the paint was still sticky. There was no litter on the touchlines, no casings, no bloodstains on the penalty spot where the condemned were shot or maimed each Friday. That didn't help much.

The dead made their presence felt, as phantoms and spirits, and Hassan sweated more than usual. Sometimes during the course of the match he thought of Latifa, and that made rage course through him. At other times, he thought he heard music rising from the pitch – pieces of Sibelius, Brahms and Mendelssohn that inhabited his arms and gestures.

When he blew the whistle for time, the sun was still burning his neck. On the way out of the stadium, he saw beggars in the streets and was afraid that he might smell bad himself. He was soaked in sweat, and changing clothes after the match had made no difference. His tunban absorbed the perspiration. He pulled it away from his skin and increased his pace. Deh Mazang was on the southern side of the Asamayi mountain, and he had kept his studs on to give him a grip on the hillside.

It had surprised him that she lived up there. When he had first heard about her, she was described as the pretty girl from Wazir Akbar Khan. But he guessed that the family must have had a tough time of it since then.

For a while, he had a gang of boys in their early teens on his tail – they wanted him to set up a match. He waved them away and continued up the hill, seeing the remnants of war here and there. Now and then, he encountered women in burkas and saw donkeys hauling carts.

As he got closer, he crept behind an abandoned barn and placed his Tokarev under the waistband of his tunban. The weapon chafed against his hip as he walked and on several occasions he considered putting it back in the bag, but he left it where it was. In the gloaming he saw the two-storey house and the meadow of yellow flowers that unfolded in front of the veranda. The house was one of the most modern in the area, with a demarcated garden and a small green tower. He looked around. There were people everywhere, but no-one seemed to be looking at him with any particular suspicion. When he had been here the first time, he had caught a glimpse of her father, the old doctor. Gamal had promised that neither he nor the brother, Taisir, would be here. But there was no way of guaranteeing that, or so he guessed. Wasn't he too early? He checked his wristwatch. It was now half past six. Gamal had suggested that he arrive much later – closer to midnight – when the neighbours were asleep and Latifa was often in her kitchen looking down into the valley.

He decided to take a walk, and paced off into the distance, increasingly nervous, the music playing in his head. When he returned some hours later, the neighbourhood was in darkness. He ventured closer to her kitchen window. A lamp shone from within the house, and he wondered whether to knock on the door. But he stayed where he was, half tempted to head back into town.

There was movement inside. The curtains suddenly opened, and when he saw her, it came as a shock. She was standing in the window with her whole face uncovered, looking straight at him, and he realised immediately that her weight had plummeted and she was hollow-eyed and slender as a bird. But her gaze was the same. He was once again lost and shy, and perhaps Latifa saw that and became less afraid. She opened the window a crack. Her lips moved.

"What?" he said.

"I recognise you."

"We've met before," he said, touching his long beard as if to help her imagine him without it.

"Where?"

"In Moscow," he said.

Her face changed. Her mouth opened, as if in astonishment or shock.

"It can't be," she said. "Is it you?"

"It's me," he said, feeling idiotic.

"Have you come back, or were you living here all along?"

He didn't know how to reply, but presumably there was something about his body language that made her anxious, because she seemed to want to close the window and disappear into the house.

"No," he said.

She hesitated, but didn't take her hand from the window.

"Should I be afraid?" she said.

"I want to help," he said, almost believing it.

She took a step backwards.

"Don't go," he said.

"What do you want?"

Her voice was scared, but perhaps there was more to it than that.

"I . . ." he said, hesitating. He had difficulty looking her in the eye.

"What?" she said.

"I want to hear you play again," he said, surprised by his own words.

She looked at him, surprised and helpless, and then he was suddenly more confident.

"I have contacts. I know . . ." He realised he didn't want to mention Gamal by name. "I can help you."

"I'm sick," she said, "and no hospitals will accept women."

"I'll do anything," he said.

She paused for thought.

"You liked it when I was playing in my room at the conservatory, didn't you?"

"I thought . . ." he said, unable to complete the sentence.

"I remember your tears," she said.

Again, words failed him.

"I just want to hear you," he said, intending to add "one last time", but thinking better of it.

It was ten to eight in the evening. Rekke was in his study, lost in the photo of Latifa Sarwani's dead body. The image was razor sharp, as if it had been taken by a professional. Absorbed in every dreadful detail, for a while Rekke thought he saw two bodies on the basement floor: Latifa's and that of the destroyed violin.

Both of them were lying there, each smashed in their own way, on wooden planks painted green that didn't reach all the way to the wall. When Rekke could no longer look at Latifa's slender body and shattered head, he examined the section of earthen floor not covered by the boards. It had been tamped down hard. Nevertheless, he thought he saw marks in it, and perhaps a white stain – a small strip – but he wasn't certain. He rooted in the desk drawer for a magnifying glass.

That didn't improve matters. He was breathing a little too heavily and steamed up the lens. "Hell," he muttered, going to sit at the grand piano, but he didn't have it in him to play a single note. It's impossible to feel this bad, he thought to himself. It's undignified, absurd. "Pull yourself together," he said aloud. "You're pathetic." Then he picked up his phone, checking that Micaela was out of earshot.

"Freddie Nilsson," said a voice on the line.

"It's Hans."

"Christ, you're panting."

"I highly doubt that," he said. "But I need more of this and that."

Freddie Nilsson remained silent and Rekke felt self-loathing at having called in every part of his body.

"Don't you have enough to keep you going for ages?" Freddie said.

"Threw it all away. Wanted to go clean and be free."

"But you don't want that any longer?"

"I want to be in your hands, amen."

"No change for the better otherwise? Something must have got you to chuck your stuff."

"I had a moment of optimism. Met an angel, you might say. Now cease your interrogation this instant, you scoundrel. I'll deposit whatever you ask into your account."

"Sure," Freddie said, preparing to take notes.

*

Micaela was talking to Jonas Beijer about Mohammad Sarwani and his son Taisir. She felt she was giving more than she was getting back, and she longed to speak to Rekke. But he had disappeared without even saying goodbye or offering an explanation. So she was wandering around the apartment thumbing through his books.

Sometimes she thought about her father. More than ever before, she felt as if an entire world had disappeared with him, as if Lucas had wanted to get rid of the old when he had taken over responsibility at home. Perhaps it was her memory failing her, though, and what did it matter now anyway? Things were the way they were, and she would have to find her path in life.

At twenty to ten in the evening, her thoughts were interrupted. Rekke returned, seemingly feeling better. He wasn't anywhere near as tense and he immediately told her she was right: they should most definitely look into whether Mohammad Sarwani had a limp like the old man in Grimsta.

"We'll go to Cologne first thing tomorrow morning," he said.

"What?" she said, surprised by his sudden decisiveness.

"Didn't you say earlier that we should pick up the pace?"

She thought.

"I suppose I did. But Jonas Beijer wants to wait and get permission to tap their phone before we approach Sarwani."

Rekke shook his head impatiently.

"We don't have time for that."

She guessed that he wanted to act before the CIA stopped him.

"My colleagues won't be happy if I head off to Germany before I've even started," she said.

"Naturally I apologise."

"But I'm not sure I care what they think anymore," she said.

Rekke smiled and made as if to touch her, but, as he had the time before, he then withdrew his hand.

333

"Perhaps we ought to call the old doctor as a matter of courtesy. To let him know we're coming," he said.

"You might discreetly ask whether he has a limp too."

"I shall," he said, heading into the living room, where he played a few anxious notes on the piano as an introduction or accompaniment to the conversation.

A few minutes elapsed, then she heard him say:

"My name is Hans Rekke. Would you prefer English or German?"

THIRTY-FOUR

Mohammad Sarwani was a widower and in exile, and he had lost the daughter he had loved more than life itself. But he was not alone. He had his son, and two grandchildren, and a wide circle of Afghans in exile who regarded his home as a gathering point. In his own way, he was a fortunate man. He was approaching eighty and still practised his profession.

Sometimes, in the good moments, he would hold his head high and feel pride. He had stood up for what was right. He had retained his dignity, and he had no intention of forgoing it now just because Darman Dirani had called to say that someone by the name of Professor Rekke had been in touch to ask intrusive questions.

Mohammad had calmed him down. He had told him that too much time had passed and that they couldn't possibly have any evidence. But afterwards he had checked the name with a doctor colleague at the University of California, and what he had been told had been both good and bad. Good because the professor had been deported and was said to be psychologically unstable, bad because Rekke was reportedly a legendary problem-solver for the San Francisco Police Department.

He switched off the news on the television. It had been showing a report on Afghanistan, on the increasing violence and oppression of women ahead of the country's first free elections in the coming autumn. There was no end to the misfortunes that befell his homeland. He stood up and caressed the portrait of Latifa on the bureau. Latifa looked up at him encouragingly, her violin clasped in her left hand, and he said to her: "I'll deal with this too." At that moment the ring of the telephone made him jump.

"Would you prefer English or German?" Professor Rekke asked after introducing himself, though he must have known that Mohammad had been raised in the British quarter of Kabul.

"English," he said.

"Splendid. I'm sorry to disturb you at this late hour."

Mohammad collected himself.

"Telephone calls from famous professors can only enliven an old man such as myself."

"Nicely put," the professor said. "Allow me to counter by saying that I was deeply moved when I heard your daughter play Bruch's violin concerto. Such heavenly beauty."

"The way she played was enough to make angels weep, don't you agree?"

"Do you have more recordings?"

"That is one of my many sorrows. The Taliban destroyed all other recordings. But thanks to Allah's benevolence, I hear her playing constantly in my head. Her music was so beautiful that no-one can kill it. Not even time."

"Beauty has a most peculiar power of resistance. I hope her assassin met with a truly terrible fate."

"I'm convinced of it. Allah sees and passes judgement. But . . . it is awful, is it not? Some people seem too beautiful to be permitted to live. All the small, stunted souls unite and come after them."

"I'm afraid so. Sometimes that is indeed the case."

"Jealousy and ingratiation are human nature."

"True, but there is more to it than that, surely? There is so much else. Especially in men such as you, Dr Sarwani."

"I am a humble man."

"I don't doubt that."

"You were a prominent pianist, were you not, Professor Rekke?"

"I had my years during which I graced the keyboard. But nowadays my work is more prosaic. I am assisting in the investigation of a murder in Stockholm of a man who called himself Jamal Kabir."

"I see," Mohammad said. "I did hear about that."

What else was he supposed to say? He looked quizzically at his daughter's portrait on the bureau and waited for Rekke's next remark. But Rekke said nothing, and he became increasingly nervous. For safety's sake, he remained silent too – but as the seconds passed and began to feel like minutes, that didn't work.

"Are you still there?" he said.

"Yes, sorry," Rekke said. "I was distracted. Where were we?"

"You were talking about the man who was murdered in Stockholm."

"Ah yes," he said. "He was beaten to death with a rock in a copse of trees just after a football match, as you may know."

What was he supposed to say now?

He settled for: "It was brutal."

"Yes," said the professor. "You aren't in pain are you, Doctor?"

Mohammad felt a new sense of unease.

"Absolutely not. Why do you ask?"

"Courtesy. You have a problem with your leg, I gather."

Mohammad looked nervously at his thin thighs.

"It was nothing more than an unsuccessful knee operation. It's better now."

"I'm pleased to hear it," Rekke said. After a pause he said: "My colleague and I are travelling to Cologne early tomorrow morning."

"I beg your pardon?" he said.

"It would be an honour to meet you, Dr Sarwani. I believe we can be with you by lunchtime."

"The honour would be all mine. But while my home is open to friends and strangers alike, I should still like to hear what the matter concerns."

Rekke was silent for a while, and Mohammad understood – the professor knew he knew.

"We wish to discuss your daughter and this murder in Stockholm."

"Nothing is dearer to me than talking about Latifa. But I know nothing of this case in Stockholm."

"I think you underestimate yourself," Rekke said. "Although perhaps it is best we invite Darman Dirani too. I'm sure he can help us to remember."

"Why should I invite him?"

"The more the merrier?"

"I don't know."

"Above all, your son Taisir is most welcome."

Mohammad felt sudden anger and it was somehow liberating.

"It sounds as if you are the host, rather than me."

Rekke was silent again.

"I apologise, it's a quite frightful breach of etiquette. But I'm afraid it's the nature of a murder investigation that exceptions to the rules of polite society must be made. It will be a pleasure to meet you."

Afterwards, his heart pounding, Mohammad turned to the portrait on the bureau.

"There's nothing to worry about, my darling, nothing at all," he said, and this time Latifa seemed to answer: *Are you sure about that, Baba? Are you sure?*

"Not on my life am I going to let them travel to Cologne."

Jonas Beijer had locked himself in the bathroom and was holding the phone away from his ear. Carl Fransson could bleat all he wanted. There wasn't anything to be done about it. Jonas had tried to stop the trip. But Rekke had found a way over their heads and was now booked onto a flight to Cologne at 9.20 the next morning, together with Vargas.

"Falkegren has already signed off on it," he said.

"What does that damned nuisance have to do with anything?" Fransson snapped, and it was a good question.

It was incomprehensible that Falkegren once again wanted Rekke to work on the case. What was more, his voice had sounded a little off when he called. It was almost as if he didn't think they'd get to Cologne. "They're most welcome to give it a go," he'd said. "Try their luck."

"I don't know," Jonas said. "There's something fishy about it. But perhaps he wants to get his own back. It feels right in a lot of ways."

"Why would it be right?"

"Well, in several ways. Not just because Mohammad Sarwani may very well be the man seen at Grimsta. His son Taisir—"

"Yes, what about him?"

"He's got a conviction for bodily harm in Germany," Jonas said. "He seems quite a bruiser, and he's got a snake tattooed on his neck, which may very well tally with what Costa saw on Gulddragargränd."

Fransson seemed to pause for thought.

"Yes, yes, OK then," he said. "Let them go. But then I'm taking over, and I hope that's clear to you. Have we informed the North Rhine–Westphalia State Police?"

Jonas muttered assent, but was already lost in other thoughts. The only thing that really concerned him at the moment was that Micaela was going away alone with Professor Rekke, and that Falkegren had sounded so odd on the phone, as if he already knew how the trip was going to end.

Kabul, the early hours of April 4, 1997

Latifa had released the canaries that afternoon, just as she was supposed to according to the new rules announced on Radio Shariat. But Jupiter and Venus didn't want their freedom. They sat on the windowsill, stiff and confused, as if longing to return to their cage. Eventually, she shooed them away and shut the window.

"You're going to die," she muttered. "We're all going to die."

She remained in the kitchen, listless. It didn't matter how much Baba and Taisir tried to make her eat. She didn't want anything and wanted to hear their encouragement even less. "I'm too sick to flee," she said. "Leave me alone." But they never left her alone. Never ever, and often they stayed with her. They were breaking her down.

Everything was breaking her down – the isolation, the inactivity, the longing, the depression. She wanted nothing anymore, nothing, and it had been a long time since she had crept down to the basement to play because there was no-one who listened or cared.

"Go," she had said several times, "go," and at around eleven in the evening Baba and Taisir had finally gone, because Taisir had heard nothing was going to happen tonight – the moron had Taliban contacts and sometimes he was almost as thick as they were.

Now she was sitting in the kitchen looking about her vacantly, wondering whether Venus and Jupiter were as paralysed and listless as she was, and she went over to the window – not because she hoped to see them, but mostly to stare down towards the town as usual and wonder how everything had become so quiet and dead, and that was when she saw him: a man of her own age, wearing a white perahan tunban, with a brown pakol on his head. Like all men these days – even her own father – he had a beard down to his chest.

It was hard to see him properly in the dark, and the vision in her left eye was poor. But he was quite clearly staring at her kitchen window. There was something pleading and anxious about his body that made her think back to the time when men had become anxious in her presence.

Should she ask him what he was doing? Absolutely not. She ought to withdraw to the bedroom and turn off the lights. She ought to raise the alarm with her brother. Yet she did nothing, staying where she was, somehow fascinated, as if something was finally going to happen to her. But that was nonsense. It was wishful thinking from a brain in need of something to grasp on to, and she told herself to go, to hide away.

But for some reason she did the reverse, making herself visible. The man

came closer and she sensed that it was more than just his posture and air
of anxiety that was affecting her. He seemed familiar. But where from? She
didn't know. The music, which had been silent for so long, came back.

She thought she could hear her own bow strokes. She felt increasingly
defiant, and while she heard a voice inside her saying Don't do it, she finally
opened the window. That startled him, and she thought: Let things go the
way they go, let him see my forbidden face. Then it was as if she forgot
everything. She realised who he was, and she could barely comprehend it.
She'd thought about him, not often, but sometimes when trying to recollect
those good years when she had been able to awaken so many emotions.

He wanted to hear her play, and that was unthinkable. She didn't know
anything about him, not back then and now even less so. But then again . . .
she thought she saw desire in his eyes, and somewhere deep down that was
exactly what she was hoping for – an audience that wasn't her father and
that wasn't forever listening anxiously for the sound of footsteps.

"OK, come in," she said, and he reacted like a schoolboy who didn't
expect to be invited in, and that was good, she thought. It had to be good.

He admires me, she thought. He cried in Moscow. I'm the one who has
the upper hand. She wrapped a shawl around her head, took a deep breath
and opened the door. The first thing to hit her was the stench. He smelled of
sweat, and she didn't like the tone in his voice when he asked:

"Do you still have the violin?"

You'll never find it, she wanted to say. Never. But instead she nodded,
thinking she couldn't take him down to the basement, not now, not ever, it
was all a mistake. Cry for help, she thought. But no, it was already too late
for that. She had received a man in the middle of the night. She had to deal
with this herself. She urgently needed to restore some form of normality.

"Do you still play?" she said.

"Not any longer," he replied, far too curtly and grimly.

"Didn't you live in Pakistan?"

"I came back," he said, and she wondered why a violist would return to
a country where music was forbidden.

"Why . . . ?" she said.

"It went quiet," he said.

"I know that," she said, without being sure they were talking about the same thing.

"But lately I've begun to hear the music again. It comes back in fragments."

He looked past her.

She thought she discerned a tremble in his shoulders.

"That's good, I suppose."

"I would very much like to hear you play again. I think it would heal me a little," he said, and she began – as if she no longer had control of her own feet – to head towards the guest room, where she had positioned her white wooden sofa over the hatch to the basement.

Micaela woke early. She was lying in the same room where she had worked the evening before, and she looked up at the bookcase to her left. It felt strange to have slept over, and even stranger to be going away with Rekke. She hadn't had time to buy a change of clothes, but Julia had lent her underwear and a couple of shirts that weren't too small a fit. Outside in the inner courtyard the rain was falling.

The sky looked dark, and she heard footsteps in the stairwell. It must be Mrs Hansson, she thought. But then she thought it sounded like several people, so she got up and pulled on her jeans and sweatshirt. It was ten past six in the morning – there was still plenty of time before they had to leave for Arlanda. She was wondering whether Rekke was up when there was a knock at the door. The knocks were hard, and she shouted into the apartment:

"Hans, are you going to get that?"

She got no reply, and when the knocks were repeated, she went to the front door and peered through the peephole. Standing outside were three men, all in suits, and she shouted again:

"Rekke."

Silence. She pulled out her phone. There was no coverage, which made her truly worried. She took a step back. At last she heard steps behind her, and the words, "I'm so sorry, I'll open it."

Rekke was approaching, freshly shaved and showered, wearing grey tailored trousers and a pale-blue shirt with a somewhat old-fashioned waistcoat. He mumbled, "I'm sorry, Micaela." He let the men in, and they immediately positioned themselves to block the door. Something about them – especially the two younger men – suggested they were prepared for violence, but Rekke could not have seemed more relaxed. He held out his arms and assumed a wide smile.

"Charles," he said. "What a treat. I've missed you."

A slightly older man with brown eyes and a well-groomed beard replied in a friendly voice:

"Likewise, Hans. Sorry to barge in so early."

"On the contrary, you're just in time for breakfast. Please do excuse my impertinence – I haven't greeted your friends. Hans Rekke," he said, offering his hand to the two men, who introduced themselves as José Martín and Henry Lamar.

"What a pleasure," he continued. "Do allow me to introduce my friend and colleague Micaela Vargas. A first-rate police officer, although you'll know that, of course."

Micaela proffered her hand and greeted them. There was clearly a showdown in progress, so she unpacked the chilly, cocksure look that Lucas had taught her early on.

"Tea or coffee?" Rekke said.

"I don't think . . ." began the man called Henry.

"No? Busy day, I suppose. But Henry . . . you'll excuse my asking. Your right shoulder – I'm fascinated. Javelin or baseball? Javelin, I should think. For how long?"

Henry looked at him in confusion.

"How did you know . . . ?" he said, before quickly regaining his composure. "Until I was twenty-one."

"You were good, I think?"

"Fourth in the US nationals."

"Impressive. But confounded bad luck having that shoulder injury. It never quite goes away, does it? Alas. Well, come in, everyone. And my apologies to you, José, I know that you too were an athlete. American football, I believe. Although naturally you were more of an intellectual. Good decision renouncing Catholicism. But you pay a price for it, don't you?"

"I don't understand . . ."

"The chain around your neck – it took a little effort to remove the cross, didn't it? The eyelet is a little bent and worn at the bottom, and I recognise a secular brother when I see one. But don't hesitate, please come in."

The older man whose name was Charles smiled slightly, as if Rekke's exhibition was amusing. But when Micaela looked closer she saw that he was still on his guard, as if before a fight or a duel, and he kept glancing around the apartment, as if looking for something.

"Hans, buddy, I'm sure you know why we're here."

"Of course. You'd prefer that we didn't travel to Cologne."

Charles nodded, almost sadly, while José and Henry took a step closer to Rekke.

"We have the law on our side, as you know, Hans," Charles said. Then, turning to Micaela: "I'm afraid we'll have to take you in too, Miss Vargas. Only temporarily, of course."

"I'm afraid she's got a prior appointment. But we were talking about sports, were we not?" Rekke said, smiling encouragingly at José and Henry, who were standing close by him now.

"*You* were talking about sports," Charles said.

"True," he said. "I'm babbling, and you're thinking about more important things, as usual. But let me keep to the subject nonetheless. I'm guessing you've got two more boys downstairs at the main door, right?"

"Maybe," Charles said.

"Sensible," he said. "You see, my good friend Micaela is astoundingly quick and explosive. Sometimes I hear her footsteps like drumbeats in my thoughts."

"Is that so?" Charles said in confusion.

"And I too – paradoxically, or possibly as a result of my neurosis – am quite capable in physical terms. My sport, as you well know, Charles, is karate. I would have preferred to box, but my mother considered it barbaric. Karate was our compromise. My mother appreciated the bowing at the beginning. A polite gesture, then off you go. That was her own method, in a way."

He made a movement with his hands that looked more like the beginning of a dance than an attack. It still made José and Henry jump, however, and put their hands inside their jackets. Micaela looked at Rekke in exasperation. Of course they were armed. What on earth was he playing at? Was he hoping to fight his way out?

"There you have it," he said with a smile. "That gave me a little more information. Not the fastest reflexes, Henry. And I'm wondering, José, whether you're starting to develop torticollis. Your left side seems a little stiff – I would most definitely work on it."

Charles shook his head and laughed or snorted – it was hard to tell which.

"Karate. That's your strategy?"

Rekke took a step back towards the kitchen.

"I currently see seven or perhaps eight options I believe would be successful. I wanted to highlight your difficulties in acting in this matter, and in that regard my martial-arts exercises are illustrative – a childish depiction of your problems."

Charles glanced anxiously around the apartment.

"What do you mean?" he said.

Rekke raised his eyebrows and smiled again.

"Yesterday evening I popped out briefly and made a few calls from a telephone I don't think you have access to. So I can pass on regards from, among others, Maureen Hamilton at the *Washington Post*."

"Goddammit," Henry said, taking a step closer.

"Calm down," Rekke said. "I didn't say a word about what I know. I honour my agreements. But I made inquiries. I discovered a little more about what is in the process of being leaked. *The New Yorker* and CBS seem to have extensive documentation of torture and degradation in your Baghdad prison, and it will be rather difficult to claim that *exitus acta probat*. It seems mostly to have been adolescent sadism exercised by bored soldiers, and obviously the *Post* and the *Times* are doing their best to catch up. Would it really be a good look if you arrested me immediately prior to such a splash?"

Charles shrugged and emitted a theatrical sigh.

"We make our own risk assessments."

"Naturally. And I'm more than familiar with them. But let me say something else. I have, as everyone does these days, lawyers – a secretive, mysterious existence, I must say. And unto one of them I have given some of what I have learned in the course of my work for you. The details are being held in the strictest confidence. Nevertheless . . . there are provisos. *Inter alia* that I must travel to Cologne as planned."

"Dammit, Hans."

Rekke checked his watch.

"Yes, quite. We all use the tricks we have to hand, don't we?"

"This changes nothing," Charles said sharply.

"No?" said Rekke. "But I haven't finished. I believe it's my colleague you should be most concerned about."

"Why is that?" Charles said, looking suspiciously at Micaela.

"Because she's part of a murder inquiry that is close to a breakthrough, and your interference would look very bad, wouldn't it? Especially given that her chief of police, the luckless Falkegren, withheld information, having been manipulated by you, my dear Charles."

A worried, almost aggressive look crossed Charles's face.

"What gave you that idea?" he said.

"I met my brother yesterday evening. Magnus explained that you and Falkegren go running together on Djurgården and like to share confidences."

Charles made a gesture that implied he wanted to strangle someone. Probably Magnus.

"Yes, quite," Rekke said. "Magnus is hopeless. You never know which side he's on. But Charles – are you quite sure you won't stay for breakfast? I'm most eager to discuss this curious idea of dissolving the Iraqi army, because surely you realise that many of the soldiers have joined a new terrorist group. They call themselves something long and ceremonious, I forget what. But I'm convinced they will find something wittier soon. An abbreviation, perhaps."

Charles Bruckner took a deep breath, as if giving up, and Rekke smiled sadly before going into the kitchen. Micaela and Charles remained in the hallway, regarding each other with mutual distrust. Micaela thought for a second: He has ill will towards me, he's looking for weak spots, then she shook off the thought and joined Rekke in the kitchen.

THIRTY-FIVE

Kabul, the early hours of April 4, 1997

I want to hear you play, he had said. Was that why he was here? He didn't know. All he knew was that he was agitated, and he wanted to shout: Cover your face, woman. Perhaps he wanted to strike her too. To thrash away the assertive light in her eyes. Nevertheless, he smiled and nodded as if to emphasise his words, and when Latifa proceeded further into the house, he noticed her shoulder blades. She seemed to be nothing but skin and bones, and without knowing why he reached out with a hand that almost grazed her. He immediately withdrew it when she turned around.

"Should I be afraid?" she said.

He could feel the weight of the pistol at his waist.

"No," he said.

"You wanted to heal, didn't you?"

"I just want to hear you play," he said.

She nodded gravely and asked him to help her push aside a white sofa, which he did. On the floor where the sofa had been was a hatch with a rusty iron handle.

"Do you keep the violin down there?"

She said nothing. Instead, she took a torch from a nearby chest of drawers, pointed to the handle on the floor and asked him to open the hatch and go down first, which worried him. Was it a trap? Perhaps she had heard what he had done to other people's instruments. Perhaps she wanted revenge and was going to lock him down there. But she would never dare, he decided. He opened the hatch. The smell of soil and damp struck him, and while Latifa shone the torch onto the steps he descended into the darkness, feeling again the anger, the longing to destroy and be liberated from what was pounding too hard in his chest.

Micaela and Rekke were heading for security in terminal five at Arlanda. They were in a hurry. The Americans had strung things out, and on the way there Rekke had stopped to buy new SIM cards for their phones. All the same, he was calmer, and not once had he put his hands to his chest as he had been doing the day before.

She had spoken to Jonas Beijer, a little surprised that the team were letting them go so easily, especially since Jonas seemed worried. "Take care of yourself," he said two or three times. There was a long queue at security, but to her surprise they bypassed everyone, taking a lane to the left, and it was a moment before she realised that it was because they were travelling business class. Behind them a young man with arrogant eyes was staring at her arse. The attention made her uneasy. But then again, she had been uncomfortable to start with.

She picked up a grey tray and put the bag she had been lent by Rekke into it before placing the tray on the conveyor belt. She was about to add her handbag, phone and jacket when the man on security shot a suspicious glance her way. It was obvious she didn't belong in business class. It may have been that glance – or just her general feeling of unease – that made her remember Charles Bruckner's eyes, which had seemed to wish her ill. Before she'd had time to think it through she grabbed hold of her bag as it was about to go into the X-ray machine.

The movement was unexpectedly aggressive. She stumbled back into the arrogant-looking man behind her, and in the space of a second a row erupted in the queue. The security attendant stepped forward, though that didn't mean anything: maybe she had just forgotten to remove something – a fumbling, anxious person. Yet she was afraid, as if her body had detected danger before her brain was conscious of it. At that point Rekke came to life, pushing through the crowd to help her. The man from security called for a colleague, who lurched forward too.

People moved to allow Rekke to stand with her and her bag, and in that moment she remembered Bruckner's footsteps vanishing into the apartment that morning when she went into the kitchen. There was muttering around her. She wondered whether to pull out her police ID to try to put a stop to it all, but she was afraid that it would only make matters worse, so she just stood there while Rekke turned around and smiled in embarrassment at the man approaching him.

"Splendid," he said. "We were looking for an expert. My wife doesn't know what to do about rolls of film. Does the X-ray camera ruin them?"

"I need you to open the bag," said the man, which made Rekke beam as if this were an excellent idea.

"Of course," he said. "We can't be too careful these days."

He bent down and opened the bag with a rapid movement. Then he lifted it up, but managed to trip and fall in a clumsy movement across the conveyor belt. It looked simultaneously comical and dramatic, and his hand shuddered as if he had hurt himself. People continued to mutter. Rekke smiled in embarrassment again and apologised. He turned towards the men on security.

"Be my guests – we haven't got much with us as you'll see," he said.

Micaela was convinced that they were not only going to search the bag but Rekke too. His behaviour was without doubt suspicious. But at that moment he was radiating such authority that the men merely nodded and went over to the bag while Rekke took a step back towards her, before unexpectedly kissing her on the cheek and saying: "Good job you're so attentive, my darling," which alone would have startled her.

She forgot about it instantly, though, when she realised that he had put something in her jacket pocket. For a few panicked seconds she wondered what to do. She took a step back just as the younger of the two men said:

"There aren't any rolls of film in here."

"That's odd. Then I really must apologise. A kitten in the house is quite wonderful, isn't it?"

The man looked at Rekke in surprise, taken aback. Then he said: "Yes – how did you know?"

"The small, fine scratches on your hands," Rekke said, throwing in some remarks about the paws of kittens. Micaela decided to act.

She set off, convinced that they would come after her, feeling their eyes on the back of her neck as she walked back the way she had come.

THIRTY-SIX

Micaela heard footsteps behind her and expected a hand to grab her shoulder. But no-one stopped her as she hurried into the toilet, locked the door and put her hand in her jacket pocket.

Her fingers closed around a plastic pouch. She pulled it out and smelled it. It was cocaine – definitely cocaine – and with trembling hands she squeezed the contents into the toilet and watched the white powder sink towards the bottom of the bowl while her thoughts raged within her. She nervously scrutinised the plastic. There were still grains inside it, and no matter how much she squeezed there would be traces left. So she threw the pouch into the toilet as well, then flushed, but it remained there in the water. She flushed again and again without success, and when someone tried the locked door handle she closed her eyes for a moment and prepared for them to force the door.

But all she heard from outside was a profanity. She forced herself to breathe calmly and wait until more water had filled the cistern. She tried again and this time managed to flush away the plastic. When she emerged from the toilets, she could see Rekke still in conversation with the men over by security. He broke off when she appeared, and smiled slightly as if it had all been an amusing little incident. Then they passed through security, retrieved their bags from the conveyor and strolled on towards the duty-free shop.

"I'm sorry," he said. "I should have realised."

At first she said nothing.

Then she hissed: "How the hell could they sink that low?"

"I don't know," he said. "But I think . . ."

His hand grazed hers. He smiled cautiously.

"What?" she said.

"They underestimated you. How did you realise?"

She grabbed a tube of toothpaste from a nearby shelf.

"Bruckner's eyes when you went to the kitchen. He looked like he was cooking up some shit. But more than anything, his eyes when he left. He seemed way too pleased with himself."

"Quite," said Rekke. "He wasn't anywhere near as resigned as I had expected. I thought about that too. But my imagination didn't extend to the idea that he might have placed something in your bag. What gave you the idea?"

She looked him in the eyes.

"I don't know whether you would understand," she said.

"Give me a chance."

She hesitated, noting the assured way he moved towards the tills.

"You don't even notice the respect you get everywhere, while I constantly feel like I'm about to be stopped. That's a burden I've carried since I was little. It's part of the package of being a dark-skinned kid from Husby."

He stared at her intently.

"And that sharpens your vision?"

"I guess so," she said.

"That's an asset, a hard-earned one. I'm . . ."

He put an arm around her to squeeze her.

"What?" she said.

"Impressed."

Kabul, the early hours of April 4, 1997

She saw him go down into the basement. Her torch illuminated his legs and football boots taking the steps carefully, one at a time, and she thought to herself: *This is wrong, this is madness.* It might look like a prison cell down there, a burial site, but it was her holy room, the only refuge she'd had during her restless, shut-in days when the passing of time did not make itself felt by any means other than her becoming paler and thinner, and her attacks increasing in frequency. In the basement she would not only play and tend to her violin, but also read some of her hidden books.

But now he was on the way down there. She had never known him properly but for a little while he had moved her because he seemed to feel every note she played more keenly than anyone she had ever met. What was she supposed to do?

She stared out across the city and mountains. Everywhere was deserted and dark. There were no stars in the sky; the calls to prayer had fallen silent. The lights were extinguished in every house, though smoke was rising in the distance. She had time to think to herself that it was probably smoke from some catastrophe when she heard him say from below:

"Are you coming?"

Flee, she thought to herself, *run to Taisir or Baba.* She said: "I'm coming," and she could feel that it wasn't just folly – she wanted to play. The risk and the danger merely reinforced her desire and she climbed down too, the stench of sweat even clearer now. The reek blended with the smell of earth and damp, and with almost no hesitation she removed one of the planks from the floor and retrieved the violin case that contained her Gagliano. She opened it and caressed the violin nervously.

"I need to add a sordino," she said. "I don't want anyone else to hear."

"That's not necessary. But perhaps you need to tune the violin?"

"Yes, I'll tune it."

She started, but it was slow work. Her hands were trembling and because she had put down her torch she could no longer see his face.

His breathing and his voice were all she had to go by. He sounded tense, as if he were awaiting a big, ceremonial moment. But she couldn't tell whether *it was good or bad. All she knew was that it was as if she were being drawn up onto a stage, as if she were about to play the concert of her life.*

The taxi stopped and they got out. Micaela looked around. They were in the Lindenthal district of Cologne, where Mohammad Sarwani lived in a white block of flats adjacent to a park with long avenues of trees. The ground floor of the block housed an Indian restaurant. It was half past twelve, and in silence they climbed the stairs to the first floor before ringing the doorbell.

It did not take long for the door to be opened and a small, hunched-over, thin-haired man with half-closed eyes looked at them. It was not difficult to understand why so many witnesses had ignored him. He looked like he wouldn't hurt a fly. His arms and legs were slender, his eyes friendly and curious. But unlike the description taken in Grimsta, he now looked distinguished, dressed smartly in a long blue shirt and white trousers, with a striking gold-embroidered Afghan waistcoat on top.

"Welcome. This is such an honour."

"The honour is all ours," Rekke said.

"I have invited my son Taisir, as per your suggestion, and also Darman Dirani."

"Splendid," Rekke said, approaching the two men, who were seated on a brown sofa suite in the living room. "Gentlemen, my name is Hans Rekke. This is my colleague, Micaela Vargas."

The men nodded stiffly and greeted them. Neither Taisir or Darman had the same friendly urbanity as the older man. Instead, they were looking at her with hostility, Taisir most of all. He looked a bit like the boys who used to flock to Lucas. He had the same guardedness in his body, and the same eyes that aimed never to show weakness.

"What a pleasure to meet you. You've been in my thoughts a great deal," Rekke said.

Taisir seemed to take the words as an insult. But Rekke did not care, instead taking a tour of the room.

"How fascinating; it's like a beautiful little museum," he said, and it was true, there were objects from different eras and from around the world. But nothing was particularly remarkable to Micaela's eyes, except that there were books scattered everywhere, and wooden statuettes on the bureaus and tables. The walls were covered in photographs, not only of Latifa, but also of other well-known violinists. Rekke seemed most interested in a book lying on top of a bureau towards the back of the room. The book was titled *The Gardens of Emily Dickinson*. Mohammad Sarwani approached, limping slightly, still smiling, but clearly troubled by Rekke touching his possessions.

"Do you like Dickinson?" he asked.

"Of course. Who doesn't? A poet of the flowers," Rekke said.

"Yes, more than anyone else."

"But she didn't just write beautifully about flowers, did she? She knew the art of pressing them too. Look at this beautiful violet . . ."

"Very beautiful," Mohammad said drily.

"Although it is a fragile flower, is it not? It takes much care," Rekke said.

Mohammad Sarwani managed a strained smile.

"Exactly," he said. "That is surely why the violet so fascinated Shakespeare."

"Quite. I had almost forgotten that. What is it that Ophelia says in Hamlet? That the violets withered when her father died?"

"A sad scene. But if we press them like Emily Dickinson did, then they live forever," said Mohammad.

Rekke laughed.

"Although not quite in the form they would have preferred themselves. What do you consider the violet to symbolise?"

"Most often faithfulness and love."

"And love is fragile, isn't it? Just like Ophelia."

"I would say that is a drastic interpretation."

Rekke appeared to contemplate this.

"You're probably right. My thoughts run away with me all too easily. And *Iris afghanica* – what does that represent?"

Mohammad did a double take, or at least Micaela thought so, but if he did it was for no more than a split second. Then he smiled with the same friendliness and self-confidence he had shown at the door.

"Nothing, so far as I know. But it is most dear to us Kabulis since it is unique to the area and was discovered there."

"I quite understand. It grows on the Asamayi mountain, doesn't it? That's where your daughter lived."

"That's possible."

"Yes," said Rekke. "I'm sure that's the case. It's a vigorous flower. Reminiscent of Latifa, wouldn't you say?" Rekke continued leafing through the book. "Do you know whether Dickinson ever pressed any?"

"I doubt it."

"I'm sure you're right. People and plants didn't travel quite so easily in those days."

Rekke returned to the others on the sofas and gestured to Mohammad and Micaela to sit down. He clearly wanted to take command.

"Aren't there an unusually high number of Anglo-Saxon references here for a man from Kabul?" he said.

Mohammad fiddled with the bowls of nuts and snacks that had been set out on the coffee table.

"I was raised in the British quarter of the city."

"Of course," Rekke said. "I think I knew that. Hence your interest in Western music."

"Then why do you ask?" Taisir said abruptly.

Rekke beamed.

"Good point. I have an idiotic passion for rhetorical questions. Let us instead speak plainly and discuss the unhappy circumstances that brought you to Grimsta IP on that rainy day," he said, reaching for the pistachios. Micaela felt the atmosphere around the coffee table grow more threatening.

Kabul, the early hours of April 4, 1997

She was sitting on the brown chair that she'd had since she was a girl, and she could feel in her whole body that she wanted to play, but also – just as pressingly – that she wanted to understand what it was all about. So she said quietly: "Sorry, I'm very nervous. I think I need to see your face. Is it alright if I illuminate you?"

"It's OK," he said.

She aimed her torch at him, not at his face – that would have felt too aggressive – but at his throat and chest, and it made his features emerge like a shadow, his eyes shining in the darkness, which did nothing to calm her. She said:

"What was it that moved you so much in Moscow?"

He took a step backwards, so that his face slipped again into darkness.

"I don't know," he said, and that wasn't what she wanted to hear.

It verged on uncivil, and he smelled even worse in the confined space. Or perhaps her senses had been heightened by fear. Once again she wondered what she was doing. Did she long so much for appreciation that she was prepared to risk everything for nothing? What had she really been hoping for? That he would praise her or cry as he had in Moscow?

"Have you heard that they're smashing instruments?" she said. "They say musicians are going missing."

"I've heard that."

"But you won't destroy my violin, will you?" she said. "My father would be heartbroken. It's not even really ours."

He shook his head in a movement that wasn't convincing, and she felt in desperate need of some friendly words of confirmation.

"But you thought it was beautiful in Moscow, didn't you?"

"I thought . . ." he began, as if he had difficulty talking.

"What?"

"That it was beautiful," he said.

She told herself that this would have to do, and she readied herself again, overcome by an eerie feeling that her life depended on how she played.

That was obviously nonsense – she really hoped it was nonsense. But she was unable to disabuse herself of the feeling. Something fateful had come to rest on the situation, and when she placed the violin to her neck and raised the bow, she stared at his silhouette in the darkness. She could see his right eye.

It shone with expectation, she thought. But that didn't help much. She had the impression that his left eye, which was concealed by darkness, was looking at her with menace and hostility, as if he were two people – one who loved her music, and another who hated it.

A drop of water fell from a crack in the wall, and she felt the blood pumping through her neck and wrists. Then she began to play. The "Méditation" from Thaïs, just like in Moscow, but it sounded hesitant and uncertain. What had she expected? She was terrified, and considered stopping and pleading for his sympathy. She tried closing her eyes and channelling her fear, which made something happen.

The notes gained life and she allowed herself to be carried away on them. She put all her despair into the piece, and eventually her upper body began to sway back and forth just like in the past. She fell into a trance-like state, and when she finished she lowered the violin and remained seated with her eyes shut, waiting to hear a bravo and applause, to receive a slap, a blow, anything. But there was silence. Only his breathing was audible. She opened her eyes and squinted into the darkness.

His right eye looked like he had been crying this time too, and that was good, she thought to herself. But he was also shaking his head, as if he were simultaneously dissatisfied, and she said in a voice that almost failed her:

"Wasn't it good?"

He didn't reply. Instead, he froze, as if her question had frightened him. But in the next moment, she realised he wasn't reacting to her words. Footsteps were audible above. For a moment she was relieved – it was Taisir. It had to be Taisir. He had come to protect her, even if he would also be furious that she had received a male visitor in the middle of the night. But that hardly mattered, not any longer. She would prefer to take a beating from her brother one thousand times over than spend another second in this silence, and she *listened to the footsteps, expecting to hear Taisir's characteristic rhythm. But the tread was heavier, stiffer. Hassan Barozai looked just as afraid as she felt, and she clutched her violin tightly.*

Rekke sat in silence, leaning forward on a wooden chair. Micaela was sitting beside him in a brown armchair, wondering whether she should start the interrogation. Well, it was hardly an interrogation. Neither of them had a tape recorder and no lawyers were present. But she wanted to take the initiative following Rekke's digressions. So she turned to Mohammad Sarwani. She said:

"I saw that you were questioned for information previously. On that occasion, you said you didn't know anyone by the name of Jamal Kabir and that your daughter didn't either. Is that still your position?"

Mohammad turned to Rekke as if it were he who had posed the question.

"It is," he said.

"And you don't know anyone by the name of Hassan Barozai either?" she asked.

Mohammad Sarwani glanced at his son, Taisir. A quick glance, nothing more, but it was enough to strengthen her. She had unsettled him. She could feel it.

"No," he said.

"Are you sure?" she said.

Mohammad nodded, and Rekke, who seemed to want to play good cop in this drama, looked as though he fully understood. He held out his arms as if to say: *Who can keep track of every name?*

"But I'm guessing you're still interested in who this Hassan Barozai might be?" she said.

"Curiosity is a virtue," Mohammad said. "Who is he?"

"A violist who briefly studied with Latifa in Moscow," she said.

"I see," said Mohammad, sitting unnaturally still.

"He also came from Elena Drugov's school in Kabul. But he returned home to Pakistan after his brief spell in Moscow and stopped playing. He only came back to Kabul in 1996 when the Taliban took over the city, and he assumed the name Jamal Kabir. He was involved in the regime's persecution of musicians."

"Really?"

"Yes, really," she said, wondering how to proceed. She could not think what else to say.

Rekke cleared his throat as if to apologise for interrupting.

"Barozai was an interesting man," he said. "My guess is that he was waging war not only on musicians but also on himself. Something we can all recognise, I suppose? The urge to kill something that once burned within us. The longing to crush our desire for what we can't have."

"I don't know about that," said Mohammad Sarwani.

"Then you must be a sounder man than I," Rekke said. "I have a worrying tendency to project myself into all human folly. At any rate, that is my vain aspiration."

"A good ambition for a detective, I assume."

Rekke held out his arms.

"Yes, perhaps. But do you know what I think?"

"No, Professor. I don't."

"I think this dark desire to crush that which is unattainable ticks away within us in secret. But sometimes – such as during the Cultural Revolution in China – a system is created that legitimises it. Our desire to destroy is given an ideological superstructure, and that's when things can go very wrong."

"Indeed they can."

"Although that is not what I want to say either. More than the killer, more than the wretched perpetrator, I'm interested in the victim and those around the victim. What do they do when no law protects them, when the jealous are permitted to run amok without punishment?"

Mohammad Sarwani fidgeted.

"I would guess that they are compelled to write their own laws."

"Quite, and that's a thought that I was somewhat taken with previously. When the rule of law does not function correctly, we create our own jury, our own court."

Mohammad continued to glance at his son.

"Really?" he said.

"Yes," Rekke said. "And while the idea mostly frightens me, I still see a beauty within it. A guarantee that decency will be upheld in times of lawlessness. When the long arm of the law clutches at air, we must use our own hands. What do you make of that idea, Taisir?" Rekke said, turning to Mohammad Sarwani's son.

"I say you're talking shit," said Taisir with sudden aggression.

"Then I must apologise. Because you see, and I hope you have noticed, you all have my deepest sympathies. I am happy, Taisir, that you and Darman Dirani are here. I had anticipated a cast of several."

Mohammad Sarwani stopped looking at his son and drew himself up, as if his pride had returned.

"You anticipated that, did you?" he said with a smile.

Rekke looked sadly at Micaela.

"Yes, actually," he said. "You see, it was my colleague, Vargas, who finally spotted the connections between the threads of this story."

Mohammad Sarwani drank his tea and looked towards the fireplace, above which there was a framed portrait of Latifa in her youth. It seemed almost as if he were pleading to her for help.

"How are these threads supposedly connected?" he said.

"I was going to come to that. *Claritas, claritas*, as I so often say," Rekke said, his left leg beginning to twitch. "But first – sorry, Taisir, I can't help but ask you, as you are surely the one who knows best what happened in the woods in Grimsta. Did Barozai get the punishment he deserved? What do you say?"

"That depends on what he did, surely?" Taisir said curtly.

Rekke appeared thoughtful.

"We all know what he did, don't we?" he said. "Or to be more precise, we know what you believe you know, because there is no exact knowledge of what happened to your sister in the early hours of April 4, 1997, in Kabul."

"No."

"But there is quite a lot of circumstantial evidence, isn't there? Overlooked by others, but not by you."

Mohammad Sarwani stirred restlessly and looked once again at the portrait of Latifa.

"Such as?"

"Small finds at the scene of the murder, for example."

Taisir and Darman Dirani nodded imperceptibly to each other. Micaela got the impression it was a signal. But she was probably mistaken. She glanced at Rekke. He was still looking at the others with a melancholy expression.

"I spent several hours last night looking at the tragic photo you took of Latifa's dead body in the basement, and there is one thing I'm wondering. Why didn't you place floorboards across the whole basement floor?"

Mohammad looked towards the window.

"We had problems with damp and rot. We had to break up part of the floor. We were worried about the violin."

"Pity," said Rekke. "But nevertheless, worthwhile for us both, don't you think? You see, yesterday I became interested in the small holes that can just be made out in front of the body and the smashed violin. I couldn't understand them to begin with – there were so many of them. But then I looked closer and I realised they were holes left by studs. By boots that had moved anxiously over the earthen floor. And yes, admittedly, there can be studs on other items of footwear too, but they felt to me like the marks left by football boots. Don't you agree? Especially given that . . . sorry, I actually have the photograph with me. Just a moment." He removed the picture from his bag and placed it on the coffee table. "Here," he said, pointing to a small white stain in the picture. "Do you see it?"

None of the men seemed inclined to look. But Rekke continued regardless.

"I was completely obsessed with this stain yesterday evening. I twisted and turned it, looking at it from all angles, and became convinced it was a strip of paint, nothing more. But that isn't what is intriguing. It's the very fact that it hasn't fallen apart, that it's still relatively intact. It's been painted with a harder, steadier pressure than would be achieved with a brush. Probably a marking machine, the kind that they use to draw lines on the streets. The very kind they use on football pitches too."

Mohammad Sarwani sipped his tea and seemed to have regained his self-confidence.

"Your powers of observation are excellent, Professor. And this is most interesting. But I'm afraid it's inconsequential as evidence."

"Quite right, of course," Rekke said. "But you are brought ever closer, aren't you? You and the unhappy violist. Isn't that the case?"

"Don't call him unhappy," snapped Taisir.

"True," Rekke said calmly. "I promise not to extend my empathy to him. I'm on your side, especially now: *in dubio pro reo*."

"What fucking language is that?" Taisir said, just as angrily.

"I apologise. It's my objectionable habit to speak Latin. *In dubio pro reo*. It means, when in doubt, favour the accused. Besides, I really do mean it when I say that you filled a void in the legal system, and personally I am prepared to forget it all. There is just one thing that troubles me."

"What's that?"

"What always troubles me when justice has been served. Was the right person punished? Or have the avengers, in their eagerness, been too hasty in drawing their conclusions? There are traces of other shoes down there, aren't there? Bigger feet."

The men looked anxiously at Rekke, and in that moment there was no doubt in Micaela's mind. They were all guilty. It was visible in their sudden uncertainty, in their unspoken question: *Did we kill the wrong person?*

Kabul, the early hours of April 4, 1997

He took a couple of steps to the side so that he was behind her instead. And not just to escape her eyes.

He wanted to see her back, just like in Moscow, even if it was no longer the same back. Latifa had grown thinner, as if drained of her blood. She must be very sick, perhaps dying, and he was moved by this, although perhaps it also pleased him as a kind of victory. He quaked. How she played! No-one else could ever have played so beautifully, he thought.

He wanted to fall down and weep. It was the same piece as in Moscow, the "Méditation" from Thaïs, but it felt different now, as if the music described captivity and fear rather than longing and sorrow, and although he didn't know it, he would later survive in the Salt Pit by summoning memories of the music. But then and there, in the basement, contradictory impulses fought within him. He wanted to go home to Mirpur and stay right there. Just as in Moscow, she played with a slow vibrato and glided between notes in a way that reminded him of his mother's lullabies and the evening sound of the sitar in the square, and he thought to himself that he wanted to listen for hours but also to silence it, to stop everything that hurt and was awakened, and he reached out with one hand to touch her back.

But his hand tensed, as if it would have preferred to strike. He withdrew it and touched his weapon, the Tokarev at his waist, and he felt a wave of agitation. Shoot her, came the thought as if from nowhere. Shoot her. But the thought frightened him in the same moment that he thought it, and he was absorbed back into the music again, losing his footing entirely, and feeling in that moment that he could do anything – shoot her or escape with her – which was probably why he couldn't say a single sensible word when she finished. Instead, he mumbled something he was barely conscious of. At that moment he heard footsteps from above and was seized with terror, convinced that her brother had returned. Then he heard a rattling sound he recognised, and he knew it was Gamal, and he let out a sigh of relief. But only for a second. He was no less afraid, but now in a different way that drew him closer to Latifa.

He looked at her and just had time to be surprised that they were breathing in time with one another, both of them agitated and panting, when Gamal came down the steps to the basement and spoke in a voice that was at once threatening and easy-going.

"Assalamu alaikum. *Don't let me interrupt. Continue.*"

THIRTY-SEVEN

"Do you know how I began to understand?" Rekke said, turning to Mohammad Sarwani. "It was the lack of gossip. A violist who played until his fingers bled and dreamed of being a conductor returns to Kabul and begins smashing instruments instead of playing them – that's the kind of thing that gets tongues wagging, isn't it? But not even Emma Gulwal, whose clarinet was smashed, wanted to say a word about it, even though she clearly knew Barozai. And Darman Dirani, who loved Latifa, didn't want to help us by guessing. I realised quite early on that a decision had been taken – a judgement, if you will – to seek revenge on the person who had not only killed Latifa but was responsible for the persecution of so many pupils of the school she had belonged to. I became convinced that many – a whole group – were in agreement over the crime. Given my predisposition towards the dramatic, I even imagine that a solemn oath may have been sworn."

Taisir moved restlessly on the sofa and made as if to stand up.

"But you don't have any evidence," he said.

"Don't we?" Rekke said, turning to Micaela.

"We have new witness statements," she said. "We know that you were on the scene, Taisir. Your neck tattoo was spotted."

"You don't have a fucking thing."

"And then there's your father's pressed flower. Deep down, you wanted the world to know. Deep down, you've been longing to explain.

Isn't that right? Because just as Professor Rekke said, in your heart of hearts you all believe that what you did was right, don't you?" she said, with an authority that took her by surprise.

Taisir stood up, looking furious. But his father signalled to him to sit back down again.

"I apologise," he said. "My son is hot-tempered."

"He has every reason to be," Rekke said. "We barge in and bring back old secrets from the grave, and well, perhaps we can draw a line under it today. You'll have plenty of time to explain yourselves. But, if you'll allow me, I have another small question for you."

Taisir leaned forward and looked threateningly at Rekke.

"We're not interested in your question. Get out before something bad happens to you," he said.

Mohammad Sarwani shook his head.

"Calm yourself, my son. Be calm. Let Professor Rekke get whatever it is off his chest."

Rekke smiled appreciatively at them both.

"I'm thinking once again about that pressed flower. It's a small but strange detail, isn't it? Why was it so important to place it there?"

"I don't know that it was important. But we do these things, don't we? Much as you said, to leave a mark. Even if it is sometimes a mark that no-one other than Allah sees. You see . . ."

He hesitated.

"Yes, Doctor?" Rekke said.

"I've always been a passionate botanist," he said. "And I have always regarded the dried flower as a protest against death, a vain protest of course, but an attempt to preserve that which is beautiful and fleeting through pressing it. Killing it in a way."

"Is that so?"

"You must understand, Professor, that after I found Latifa shot dead I was inconsolable. It felt as if my life too had ended, and yet I was unable to cry. It was as if I were petrified, and only when I emerged into the sunlight and saw the small meadow of irises growing in front of her house did I break down. I fell to my knees and picked one of the flowers. Afterwards, I pressed it. The flower became important to me. As if a small part of Latifa's soul was in it. I can't explain it any better than that."

Rekke looked at Micaela.

"That's a beautiful, comprehensive description," he said.

"Well, I now realise that it was a mistake to leave the flower. We should keep our feelings to ourselves rather than spread them through the forest as memorials. Unfortunately I'm not as rational as I'd like to be."

"We are contradictory figures. It's what makes us interesting. I apologise, Doctor. This has been a trying day for you," Rekke said, which somehow annoyed Micaela.

These were empty phrases, she thought. Puffed up words. Her tone changed and she spoke with restrained anger.

"So you confess to your involvement in the murder of Jamal Kabir?"

Mohammad Sarwani looked towards the portrait of his daughter and put his hands to his chest.

"I confess it," he said. "And I admit there were many of us involved. You were right about that too. We regarded ourselves as a court, a jury. We wanted to punish the man who killed my daughter simply because he had himself failed and had never been capable of producing anything divine, or remotely close."

Rekke appeared to consider this, and placed his hand on his left leg as if to still the twitching.

"You may be right – although he probably didn't see it that way. We are all skilled in the art of self-deception, are we not?"

Mohammad Sarwani looked down at his hands again, then cast a placatory look at his son.

"Yes, that may be true. Although it was not our task to take into account the murderer's lies to himself."

"True, of course. But was he really a murderer? That is the question."

"Naturally, it worries me when you say that. But for us there is no doubt."

Micaela leaned forward and said:

"Would it not be best if you told us why you are all so certain?"

Mohammad Sarwani closed his eyes and appeared to be choosing his words with care.

"I saw him standing outside her house the day before," he said haltingly. "I didn't know who he was then, and I didn't care either. He seemed harmless and rather comically dressed, and detached from the scene somehow. But after the murder it began to dawn on me, and I didn't have to go far to get answers. He was the football referee who moved so strangely. I'd heard he was liked, but also that he was involved in the Taliban's war on musicians. Then I called around and eventually got the whole story from Emma Gulwal. Latifa had told her about the violist who had rushed into her room in the small hours in Moscow. Darman Dirani, my dear friend here, filled in the remaining gaps in the story. I also heard that Barozai was in a state of crisis following the murder. He barely went out, and officiated at no matches for several months. Latifa's neighbours, the Ghani family, told me that he had shown up on the night of the murder too. And then, well . . . I saw the marks left by the studs on the earthen floor and the small strip of paint that you so perceptively identified. But above all – and this was crucial – I knew that the murderer must have been someone she knew and trusted. She would never otherwise have gone into the basement and taken out her violin."

Mohammad Sarwani fell silent and Micaela looked at Rekke, who seemed to be searching for words, as if he wanted to ask another question. But in the end he said nothing. In that pause, Mohammad Sarwani stood up and declared that he was going to call his lawyer.

Kabul, the early hours of April 4, 1997

When Gamal came down the steps into the darkness with his Kalashnikov and his white tunban, Barozai felt it with absolute certainty: he was not affiliated with either of them. He was no longer a musician like Latifa. But he was not like Gamal either, and he wanted nothing more than to drive the man out. That was now impossible.

To maintain the illusion that he represented the regime, he replied: "Wa aleikum as-salam. Latifa has been showing me her violin." Gamal took a step forward.

"And she played it for you, no?"

"Just a brief piece," he said, putting his hand to his weapon, the Tokarev at his waistband, as a nervous reaction. Or perhaps to demonstrate that he had the situation under control and hadn't lost his head and become consumed by the music. But he failed in that regard.

The hand on his weapon was trembling. He didn't feel at all like a faithful warrior.

"Isn't she going to play for me too?" Gamal said.

Latifa shook her head anxiously, and Hassan thought to himself, I have to prevent it. But he didn't know how. He could hardly plead for Gamal's sympathy. In his eyes, Latifa was a whore. It was impossible to say. Let's leave her be, let's go. He had to find another way out, and the best he could think of was to let her play. Gamal had been a musician too, once upon a time. Perhaps he'd understand – at least on some level.

"Won't you play the piece again?" he said. "We won't harm you."

But that didn't sound good now – not in front of Gamal with his huge stature, and his eyes shining with that unforgiving gaze that had frightened Hassan the first time he had seen it. It didn't surprise him in the slightest that Latifa shrank away as if terrified.

"You don't have to," he said, but Latifa was no longer listening to him.

Gamal was the new centre of power in the room. When he gestured to her to begin, she did, even more hesitantly than last time. Within minutes she moved on to something new, another disconsolate piece. It was as if she couldn't summon anything that didn't move the listener, and Hassan looked pleadingly at Gamal.

Gamal's face shone with an uneasy, excited glow. There seemed to be something else there too, but perhaps Hassan was imagining it because he couldn't understand how a single person, even a warrior in the middle of their jihad, could listen to the music without being moved.

In the dim torchlight that spilled across the floor Gamal looked around. His gaze settled on the Tokarev at Hassan's waist. It made the weapon feel heavier, and a sudden and unexpected thought came to Hassan: Latifa is playing her requiem. He pushed the thought aside. But it returned and made the piece sound even more alive. He thought to himself: Nothing must happen to her, not now, not ever.

He couldn't help looking back at Gamal, and Gamal looked at him as if he had been reading his thoughts, and whispered, "Allahu akbar," which sounded both ghostly and imperious. At the same moment, Gamal took hold of his Kalashnikov and aimed it for a scant second not at her but at him, before lowering it again.

Hassan's whole body shook, as if he faced a choice between his own life and hers. It was perhaps just in his head, an overheated reaction in a moment of madness. He would think about it often afterwards. But it seemed real, and somewhere inside him fluttered memories and disappointment from Moscow. A whole life flashed by as Gamal cleared his throat, took a step towards him and touched his Kalashnikov again. Hassan drew his weapon and shot.

He shot her in the back of the head with a feeling of complete estrangement from himself, surprised at the slowness of the event, at the fact that the violin hit the floor first, letting out a bang as a string snapped and the bridge came loose. A second later Latifa collapsed, more quietly, as if she were carefully settling onto the floor.

"Allahu akbar," Gamal said again. Hassan repeated the words, turned away from the body and began to climb the basement steps.

Behind him, he heard Gamal's breathing and the sound of him trampling the violin to pieces.

*

When Mohammad Sarwani returned from his telephone call, he looked composed and asked whether they had any more questions. If not, he was going to withdraw, he said, to pray.

"I assume," Micaela said, "that the Taliban did nothing to apprehend the killer."

"No. In their eyes, Latifa had received the punishment she deserved."

"So you began to plot your revenge?" Rekke said.

"What would you have done, Professor Rekke?"

"My self-knowledge does not extend that far as yet."

"But some day it may," Taisir said ominously.

"Perhaps," Rekke said with a smile.

Micaela drew them back to the subject.

"Wasn't it possible to deal with it in Kabul?"

Mohammad Sarwani looked dejectedly at the portrait of Latifa on the bureau.

"After we buried Latifa, my son and I and his family were harassed on a daily basis, and when we had the opportunity to flee to Peshawar, we took it. But we swore we would find Barozai, and one day, much later, thanks to Allah's benevolence, we heard he was in Sweden."

"You were set on his trail by the TV report, weren't you?" Micaela said.

Mohammad Sarwani looked towards his son and Darman Dirani, who hadn't yet said a word.

"Yes, we had friends in Sweden who told us about it, and we managed to get hold of the report through the Deutsche Presse-Agentur news agency."

"How many of you travelled to Sweden?"

Mohammad Sarwani looked at Rekke again, as if he had posed the question.

"We were well represented, and Allah gave us rain and thunder as protection."

"And an innocent man whom He was benevolently able to point the finger at," Rekke said with the same mild smile as before.

He stood up as if he had suddenly tired of listening and looked at Micaela, who nodded. She said that she was going to make a phone call and went into the stairwell. For a moment, she wondered whether the men would try to prevent her. When she returned, she told them that they were under arrest for the murder of Hassan Barozai in Grimsta, and that the local police were on their way. Rekke proffered his hand and said:

"We must thank you for your hospitality. I hope you will be treated with understanding. I wish you the best of luck."

They went downstairs to find a taxi, but first they stood in silence on the pavement, taking in what had happened. Rekke looked at her with an absent smile, then disappeared into his own thoughts. As if to himself, he mumbled: "*Nunc est bibendum.*"

Micaela couldn't summon up the energy to ask what he was talking about.

Later that afternoon, in the bar of the Excelsior Hotel Ernst by Cologne Cathedral, they shared a bottle of wine and reviewed what they had established, but before long Rekke seemed to tire. It was as if he had already moved on from the case and would rather scrutinise the people around them than the details he had identified in the investigation.

"Do you see anything interesting?" she said.

He turned back to her again.

"Yes, perhaps," he said. "The man over there with the chapped red cheeks – he's just returned from sailing in the Arctic Ocean. You can tell from his hands that he's buried a bounty in the harsh cold, thirty pieces of silver by my count, which he received when he sold his sister to a travelling circus."

"What does the sister do? Lion tamer?"

"I believe she is able to teach the elephants to stand on one leg. But it's hard to be certain."

She smiled and he smiled in reply. Then he brushed an invisible piece of dust off her arm and looked at her with his intense blue eyes. For a moment, she had the impression he wanted to draw her close, but she dismissed that as her imagination.

"You didn't seem certain that it was Kabir who shot Latifa?"

He looked down at his hands.

"I'm fairly certain. The shot appears to have been fired from the angle where the person wearing studs was standing. But I suppose I wanted to exploit that uncertainty to make them talk."

She fell into a thoughtful silence.

At last she said, "What was the Latin phrase you said in the street earlier today?"

"I don't remember."

"*Nunc* something."

He smiled again and looked at her with the same intensity as before.

"*Nunc est bibendum*," he said. "Now is the time for drinking. Horace's words after the Roman victory over Cleopatra. 'Now that Cleopatra is defeated and dead is the time for celebration,' he writes."

He refilled their glasses.

"What did you mean by that?"

"Perhaps that Mohammad Sarwani's grief was a triumph. Let him doubt. Let us raise a glass."

"Cheers," she said.

"Cheers."

"But you always secretly sympathise most with the defeated, don't you?"

"Yes, perhaps. *Gloria victis.*"

"What is it with you and Latin phrases?" she said.

Rekke leaned in again.

"*Quidquid latine dictum sit, altum videtur.*"

"What?"

"Everything said in Latin seems deep. Although nowadays I ought to blame habit," he said. "It is as if the phrases are part of me. But once upon a time I used them to make myself seem more interesting than I was."

She leaned forward too.

"You wanted to show off."

"Definitely."

"Snob."

"Yes, of course," he said.

"Why don't you ever strike back?"

"My false modesty does a pretty good job of it. Now, what do you say, shall we go out for an early dinner?"

She nodded and stood up, and went to her room to get ready. For the first time in a long time she brushed her fringe back.

THIRTY-EIGHT

May 10, 2004

Martin Falkegren had called a press conference. He would have preferred to hold it by himself, but he had felt obliged to bring along Chief Inspector Fransson. That was why he was sitting there, chunky lump of a man that he was. On the other hand, Falkegren could hardly complain. They'd got good press out of it in the end. Taisir Sarwani had confessed to the crime and was, together with his father, in custody for the murder – and no shortage of spectacular details had emerged over the course of the past five weeks. There were at least forty or fifty journalists here. They had been compelled to provide additional chairs and two fans. It was an unseasonably hot day, and Falkegren was wearing a new light-blue suit and a pair of brand new Alden shoes.

"Welcome. As everyone knows, police work takes teamwork," he said, dissatisfied with the clunky wording but pleased with the overall sentiment.

It wasn't headline-grabbing. But it ensured there was no need to name any one individual, which allowed him to outline in sweeping terms the observations that had led to the breakthrough, and not until he had hit all the high notes did he cede the floor to Fransson, which was sensible. Fransson was a terrible public speaker, and got bogged down in excessive detail. Falkegren thus concentrated on looking decisive and handsome. He thought he had succeeded in this, not only because he had made an effort in front of the mirror that morning, but because he had been able to turn quite naturally towards Fransson, thereby displaying his left profile, which was his better side.

Once again, he fell to thinking about Rekke and the Chilean girl – about how wrong Bruckner had been when he assured them that they would never get to Cologne. Instead, they had solved the murder in no time at all. There was something so dreadfully sneering about the Americans' attitude. He hoped to God that it wasn't widely known and that his own role in the drama wouldn't leak out. Hearing his name mentioned, he surveyed the assembled journalists to see who had addressed him.

"It's reported that you uncovered Kabir's true identity when you found scratches from a viola on his left hand?" said a young, dark-haired girl he thought might be from Sveriges Television.

"That's not the case," he said. "There were no specific details that sealed matters. It was teamwork, as I said. Wide-reaching work under wise leadership," he said, once again managing to stumble on his words.

He moved on quickly, taking a question from an older reporter from *Dagens Nyheter*.

"What's your view on the government's handling of the asylum case? Kleeberger appears to have knowingly allowed a security risk to enter the country to appease the American administration . . ."

For a moment, he was uncertain. On one hand, he was eager to distance himself from the foreign minister. On the other, he was reluctant to rile Bruckner, who had his back. In the end he adopted convoluted phrasing similar to that deployed by Undersecretary Rekke, who had somehow managed to come out of the crisis untouched.

"The government is in a difficult position. While I can see the unfortunate consequences of that decision, I also note that it took courage to let in Kabir. It was thanks to him that it was possible to track Mullah Zakaria to Copenhagen, where he was shot. Unlike Kabir, Zakaria was a genuine security risk and terrorist."

He continued in a somewhat forced manner, hoping to avoid follow-up questions, detailing the valuable assistance afforded them by the American intelligence services in Kabul, ignoring the fact that American intelligence was far from flavour of the month given the recent revelations about torture at Abu Ghraib.

Rekke was sitting at the grand piano. He wasn't playing and he seemed listless again. But Micaela didn't think he was under the influence, or at least not much. It was more that he was paralysed by inaction, lost in his own thoughts, in his own Prison of Darkness, as Julia had put it. Micaela had settled down on the green sofa behind him and was reviewing an investigation into a shooting in Rinkeby, while occasionally glancing at Rekke. What exasperated her was how passive he was. In the last few days, he hadn't even read his books, choosing to linger over the keys instead.

Of course, she could always withdraw and look after herself rather than worry about him. She had been living here, on and off, for around a month – to Mrs Hansson's great delight. Lucas was less pleased, of course, and her mother and Vanessa complained about how little they saw of her, but right now she didn't have it in her to care. It felt like a new chapter of her life.

It seemed to be raining again. Rekke said something. She tore herself away from her investigation and her thoughts.

"What?" she said.

"A man's coming, slightly obese, middle-aged, alcoholic, hunched over, nervous."

She didn't bother to ask how he could possibly know. She listened for sounds from the landing and heard footsteps approaching. She could understand why Rekke had described the footsteps as nervous. They seemed a little lost and cautious. Now they stopped, and a cough was audible. Then the doorbell rang and she looked at Rekke. He held out his arms, apologetically. She muttered: "Lazybones," and went to open the door herself. Standing outside was a man of forty-five or fifty. It was perhaps true that he was an alcoholic, and that his posture was far from upright, but it was also clear that he had once been an athlete, a strongman, and – before all the drink and worry – handsome. He wore a brown corduroy suit and blue shirt. He was clutching an old-fashioned attaché case.

"How can I help you?"

"I'm looking for Professor Rekke."

"What's it regarding?" she said, a little uncomfortable with the situation, feeling like Rekke's secretary or gatekeeper.

"My name is Samuel Lidman," he said. "My sister studied under Professor Rekke, and she says . . ."

He hesitated, as if embarrassed by what he was about to say.

"What does your sister say?" she said.

"That if you have a mystery, there's no-one better than Professor Rekke."

"I'd probably start with the police."

"They don't believe me. May I come in? Is the professor at home?"

They heard footsteps approaching and Rekke was suddenly there, looming over them, giving them his full attention.

"I'm here," he said. "Please come in. Someone has gone missing, haven't they?"

The man looked at Rekke in astonishment.

"How could you know that?"

"I had that feeling. Do sit down and tell us."

The man sat on the green sofa, opened his bag and produced a photograph that he placed on the coffee table. The picture was of a square in front of a magnificent church with a tower and spires and huge arches. In front of the church thronged people and pigeons.

"St Mark's Basilica in Venice," said Rekke. "A fairly recent photo, I should think?"

The man looked at Rekke with his sad brown eyes.

"Yes," he said. "Taken at the end of March, if I understand correctly. But what I want to talk about is this woman here."

He pointed to a woman in her forties in an expensive-looking red coat. She was standing in the foreground, in front of a group of Japanese tourists who appeared to be listening to a tour guide.

"That's my wife," he said.

"She's beautiful," Micaela said encouragingly.

"She was far more beautiful than I deserved. But she died fourteen years ago."

"She looks very alive."

"That's the thing," said the man. "I have a death certificate. But that really is her."

"You're certain of it?" she said.

"Absolutely certain," he said. "Do you see the birthmark there by her ear? Well, there are several details. I've got old photos with me too. You can see for yourselves."

Rekke glanced at Micaela, then said with renewed energy:

"Do tell."

And so, at twenty past five on that warm spring afternoon, Samuel Lidman began to tell his peculiar story, one that kept Rekke and Micaela up long into the evening.

ACKNOWLEDGEMENTS

I have received incredible support from my publisher, as well as from my agent Jessica Bab, who has always been there to help.

My editor, Eva Bergman, offered a series of smart and creative solutions – both big and small. My friend Johan Norberg helped me with the musical elements, ensuring through his expertise that the story expanded and gained depth.

No-one can possibly doubt the debt of gratitude I owe to Conan Doyle and his creation Sherlock Holmes, and I have ensured that I nod to them as often as possible. It was through reading Lena Sundström's *Spår* that I learned about the Salt Pit prison, which led me to read about Gul Rahman, who froze to death at the site following days of torture.

An event of great significance to me was the dinner I attended at the Grand Hôtel in Stockholm, where I saw Ahmad Sarmast and his Afghanistan National Institute of Music (ANIM) receive the Polar Music Prize for their efforts to preserve Afghan musical heritage and to educate young musicians in the country. The ceremony opened my eyes to the oppression of musicians in Afghanistan since the civil war in the 1990s.

The violinist Christian Svarfvar taught me much, including what violinists' fingertips look like. Erika Pérez showed me around Husby and told me the incredible story of her family's escape from Chile. Frédéric Brusi and Estella Burga read early drafts and offered valuable input. Fulsome thanks are also due to Linda Altrov-Berg and Catherine Mörk at Norstedts Agency.

And from the depths of my heart, thanks to my dear Anne.

DAVID LAGERCRANTZ had his breakthrough as a novelist with *Fall of Man in Wilmslow*, a novel about the British mathematician Alan Turing. The biography *I am Zlatan*, which he co-wrote with international football star Zlatan Ibrahimović, was published in 2011, selling millions of copies worldwide. In 2013, Lagercrantz was asked to write a free-standing sequel to Stieg Larsson's Millennium Trilogy. *The Girl in the Spider's Web* (2015) became a global publishing phenomenon with simultaneous publication in twenty-seven countries, and was followed by *The Girl Who Takes an Eye for an Eye* (2017) and – Lagercrantz' final book in the Millennium series – *The Girl Who Lived Twice* (2019). The Millennium series has sold 100 million copies to date and has topped the international bestseller charts all over the world.

IAN GILES has a PhD in Scandinavian literature from the University of Edinburgh. Past translations include novels by Arne Dahl, Carin Gerhardsen and Camilla Läckberg. His translation of Andreas Norman's *Into a Raging Blaze* was shortlisted for the 2015 CWA International Dagger. He is Chair of the Swedish-English Literary Translators' Association and lives in Edinburgh.

31/8/22 CENT.